From

A BOY

To

A MAN

ALAN WHICHELLO

Order this book online at www.trafford.com
or email orders@trafford.com

Most Trafford titles are also available at major online book retailers.

Print information available on the last page.

ISBN: 978-1-6987-1250-5 (sc)
ISBN: 978-1-6987-1252-9 (hc)
ISBN: 978-1-6987-1251-2 (e)

Library of Congress Control Number: 2022914192

Trafford rev. 08/03/2022

 www.trafford.com
North America & international
toll-free: 844-688-6899 (USA & Canada)
fax: 812 355 4082

From a Boy to a Man

I would like to dedicate this book to my wife Gillian who has supported me for over 50 years

I would also like to thank my close friend Jacquie Cook who helped with the editing and of course Trafford for publishing this book.

CONTENTS

PREFACE

FROM A BOY TO A MAN

This is loosely based on a true story. Although most of the facts are true, I have exaggerated on some to make the story more interesting reading.

This book is not suitable for children and is adult themed. In the first part of the story, there are a few words that are sexual and explicit. Some readers may find them offensive and vulgar, but I kept them in the story as they were relevant at the time this story was written. I do apologize if I offended or upset anybody—this was not my intention.

PROLOGUE

Christmas 2003, my wife Gillian and I were walking through the streets of Oxford. Christmas was only a week away, and we were getting the last presents for our youngest child. We walked past Debenhams and noticed a shabbily dressed man sitting on some cardboard in the shop doorway. "Give us a few bob for a meal, governor," he pleaded. "I haven't eaten since this morning."

I felt sorrow for him. I bent down and said, "Can't you get food at your lodgings?"

He coughed several times, clearing his throat, and Gillian moved away. I could see she didn't want to get to close to the man. "My only lodgings is the bus shelter if nobody else is sleeping there," he replied.

"But can't you get help from Social Services?" I asked.

"I could but I am an illegal immigrant," he said, "even though I was born and bred here." I was intrigued and could tell he was a well-educated man, but Gillian was getting impatient to go home. I gave the man £5 and asked if he would meet me here the next day at 10:00 a.m. "For £5, governor, I'd meet you on the moon." He laughed then tried to get up. I could see it was a struggle, and the effort made him wheeze. So I grabbed his arm and helped him to his feet. "You're a real gent, sir," he said then picked his bit of cardboard up and stuffed it in his old army coat and shuffled off toward McDonald's. Gill was tugging at my arm so I relented and we walked back to the car.

The next day, I was outside Debenhams at 9:30 a.m., hoping to see where the man had been sleeping, but he was already there sitting on the ground with a plastic dish on the ground, asking people for money. Most people walked by and ignored him as if he wasn't there. "Come on," I said, "let's go and have some breakfast." He got to his feet, picked up the few coppers that were in the dish, and we walked to a little café down the road. His clothes smelt a bit, but you could see he'd washed and kept himself clean. We sat down in a quiet corner away from the other tables. "What's your name?" I said.

"Jones—David Jones," he replied, "but my friends call me Davy."

"Well, Davy, I'm Alan." I called the waitress over and ordered two English breakfasts. "Davy would you be willing to tell me your life story?"

"Will I get paid any money?" he asked, with a twinkle in his eye.

"I can't promise anything but if I publish the book and it's a success, then you would be paid some reward." After we had eaten the breakfast, I took out my tape recorder from my case and set it on the table. Davy looked a bit suspicious. "It's all right," I said. "I can't do shorthand writing and have a poor memory so I have to tape things." After he had drunk his tea, he began telling me his story. As his story unfolded, I was moved by how much he remembered from such a young age. His graphic account of his abusive and violent past brought tears to my eyes. We spent all day at the café after buying him lunch and tea and changing tapes on the recorder. We finally left, when the café closed. I shook hands with Davy and gave him my card with my contact details, eager to get home and write his story.

CHAPTER

The Early Years

David William Jones, born on July 20, 1945
Location: London, England
Mother: Edith Elizabeth Thomson
Father: Trevor Martin Jones
Registered July 8, 1948

That's what I'd first seen written on my birth certificate.

I was nearly three years old when we moved to our new house in the summer of 1948, well, it wasn't a new house as such but a 1906 detached cottage with two bedrooms and landing upstairs with a large kitchen downstairs. A passageway led off to a large lounge with inglenook fireplace. An old toilet and wash hand basin had recently been built into the corner, which was a luxury as most old properties had their toilet outside. From the passageway, a door led down a stone stairway into a cellar. This was originally an old pub but had been converted to a living accommodation by the farmer who owned quite a few houses in the village. Most of them were tied cottages for the farm laborers. The village was divided by a large stream with Upper Balding on one side and Lower Balding on the other. Trevor Jones, my father, had married Edith, my mother, a few months before at a registry office, and as he worked on the farm as a tractor driver, it entitled him to a house, which was in Lower Balding.

Trevor was twenty-five years old and was a huge man with a beer gut, with fiery red hair and beard. He was also a bully with a short temper. Edith was twenty years old, tall with a slight frame, quite pretty but was eight months pregnant and had a massive belly. She too was very irritable from carrying the baby and snapped at the slightest thing. As I think back, they did not make a suitable couple, and they argued a lot.

My first memory was being upstairs with my father. I was excited because it was my third birthday and my mother had promised me a birthday cake for tea. I remember falling down the stairs but couldn't remember whether I slipped or was pushed. I lay at the bottom of the stairs. I was conscious but ached all over. My mother came rushing through from the kitchen after hearing the bumps, and picked me up,

"Are you all right, Davey?" asked Mum.

"'Course he's all right," shouted my father, peering over the stair rails. "He shouldn't be so clumsy."

Mum removed my jumper, and I winced at the pain. Bruises were already starting to show on my thin body. Mum quickly pulled my jumper back over my head. "You'll be all right. Nothing's broken. Go back in the lounge. Dinner will be ready soon and then you can have your cake." I stumbled back into the lounge and slumped into an armchair. My arm really hurt, but

I knew I shouldn't complain. It would only make things worse with my father.

My father came stomping down the stairs a few minutes later, demanding if the dinner was ready. He had got changed and was itching to get to the pub. Mum ignored him and laid the table. "Davy, come and get your dinner," she shouted, but before I could move, my father charged into the room.

"Are you deaf, boy, didn't you hear your mum calling?" I was about to raise my aching body, but I couldn't avoid a clip around the ear from my father. I hurried into the kitchen and sat down, my head just above the tabletop. A bowl of stew and a slice of bread were placed in front of me.

My father exploded into a rage. "Is this all you can dish up, woman? I need a healthy meal, not pig slops."

Mum shouted back, "If you were to give me more money, I could buy some meat, instead of you pissing it up in the pub." I held my breath, expecting Mum to get a slap, but Dad smirked and carried on eating his stew. After we had finished, Mum proudly brought the small birthday cake she had made, to the table. Three small candles were pushed into the center. She lit the candles and said, "Blow the candles out, Davy, and make a wish." I made a wish but was glad my father couldn't read my mind.

My father cut the small cake in half and ate the biggest bit before Mum could offer me a slice, but I was grateful to share the other half with her. After stuffing the cake into his mouth, my father stood up. "I'm going to the pub," he mumbled. "Don't wait up." Then he stormed out of the house. By seven o'clock, I was tucked up in bed with my thumb in my mouth and a tucker rag squashed against my nose. My tucker rag was an old nappy, which smelt revolting from the dribbling of my thumb, but this relaxed me and I felt safe. I fell into a deep sleep. After some time, I was awoken by the door being slammed and my drunk father stamping up the stairs. I slid down the side of the bed between the wall and the old flock mattress, still wrapped in the sheets, and listened. He went straight to Mum's bedroom and tore the sheets off the double bed. I heard my mother cry out, "No, Trevor, I'm over eight months pregnant." I heard a slap then some groaning. My mother cried out a few times then it all went quiet. I pulled my tucker rag tighter and dropped back off to sleep wondering what had happened.

I dreamt I was on a big red bus, looking out the windows at the rubble and damaged buildings. Kids were playing amid the rubble. I wanted the bus to stop so I could play with them but the bus never stopped, and then I woke up. I had experienced this dream many times before, but I did not understand what it meant.

The next morning, I got dressed in my old shirt and shorts, pulled on my socks and shoes. My father had already gone to work. When I came down the stairs, Mum was in the kitchen, bent over the sink. I could see she was in pain. "Are you all right, Mum?" I asked, concerned.

"Quick, Davy, run and fetch the midwife, and hurry." I ran out of the house and down the street. I knew where she lived as we had passed her house many times when Mum took me to the local co-op store. I banged on the front door, and thankfully, she was in. I told her what had happened. She hurried to get her bag then chased after me down the street. When we went into the kitchen, Mum was lying on the floor, bleeding badly. I burst out crying.

"Quick, Davey," said the midwife, "get me all the towels you can carry." When I returned, the midwife made my mum as comfortable as possible, then told me to wait in the lounge. I listened and heard my mum screaming. "Push," I heard the midwife shout. I heard another scream and then a baby crying. "You can come in now," the midwife said. I peered around the kitchen door and was relieved to see Mum still on the floor, propped up against the kitchen sink, holding a small baby.

"Come and meet your little sister," she said. I looked and was a bit concerned how tiny and wrinkly it was.

"Don't worry," said the midwife. "She was born a bit early but is healthy and will soon put on a bit of weight." She tidied up a bit, packed her bag, and told Mum she would call in tomorrow to see how she was managing. (In the late forties and fifties, most women had their babies at home.) I thought with a little sister at home, things would get better between me and my father, but it only made things worse, much worse.

Mum coped as well as could be expected. She adored little Sheila, but I was getting more and more neglected.

CHAPTER

The Headless Chicken

The villages were connected by a narrow road. Lower Balding was the smallest, about half a mile long with about 250 houses, a chapel, two pubs, and a large farm, which most of the farmhands worked on, including my father. There was also a small school and recreation field just off the main road. A bridge over the large stream separated Upper Balding, which was slightly bigger, about three quarters of a mile long with three pubs and about 400 houses. In this village, there was the co-op, a baker's, butchers, and a smithy, as most of the farms still used some horses. There was a large council estate in the middle of the village with a primary school and police house to one side. On the other side stood the village hall and church. On the outskirts of the village lay Beal's sawmills. Most of the people did all their shopping in the village or caught the daily bus service into the next town about two miles away. In 1948 there were very few cars about in the village.

Our house was the first house in Lower Balding, built on the corner of the main road through the village. It had a large garden bordering on fields at the back and a small wood to the side. A public footpath ran alongside our property, separating the woods. The woods had barbed wire around the perimeter to keep out intruders, as the woods and land beyond were all owned by the local farmer Giles Bedford. Our garden was divided by a track, which some of the farm vehicles used as it was the quickest way into the fields beyond. The farm had two tractors and the very first combine harvester, as well as shire horses although these were being used less and less. On one side of the track, we had a large wire run for the chickens, a small tin grain store, and an old wooden shed, while the other side contained our vegetable patch, some small fruit trees, and various fruit bushes. The whole garden was surrounded by a chicken wire fence, except where the track went through.

I loved our garden and felt quite safe when I was left alone, which was quite often. I would help Mum feed the chickens and loved handling the young chicks. Being in the countryside, we did have foxes, badgers, and rats coming into the garden after the chickens or their corn. My father had a twelve-bore double-barrel shotgun, which he used to kill the vermin if he was quick enough. He did go out shooting for rabbits and pheasants and sometimes pigeons, although this was not often as it took five or six pigeons to make a pie as only the breast was usable. The next thing that stuck in my mind was just before Christmas. Being only three and half, I didn't know what Christmas was all about, but everybody seemed to cheer up so I did too, until my father suggested I go with him to get the cockerel on Christmas Eve. I followed him to the chicken run, and he closed the gate behind me. He caught the largest cock bird in the run and told me to stand behind it. He put the bird's neck over a wooden block, and as quick as a flash, he chopped its head off with a small axe, then he let the bird go. I screamed and watched the headless bird run around, blood oozing out of its neck. I ran and tried to get out, thinking the bird was after me. My father was roaring with laughter as I tried desperately to get away, but a few seconds later, the cockerel lay dead on the ground. My father was still laughing as he picked the dead bird up and opened the chicken run gate. I had nightmares for weeks after. I didn't learn until much later that it was only the bird's natural instinct to run for a few seconds, even though it was dead.

Christmas was all over very quickly. We ate the cockerel, but I left the meat and only ate the potatoes and greens. I couldn't forget that poor chicken running around with no head. Christmas pudding was a small piece of homemade cake, which my father ate most of. I did open my only present after dinner, a wooden lorry with a tipping back. I didn't see any presents for Mum. My father stood up, belched, and then said he was going to the pub. He left without even thanking my mother for the meal. Mum played with my little sister Sheila for the rest of the evening. I played with my lorry, wishing I had a brother to play with. That was Christmas 1949. (Although rationing was still strictly enforced in the cities and towns, in the countryside this did not affect us so much. We grew most of our greens, potatoes, fruit, and eggs were plentiful so we ate quite well.) My mother would often walk up to the Baptist chapel on Sunday mornings for the service at ten o'clock and took me along with Sheila in the pram. I did like the singing part but got bored with the talking part. This didn't last long as Father objected to Mum going. "Why do you waste your time going there?" he said one night. "There's plenty of work to do in the house."

My wish came true. Mum was pregnant again and had the baby in the summer exactly a year later. Mum called my little brother Tommy and to my surprise Father adored. He seemed a changed man, picking the baby up and tickling him. But that didn't last long. He still treated my mum like a servant and kept her short of money. I had learned to stay out of his way especially after he came home from the pub, but he still hit me if anything went wrong. I always seemed to get the blame.

I was left to my own devices for most of the summer. I had found a hole in the fence and ventured across the footpath and into the woods. This was a whole new adventure for me. I loved the woods and played for hours with my lorry, filling it up with twigs, imagining they were logs and I was in a timber yard. That was my best summer ever, until one day I was so absorbed in playing, I was a bit late for tea and heard my father shouting. I didn't know if I should hide or answer him. I decided to keep quiet and slip home later. But that only made things worse. He found the hole in the fence, and it wasn't long before he found me. "Didn't you hear me calling, you little bastard? Get off home before I take my belt to you."

He looked around and saw my lorry loaded with logs. He smirked and stamped on it, smashing it beneath his hobnail boot. I stood there and, for the first time, cried. "You little crybaby," he said and then booted me up the backside. "Get off home and don't say anything to your mother, or else you'll be sorry." I went home crying, having lost the only thing I really cared about. I can't understand why my mother didn't see how unhappy I was. I always kept quiet when I came in, but she asked how I had gotten the bruise on the side of my head and when I did tell her the truth that Dad had hit me, she always said, "Well, you probably deserved it." So that's why I didn't tell anybody. When the district nurse came on her monthly rounds to check on Mum, I was either out playing in the woods or in bed with a cold. Nobody checked. I did manage to persuade Mum to buy me some wood glue to see if we could try and repair my lorry. Mum stuck the wheels back on and the sides, but it never worked the same.

Once a month my mum had started taking us to see her mother at Gifford, a small village about two miles north of the town. We caught a red bus at the top of the road (it looked like the bus in my dreams, only smaller). It stopped at the town square for a few minutes and let people off and on then carried on to Henley. The bus stopped right outside my gran's house, so Mum didn't have to walk very far. Gran was quite old. My granddad had been killed in the war, so she was living alone in a big council house. But she had a son, William, who lived next door. Most people called him Bill, and he kept an eye on her. Gran welcomed us all; she especially liked me and gave us all a bar of chocolate. I liked her too, but she wasn't very clean and smelled of pee when she got close. We stayed for about two hours before we had to catch the bus home.

I was four and half, just before I started school when I discovered just how much my father hated me. I was in the garden early one morning. Mum had fed the chickens and had left the flap open on the corn bin. It was about four feet square and held two large bags of corn, which my father pinched from the farm. I climbed up on a log and peered inside. It was nearly empty, so I climbed up on top and lowered myself down. It was high enough for me to stand up in this was great. I had found myself a new camp. I settled down on the bottom when I heard footsteps outside. The flap was suddenly pushed down and a large concrete slab placed over it. I screamed and banged on the side of the steel bin. Whoever was out there must have heard. I listened again and heard footsteps walking away, I pushed on the flap but it didn't budge. I was trapped. I panicked and screamed and banged on the side of the bin for about an hour, but nobody came. I sank to the bottom of the bin, tired out, and must have fallen asleep.

This time, I dreamt I was on the big red bus. I was looking out of the windows at the children playing in the rubble. All the buildings were falling down around them. I wanted to get off the bus and help them, but I couldn't. The bus never stopped. I woke up sweating. I looked up and the flap was open, but before I could stand, one hundredweight of corn cascaded down, burying me. I struggled to breathe and forced my head above the corn, gasping for air. Then the flap was shut, I heard the slab being pulled back over, then all was quiet. The corn bin was about half full. I stretched and pulled my body free, and finally,

I lay on top of the corn. It was pitch black, and the air was full of dust. My breathing became labored. I pushed my head against the flap. There was a slight gap where the flap wasn't seated properly, but enough for me to breathe. I settled down and waited for somebody to save me.

My mum had been worried sick. She had searched the woods and surrounding areas "Have you seen Davy?" she asked my father when he arrived home that evening. "Only he didn't come home for lunch and I haven't seen him all day." He said he hadn't but agreed to help search. He went and searched the woods again, while Mum went to feed the chickens. I heard the concrete slab being pulled off the flap and then opened. Mum screamed when she saw me, I was only semiconscious and wasn't moving. She pulled me out, and I took a deep breath. After only a few minutes, I had recovered enough and told her what had happened. Of course, my father denied any knowledge that I was in the corn bin and Mum believed him, but I knew the truth.

CHAPTER

The Early School Years

In September, I started school. I had been looking forward all summer to meeting other children and playing with them. My mum walked me to the junior school in Upper Balding. She told me to be a good boy and behave myself. She kissed me on top of the head then left me in the playground, surrounded by screaming boys and girls running around like mad things. I stood there frozen to the spot, not knowing how to interact with the other children. A pretty young girl came over and said, "My name's Alice. What's yours?" I told her my name, and that was the start of a friendship that lasted all of my early school days.

It became quite clear there was a hierarchy in our school. Which boys and girls held the most power over the others? Edward Stevens was the biggest and loudest boy in our class, and most of the schoolkids were scared of him. The girls were dominated by Tracy Monk. She wasn't the biggest, but she had a foul mouth and bad temper. We picked up most of the swear words from her. Our class had the best female teacher in the school, Miss Shaw. I liked her from the start. I enjoyed the lessons and was eager to learn. I was a bit backward, having never learned to read or write and could not tell the time. I could count to ten, but that was my limit of ability. This was my downfall. It soon became clear I was the dunce of the school and was placed in the lowest grade. Eddy Stevens picked up on this, and the bullying began. I hated fighting and would rather walk away. If it wasn't for Alice, who stuck by me when I felt depressed, I don't think I would have coped. In fact, I got on better with the girls than the boys.

It was a very strict school with corporal punishment quite commonplace, especially among the boys. It ranged from a clip around the ear, which was a favorite with Miss Smith. Mr. Kiddie favored the ruler (he was the butt of many jokes with a name like that) and used the ruler quite often across the palm of your hand. But the person we feared the most was the headmaster. If you were sent to him, the slipper was mostly used. He would make you bend over and whack you as hard as he could across the bottom, often more than once. (These methods of punishment were widely used in the late forties and fifties.) I soon caught up with the others on education, apart from a few fights in which I always came off worse. On one occasion, Jimmy Hoskins and I ended up in front of Mr. King the headmaster. "I will not tolerate fighting in my school," he bellowed. Then he made Jimmy bend over. After I witnessed the slipper being given to Jimmy, I made a bolt for the school front door and was gone before the headmaster realized what was happening. After dodging my father for so long, I could run like the wind. But I got no sympathy when I got home. After I had explained what had happened, my mum said her favorite saying, "Well, I expect you deserved it," and promptly put the two kids in the pram and marched me back down to school, where

I received four whacks of the slipper instead of two. I never ran away from school again.

Another thing I remembered most was the mobile school dentist and nit nurse who came once a month. I wasn't sure what to expect as I walked up the steps into the back of the van. The nurse examined me first combing through my hair, then looking for any head lice or their eggs (commonly called nits). Although I was dressed scruffily, Mum always made sure I was clean, so I was given the all clear (even the cleanest of children could still get nits). I then sat in the dentist chair quite confident that all would be well, until the dentist opened my mouth. "I will have to remove one of your teeth at the front," the dentist said. "They are overlapping badly." It was common practice to pull milk teeth with no anesthetic in those days. I have never felt pain that much, even when my father hit me. My mouth was filled with blood and ached like mad. That experience put me off dentists for the rest of my life. School passed very quickly that year.

My sixth birthday was rapidly approaching. I asked Mum if I could invite Alice around for tea. "I don't think that's a good idea, Davey, what with all the kids running around." I think she was a bit ashamed of the mess, so I didn't argue. Sheila, my sister, was now three, and Tommy was two. We now had bunk beds for me and Tommy in our bedroom, and Sheila had a single bed on the other side. My father had erected a blanket stretched across the bedroom to give Sheila some privacy, but it was getting a bit cramped. Unbeknown to me, Mum was pregnant again and looked very tired. When I told Alice that Mum wasn't feeling very well, she invited me around to her place for tea. I felt a bit nervous as I had never been to anybody else's house. I put my clean clothes on, which were really my school clothes as I only had two of everything: one to be worn, one to be washed, as my mother used to say. I needn't have worried. Mrs. Kimber, Alice's mother, was the nicest person I had ever met. She told us to go and play in the garden. Alice's friend Susan joined us soon after in the garden. "Come on, let's go and play in my tent," said Alice, so we all squeezed into the tent and pulled down the flaps. It was bigger inside than I thought. The girls started playing with their dolls, and I soon became bored. Alice looked at me and said, "If I show you mine, will you show me yours?"

I hadn't a clue what she was talking about until they both lifted their skirt and pulled down their knickers. I stared in amazement and blurted out, "How do you go to wee if you haven't got a Willy?"

They both burst out laughing. "Come on, show us yours, then," said Susan. I felt my face reddening up, but dropped my shorts and pants so they could see. They didn't laugh, so that was a relief. Then Alice's mother came into the garden and called us for tea. We quickly got dressed and went through into the dining room. Sandwiches, cakes, cream biscuits, jelly, and ice cream were spread on the table. I had never seen so much food. That was the best birthday I have ever had, and I never forgot that first sexual experience.

All too soon, summer was over. I had a few run-ins with my father, but I was quite good at avoiding his blows. I usually ran away before he could catch me, He never hit me in front of my mother. But on one occasion, he caught me in his shed, using his handsaw. He closed the door. "What the fuck do you think you are doing, you little bastard," he said angrily, "using my tools without asking?" I backed away, thinking he was going to punch me, but instead, he removed his belt, folded it in half, and began thrashing me. He didn't stop until I collapsed on the floor. "Don't you dare tell anybody, or else you'll get some more of that," he said as he opened the door and left. My body battered, I lay there weeping. (Why was my father doing this? I kept asking myself.) It was two hours later when my mother called out that tea was ready. I pulled myself up and brushed myself down. I had no marks on my face, but my legs were covered in red weal marks and my body ached all over. I straightened myself up, opened the kitchen door, and sat down at the table. My father glanced across the table and smirked.

CHAPTER

Life at Home

I expect you are wondering how we all kept clean with no bathroom. We did have a flannel wash in the kitchen sink every morning and night. But I will tell you my mum's weekly routine. Monday was washing day. Mum had to do all the washing in the boiler, a large round aluminum tank on legs, which plugged into the electric socket in the kitchen. It held about six or seven buckets of water. (This was the only hot water we had, apart from a small Sadie electric heater above the kitchen sink, which wasn't very efficient.) Mum would then boil the soiled nappies first as these were the dirtiest. With two kids, there were loads of them. Then they were put through the old wooden mangle to squeeze all the excess water, then hung on the line in the garden. My mum then had to empty and clean the boiler, fill it back up with fresh water, to boil the working clothes, etc. She then had to repeat the process with clean water. Then the sheets were boiled after she had hung them on the line. This took Mum all day and most of the evening. Then she would drag the old tin bath into the kitchen or in front of the fire in the lounge if it was cold and drain the hot water from the tap at the base of the boiler and use the recycled water to have our weekly bath. I was lucky as I went first. (Mum usually left the room so I wasn't embarrassed.) Then Tom and Sheila went in together. By that time, the water needed emptying. It was bedtime before she was finished. She then had to boil up a fresh lot of water for her and my father to use.

On Tuesday, she would do the weekly shop at the co-op, taking both Sheila and Tom with her in the pram. In the afternoon, she would do some gardening, picking the greens and potatoes, feeding the chickens, and collecting some eggs. (My father sometimes helped in the evening with the gardening.)

Wednesday usually involved more washing and mending clothes. Mum rarely threw anything away. On Thursday after breakfast, which was usually porridge made with water and a splash of milk or cornflakes or Weetabix, she then took Sheila and Tom down to the recreation ground to play on the swings. This was the only day she relaxed a little, talking to the other villagers who were also playing with their kids. When she got home, dinner had to be started. My father liked the dinner to be waiting for him when he got home. Mum would be in trouble if it was late.

Friday was for boiling nappies, cleaning the house, and darning socks or any other clothes that wanted repairing.

Saturday, Mum was in the garden most of the day, digging, planting, and weeding.

Sunday she made pies, cakes, and scones. Rock cakes were our favorite. We used to eat them before they got cold, but she always made sure there was some left for my father. That was Mum's routine for the week.

It was about this time my father bought home a dog, a black Labrador. This surprised us all as he had not showed any interest in animals or birds, only the ones he could shoot and eat. We named him Bruce, and he became my best mate. The farm manager had asked my father if he could look after him as there were too many dogs around the farm. Mum protested, complaining about the extra cost and time needed to look after him, but she relented after seeing how disappointed I was. Bruce became my dog, and we did everything together. I took him into the woods and showed him all my camps and hiding places, then I took him for a walk across the fields. I was very happy for about two weeks, until I returned home from school one day and opened the kitchen door.

Sheila and Tom were crying. Bruce was barking. Mum was bent over the kitchen sink and had been washing her hair. My father was standing behind her with both hands around her neck, holding her head underwater. Her arms were flailing, and water was everywhere. I shouted, "Dad, stop!" But it made no difference. So I kicked him as hard as I could in the shins. He let go of Mum, turned around, and made a lunge for me. I ran out of the kitchen as fast as I could. He was yelling behind me, "Come back, you little bastard," but I was gone like the wind, straight into my second home, the woods. One of my camps was inside a massive heap of grass cuttings bordering on the large lawn owned by the farmer Giles Bedford. His mansion lay behind the gardens at the back. The day, my father had caught me in his shed and beat me. I had just finished building my camp with planks holding up the sides and roof, which I had taken from my father's wood store and then covered it all with grass cuttings. I crept inside and pulled down the sack cloth hiding the entrance. The space was cozy and warm. I had one of the corn sacks on the floor. I kept a small torch inside as it was quite dark. I switched it on and waited.

I dreaded my father finding me because I knew he would beat me with his belt. I was tired and hungry but I still fell asleep. I had a nightmare Mum was lying on the kitchen floor.

Sheila was shaking her, trying to wake her up. Tommy was screaming. I awoke sweating and cold. I was in darkness. The torch had gone out, so I pulled back the sackcloth, but it was still the middle of the night. At least nobody had found me. I wondered how my mother, brother, and sister were. Had he harmed them? I decided to wait until I was sure my father had gone to work before I would venture back, I snuggled up in my camp and dozed off.

I was awoken by a rough wet tongue licking my face, Bruce was standing over me, wagging his tail. We crawled outside, and there was Mum. She ran over, lifted me off my feet and gave me a huge hug, then kissed me. She was crying. I had never seen my mother so emotional before. Mum never told me why my father reacted like he did, but things changed after that, and for the better.

Mum had the baby a little girl in September at home, although there were some complications at the birth and the doctor had to be called to assist the midwife. Mum was advised not to have any more children. Mary was a bonny baby, never cried much and slept through the night in a cot in Mum's bedroom.

Christmas that year was the best so far. My father had got an extra job on Sunday mornings working as a gardener at a posh house in the village. He was paid cash and gave the extra money to Mum. That's the only time I saw Mum kiss him on the cheek and say thank you—she was so happy. Father still ignored me, but at least the hitting became less, with only a clip around the ear every so often. But everybody was very excited on Christmas Eve. My father had dug up a tree from around the farm, which we put in the lounge. I helped decorate it, and the presents were placed around the tree. I noticed there were six presents and guessed one was for Mum. Christmas morning and we were all up early. We raced down the stairs, eager to open the presents. Sheila had a pushchair and a doll. Tommy had a pull-along wooden train and carriages, and I had a dinky toy car. My mum had come down the stairs and was watching us open our presents. We were all happy and thanked her, although she could see I was a bit disappointed. "Why don't you come into the kitchen and help me with the breakfast?" She said, smiling to herself, I followed her into the kitchen, and there it was. I stood in amazement. A red bike was leaning against the sink. "It's not new, but your father got it off Mr. Primrose," Mum said, "the man he does the gardening for. His son is two years older than you and has outgrown it." I didn't care how old it was. It was the best present ever. I kissed Mum and thanked her. "You must thank your father," she said. "He brought it home." So when my father came down the stairs for breakfast, I thanked him for my bike. He only grunted, but at least he acknowledged me. Mum got a new coat and scarf. Knowing my father, it was probably one of Mrs. Primrose's discarded coats, as he had been bringing back hand-me-down shorts and shirts from her house for me to wear, but Mum looked good in her coat and scarf, and she was happy with her present.

CHAPTER

My Dog Bruce

I rode everywhere on that bike, all through the villages to the sawmills at the end, and even to the town two miles away, although I had to stick to the footpath across the fields. Mum wouldn't let me ride on the main road. I told Mum where I had been, and she asked me if I had met my uncle. "What uncle?" I said, not understanding what an uncle was. "Mr. Beal," she said, "the man who owns the sawmills." I didn't know we had relations in the village and found out I had two cousins, Jimmy and Johnny. They were three years younger than me, but the Beal family was to play a big part in my life in the years that followed.

Those were the best months in my life so far, apart from one incident and it didn't involve my father. I had been teaching

Bruce some new tricks, throwing stones and him bringing them back to me. But sometimes he never bought them back and just sat there looking at me. This went on for a few weeks before Mum noticed a large swelling in his stomach and Bruce had stopped going to the poo. Mum took him to the vets, and he had an operation to remove nine large stones from his stomach. Apparently the stones he hadn't brought back to me, he had swallowed. The vet told Mum that Bruce had hard pad or distemper in both front paws, which were very tender. She gave Mum some cream to apply to the paws. The next day I was playing with Bruce, I knelt down to give him a cuddle and accidently knelt on one of his paws. Bruce reacted with a bite to the side of my face. Mum heard me cry out. When she saw me, my face was covered in blood. She quickly bathed my face but couldn't stop the bleeding. Mum ran to the neighbors to phone for an ambulance. (We didn't have a phone.) And I was taken to the hospital. I had four puncture wounds that needed stitches, one just below my eye. But I came home the same day and recovered very quickly. I still have the scars to this day. I never blamed Bruce. He must have been in real agony, but his paws soon healed and we were best buddies again.

My eighth birthday was not very exciting. I remember the cake most because Mum let me make it and I liked helping her on Sundays when the rock cakes, Flapjacks, and other cakes were made. I know I had some books. One was all about the wild British birds and animals. The other about wild British trees and flowers, and before the week was out, I could name all the trees in my woods, especially the biggest and tallest and my favorite, the *Wellingtonia gigantea*. I had to ask Mum to pronounce it, but I couldn't remember. So I called it the Wellington tree.

It was the Queen's coronation that year, and in the summer, a national holiday was declared. The queen was actually being driven through our village on her tour of Oxfordshire, and every village was organizing a street party and celebrations afterward. Everybody was excited. Bunting was stretched across the streets, grass verges cut, gardens tidied, roads swept ready for the big day. The next day was warm and sunny. Everybody was up early to get the best spot on the side of the road through the village. At noon, the first cars arrived, followed by the queen's car. We all had Union Jack flags to wave as the queen passed by. I caught a fleeting glimpse of her in the back seat, and that was it. The moment had passed. I thought it was all a lot of work and effort to see a few cars drive by, but then I was only eight. The following day, tables started being erected down the main street. All the adults seemed to be rushing about, laying out food and drink. Everybody had contributed something. The pubs were open all day (which pleased my father) and they had supplied all the fizzy pop. Mum and some of the neighbors had supplied the cakes while others had made sandwiches, sausage rolls, and jelly. In all it was a massive amount of food and drink. The whole village, whether rich or poor, all sat down at twelve noon and tucked into the food, even my father. But as soon as the meal was over, he slunk off into the pub.

After the meal, all the children were ushered off to the recreation ground, where all the games were being organized. There were fairground rides, swing boats, and a helter-skelter, a wooden tower that you climbed carrying a coco mat and slid down on. Most of my school mates were there, but I was only looking for one girl, Alice. When I found her, she looked beautiful. We had a few rides on the swings and then the tournament began. My sister Sheila was entered in the fancy dress composition as the World's Beauty Queen. Mum had made a paper dress out of the *News of the World* showing pictures of the queen, and Sheila won first prize. I won the 100-yard sprint race. I didn't come anywhere in the sack race. We kept falling over. Then we had the children's wellie-throwing competition, and I came third. The games went on well into the evening, but I didn't see my father at all. I so wanted him to see me win the sprint race and make him proud. But we all had a smashing time and when I finally crawled into bed that night, I had the best night's sleep ever and no dreams.

On the Sunday, there was the annual steam-engine rally at Barclay Fields about two miles away. My father and all the local farmers drove their tractors and trailers into the main street at 9:00 a.m. My uncle drove his old army flatbed truck. Then we all climbed onto the trailers and sat on straw bales. We set off in convoy with my uncle leading. It took nearly an hour before all the tractors assembled in the field.

That's the first time I'd seen a traction engine in full steam going around the arena in the center of the field. It was thrilling. They even had miniature steam engines pulling trailers, taking kids for a ride. We ended the day on the fairground rides, then returned on the tractors and trailers in the evening. That day was the most exciting day ever. And it was the first time we had all been together as a family, although I noticed my father sneaking off for a quick pint in the beer tent.

On Monday, it was back to school as normal. I had made a lot of friends over that week and had showed some of them my camps in the woods. But only one of them wanted to come back, and Billy Monger became my best friend. He showed me how to make a bow and arrow out of a hazel wood, then sharpened the arrow with his penknife. We played cowboys and Injuns until he shot me in the leg with an arrow. I howled in pain as the arrow had gone in quite deep. Billy pulled it out, and I yelled some more. It bled for a while but he wrapped his hankie around it, and by the end of the day, it had healed over. We never played Injuns again, just cowboys.

CHAPTER

The Alternative Accommodation

The next year was the worst for the whole family. It started off all right—well, Christmas did, and I got a model steam traction engine. You filled the boiler with water then put methylated spirits into the little tank under the boiler, lit it with a match, and waited until the water turned into steam. Then you opened the valve and off it went. It was brilliant and my father showed me how to do it, but sadly, it didn't last.

That year was one of the coldest. It snowed then froze all week. The roads became treacherous. Cars were skidding into ditches, trees, and each other. Then late one night, we were all in bed, and there was a loud crash. My father and mother raced down the stairs and opened the cellar door. A car had come through the wall into the cellar. The car was pretty smashed up, but the driver crawled out. He was drunk as a lord but unhurt apart from a few scratches. My father helped him up to the kitchen, and Mother made him a cup of tea. I remember his posh voice when he spoke: "You'll be rewarded well, my good man, for your kindness." There was nothing we could do that late at night, so he slept in front of the fire on some blankets. The next morning, the police turned up with the farmer Giles Bedford and his architect. The drunk driver turned out to be Earl Spencer, a friend of the farmer, and well known to the police for his donations to the Policeman's Ball, held every year. A crane arrived and pulled the Rolls Royce out. The whole wall had to be shored up to make it safe. "You and your family can't stay here. It's not safe," said the architect. Farmer Giles Bedford assured my father he would find us alternative accommodation until the building work was done. As far as we know, no charges were bought against the earl, and we never got a reward. My father muttered, "One law for the rich, one for the poor." I never did know what that meant until much later. We stayed in the house that night. The next day, the farmer organized some farmhands with a tractor and trailer to help my father move all the furniture. They had moved all the stuff by midday, and we all moved in that afternoon.

The alternative accommodation was just around the corner at the back of the farm, a wooden bungalow that looked like a prewar barrack block. It looked depressing from the outside, but once inside, it was worse. We immediately felt the cold and damp. Even with all the furniture moved in around the bungalow, it didn't feel like home. As we all stood in the lounge and looked around, we noticed all the walls and ceiling were covered in asbestos sheets. Some were bare, and some had been wallpapered over. All the ceilings were covered in white distemper, with a single light bulb hanging in the center. There were no carpets on the floors, only linoleum. The only heating was a small fireplace in the center of the back wall. There were three bedrooms and a small kitchen off the lounge with a Belfast sink and wooden draining board. There was no hot water. An old three-ring electric cooker with a wooden worktop at the side, two shelves underneath for the saucepans, and a tall unit at the end held all the plates, dishes, cups, and saucers, with two pull-out drawers for the knives and forks. There was no bathroom or toilet inside.

Mum burst out crying. "How are we supposed to manage in this dump?" My sisters and brother all started crying as well. That's the first time I ever saw my father give my mum a hug, and I had tears in my eyes. My father opened the back door, and we all ventured out to explore. It was a very small back garden with a vegetable patch. On the side, a long brick shed divided the garden from next door with a gate connecting the properties. There were three properties in total. I opened the shed door, and there was the toilet. Wood had been stored in one corner, and there was a coal bunker in the other corner (at least it was filled with coal). I remember my father lighting the fire, and we all huddled around it to keep warm. Little did we know this would be our home for the next three years?

The freezing weather lasted all through January. My father did complain to the farmer about the cold, but he made excuses that the builders couldn't start work on our old house until the weather got warmer. However, he did give Dad a one-off payment to buy more sheets and blankets. But it was still freezing in the house, with ice forming on the inside of the windows. We even kept the fire going all night. It kept the lounge fairly warm, but that was all. Mum had to boil up water in an old kettle to make a cup of tea. We still had the electric boiler for washing clothes, so we had our weekly wash in front of the fire. Life was hard through that winter with the water pipe to the toilet regularly freezing up, but we managed.

We met the neighbors John and Jessy Williams with their son Adam, who was two years older than me. Mick and Val Turner and their two daughters Elizabeth, who was sixteen, and eight-year-old Pearl lived in the end bungalow. She must have gone to another school as I didn't know her. John and Mick both worked on the farm. John worked at the piggery (boy, did he stink sometimes), and Mike was the head herdsman looking after the cows. Both families became very friendly and helped us out, which pleased Mum.

Winter finally turned to spring, and the builders started repairing our old house, which made my father a bit happier. But a few weeks later, my father was told the new farm manager would be moving into our old house. When my father confronted the farmer Mr. Bedford, he replied, "Now you are a family of six, we decided the house simply wasn't big enough for you. The manager does not have any children, so it would be more suitable for him." When my father told Mum after work what Mr. Bedford had said, she burst out crying. We all tried to comfort her, but she was devastated. My mother and father changed after that.

My father started drinking more heavily, especially whiskey, which made him more violent, and Mum became more depressed and angry. Money was tight as my father hadn't done any gardening all through the winter, and Mum missed that extra bit of cash. The abuse began all over again. We all tried to help Mum with the housework—well, me and Sheila. The other two got in the way. I used to put the clothes through the mangle, and Sheila would hang them on the clothesline. One morning, my father returned home in a foul mood and argued with Mother, shouting and then storming out of the house. I was winding the sheets through the mangle. My father snatched the handle and turned it very quickly. I screamed as my hand went under the wooden rollers. He laughed and walked off. Sheila came over and helped me unwind the roller. Nothing was broken, but my hand felt squashed. Sheila asked, "Why does dad keep picking on you?" "I don't know" I replied but I wished I knew why.

My mother turned violent as well, but I think it was more frustration than anything. Up until then, she had never hit me, apart from a clip around the ear, which I probably deserved. But on this occasion, it was Monday, washing day, and the most stressful for Mum. I can't remember what I said to Mum, but she must have taken offense as she picked up the first thing that came to hand, the wooden copper stick and whacked me across the arm. I thought she had broken it and cried like a baby. It hurt, but it hurt more knowing Mum had hit me. We were never as close after that. Although my father had started the abuse again, it wasn't all bad for me. Billy Monger started coming around again as summer approached and the weather got warmer. We still went to the woods and played. I got quite good at climbing trees and we found a large badger's hole in a bank, but we never saw any badgers. Then Billy had this great idea. We would build a soapbox. He would supply the wood if I could get the wheels. I didn't know where I could get any wheels and then thought of Mum's old pram. She never used it now, as the kids could all walk so she used the pushchair. The next day, I pleaded with Mum until she finally relented. "You can have it, but you must build the soapbox around Billy's place," she said. "I don't want you using any of your father's tools. You know how angry he gets."

I pushed the pram over to Billy's house. It took all the next day to build it. We then stood back and admired our handiwork. We had the two large wheels at the back and the smaller ones at the front connected to a T-shaped piece of wood. This was connected with a bolt through both pieces of wood, which let the wood swivel. You then used a rope tied around the ends of the wood to steer it. We sat our bum down on a box over the back wheels. If you wanted to slow down, you put your feet down on the road. We tried the soapbox out the next day down the hill on the council estate. It went brilliantly. Some of the estate kids came out and wanted a go. The craze took off, and after a few weeks, there were half a dozen soapboxes racing down the hill.

Summer passed quickly; my ninth birthday came and went. I don't even remember getting any presents, but then times were hard. Then toward the end of the summer, I had been playing on my own in the woods. I was walking along the path on my way home, when three teenage boys approached me. I remember they were all smoking. The biggest boy said, "Do you want a fag, son?"

I retorted, "You're not my father." He bent down as though he was going to whisper in my ear. But then I felt a searing hot pain in my ear. He had stubbed his hot cigarette out in my ear. They all ran off laughing. I ran home, crying, clutching my ear. Mum removed what remained of the cigarette stub and bathed the inside of my ear with cold water. My ear blistered but cleared after a few days. That put me off smoking, until I started work.

CHAPTER

In Trouble with The Police

That Christmas was not very joyful. My mother and father were still arguing a lot over the slightest thing. I am sure the next-door neighbor, John and Jessy, heard all the shouting going on, with the paper-thin wall separating the properties, but they never said anything or interfered. We all got a present. Sheila had a doll, Tommy a farmyard puzzle, Mary some square stacking blocks with letters on the sides, and I got a Lone Ranger cowboy gun and holster that fired caps. I think I got the best present. Perhaps Mum felt guilty about whacking me with the copper stick. However, the following year was a bit better. Sheila had started school. Unfortunately, I was moved up to the senior school in Lower Balding about half a mile away, as were all my classmates, so I never saw my sister at school.

That summer, I made a friend with a hedgehog that had wandered into the garden. I made a run for him. (I think it was a male and not a female because of the size of it.) I found a cardboard box for a shelter and put some straw inside. I fed him some cat food and a drink of water, which he soon scoffed down. Sadly I only had him for two days, before my father found out. "What do you want a flea-ridden thing like that for? Get rid of it," he snarled. The next morning, the run and shelter had all gone and so had the hedgehog. I do hope he escaped before my father got to it, but I never saw it again.

We did have a white cat that kept coming around from the farm, obviously after food. When Mum saw it, she said, "Don't even think of keeping that as a pet. Your father will go mad." But we did keep it, and it stayed well away from my father, after he'd kicked it. Why did he always have to kick things? We had Snowy for many years, but he never came into the house.

That summer saw many changes in the village. All the horses on the farms had gone. The old smithy was pulled down and a new hardware shop built in its place. More houses were being built, and there were a lot more cars about. A new thirty-mile-an-hour speed limit was introduced through the village. The old village bobby retired, and Mr. Bartlett and his wife moved into the police house. (I was soon to meet the new village bobby, but not on friendly terms.) My friend Billy Monger and I began to get in a lot of mischief that summer, knocking on people's doors and then running away before they opened the door, riding our bikes through the village when it had rained, and going through puddles, splashing people on the pavement, but our favorite pastime was apple scrumping. We knew where all the best-eating apple trees were in the village. Unfortunately, they were all in private gardens. This particular garden had the best Cox's Orange Pippins in the world. They also had a Jack Russell, a snappy little dog, and there was always a danger of getting bitten. But that made it more exciting to get into the garden, pick the apples, as many as we could cram into our pockets, and then escape without being caught. We had done this many times. But one day, our luck ran out. The owner must have been waiting for us. As soon as we were up the trees, he let the dog out, and we were trapped up the tree with a barking snarling dog standing guard. He must have called the police because Mr. Bartlett came cycling up the path. He took our names and addresses and said he would be speaking to our parents later. We rode home, dreading what our parents would do, especially my father.

That evening, there was a knock on the door. My father answered it, and there was PC Bartlett standing on the step. My father invited him into the lounge, where we were all sat listening to the radio. Mum turned it off, and PC Bartlett explained what I had been up to. "I am only giving the lad a caution today," he said, "but don't let him get into any more trouble or else I will have to take this matter further. Trespassing and theft are serious crimes. It's lucky the owner doesn't want to press any changers. I am sure you can deal with the situation, Mr. Jones." He shook my father's hand and left. I froze. My father's face turned bright red with rage. He grabbed my arm and marched me outside. I heard my mum shout, "Don't be too hard on him, Trevor!" He pushed me into the shed and closed the door. I knew what was coming as soon as he undid the buckle on his belt. "You embarrassed me, you little bastard, and now you must be punished." I pleaded with him as he removed his leather belt, but he only smiled then began thrashing me with the belt. I don't know how many times he hit me, before Mum opened the door. "Stop it, Trevor. The boy's had enough." I was slumped on the floor. My father kicked me before he left. My mum helped me up and took me indoors. My father had left and probably gone down the pub. Mum stripped me down to my pants and bathed the weal marks on my body and legs. With tears in her eyes I could see Mum was upset. All the kids were in bed except Sheila. "Why is Dad so horrible to Davy?" she asked after seeing the bruises covering my body.

"I don't know, love," my mother replied, "but you know what he's like when he's been drinking." But Sheila and I both knew my father was not drunk.

Mum kept me off school until the weal marks and bruises had nearly vanished. Billy Monger came around to see where I was, but Mum made an excuse that I had caught chickenpox and needed to be isolated. The school never enquired why I was absent. It was two weeks before I went back to school, but I never told anybody what had happened.

The new school taught children from nine to eleven. We were classed as seniors, but we were still only children. Alice was not in my class but one above. But I still saw her at lunch break. However, my worst tormenter was Edward Stevens, who was in my class. But he had found a new boy to bully. Brian Thomas and his family had moved into one of the new houses in the village. At assembly that morning, the headmaster Mr. Quick announced that Brian Thomas was starting the new term with us. "Brian was born with one leg longer than the other," he said, "and consequently has to wear a club shoe. I will not tolerate any bullying in this school. Is that clear?"

There was a combined voice of "Yes, sir," by all the children. The headmaster stood there a moment longer and picked up a long cane that was behind his desk. He held it up and gently hit himself across the hand, so as to show us what to expect if we disobeyed him. "That we be all, children. Dismissed." We all filed back to our classrooms. Brian was in my class and sat in front of me. Edward Stevens sat right at the back. His favorite trick was to flick things at you with his ruler. Nobody liked him very much, but he did have some followers. At lunch break, everybody in my class wanted to see Brian's club shoe. He explained why he had to wear the special shoe, but soon everybody began to lose interest and walked off. That was Brian's moment of glory. (Little did we know that in the seventies, platform shoes were all the rage.)

It wasn't long before Steven Edwards began harassing Brian, or Clubby as he soon became known (children back then could be so cruel). He became very withdrawn. I had been told to stand up to bullies by both my parents, but when they are much bigger and stronger than you, it's hard to do that. I preferred to run away. It was about a week later when there was a commotion at the back of the playing field. There was a gang of children surrounding the ruckus. I pushed my way through only to see some boys holding down Brian. Edwards had removed Brian's club shoe and sock. They were all laughing at his shortened leg. I lost my temper and threw myself at Edwards and caught him off guard. We rolled about on the ground. With all the children shouting, "fight, fight," it wasn't long before Mr. James, our English teacher, came running over and stopped the fight, but it wasn't before Edwards landed a punch in my stomach. We were both marched off to the headmaster, Mr. Quick. He looked at us both and said, "I don't want any excuses. You were both fighting, so you will be both punished."

We were both expecting the cane across the palm of our hand. But he made us bend over and whacked us twice across the backside, and boy, did that hurt. I didn't cry—well, not in front of Edwards but I did in the toilets. Clubby became my second best friend after Billy although I never saw him outside of school. We still had our arguments with Edwards and his so-called gang but not so often. That first year passed very quickly, and I never got the cane again. But Steven Edwards did, more than once.

CHAPTER

The Day Trips

Christmas that year, the weather was mild, and it wasn't as cold as the previous year. I had not argued with my father much and kept well out of his way. I think Mum kept a watchful eye on him when he was drunk, but it was when he was sober that the sneaky cuff around the ear took place out of eyesight. I had some building bricks. Lego had just come on the market. Soon I could build little houses with windows and tiled roofs (this probably influenced my future career). Sheila had a scooter. Tommy got a clockwork train that went round and round on a circular track, which I thought was boring. And Mary had a toy trike, which she pedaled with the front wheels. I don't know what my parents gave each other, but I remember them both getting drunk that evening and snoring their heads in front of the fire.

I was nine and a half and looking forward to my tenth birthday. Billy had got a new bike for Christmas. As I was getting too big for my bike, even after raising the saddle and handlebars, he gave me his old bike and I let my sister Sheila have mine. Even though it had a crossbar, she still rode it. Snow began falling at the end of the month for a whole week. Everybody was out on toboggans heading for the hill at the back of the farm. Billy and I found an old galvanized sheet from around the farm. We bent the front up, then dragged it up the hill. Billy sat in front with me behind, then we set off down the hill. Trouble was we couldn't steer it. We bowled a few people over on the way down then went straight into the hedge at the bottom. We had a few more trips up and down the hill that day, then went home tired but happy.

The only other thing that I remember happening was the storm in April. It rained for a week then thunder and lightning streaked across the sky. That night while in bed, I was petrified when the lightning lit up the bedroom and seemed to shake the whole bungalow. The next morning, the storm had passed. After breakfast, Billy came over on his new bike and we set off for the woods, we hid our bikes and sneaked in under the barbed wire. We made our way to the camp only to discover it wrecked. Lightning had struck my favorite and tallest tree, the Wellington. The top half had completely gone and landed on top of the camp. There was nothing we could do. We got on our bikes and went back to my house. We collected up some jam jars and nets and went fishing for minnows and sticklebacks in the stream.

Summer came, and my father had booked up a day trip to Hayling Island, a seaside resort on the south coast, with the local coach service. This was a complete surprise to all of us. In nine years, we had never been on holiday, not even a day trip. We were all so excited when the coach picked us up at the village bus stop. We set off and, two hours later, arrived at the coach park. It was very hot. Mum had packed some food and drink in a carrier bag and our costumes and towels in another. We lugged all the bags down to the sand banks overlooking the beach. Mum set up a blanket to sit on then we tucked into the food and drink. "Are you going to have something to eat, Trevor?" asked my mother.

He just stood there, looking out to sea. "If you think I'm going to sit out here in this bloody sun after sitting on a tractor all day, then you must be mad. I'm off to the nearest pub." And off he went. Mum was disappointed, but I wasn't. We all went off paddling and messing about in the sea. After a smashing day out, it was time to make our way back to the pick-up point in the car park for the return journey. My father was nowhere to be seen. When everybody was on board, the coach driver stopped at the nearest pub to the beach. Mum went in, and a few minutes later, my father came staggering out, resting on Mum's shoulder. He was helped into the coach and promptly fell asleep across two seats. Mum was clearly embarrassed, but he never woke up until we were dropped off outside our home. We were all tired out and slept well that night.

My tenth birthday was not very exciting. Mum made a cake, and I had some more Lego bricks, but I loved building houses. The trouble was they never seemed to last up overnight. I suspect my father had something to do with that.

About two months before Christmas, Mum had got very friendly with Val Turner and her two daughters Elizabeth, eighteen, and Pearl, who was ten. I knew Elizabeth quite well because she had babysat for Mum when we first moved into the property. She was quite pretty but small and plump. She didn't go out much, and I don't think she had a boyfriend. Val and Mick wanted to go out on their wedding anniversary one night and take both their kids with them, but Elizabeth didn't want to go because she had a headache and preferred stay in bed. So they went without her. About eight o'clock that evening, Mum asked me to pop around Val's to borrow some washing powder. I knocked on the door and Elizabeth opened the door, dressed in a bathrobe. "Mum wants to borrow some washing powder," I blurted out. She invited me into the lounge, and I noticed there was a small tin bath full of hot water in front of the fire. "I was just about to have a wash," she said, "and I don't want the water to get cold. Sit over there until I have finished and don't look." I sat on the sofa and saw the bathrobe fall to the floor as she stood in the bathtub. She carried on chattering while washing herself. I kept my eyes on the floor but she asked me a question and I immediately looked up. I had never seen a naked lady before, and I stared at her hairy fanny. "You naughty boy," she said, "Now you must wash my back." I asked where the flannel was. She replied, "I don't have one, use your hands." So I picked up the soap and washed her back. When I stopped, she said, "You haven't finished yet. Wash my front." I was very nervous, so she held my wet soapy hands and placed them over her breasts, moving them around. Even at ten years old, I could feel my Willy getting hard. She quickly moved my hands around her fanny area and moaned. It seemed to go on for some time before she suddenly stopped and let go of my hands. "It's your turn now," she said. "You have seen mine, now let's see yours." It reminded of Alice when we first met in the tent. I nervously took off my shorts and pants and stood there "Take off all of your clothes," she said. "I want to give you a wash." I did what she said and stood there naked. Then she told me to stand in the bath and she proceeded to wash me with her hands. I remember she didn't wash my back but concentrated more on my Willy and I was enjoying it. She dried me off with a towel and led me through to her bedroom and lay on the bed. "Climb on top of me," she said. I did what I was told then she grabbed my buttocks and pulled me into her. Suddenly there was a loud knock on the back door. She pushed me off and grabbed her bathrobe and whispered, "Keep quiet" then went to the back door and opened it. I heard Mum say, "Where's Davy? I sent him around here an hour ago for some washing powder."

"I'm sorry, Mrs. Jones. Mum and Dad have gone out. Davy's been helping me sort out my record collection," said Elizabeth. "He will be finished in a few minutes then I will send him home with the powder."

My mum replied, "Make sure you do. It's nearly his bedtime," and then left. Elizabeth shut the door and told me to get dressed. She then gave me a packet of washing powder. As

I was leaving, she whispered, "Don't tell anybody. It's our little secret." I never did tell anybody but often wondered what would have happened if Mum hadn't knocked.

For the next few weeks, I kept thinking about what had happened that night. I had certainly enjoyed the experience but knew something was wrong. But who could I ask? It would be too embarrassing to ask Mum, and my father, well, he would probably have laughed. My current teachers were mainly elderly, well old to me. Then Miss Shaw my favorite teacher came to mind, but I hadn't seen her since I left primary school and didn't know where she lived. I thought of telling Billy, but he was only a few months older than me. The only person I could ask was Elizabeth herself, but that was difficult because I hardly ever saw her. And I think she had a new boyfriend as I had seen a young man going into her house. But I wanted to find out more. I had kissed Alice and tried to touch her small boobs, but she pushed me off. My frustration built up. What had Elizabeth done to me? Her younger sister Pearl was the answer. I had never fancied her, but she tried to look and dress like her big sister. She did look kind of sexy, and she was the same age as me. When I saw her alone one Saturday, I asked her if she wanted to go for a walk in the woods to see some flowers. She agreed and we set off. I showed her the secret way in under the barbed wire. We walked to our old camp. The farmer had cut all of the fallen tree and stacked the logs up in a heap. My old sackcloth that we had used in the camp was still there. We sat down. I leaned on her and kissed her on the lips. I then lay on top of her and pulled her knickers off. She didn't object. So I took my shorts and pants off and lay back on top of her. I fiddled around with my hard Willy. She suddenly shouted, "Stop! You're hurting me," and pushed me off. She quickly got dressed and said, "I want to go home." I was a bit embarrassed but got dressed and took her home. What had gone wrong? Elizabeth hadn't reacted this way, and she seemed to have enjoyed it. I just didn't understand.

That night, Pearl's father knocked on our back door. When Father answered it, Mick said, "Can I have a private word with you outside?" They went outside in the backyard. Mum looked across at me. "Have you been getting into trouble again?" She asked.

I looked a bit sheepish but said, "No, Mum." But I was thinking Pearl must have told her mum. When my father came back in the house, I was petrified. "Outside now!" he shouted.

I remember Mum saying "Whatever he's done, Trevor, don't lose your temper." I went outside, and my father shut the door. I was quite expecting him to remove his leather belt, and get another thrashing, but he didn't.

"Mick told me what you did to Pearl, you fucking pervert." Then he grabbed me around the balls and squeezed hard. I cried out and fell to the floor. He then kicked me hard in the ribs. "That will teach you not to interfere with young girls," he said and stormed off back inside, slamming the door behind him. I lay curled up on the path. I didn't know which hurt the most, my balls or my ribs. I was struggling to breathe when Mum came out and helped me to my feet. "What's he done to you this time, Davy?" I felt embarrassed to tell her that he had squeezed my balls, and just said he had punched me in the ribs.

My balls didn't ache so much when I went to bed that night, but my ribs did. I could hear my mum arguing with my father in the night, but couldn't hear what they were saying. My balls may have healed. But my ribs took a few days before I could breathe normally without it hurting.

I worried over the next few days, wondering why my father had called me a pervert. Was it some disease I had? Did other boys get it? I had done the same to Pearl as I had to Elizabeth and she seemed to like it, so why didn't Pearl? It was about twelve months later that I had another sexual experience, but this was entirely different.

(In those days, there were no sex education classes at primary school. If your parents didn't tell you about the birds and bees, which most of them didn't or were too embarrassed, you only relied on the whispers in the school playground.)

CHAPTER

My Auntie and Uncle

That Christmas wasn't cold and didn't snow, which was disappointing, for me anyway. But we did have a nice tree, which father had dug up from around the farm. My sisters and brother had various small gifts. I had another small box of Lego, a painting book and box of paints, and a book about the human body. I think this was Mum's way of telling me about the birds and bees. I found this fascinating, especially the pictures. But it didn't tell me what a pervert was. When I showed my sister Sheila a picture of a naked adult male, she giggled and wanted to look at the other pictures, so I let her borrow the book.

For Christmas dinner, we had chicken with all the vegetables. For an extra treat, we had trifle and ice cream. I sat as far away from my father as possible. I hated him so much and vowed one day to get my revenge.

The New Year started off well. Mr. Giles Bedford had informed my father that he had got planning permission to build a new three-bedroom house and it was for us. My mum was overjoyed when my father told her, but Father was doubtful. "We have been in this dump for three years," he said. "I will believe it when I see it." He always was a miserable old sod.

I was a bit bored one Saturday. Billy hadn't turned up, so Mum suggested I cycle over to my cousin's house and meet the twins Johnny and Jimmy Beal. They were a bit younger than me, but I agreed to go. It was a large detached house at the end of the village, just over a mile away. When I got there, Auntie Stella invited me in, and I met Johnny and Jimmy. They showed me around the house. I could see they were much richer than my mum and dad and even had carpets in most rooms (we only had linoleum on our floors), but the most exciting thing I saw was a television. The kids at school had talked about them, but not many had seen one. I was fascinated. I sat down with Johnny and Jimmy on the sofa, and watched a western called *The Lone Ranger*. It was so much better than listening to the boring radio and the Archers every night. That evening when I got back home, I told Mum all about the television that Auntie Stella and Uncle Jim had in their house. She just said only rich people could afford a television. I made up my mind then I was going to be rich one day. But I never got invited back until much later.

Early that summer, the workmen started building the new house for Giles Bedford. My mother was excited, but my father was optimistic. "Don't count the chickens before they're hatched," he said to Mum. "He will probably give it to the new farmhand, knowing him." But Mum never gave up hope.

This was the last term at school, and I was not doing that well in class. Clubby helped me out as much as he could, but I had a poor memory and did not understand all that was said. But we stuck together. The name-calling became an everyday thing. "The freak twins" was the most common. Alice was comforting in the lunch breaks, and Edward Stevens and his gang left us alone during school hours, apart from the name-calling and taunting. It was when we left school to go home that we had to run the gauntlet. Clubby was all right, after his dad heard about the bullying. He would meet him at the school gates and walk him home. Unfortunately, it was in the opposite direction from my home. I never took my bike to school, as it was only about a half mile. And I know Stevens would have damaged it if he knew it was mine. I knew at some stage I would have to stand up to him and fight. And that is just what happened about a week later.

I had said goodbye to Clubby and his dad after school. I looked around for Stevens but couldn't see any sign of him or his gang, so I made my way home. But they were waiting for me. My journey home took me past some trees and bushes on either side of the road. But there were no houses on that part of the road. I had always hated going past this spot. When I was younger, I imagined the place was haunted as the trees' branches touched each other over the road, making it seem quite dark. The trees seemed to whisper and groan to one another, and the bushes rustled as though somebody or something was hiding behind them. I always ran past this section of road, but on this occasion, I ran straight into Stevens. He and his buddy had been hiding on either side of the rode and they jumped out on me, blocking the road. I stopped and look around for an escape route. But two of his other gang had crept up behind me. There was nowhere to run. He stood in the middle of the road, legs apart with arms up and fists clenched, like a boxer's pose. "Come on, freak, let's settle this once and for all," said Stevens, smirking.

I knew I would be no match for him or his gang, then a thought crossed my mind: my father squeezing my balls—it was so painful. I didn't hesitate. I kicked him as hard as I could in the crotch. He hadn't anticipated this and crumpled to the ground, groaning in agony. I then ran like the wind before his gang could grab me. Some of them gave chase, but I was the school running champion and soon left them behind. That night, I lay in bed dreading of going to school the next day. I thought of telling Mum I had a stomachache or had a cold but then remembered how many times I had missed school apart from the last thrashing my father had given me. I had never missed school through illness. Even when I got infected with boils on my legs and could hardly walk, Mum just put a hot flannel over then squeezed them until all the pus was out. It hurt but she always said, "You can still walk, so you can still go to school." As I look back, my mum was so strict.

The only way was to face Stevens and take whatever punishment he and his gang had in store for me. But I got a pleasant surprise when I arrived at school. Stevens just ignored me; they left me and Clubby alone for the rest of the term. Perhaps a good kick in the balls did the trick.

My birthday was not very exciting that year. I don't even remember what I had apart from the Collins English Dictionary and finally found out what a pervert was. Mum did make a cake, but that was all. However, to our surprise, my father had booked another day out with the coach company, this time to London Zoo. I didn't know what a zoo was. I knew they kept animals and birds and things, so I asked my mum. "You will see when you get there," she said. I don't think Mum had been to a zoo either. But before that, I had one more encounter with my father. The harvest was in full swing. Dad was doing a lot of hours, often coming home at dusk, covered in dust from the corn. There was no health and safety in those days. The combine harvester my father drove had no cab. He didn't wear any goggles or breathing masks or ear defenders (no wonder he suffered later on in life). When the corn was cut, he drove the bailer to pick up the straw in the rows. A steel sled was towed behind to stack the bales into groups of six. A man usually stood on the sled and did this job, then he would pull a lever and the bales would slide out, ready for the next stack. I often watched my father when he rode the combine sat up high on the driver's seat. I suppose I was a quite proud of him driving the largest machine on the farm, but I never showed it and always kept out of sight when watching him. This particular day just before our day trip, my father forgot to take his lunch box to work. My mother asked me to take the lunch box to my father. I made all the excuses I could but, in the end, agreed. "He's in the large field next to the footpath," she said. "He's doing the baling today."

I set off on my bike, with the lunch box in my backpack. It wasn't very far. I could see that all the bales were stacked and the field finished when I arrived. I looked across, and he was sitting on his tractor alone. He must have seen me and beckoned for me to come over. I leant my bike against the fence and made my way over to him. He was drinking from a thermos flask. "I hope you have brought my lunch," he said. "I'm getting bloody hungry." I handed him his lunch box. He opened it and stuffed the sandwich into his mouth. I stood there watching as he devoured the rest of his lunch. He belched, handed me his empty lunch box, and said, "Do you want a ride on the sled?" I hesitated, knowing what my father was like. He said, "Well, make your bloody mind up. I haven't got all day."

So I accepted and climbed on board the sled. There were no bales to sit on, so I just stood and clung onto the back. My father drove off at a steady pace, and I was quite enjoying it watching the stubble slide under the sled. But then he started going faster, the sled was bouncing over the field, and I had to hang on for dear life. He looked back and was laughing. He suddenly swerved, and the whole sled tipped to one side. I was thrown out and landed on my back. I sat up bruised but unharmed, and my father just drove off laughing and left me there. I sat there a few minutes before I made my way back to my bike and rode home. I had to laugh after Mum took out his tin lunch box and it was squashed where I had fallen on it. "How did this happen?" my mum said. I told her I'd fallen off my bike, but I never told her the truth.

CHAPTER

The New House

The zoo trip went very well, because my father was too busy
with the harvest and had to work all weekend. My mother and
the kids were disappointed, but I was delighted. I held Tommy's
hand and Sheila held Mary's. We looked quite a grown-up
little family, walking around the zoo. I liked all the animals,
but didn't think the lions and big cats looked very happy on
their concrete floors and black metal bars surrounding the cage.
We then came across the camels, but these were not in cages.
These were camels with two humps that you could ride on.
We all begged Mum for a ride. We all climbed up the wooden
staircase to a platform level with the camel's back. The guide
then lifted me and Tommy and put us between the two humps;
he did the same with Sheila and Mary. Then the keepers led the

camels around a grass track and back to the start. My brother and sisters were thrilled at being up so high and looking down at all the kids waiting for a ride. There was an elephant ride next door, but I don't think Mum could afford both rides as they were quite expensive. "Maybe next time," she said. We were all disappointed, but we didn't argue. We then had a picnic on the lawn and an ice cream for desert. Our next stop was the reptile house. None of us enjoyed this much, seeing all the big snakes coming up to the glass with their fangs poking out and hissing at you. We carried on around the zoo, until my mum said, "Hurry up, let's get over to the chimpanzees' tea party before it starts."

I didn't know what that was, but we followed Mum over to a roped-off arena. There was a long table in the center and about eight chimps sat on benches either side of the table, all with spoons in their hands. The keepers then came out with plastic dishes filled with food. The chimps tucked into their food with their spoons. I had never seen anything so funny, and we all laughed. There was more food going over the table and on the grass than in their mouths. The chimps finished off with some drinks in plastic cups. We came away from the zoo feeling happy and caught the coach home. We told Dad all about it when we got home, but he didn't seem very interested. (I think the chimpanzees' tea party in the late fifties and early sixties was the inspiration of the PG Tips television adverts.)

At the end of the school term we all took the eleven-plus exam. This determined what school you would be attending when you started the new school in September. Billy passed but only just. Alice passed easily and was top of the class, but I always knew she would. I gave her a hug and kissed her as I knew I would probably never see her again as she was going to a private girls' school in Oxford, and Billy was going to the grammar school in Abingdon. Clubby and I failed the exam and were destined for the secondary modern school in Wallingford. I never did know what school Edward Stevens was allocated to because he never came to ours. That summer, Clubby and his family moved out of the village, and I never saw him again.

It was nearly the end of summer before the new house was finished. Mr. Giles Bedford kept his word and told my father we could move in on the weekend. The same farmhands helped my father move the furniture back into the new house. Mum was overjoyed at moving from the cold damp bungalow into the new warm house. We had central heating, well, sort of. Two radiators, one in the lounge and one in the kitchen ran off the back boiler in the lounge, but you had to keep the coal fire burning or else the radiators went cold. It wasn't very efficient, but it was better than nothing. We had an upstairs bathroom, with an immersion heater in the cupboard on landing, so we had hot water. We still had three bedrooms but they were much bigger. So the girls had one, Tommy and I had the other, and Mum and Dad had the largest room on the end. But the best surprise was the kitchen. It had proper units around the walls with built-in sink and wall cupboards with a kitchen table in the middle, but compared to the old bungalow, it was a palace. We soon settled into our new surrounding in fact the new house was right next door to our original house on the corner, a stone's throw from the woods.

September soon came around. Sheila moved up to the senior school. Tommy was in the last year of primary, and Mary had just started school. I was not looking forward to starting the new school. None of my best mates would be there, and I felt alone. My mum tried to cheer me up. "There will be lots of other boys and girls you can make friends with," she said. "You can bring them back here if you want." But I wasn't very confident. The first day, Mum let me ride my bike to school. I put the bike under the cover where all the other bikes were and went into the school assembly hall where all the kids were milling around. Several large boards were on display, which told you want class you were in. Year 1 class A was the top class then B, C, and D. I was in class 1 D, the bottom. I was a bit disappointed, but I found my way to the classroom and sat down in an empty seat. I looked around and recognized some of the boys and girls from our old school. The class master came into the room, and everybody stopped talking. "I am Mr. Harding, your math's teacher," he said. He was a tall thin man with thick black hair (we later found out it was a wig), and he wore glasses. "If you open your desks, you will find a list of all the classes you will be attending and what rooms they are in," he continued. "You will have a different teacher for each subject, so in your break time, find out where they are." I liked him. He smiled and seemed friendly.

I met all the other teachers in the weeks that followed: Mr. Thomas (geography), Mrs. Goodall (English), Mrs. Hepworth (science), Mr. Beaching (technical drawing), Miss Charleston (religious education), Mr. Tim's (woodwork), Mr. Granger (metalwork), Mr. Travis (music), Mr. Duckworth (arts and crafts), and of course, our math's teacher, Mr. Harding. The PE teacher was Mr. Grinder and for the girls Miss Becker. The headmaster was Mr. Davis and his secretary Miss Proctor. It was a large school, and remembering the teachers' names and classrooms took a while.

It was a bit confusing the first day. The school was huge compared to the junior school. It consisted of four separate blocks with corridors connecting them. The two blocks were for main studies: math's, English, etc. One block had the assembly hall, gym, shower and changing rooms. The last building contained arts and crafts, woodworking, metalwork, the science lab, and girls' domestic science room. Each block had a large cloakroom for hats and coats etc. it could take ten to twenty minutes to change classes. Although it was a mixed school, the girls played at lunchtimes in the netball and tennis courts areas, which were fenced in, and the boys played in the tarmacked area used for playing football when it was wet—this was also fenced in and was on the opposite side to the girls'. So the only time you saw the girls was when you were changing classes or in the classroom. Obviously you could meet outside of school hours, as many did. I did speak to a few boys and noticed that most of them were wearing long trousers, and I was the only boy in my class to have shorts on. When school had finished, I went to get my bike, but it was gone. I looked everywhere but couldn't find it. Of all the hundreds of bikes, why did they have to pick mine? When I complained to Mr. Harding, my math's teacher, he said, "Did you lock it up with a chain?" I told him I hadn't. He was sympathetic, and took my name and details. But I never saw my bike again. Mum wasn't very pleased when I told her. "Well, we can't afford to get you another bike. You will just have to walk to school," she said. "Maybe you will get one for Christmas." I was disappointed but knew Mum was struggling with money problems again, so I didn't argue.

So I started walking to school. It was only two miles by road, but it didn't take me long, and I soon got used to it. About a week later, I was on my way back home, and it started to rain. I didn't have a raincoat, so I held my backpack over my head. I thought I might try and thumb a lift. I'd seen other people stick there arm out and wiggle their thumb, so I did the same. I didn't have much success and was about to give up, when a car pulled up and a lad opened the back door and said, "Hop in. you look soaked." So I got in and was glad to get out of the rain. I pulled the door shut and the car pulled away. There were three lads, two in the front and the one sitting next to me. They all seemed friendly, but I immediately felt frightened when they started talking dirty and laughing. "I wonder how big his dick is," the front passenger said, and the driver replied, "I bet he hasn't even got any hairs around his balls."

I looked out the window and saw the turnoff for my village up ahead. I said, "Could you stop here please? I just live down that road." But they just laughed and drove past the turning. I panicked but kept quiet and tried to ignore them. Then the lad sitting next to me grabbed me and tried to take off my shorts. The front passenger was leaning over the seat, trying to hold my legs. But I was kicking and punching, trying to get away. The car slowly pulled up at the crossroads near my uncle's sawmills. I saw my chance, grabbed for the door handle, and opened the back door. I half stumbled then fell out of the car just as it was pulling away. I lay on the road, bruised and my legs crazed, but

I had not broken any bones. I stood up and realized I had left my backpack in the car with all my school books and things inside. I glanced up the road, but the car was nearly out of sight. I walked back home wondering what excuse I could give to my mother. She did ask why I was late and why my shorts were torn and dirty. "I will have to wash and repair them before you go to school tomorrow," she said, rather annoyed. I thought about telling her what had happened but decided against it, as it would only worry her. I lay in bed that night thinking what excuse I was going to tell Mr. Harding and then realized all my books had my name and address in. I did explain to Mr. Harding what had happened, and he asked if I wanted to contact the police. I was a bit scared of the police, so I declined his offer. He told me not to worry about the lost school books and would give me an overall score in my exam, at the end of school term. He did say just before I left, "You haven't had much luck since you started school, David, first your bike and now this. I hope your luck changes in the New Year."

With all the kids at school, it was getting harder to keep us all in clothes. Mum had opened an account with a company called Freemans, where you could order clothes from the catalog and pay weekly, when the man came around to collect the money and take your orders.

To cheer me up, Mum suggested I walk over to my uncle Jim's sawmills and see if I could do any odd jobs around the wood yard. It was about one and half miles, but it only took about half an hour if I walked and ran. When I got to the yard, I was quite nervous, but went into the office to see my uncle. At first he said I was too small, and didn't have any work. Although I was still skinny, I was quite tall. As I thanked him and turned to leave, he said, "I suppose you could try and bag some blocks, but they're quite heavy." I said I would try anything. He then took me over to the block shed. One of his workers was cutting tree branches on the big tabletop saw into logs and throwing them onto an enormous pile. Two other workers were putting the logs or blocks, as they called them, into sacks, then weighing them on the scales. I watched them for a few minutes, until my uncle said, "Well, lad, do you think you could manage this job? I will pay you a penny for every sack you fill."

I was thrilled I had a job and was going to get paid for it. Bill showed me how to hold the sack and put the blocks inside. I managed this but couldn't lift the sack onto the scales to weigh them. Each sack weighed half a hundredweight. "You will need bigger balls to lift them," joked Tom, the other worker.

I laughed but didn't know what he meant. They loaded the lorry with the bagged-up blocks and set off on the block round, which they did every Saturday. I was left bagging up some more blocks on my own. Toward the end of the day, my back ached and I was tired. I had bagged twenty-four bags. I decided to finish and went over to the office. My uncle sat smoking a pipe. "How did you get on, lad?" he said.

I proudly replied. "I bagged twenty-four bags, sir."

"Ah, but did you weigh them as well?" he said. I told him I hadn't. "Well," he replied, "you have only done half the job, so I will give you half the money." He put his hand in his pocket and pulled out one shilling and gave it to me. He asked if I was coming next Saturday, and I said I would and left to walk home. I had enjoyed doing the work and did earn a shilling, so I was quite happy.

On my way home, I passed my Auntie Stella's house and decided to call in see Johnny and Jimmy, the twins. Auntie answered the door and invited me in. The twins were sat watching the television. They were watching *Andy Pandy*, which I found a bit childish, so I soon became bored. "Would you like to stay for tea?" my auntie asked.

I replied, "Yes, please," knowing it would be a better meal than we had at home. Then we all sat around the kitchen table and had the meal. The twins bolted down their food. "Mum, can we watch *The Lone Ranger*?" said Johnny.

"And Tonto," said Jimmy.

"If you stay quiet," she replied. (Although they were twins, they were not identical.) So we all sat in the lounge and watched the cowboy film. I was rather hoping Uncle Jim would come home for tea and then take me home in his car, but he never arrived. "You have to go home now, Davy," my auntie said. "Time's getting on, and the twins need a bath." I thanked my auntie for the meal. It was quite dark when I left and quickly made my way home, until I came to the stretch of road that I dreaded, the haunted section. I stood by the last house illuminated by the lights in the windows. There was a slight breeze as I looked down the dark road, already imagining what creepy beings were hiding in the bushes. I hesitated whether to run or wait for a car to come by so it lit the road in front, and then run. I waited and waited, but no cars came. So I ran as fast as I could. I could hear the branches above me talking to one another as they rubbed against each other, the bushes swaying as if something was moving them. It was probably one hundred yards to the next house and light, but I must have cleared that distance in less than four minutes. There was nothing there really, but to an eleven-year-old's imagination, the mind creates strange things. I arrived home after seven. My mother was worried. "Why didn't you let me know you were going to be late?" she said. But how could I, without a phone?

Mum soon calmed down when I told her I had a job and showed her the bright shilling coin. "When I earn some more, I will give you half," I told her. I got a big cuddle for saying that.

The following Saturday, it rained, so I never went to my uncle's but stayed indoor playing with the Lego. Billy paid me a visit on Sunday and we played in the woods with Bruce. He was getting quite old now but still jumped around when we threw him sticks. I hadn't seen Billy since I started the new school, so we had a lot to chat about. I told him about my stolen bike and that I was saving for a new one. He said he would come next Sunday when I explained about the job I was doing on Saturdays. He left early afternoon, still a good friend.

CHAPTER

My First Real Job

That first term at the new school dragged by. I did get the mickey taken about my short trousers especially as it was getting quite cold, but it didn't bother me. I was more interested in going to the sawmills and earning some money. After a few weeks, I could fill sacks, lift them on the scales, and weigh them. And just before Christmas, I was filling up to forty bags a day. But my uncle was crafty; he seldom gave me more than one half-crown coin, or two and sixpence, no matter how many sacks I had filled. But I didn't mind. I gave Mum half the money and kept the rest.

Christmas was cold. My father and mother had dug the garden, and it was ready for planting in the spring. The house was warm downstairs if we kept the lounge fire going but a bit chilly upstairs until you got into bed, then you soon felt warm. The same cat that we were feeding around the old bungalow followed us and sneaked into our new house and became very friendly; even Bruce our dog accepted her. My father must have softened a bit because he let us keep her. She was a pure-white cat, so we called her Snowy.

We erected the Christmas tree and decorated the lounge with tinsel and holly. Presents were stacked beneath the tree, and we were all very excited when we went to bed that night. We all awoke early and crept downstairs. I hoped I might find a new bike in the kitchen but was a bit disappointed at not finding one. Shelia suggested we take Mum and Dad a cup of tea in bed as a surprise. I made the tea but asked her to take the cups up on a tray. (I didn't want to face my father this early in the morning.) She came down a few minutes later, smiling. "Mum thought that was a lovely surprise," she said, "but Dad didn't say anything."

I wasn't surprised, knowing how grumpy my father was in the mornings. We waited until Mum came down the stairs. Dad decided to have a lie-in. We started to open all the presents, with squeals of delight from Sheila and Mary as they unwrapped some more dolls, a teddy bear, and puzzles. Sheila also had a dolls pushchair. Tommy had a toy rifle that fired corks and some more track and carriages for his clockwork train. I had new pair of shoes and long trousers (at least they weren't secondhand from Mr. Primrose) and I had a Meccano set with instructions of how to build a lorry with small strips of metal that bolted together. I was fascinated by this and soon began bolting the pieces together, completely forgetting about the bike I'd wanted. After dinner, which my father did get up for, we played with our toys. I didn't see any presents for Mum; perhaps she had spent all the money on us. But it was a great Christmas and warm in front of the fire.

In the New Year, I continued working at the saw mills on Saturdays for my uncle, bagging blocks and weighing them. I began pacing myself and found I was not as tired at the end of the day. I was regularly filling forty to fifty sacks, but my uncle never paid me the full amount we agreed on. Winter turned to spring, and I was looking forward to my twelfth birthday. A new sweet shop opened up in the village. I say new but it was a council house that the tenant had bought off the council and converted the downstairs lounge into a shop. It was an instant success on the estate, with the kids queuing up to buy sweets. My favorite was the two-penny pick-and-mix bag. You never knew what was inside, but usually there was a gobstopper, four small chews either fruity or liquorish, four small aniseed balls, and a penny lollypop. If you bought them all separately, they cost a lot more. The shopkeeper must have done well because he was always running out of the most popular sweets.

It was about this time that the Browning family moved onto the estate. They had ten children; most of them were little tearaways. Both parents were alcoholics and neglected the children. The eldest girl, sixteen-year-old Bethany, looked after the kids as best she could, but they soon got into trouble with the police. Mr. Bartlett the village bobby spent more time around their house than he did in the whole of the village.

It was just my luck that twelve-year-old Gary, the third oldest and most troublesome of the family, ended up in my class. He was instantly disliked by all the children when Mr. Harding introduced him. At least I didn't have to sit next to him in class. By then, I had made friends with Brian Bennett. He was staying in a children's home in the town. I felt sorry for him after he told me about his mother and father abandoning him at a young age and he had been in care most of his life. Brian was big but very insecure and quite shy. Because of his size, he didn't make friends very easily and most were afraid of him, but he was a big friendly giant to me. So Gary Browning didn't bother me too much at school. But out of school was a different matter. (Wherever I go, I seem to attract bullies.) I had started walking home from school across the fields after the experience from the lads in the car. But Gary had started taking this route as well, and one afternoon, he was waiting for me. I didn't see him until the last minute; he'd been hiding behind a bank and jumped out on me. He wasn't any bigger than me, perhaps a bit heavier. But he was a ruffian and knew how to fight. I suddenly remembered the last fight I'd had with Edward Stevens and tried to kick him in the balls. But he turned just as I was off balance and struck me with a punch to the side of the face. I went down then he sat on me and continued punching me. I tried to protect my face with my arms and begged him to stop. I'd had enough. He punched me once more in the stomach and got off. He had winded me, and I was struggling to catch my breath. Gary just stood there and laughed. "You fucking little wimp, not so big now you haven't got your big dopey friend with you," he said. He walked away, leaving me lying on the ground. I waited until I was sure he was well ahead of me before I struggled home. Funny enough, he didn't bother me much after that. Now I was beaten he moved on to other kids to bully.

The summer had arrived and sadly the job at the sawmills finished. My uncle informed me people did not want any more blocks now the warm weather was here. I was disappointed but had saved up just over a pound, which was a huge amount for me. It was the last day of school. I said all my goodbyes to my friends that I would not be seeing until next term at school. I had had no more trouble with Gary Browning since he beat me up. I suppose I was a bit of a coward but wasn't ashamed. Billy started coming around on Saturdays, and we played in the woods, mainly climbing trees. We did find a large badger's set in the bank and decided to dig it out so we could crawl inside. I had a little trowel and was digging at the back. Billy was taking the soil out, when suddenly the tunnel collapsed and I was buried. It was a few minutes before Billy pulled me out by my legs. I was fine but often wondered what would have happened if Billy hadn't been there. We were both getting bored and wanted something else to do. I did miss my bike and wondered if I might get one for my birthday. I needn't have worried because Billy had a new bike for his birthday and his father said I could have his old one for a pound. So it worked out all right.

We were all wondering if Father had booked a day trip with the coach firm this year. Sheila and I wanted to go to the seaside, but Tommy and Mary wanted to go back to London Zoo. But when Mum asked my father, he was a bit grumpy. "I've got to work all the summer with the bloody harvest," he moaned. "Anyway, we can't afford it this year. Giles Bedford has put up the rent, and you keep spending money on that bloody clothes catalog."

Mum replied, "We have to keep the children in clothes, Trevor. They are growing up so fast."

"Well, why don't you get off your fat arse and get a job?" he shouted, then got up and stormed out.

I could see Mum was upset and gave her a cuddle. "Don't worry, Mum. In two months, I will start working at Uncle Jim's again, so I can pay you a bit more."

She smiled. "You're a good boy, Davy." And she ruffled my hair.

One Saturday, I was around Billy's house, and his mother said, "Why don't you ride over to the town and go to the cinema? They have a matinee on Saturday afternoons, and it's a lot cheaper." We thought that was a great idea and set off across the fields on our bikes. When we arrived, we chained our bikes together and locked them. I always carried a small chain and lock in my saddlebag after my other bike was stolen. We paid the five pennies entrance fee (I still had two shillings saved up) and sat on the back row of seats. We looked around. There were six or seven other kids and their parents, but apart from that, the cinema was empty. We sat back as the lights dimmed. Path News came on first about what was happening around the world; we found that a bit boring. Then there was a cartoon starring Mickey Mouse and his friends, then the lights came back on and the usherette came around, selling popcorn drinks and ice cream. I didn't want anything, but Billy bought me a drink. The lights dimmed and the main film started: *Wagon Train*, staring Pat Boone. We sat through the whole film mesmerized. We both loved cowboy films and came away very happy. That was a great afternoon, and we decided to go the following Saturday.

Billy, however, couldn't come the following Saturday. His parents were visiting their relations for dinner, and Billy had to go along. So I decided to go alone. I was a bit scared to start with, but sat down in the back row as before. Again there were very few people in the cinema. After the news, the cartoon started. I found it a bit boring and waited for the main film to start. The usherette came around as before, but I didn't want anything. The lights dimmed, and another cowboy film started, starring John Wayne. I settled back in the seat and relaxed, completely mesmerized by the film. I didn't notice a man come along the aisle, until he sat down next to me. He was dressed in a raincoat, which I thought a bit odd as it was a warm day. I carried on watching the film and didn't notice him gradually slide my arm over his knee until my hand touched a warm hard thing. I looked across. He had his Willy out, and my hand was touching it. I quickly pulled my hand away and dashed to the toilets. I washed my hands and stood there a few minutes, wondering what to do. Was this a pervert, that my father had called me? I didn't know. I decided to go back inside to see if he was still there. The whole back row of seats was empty. He had gone. I sat back down on the seat closest to the aisle, ready to run if he returned, and watched the rest of the film. When Billy came over the following Saturday, I told him what had happened. He thought it a huge joke and laughed, but we still went to the cinema the following Saturday. I never saw the man again.

CHAPTER

Growing Up

September soon came around, and I went back to school. I decided to walk, although I had a bike and could lock it up. I didn't want to risk my bike getting damaged especially if Gary Browning found out which one was mine. But I had a pleasant surprise when I went to the information boards and found what class I was in. It read David Jones class 2C. Good old Mr. Harding had kept his promise and given me a higher mark-up. It did mean I had a new class master, which turned out to be Mr. Goodall the English teacher. He was a short man with thinning hair and was quite fat. He was a bit older than Mr. Harding, but I liked him. When I sat down and looked around, I couldn't see Brian my school mate, or Gary Browning. I did recognize some of the other kids from year 1, but at least Gary wasn't in my class, which was a relief. I made a new friend who sat next to me in class: Michael Bolton, or Mickey, as he was soon called. We hit it off right away as I found out his father owned a farm and lived about five miles away in a village called Whittingham. He was lucky because he came to school on a chartered coach, which picked up children as far as ten miles away. I still saw Brian Bennett at school lunch breaks, and we all became firm friends.

There were a few girls in our class that I quite fancied. I suppose I was quite good-looking with long blond hair and muscular arms. And some of the girls kept looking at me and smiling. So I decided to get to know them better. It started off in the lunch break before the girls went to the playground, with a cuddle in the back of the cloakroom, where all the coats were hung up on pegs and nobody could see you. A kiss on the lips then I slowly put my hand over her breast and squeezed. If she didn't push me away, I then slid my hand up her dress and felt between her legs. Some girls pushed me off and called me a dirty bastard. But other girls didn't mind me groping them, so I mostly went with them. (This may sound disgusting behavior, but it was all part of growing up in those days and a lot of boys did it.) But this didn't happen every day. I did get caught one day when I met Mary Welch, one of my regular girls on the stair landing at lunch break. I looked around, and there was nobody about. She was on her way to the playground. She stopped and I put my arms around her and gave her a long smouchy kiss. I then put my hand up her dress and felt between her legs. We stood like this leaning against the wall for a couple of minutes, when all of a sudden a loud voice said, "Are you enjoying yourself, Jones?"

I looked around, and Miss Proctor stood in the doorway, watching me. I didn't know what to say or do but then said, "This is my girlfriend, miss," and she replied, "Well, you can do that sort of thing outside of school hours. Now get along, both of you." And then she went back into the classroom. She didn't reprimand me or Mary, so I got off lightly.

One of the games we used play in the lunch break was British Bulldog. One boy would bend over and push his outstretched hands on a wall or fence for support. The process was repeated with the next boy pushing against the first. So you ended with a whole row of boys bent over. Then you had to leap across all the boys and get up the line as far as possible before another boy leapt on behind you. The object of the game was to have the longest line before you all collapsed. The record was ten. The other game was Tic Tac. One boy in the group would be the starter then have to touch another person's head before he could pass it on. It usually ended with the fastest boys never getting caught.

The colder weather started at the end of September, and I started working at my uncle's sawmills, filling the sacks with blocks. I became quite confident after a few weeks, and I could even lift the half-hundredweight bags onto the back of the lorry. The trouble was the more I exerted myself, the faster I became tired. "Pace yourself," Eddy the lorry driver kept telling me. "Slow down and take your time." He was right. I don't think Uncle Jim thought any more of you however many sacks you filled. I certainly never got any extra money. But I loved the job, and Tom even showed me how to hold and saw logs on the table saw, which on hindsight, was a bit dangerous. I could easily have sawn my hand off, as there was no guard on the saw blade.

As the saw mills were so remote, there had been a couple break-ins at the office. Uncle Jim had bought got a guard dog to protect the property. He called it Satan, a massive black German shepherd. At night, it would wander around the yard, barking at anything that moved. But in the daytime, it was tethered to a long running chain that let the dog have limited freedom. At first I was terrified of it and glad it was secured by the chain. But as the weeks went by, it got used to me and became very friendly. He even wagged his tail when I arrived for work on Saturdays and would let me stroke him. Sometimes I called into my auntie's on the way home from the sawmills and watched television with the twins. But after an hour, she usually said I must go home, "or your mum will be worried."

Now I had a bike I didn't mind riding past the haunted section of road at dusk, but I still imagined there was something lurking in the bushes when the wind was blowing. I did have an active imagination. I gave Mum most of my money and just kept a bit back for sweets. When I did venture onto the estate to buy sweets, there was always the possibility I would bump into Gary Browning and I did once or twice and both times he stole all my sweets.

I thought my father had softened a bit because he did not hit me as often as before. But he hurt me in other ways, teasing me as much as he could, usually when Mum was out of sight. Sometimes he would bring back small bars of chocolate for Sheila, Tommy, and Mary and give them a bar each, then say, "Sorry, that's all there was in the shop." But I caught him feeding Bruce our dog with chocolate a few times and he just smiled. But Sheila noticed and always gave me a few squares when he went out. I was a bit cheeky sometimes and usually got a clip around the ear. He never beat me with his belt again. But as I got older, the punching started.

That Christmas we did have a tree and we all got a few presents but the atmosphere wasn't very joyful. There were no gardening jobs at Mr. Primrose's house, Mum still hadn't found a job, and money was tight. In the New Year, Bruce our dog became ill. He wasn't eating, and the mouthfuls he did eat he vomited back up. Mum called the vet out and he diagnosed it was cancer. "He's an old dog," said the vet. "He's suffering and it's cruel to keep him alive. It's best if we put him down."

I said to Mum, "Is Bruce going to be killed?" When she replied that was the best thing for him, I burst into tears. I was devastated. He was my mate, when he found me in my camp and licked my face. The times when I had thrown sticks and he bought them back, the times I'd hugged him when I was upset—all these thoughts came flooding back. I just cried when the vet injected him in the leg. He looked up at me just before he closed his eyes. Then the vet covered him with a blanket. I ran outside across the path to the woods, the place where Bruce and I had played together for all those years and cried. I'd never felt so alone. Mum and I buried him the next day in the garden under the apple tree.

One Saturday, Billy wanted to see what job I was doing. So we both rode over to the saw mills. We parked our bikes against the fence and walked over to the blocking shed. Satan was tethered to the running chain and immediately began to bark and looked aggressive, but when I went up to him and stroked him, he calmed down. Billy followed me over, and as soon as he was in range, Satan jumped up at him and knocked him over. He then jumped on his back and began humping him. Billy was crying out, and Eddy came running over and pulled the dog off but not before Satan had ejected all over Billy's back. It was funny to watch, but Billy didn't think so. He wasn't hurt but soon went home on his bike. I found out later that Billy's parents had a Labrador bitch that was on heat, and Satan must have smelled it on Billy.

As the weeks went by, I was getting quite strong and muscly especially around my back and arms with all the bending and lifting the sacks of blocks. I was hoping that Uncle Jim would let me go with Eddy and Tom on the lorry and deliver the blocks, but when I asked him, he said, "Maybe next year, lad. You may be able to lift the sacks, but it's a lot harder to carry them down a narrow path," so I was a bit disappointed. When I arrived home, Mum was very excited. "I've got a job, Davy," she said as I came indoors. We sat down at the kitchen table, and Mum told me the job was cleaning for the lady across the road. Mrs. Davis was quite elderly and struggled up the stairs. Mum had to work one hour a day for two days of the week and could work when all the kids were at school, so it suited her. But it wasn't long before word spread, and Mum was soon cleaning for three other people. My father was pleased when Mum told him. "I've also started the gardening work for Mr. Primrose," Father said, "so we will be able to afford a day trip somewhere." But he never told us where or when. It was two weeks later that Father informed us he'd booked a coach trip to Hampton Court and Kew Gardens. We all looked puzzled. "What's that?" Sheila asked.

Mum explained, "It's a great big historic house that you can explore and a big glass building with all sorts of tropical plants." We had all hoped to go back to the seaside, but at least we were going somewhere. When the day arrived, it was raining. We stood sometime before we boarded the coach, and were all quite wet and miserable. "Cheer up," Mum said. "It's a good job we are not going to the beach. At least where we are going will be warm and dry."

When we arrived at Hampton Court, my father said, "I'm not interested in historic buildings. I'll see you later" and strode off to find the beer tent. It was left to Mum to drag us around the palace, trying to explain who stayed there and what all the rooms and suits of armor were used for. It wasn't long before we were all totally bored, and for once, wished I'd gone for a drink with my father. At least when we set off for Kew Gardens, it had stopped raining and my father was in a better mood with a few beers inside him. We found Kew Gardens a bit more interesting. Well, Sheila and I did. Tommy and Mary were bored very quickly, but cheered up when Mum bought them ice creams. Even Father seemed interested in the exotic plants. The sun was shining when we went outside and walked around the gardens, and beneath the trees, we all sat down on the grass and ate the sandwiches and apples Mum had brought with us. "The flower Borders look very pretty. I wish our garden looked like that," said Mum.

"We need to grow vegetables," my father replied. "You can't eat bloody flowers." When we eventually got back on the coach, we were all tired. Sheila, Tommy, and Mary fell asleep on the back seat and didn't wake up until the coach dropped us off at our house. We all agreed it was a nice day out, but not as much fun as the seaside.

CHAPTER

Racism

At last I was a teenager; my thirteenth birthday had arrived. The work down at the saw mills had finished. But my uncle asked if I would like to accompany the team out on a few days' work felling trees in the forest, before I went back to school. I had never seen a full-size tree being cut down, so I agreed immediately. I rode over to the yard at eight the next morning and got in the lorry. I sat between Eddy and Tom; my uncle drove the crane with Bill. It took nearly an hour to get there, but it wasn't long before the first tree was felled. I had to stand behind the lorry to watch it fall with a huge crash. "Come on, lad. You can help start a fire," my uncle said, "then you can burn all the brushwood that's left."

While Tom cut all the branches off the tree and Eddy loaded them on the lorry, I was left to pick up the brushwood and put on the fire. When the lorry was loaded, we set off back to the saw mills. Before I left for home, my uncle said, "If you would like to come tomorrow with us, it will be an exciting day out for you." Of course, I agreed. I met him at the yard at 8:00 a.m., wondering what exciting thing my uncle had in store. When we arrived at the forest, Tom went off with some boxes and a coil of cable. Jim let me sit in the crane and watch him load the felled trees that we had stripped all the branches off. The lorry could only carry five tree trunks. "Any more than that," said my uncle, "and we will be overweight." Tom returned sometime later, unrolling a reel behind him. "All set, Tom?" my uncle asked.

Tom nodded. We then all sat around the lorry and had a packed lunch. About half an hour later, Jim told me to sit under the lorry and watch the five tree stumps about fifty yards away that had been felled the day before. "Don't take your eyes off the tree stumps," he said, grinning, before joining Tom, Eddy, and Bill behind the lorry. A strange noise like an air-raid siren wailed over the forest, then it all went quiet. I kept my eyes on the tree stumps, and suddenly, all the five tree stumps were uprooted and flew into the air. It was strange there was no noise or explosion, then less than a second later, the sound wave hit us with a huge *whoosh*. Clods of mud and bits of wood rained down about twenty yards from the lorry. I was stunned but thrilled. I never expected anything like that to happen. My uncle came around the lorry and stood beside me. "What do you think of that then, lad, amazing, wasn't it?" I never forgot that day; it was the most exciting ever. Why couldn't my father be more like Uncle Jim?

September came around, and it was back to school. Billy hadn't been around for most of the summer as I'd been at the saw mill most of the time. But all my old school friends and enemies were there, including Gary Browning and his gang. At least we all moved up a year to 3C and Gary was still in D.

At assembly that first morning, the headmaster stood up with a young lad at his side. "This is Ian Mackenzie, and he has come all the way from Jamaica," the headmaster said. "I would like you welcome him and make him feel at home. He may look different but he is the same as you, so be friendly."

Ian then sat down with the kids in the front row. This probably was the first black pupil the school had seen. It was for me. I had seen them in movies but hadn't taken much notice as most of the old films were in black and white. Ian was a celebrity for the first day. Everybody wanted to meet and touch him. He was not in my class but one above, 3B, so we only met him in the playground the next day. He told us that he had come over with the Windrush generation two years before and had lived in London. His father was a bus driver, and his mother was a nurse. He was the only child, and his family had moved from London to the country to escape racism. When we asked him what racism was, he started to explain, but before he could finish, we heard Gary Browning's booming voice: "Hey, what are you talking to that nigger for? Why doesn't he bugger off back home where he belongs?" All his gang sniggered.

Then Ian said, "That's racism." After he had told us about himself, it seemed he had the same likes and dislikes as us. The only difference was his skin color and tight curly black hair. He joined in with the game we were playing, so he became one of our gang. He was safe in the school playground apart from the racist remarks, which he ignored, most of which were from Gary Browning and his gang. But it was after school, while waiting for the school bus, he was most vulnerable to the lurid remarks. It seemed racism followed poor Ian wherever he went.

It wasn't long before I met Gary Browning again. It seems he had taken offense to me making friends with Ian and was hiding behind the bank on the way home from school, in exactly the same place as before. "I don't like nigger lovers," he spat at me, "and now you're going to pay." He stood to one side of me, with fists raised. I think he thought I would try and kick him again. I knew he would easily beat me in a fistfight, so as he threw the first punch, I dodged and grabbed him around the neck with my right arm and pulled him down to my waist and squeezed as hard as I could. With his arms flailing and trying to punch me, I held on and squeezed harder. It was deadlock. I couldn't hit him, and he couldn't hit me. After a couple of minutes, he was struggling to breathe, so I let him slump to the ground. He got up and I thought he would come at me again, but he only called me a bastard and threatened to get even with me one way or another then he walked off. That was the last time Gary picked a fight with me. All that bagging and lifting of blocks at the wood yard had made my arms very strong. Despite the name-calling, Ian seemed happier when playing with us and told us most of his class were friendly too. But Gary Browning did have his revenge a few days later.

The school tuck shop was a table on wheels with a shelf at the back and sold crisps, biscuits, chocolate bars, and small bottles of pop. It served pupils that didn't want school dinners or anybody that was hungry. It was run by prefects usually in their last year who could be trusted to handle money. It was handy but sometimes you had to queue up because it was so popular. I was standing in the queue one lunchtime, and one of the prefects shouted, "Somebody's stolen a bar of chocolate."

One of the teachers came over. "It's him, sir. I saw him put it in his jacket pocket." I turned around. Gary Browning was behind me and pointing his finger at me. The teacher told me to stand with my arms out straight. He then put his hand in my jacket pocket and pulled out the chocolate bar. I don't know how Gary had put the chocolate in my pocket. But I was marched to the headmaster's office. I protested my innocence, but the headmaster said, "The stolen bar of chocolate was found in your pocket, Jones. That's proof enough for me," and I received a whack across each hand with the cane, for stealing. When I came out clutching my hands, Gary and his gang stood outside, laughing.

There were at least thirty pupils to each class, roughly half boys, half girls. Mr. Grinder held a football match twice a week. The best boys were usually the captains, and they picked whose side you played on. There were normally sixteen boys in our class. So we played eight a side. Now I might have been good at running. In fact, I was always in the top three in the cross-country race. But I was useless at football, so as the boys were picked, I was always the last and always lost the ball in a tackle. Usually, our side lost.

But it was in the changing rooms, especially the showers, that I noticed my Willy was different from most of the other boys. Nobody had said anything, but I was worried, so I asked another boy who had a Willy like mine. He laughed. "I'm a Jew, so we are all circumcised at birth. It's our religion," he said, but it still didn't answer my question. I was still worrying when I arrived home that afternoon. So when Mum was alone and my brother and sisters were out of earshot, I plucked up enough courage to ask her. "Mum," I said, "am I a Jew?"

She looked at me, puzzled. "Of course not," she replied. "You're a Christian."

"Then why is my Willy like Atom Abner's and he's a Jew?" I said.

Mum's face turned bright red. This was the first time I had asked her about sex, and Mum looked embarrassed. But she collected her thoughts and replied, "When you were born, you had difficulty in peeing and the doctors up in London recommended you have a circumcision to make sure you had no complications when you got older. That doesn't mean you are Jewish." She looked relieved when I didn't ask her any more questions and I went outside.

CHAPTER

I Join The Scouts

The weather was getting colder, and I started working back at the saw mills. I got straight into the job, and by 10:00 a.m., I had bagged nearly as many as Tom or Eddy. Uncle Jim came out just as we were loading the last sack onto the lorry. "So do you still want to help on the block round?" I nodded and he said, "Watch how Tom carries the sack on his back, and if you think you can manage it, you can have a go."

"I'll keep an eye on him, Jim, and make sure he doesn't overdo it," said Tom. So I climbed aboard the lorry and we set off. The first few houses only had two bags each. So I sat in the lorry and watched. They tipped out the logs on the path and then knocked on the door for the money. An old woman came out and paid Tom. "Would you be so kind and stack the logs against the kitchen wall?" she asked.

They did as she asked and came away smiling. "She's a crafty old bugger," Tom said. "She'll be asking me to light her fire next." They were both chuckling as they got back in the lorry. I had a go next. It was a short walk to the garage where the blocks were stored, and they wanted six bags. "That's twelve shillings, sir," Tom said to the owner when he came to the door.

I did a quick calculation in my head. "That's two shillings a bag, so one bag nearly covers my day's money," I said aloud.

Tom and Eddy both laughed. "That's why you're working your bollocks off and your Uncle Jim's sitting in the office, smoking his pipe." I didn't quite get that, but laughed along with them. It was early afternoon. I sat in the lorry feeling a bit tired. I'd carried in about twenty bags. "You stay here, lad. We'll do the last house," said Tom as he and Eddy carried the last sacks into the end house.

I sat in the lorry for half an hour before they came back. "You were a long time," I said.

"The lady couldn't find her purse," Eddy replied, "so we had to search for it before we got paid." He winked at Tom and smiled. It wasn't until much later that I found out what they were up to. But I still went home with half a crown.

School term came to an end, and I said goodbye to all my friends Brian, Peter, Mickey, and Ian. We had no more trouble from Gary Browning; he was probably bullying some other small boy. I wish sometimes I had been a bit braver and punched him on the nose.

That Christmas was good. Over the last year, my father had hardly laid a finger on me. Perhaps he could see I was filling out and getting quite muscular, but he was still mean and hardly ever spoke to me. Mum was still working and had saved her money for presents. And we had a nice surprise just before Christmas. Father had a television installed by Radio Rentals. It was nearly new, and Dad had to pay the rent collector once a month when he called. It was great. We hardly moved from the lounge over Christmas and watched the queen's speech for the first time. I was so excited about the television. I don't even remember what presents we had that Christmas. New Year's Eve and Mum let us all stay awake to watch the New Year in on the television. But it was only me and Mum awake when Big Ben struck twelve at midnight. All the others were asleep curled up in front of the fire. Even my father sat in the armchair, snoring his head off. Yes, that was a great Christmas.

New Year's Day didn't start off that well. It was bitter cold and then it snowed for about a week. It was fun for us but not for the farmers. My father was at the pub most evening and came home drunk most of the time. As long as he just drank beer, he wasn't violent, but as soon as somebody offered him a whiskey, he was unpredictable. As far as I know, he never hit my brother or sisters. Sheila did have a few cuffs around the head. He did want to fight me, however, one night after coming home drunk. We were all in bed. I had gone downstairs to get a drink of water just as Father let himself in the back door. He stood in front of the stairs so I couldn't get back to bed. I stood there shivering in my pajama's. "What the fuck are you doing up at this time?" my father slurred. "I'll soon make you sleep." And he suddenly threw a punch.

I ducked, but he caught me on the top of the head and sent me flying. Mum heard the commotion and came running down the stairs and saw me lying on the floor. I was dazed but aware of what was going on. "Leave the boy alone, Trevor," Mum screamed. "You're drunk and don't know what you're doing." She managed to get me up the stairs before my father could injure me anymore. I was all right but could hear Mum arguing with him when he came to bed. That was the first time my father had actually used his fists and not his belt.

On Thursday evenings, the local scout group held their weekly meeting in the village hall. Mum suggested I go along one evening to see what it was like. The scoutmaster's name was Kelvin Richards. He was about thirty-five but looked younger, with thick blond hair and light build. He didn't look mature enough to be a scoutmaster, but he made me welcome and seemed very friendly. He introduced me to the other scouts. There were about twenty ranging from eleven to sixteen, although the oldest, Paul, was also a senior leader. But he didn't look sixteen although he was quite tall. Both of his shirtsleeves were covered in badges. I also noticed that Kelvin and Paul were the only people in long trousers. That put me off a little as I had only just started wearing long trousers and felt it was a step back from being an adult. I got chatting to some of the older boys, and they explained all the activities they did in the evenings and what badges you could earn. "It's better in the summer," one of the scouts said. "We go camping up the woods some weekends and cook sausages on the campfire." This sounded fun to me, so I signed the form and joined the Balding Scouts Group.

I still went to the saw mills on Saturday for the block round, and toward the end of April, I found out the scam that Tom and Eddy were doing. When we had loaded the lorry and counted the number of sacks on board, they would slip an extra five or six bags on before we left the yard. These bags would not be accounted for, so they pocketed the money. But they kept the last four bags back for the last house on the council estate, where they had the half-hour break at the end of the round. I had been invited in for a cup of tea, so I joined Tom and Eddy. When I sat at the kitchen table, Phillis made us all a cup of tea. Tom and Eddy drank theirs very quickly and sneaked off upstairs, leaving me to talk to Phillis. She was probably in her late thirties, not much older than Tom or Eddy. But she looked a bit of a tart, with lots of eye make-up and bright-red lipstick with a fag dangling from her mouth. She obviously smoked a lot because she had yellow nicotine-stained fingers but the most off-putting thing was, she kept putting her hand up her skirt and scratched her fanny. Whether this was to excite me I don't know. When she did sit down, she asked me some embarrassing questions. "Have you got a girlfriend, Davy?" she said, smiling still with a fag in her mouth. When I told her I hadn't, she said, "What, a good-looking boy like you? I bet all the girls would want to hop in bed with you." I could feel my face turning red and was glad when Tom and Eddy came back down the stairs looking a bit flustered, but two young girls followed them down. "These are my daughters, Tracy and Emma," said Phillis. They both looked at me and smiled. I recognized one of them immediately. She was a pupil at my school, in the sixth form, and couldn't have been any older than fifteen. (The lads at school used to say she was the village bike. I never knew what that meant until much later.) And her sister was not a lot older. They both looked a bit worn out, and their lipstick was all smudged. "Have you put the four bags of blocks in the garage for me?" said Phillis. When Tom nodded, she added, "Same time next week, then, lads."

We all left and got back in the lorry. "Did Phillis try and come on to you, Davy?" said Eddy.

"I don't know what you mean," I said, "but she kept putting her hand up her skirt and scratching her fanny."

They both roared with laughter. "You'll learn," said Tom, still laughing.

I worked it out that night. Phillis never paid for her blocks because she let her daughters have sex with Tom and Eddy and their mother had arranged it, no wonder the whole family had a bad reputation. It wasn't long after that the block round finished. When we came to the last house on the estate, I made sure I stayed in the lorry when Tom and Eddy delivered the final bags of blocks to Phillis's house.

I did miss the block round but concentrated more on the scouts. The weather was getting warmer and it was nice to get out of the village hall in the evening and do some activities outside, but it was the weekends I enjoyed the most. Some of the older scouts wanted to go for a swim in the river at Wallingford on Sunday, so I joined them, wondering what they were up to. It was a very hot day, and we left our bikes under the bridge, then got undressed and slipped on our swimming trunks, then we all jumped in the water. It was cold at first but I soon got used to it after splashing around and swimming under the arches. The oldest scout, Jerry, dared us to jump off the bridge. "Come on," he said. "I've done it loads of times."

I knew the water wasn't very deep under the bridge as I could stand and touch the bottom, but I didn't want to be a sissy so I followed the rest of them up the stone staircase to the road above. We climbed onto the top of the stone balustrades and stood looking down over the twenty-five-foot drop. One boy jumped and the others followed. I stood there petrified all on my own. "Come on!" they shouted as they surfaced in the water below.

I had to jump or else be laughed at for being scared. I held my nose and jumped. I hit the water hard and sank to the bottom fast. I pushed off with my feet when they hit the riverbed and immediately felt a pain in my foot. When I surfaced, I swam to the bank and pulled myself out. One of my toes was pouring with blood. I must have landed on a broken bottle or something. The other scouts got out and bandaged my foot with my neckerchief. It seemed to stop the bleeding, and I was able to ride home. When I got home, Mum found I had a gash on my little toe and put a plaster over it. The wound soon healed, but that was the last time I jumped off Wallingford Bridge.

The scout group had an old Morris bus that held twenty people, and this was used to take us up to the woods about two miles away. Sometimes we would stop over on Saturday night and come back Sunday afternoon. We had two massive tents that slept ten scouts in each. It was a bit cramped but it was fun. Kelvin Richards, the scoutmaster, had his own tent. It was quite big, but nowhere as big as ours. The first day after we had erected our tents, Kelvin showed us how to build a shelter out of brushwood. Then we built a zip wire, but we made ours out of rope. Somebody had to climb the oak tree to attach the rope at the highest end. It was decided that Paul, who was the oldest, would climb the tree, but I volunteered. I had so much practice in my woods over the years and found it easy. After the rope was pulled tight and fastened to a tree stump about thirty yards away, we all had a go sliding down the rope on a block-and-tackle pulley connected to a seat made from a branch. That was great. We ended the evening lighting a campfire and cooking sausages in bread rolls and drinking hot chocolate before curling up in our sleeping bags. The next morning, we relit the campfire and had a bacon-and-fried-egg sandwich and a cup of tea for breakfast. In the morning we had a competition about how many different trees you could name. I found this easy and named all of them. We then had a knot-tying lesson and finished off the morning on the zip wire before dismantling it. Over the weekend, I won three badges for fire lighting, building a shelter, and naming all the trees. When I finally arrived home that afternoon and told Mum everything we had done, she smiled and said, "I knew you would enjoy it."

I didn't say anything to my father when he came home from work because I knew he wouldn't be interested.

Kelvin told us at the next scout meeting that he had organized a week's trip in Devon. Anybody that wanted to go had to get both their parents' written permission, and the cost was six pounds each, including all expenses. I went home that evening very excited and asked Mum if I could go. She read all the rules and the places we would be visiting. "I don't know, Davy," she said. "It's very expensive, and I don't think your father would agree."

"Couldn't you persuade him?" I pleaded. Mum said she would ask him when he was in a good mood. (I thought to myself that could be some time.)

She did ask him a few days later when he came home from the pub. He was merry but not totally drunk. He still refused at first, but Mum was crafty. "Davy's birthday is in two weeks. What if he paid some money toward it and we paid the rest as a birthday present?" He eventually agreed and signed the paperwork.

CHAPTER

Scout Camp

The trip was a couple of days after my birthday, and I couldn't wait to go. We set off early Saturday morning. Kelvin and Paul had already loaded the bus with all the equipment the day before. The bus picked me up on the top road, and I clambered aboard. The bus was full of excited scouts all talking of where we would be going and what we would be doing. The trip down to Dartmoor in Devon took nearly all day, arriving on the campsite early evening. We unloaded the bus and set up all the tents. By the time we lit the fire and cooked the sausages for supper, it was 11:00 p.m. before we crept into our sleeping bags and fell asleep.

Kelvin had to wake us up, as we all overslept. We spent the second day trekking across Dartmoor and ended up at

Huckleberry Bridge. We all stripped off and put on our trunks. I noticed Kelvin was keeping a close eye on all the boys and he didn't come into the water. The water was cold, but we had a great time chasing and splashing one another. We all went to bed tired but happy. I got disturbed during the night as one of the boys trod over me to undo the tent flap and go out. As I was the nearest to the flap, I peered outside. It was quite dark but I could see a shadow undo the flap of Kelvin's tent and go inside. I looked around inside the tent but it was too dark to see who was missing, so I went back to sleep. There were facilities on the site with toilets, sinks, and an old shower block, but not many used this as there was only cold water.

After breakfast the next day, we had to call into a food store to pick up supplies. We then drove over to Hornsworth Dam and spent the day exploring the woods and wildlife. We did see a lot of wild Dartmoor Horses and ponies on the way back to the campsite. That night, we drank hot cocoa and sang songs around the campfire. I wasn't disturbed that night and slept well. The next day, we all went on the Dartmouth steam train to Totness. I had never been on a train before and enjoyed chugging along with the windows open, occasionally getting a whiff of smoke when the train passed under a bridge. We walked around the historic town then visited Totness Castle before it was time to get back on the train for the return journey. I thought that was one of the best days of the holiday. That night, I didn't sleep that well. It was so hot we had the tent flap open to let the breeze in, but I think a lot of the boys slept outside their sleeping bags. Again somebody trod over me and went outside. It was still dark, but with the tent flap open, I could see all the eight boys asleep and one empty sleeping bag, Paul's. I never heard him come back in the night, but he was asleep in his sleeping bag the next morning. I thought about asking him where he had gone, when we were in the shower block, having a wash the next morning. But he looked a bit grumpy, so I didn't bother.

It started to rain on the fourth day, so the beach trip was canceled so we all voted to spend most of the day driving around

Dartmoor sightseeing. We visited a pottery museum and had a go at making cups, but we were all useless. Then Kelvin suggested we visit Dartmoor Prison. On the way, we passed Haytor Rocks, a massive pile of huge boulders jutting out of a hill. I asked Kelvin if we could climb up them. It had stopped raining, so he agreed. "Be careful," he said. "The rocks might be slippery." He and Paul sat in the bus as all the scouts scampered up the hill. When we sat on the highest rock and gazed out over the moors, it was a spectacular sight. You could see for miles.

As the other boys were climbing down, Gregory and I were the last to leave. He was a bit older than me and had been in the scouts for three years. So I asked him about Paul, how I had seen him go into Kelvin's tent the previous night. He chuckled. "Didn't you know Kelvin's gay and Paul's having an affair with him? But don't worry. He's a great scoutmaster as long as he doesn't make a pass at you."

I didn't quite understand and would have questioned him some more, but he was already climbing down the rocks to catch the other boys up. When we had all got on the bus, Kelvin drove over to see the Dartmoor Prison. We had a little walk around with the warden, who showed us parts of the prison that weren't occupied. There were inmates still imprisoned there, but that section was sealed off. We then drove back and had cream teas in Princetown. We all agreed we'd had an interesting day out when we arrived back at the campsite.

On the last day, it was hot. We all voted to have a day on the beach and ended up at Thurlestone. It was a lovely beach but a bit of a walk to get to it. It was great playing in the rock pools; even Kelvin and Paul joined in, trying to catch the crabs stranded in the pools, but it was cold when we went swimming and we didn't stay in the water for very long. We had to trek back to a café to get something to eat in the afternoon before we finally went back to the campsite. We were all exhausted and lay in our tents. In the evening, we lit the campfire and cooked more sausages. We heated baked beans in a large saucepan and had sausage sandwiches with baked beans, all washed down with a mug of cocoa. It was brilliant.

About midnight I had to get up for a pee and walked across the campsite to the latrines in just my pants. It was still very muggy. On my way back, Kelvin stood outside his tent with just his pants on, smoking a pipe. (I didn't know he smoked.) "Is that you, Davy?" he said as I approached. "It's a bit humid tonight. Can't you sleep?"

"No, sir," I said, "it's a bit stuffy in my tent."

"Well, you're welcome to come in my tent. It's really cool in there and not at all stuffy." Was this a pass that Gregory had told me about? He eyed me up and down, waiting for an answer.

"That's all right, sir," I said. "I'll sleep with the flap up." I didn't know what else to say. I carried on walking and crept inside my tent. I didn't tell anyone, because nothing actually happened, and it may have been an innocent remark. The next morning, we were all up early. After a wash and breakfast, we began taking the tents down and packing all the gear into the bus. We stopped at a café on the way home and had fish, chips, and a bottle of pop. The bus dropped me off at my house at nine in the evening. Mum was eager to know what I had done and where I had been. My father just sat in the lounge watching television. "I'll tell you all about it tomorrow, Mum," I said, "but right now, I need some sleep." Then I went upstairs and slumped on my bed still dressed and fell asleep. The next morning, I was woken by Tommy jumping all over me. At least he'd missed me. I told Mum all about the trip the next day. "That's the best birthday present ever," I said.

She replied, "You deserved it, Davy."

A month later, I finished with the scouts. It was nothing to do with Kelvin Richards; he was a dammed good scoutmaster. After the trip to Devon, I had been rewarded with another four badges, which my mother sewed on the sleeves of my shirt and I was very proud of. It was the short trousers. When I walked home after scouts in the evening, I passed one of the village pubs. There were always teenagers outside drinking and flirting with the local girls. One of the girls remarked loudly, "Here comes the Jones kid. Look at his chicken legs. Is he in the Brownies or Cubs?" They all burst out laughing as I hurried past. I suppose I did look childlike with my gangly legs sticking out of my shorts. But that was the last time I attended the scout meetings.

After I told Mum why I was leaving the scouts, my mother suggested I should join the Army Cadets if I wanted to wear long trousers. "They look very smart in their uniforms," she said, "and nobody laughs at them." So I joined the Army Cadets at Wallingford. When I was finally kitted out in full uniform, my mother was very proud. "You look like a young man now, Davy." She beamed as I stood in the kitchen.

My father came in and snidely remarked, "He'll never make it in the army as long as he's got a hole in his arse."

"Don't be so rude, Trevor," Mum replied. "At least he's joining something worthwhile and not drinking his money away." My father didn't reply to that and walked out. I did enjoy most evenings practicing the marching, and we even went on a training course one Saturday with real live land mines. Well, they sounded real anyway. I also learned to strip down and fire a .303 rifle at an army rifle range at Blewbury. But what I didn't like was the constant polishing of my boots and brasses until they shone like the sun. The sergeant major continually complained that they were not clean enough. The uniform always itched no matter how much Mum ironed it. So after six months, I packed it in, much to my father's amusement.

CHAPTER

Falling in Love

The summer came to an end, and I started back to school in September. Peter and I were moved up a year to 4B and sat next to each other in class, which meant we had a new class teacher, Miss Charleston, who taught religious education, or RE. She had an awful habit of sitting on the front school desk with her feet on the seat when she talked to the class. If you sat in the second row of desks directly in front of her, which Pete and I made sure we did, you could see directly up her skirt. This would have been ideal to any male teenager if Miss Charleston had been a twenty-year-old blonde bombshell. But she was a sixty-year-old spinster with white hair. I suppose she wasn't bad-looking for an oldie. The reason we sat there is we had a bet on what color bloomers she would be wearing each day. If you picked the right color, then the loser would have to buy a chocolate bar at the tuck shop. They ranged from yellow, white, pink, light blue or green. I usually won, but I am surprised Miss Charleston never cottoned on to what we were doing. Perhaps she thought we were very keen students and eager to learn. In truth, we both thought RE was the most boring lesson in school.

However, we did quite like science, heating things up with Bunsen burners, blowing up tin cans, etc. Mrs. Hepworth taught science. She was young, about twenty-five years old and quite good-looking. I expect many boys had sexual fantasies about her. Mrs. Hepworth had her own classroom, which was next to the science lab. It was a bit strange as all the boys sat next to each other on long wide benches and the girls sat on the opposite side. There were Bunsen burners and other equipment down the center of the benches. This was a bit off-putting especially if you fancied the girl opposite.

One day, I sat next to Timothy Anderson. Although he was in our class, I didn't know him that well. He lived in Pangbourn about ten miles away and came on the school bus. Everybody called him Tugger, but I don't know how he got that nickname. Mrs. Hepworth was at the front, drawing a diagram on the blackboard. We were sitting at the back row of benches, when suddenly Tugger said to the girl opposite, "Quick, look under the bench." When she did, I glanced under the bench as well. Tugger had his Willy out and was vigorously rubbing his hand up and down it. The girl giggled and whispered to her mate. I smiled as well, thinking he had an appropriate nickname. Nothing very exciting happened after that. Then I spotted a new girl that was in our year but in class 4C. So as we changed classes, I just happened to bump into her. "I'm sorry," I said, looking all embarrassed. "My name's David, but everybody calls me Davy. What's your name?"

"Brenda," she said and hurried off to her class. That was short and sweet, I thought, but at least I knew her name. I couldn't get her out of my mind. She wasn't like the normal girls that I had groped behind the coats, but I decided to try it on with her. So the next time I spotted her going past the cloakroom, I asked if she wanted to see my new leather coat. She hesitated but stepped behind the coats with me as soon as we were hidden. I pulled her toward me and gave her a kiss full on the lips. She didn't pull away so I slipped my hand over her breast and squeezed gently. She did push me off then and said, "No, Davy, I'm not that sort of girl."

I was disappointed, and I said, "Sorry, my hand slipped."

She grinned. "I bet you say that to all the girls," she said, and before I could say any more, she hurried away. I worried all day that she wouldn't speak to me again. I really liked her and hoped I hadn't blown it.

I was hooked. I had never met a girl like Brenda before. I liked Alice from primary school, but this was entirely different. She wasn't the prettiest girl in the school, but there was something about her that made my heart beat faster. She smelled gorgeous and had long blonde hair. Her eyes were brown and her lips were full, with a light shade of lipstick, and she was by far the best kisser. I think I was in love. I never made any play for the other girls after that first kiss.

I looked out for her the next day and waited by the cloakroom at lunch break, hoping she would pass by. She did and spoke first. "Hello, Davy, I learned a lot of things about you from the other girls."

"All good things, I hope," I said.

She laughed and I knew we were still friends. We sat on the benches behind the coats and chatted. I told her where I lived and what my parents did. She told me her name was Brenda Watson. She was living with her gran on a caravan park at Shillingford and caught the bus to school. She had moved down from London. When I asked her if she was here to stay, she replied, "Well, sort of, but I don't know how long for." I thought that a bit strange, but before I could question her some more, the bell sounded for the classes to begin. She started to leave, but I pulled her close and kissed her and she responded but then pushed me away. "I will be late for class," she said and hurried away. I waited after school to see her before she boarded the bus. She did wave when she saw me but had no time for anything else before the bus drove away.

Mum knew something was on my mind when I was quiet all evening. And when the others were in bed, she said, "Is something troubling you, Davy?" I told her I had met a girl at school and really liked her. "Why don't you bring her back here so I can meet her?" she said. When I explained she had to catch the school bus home, Mum seemed disappointed but said, "Maybe it was for the better." But I didn't understand who it was better for.

Billy came over on Sunday, and we went for a bike ride up Wittenham Hills. We sat on a bench overlooking the fields, and I told him about Brenda. "Have you tried it on with her yet?" was the first thing he asked. When I told him she wasn't like that, he said, "Oh, she's not a lesbian, is she?"

"Of course not," I replied, not quite sure what a lesbian was. We chatted some more, and I changed the subject. "Do you want to come to my place for some cakes? Mum bakes on a Sunday. I am sure she'll have some spare." Billy agreed. We had a race back home and Billy won, but then he did have the best bike. Mum had just taken a tray full of rock cakes out of the oven as we entered the kitchen. My sisters and brother were all there equally waiting for a hot rock cake, and before they had cooled down, most of them were eaten. Billy admitted afterward that was the best rock cake he had ever tasted.

Monday morning came and I got to school early, hoping to see Brenda before school started, but the bus must have been late as I never saw her. We did meet at the cloakroom but didn't have much time together, so we agreed to write messages to each other. I suppose they were our first love letters, but they were to get me into trouble. Mrs. Hepworth was very strict, more like a sergeant major. She was a well-built woman, quite tall, short black hair, and she wore horn-rimmed glasses and always carried a short cane that she used for pointing at things. She had a nasty habit of walking around the classroom when you were working, then creeping up behind you and looking over your shoulder to see what you were doing. On this one occasion, I was bent over writing a short love letter to Brenda and drew a heart and lots of crosses, completely engrossed in what I was doing. I suddenly felt a whack across my shoulder. "What are you writing, Jones?" Mrs. Hepworth boomed out.

"Just some notes, miss," I said.

"Let me see," she said and snatched the piece of paper from the desk. My face reddened as she read the letter to herself. Then she smiled. I breathed a sigh of relief, thinking that was the end of the matter. But no, Mrs. Hepworth went to the front of the room, turned, and read the letter aloud to the whole class. I wanted to curl up under the bench when the whole class started giggling. "Well," she said, "who is this Brenda?" expecting one of the girls to stand up.

"She's not in this class, miss," I blurted out.

"Well, I don't care whose class she's in," she stormed. "I will not tolerate you scribbling love letters when you should be concentrating on your work. Go and stand outside the headmaster's office, tell him what you were doing when you should have been working." I got up and left, glad to get out of the classroom and away from the giggling girls.

I stood outside the headmaster's office for ten minutes before he opened the door and let me in. After I explained why I had been sent to him, he smiled, but he still made me hold my hand out and whacked me across the palm with a cane. "I don't want to see you outside my door again," he said, "or next time, I won't be so lenient." I never went outside his door again.

Brenda and I still met behind the coats for a quick snog, but I wanted more time with her, not just for a kiss and cuddle. But I would have to wait until the following year for that.

CHAPTER

My First Driving Lesson

I started work at the saw mills again, bagging blocks. The twins had started coming to the yard at the weekends. Jonny and Jimmy were now twelve. And their dad, Uncle Jim, had let them do some small chores, one of which was to empty the sawdust pits under the massive bench saw, which was used to slice whole trees into planks or pit props for the coal mines or railway sleepers. The boys loaded the sawdust into an open-backed van that was old and battered. My uncle had taught both the boys to drive the van down the yard and empty it onto the sawdust pile. This massive heap of sawdust built up over the years and was alight but only smoldered its way through the pile very slowly and never went out.

I was quite envious of the twins driving this old van around the yard, and one Saturday afternoon, I asked if I could have a go. After a couple of weekends, I was helping them emptying the pits and driving around the yard. I decided then when I left school, I would save up and buy a car.

Back at school, there were quite a few subjects I was good at and enjoyed doing. One was technical drawing with Mr. Beaching. He taught us how to draw things to scale, such as plans for a house or parts of an engine, which I found interesting but a lot of my class found it boring, including my mate Peter. Mr. Beaching often remarked, "You would make a good architect, Jones, when you leave school." The other thing I enjoyed was woodwork, making things with my hands then taking them home and showing Mum. But I was also good at gymnastics and even represented the school once, in the annual Midland Championship. We came fourth in a total of eighteen schools. I continued to see Brenda through the school term and was getting frustrated at the limited time I had in the cloakroom with her. Over that time, she told me she was living with her gran because her mother couldn't cope. She had an older brother that had left home at sixteen. Her mother had turned into an alcoholic. That was when her father had left home, and her mum had taken a lodger in, to make ends meet. Brenda stopped then, and I could see she was struggling to tell me anymore, but she carried on. "Brenden the lodger was a horrible man," she said, "and often slapped Mum around, especially if he was drunk as well." I gave her a cuddle then she said, "He tried it on with me one night, and I ran next door crying. The police were called and then the Social Services turned up and took me into care. They found out about my gran, and arranged for her to look after me." She then burst into tears. I put my arms around her and kissed her wet eyes. I so wanted to protect her, and wished we could spend more time together.

I think my father had a little more respect for me that year. I had grown a lot taller and put on a bit of weight. It was about four weeks before Christmas I was walking back from school along the road and I passed a garage. The side door was open, and I saw a man lying on a bench, pushing up weights. He stopped when he saw me watching him. "Come in, lad," he said. I hesitated but when I saw other lads inside, I went in. The garage seemed much bigger once inside. There were two benches, a large frame at the back that held a cross bar and weights and a pull-up bar. There were two other boys bending down and picking up weights. "I'm Brian," the man said. "I'm starting up a weight training course. Its two shillings a week. Do you want to join?" I looked at him closely. He was built like a brick shithouse. Standing in his shorts and string vest, he was not very tall, but he had bulging muscles on every part of his body. I imagined me one day looking like that and facing up to my father. I snapped out of it when he said, "Well, lad, what do you think?" I agreed and started the following week. I later learned from the other lads that Brian was once the Midland weightlifting champion but had retired and started this gym. It was one of the first in Oxfordshire. But not many people wanted to pick up weights and pump iron until you were sweating your nuts off, so it wasn't very popular.

I don't think there were ever any more than six people who joined, but I went along on Tuesday and Thursday evenings for one hour, pushing weights on the bench and free weights. Brian taught me how to do a clean and jerk, a shoulder press, and a dead lift. I was growing more and more confident as the weeks went by. With me filling the sacks of blocks and doing the block round once a week, my whole body ached some days, but when I stood in front of the mirror, I could see the difference to my body.

I also got a pay rise at the sawmills, but not by my uncle, who still paid me the same as when I started. When I complained to Tom and Eddy, they said, "Don't worry, lad. I think you will get a pay rise this week." and I saw them lift another sack of blocks onto the lorry before we left, and knew what they were up to. So that week, I got two shillings and sixpence from my uncle and two shillings from Tom and Eddy. So Mum got a pay rise as well.

I said goodbye to Brenda on the last day of school and had the longest and wet kiss ever, and she even let me feel her breasts and give them a gentle squeeze. I also said goodbye to Ian, Brian, Pete, and Mick. That was the last time I saw Brian. I think he went back home to live with his parents. I walked home, thinking of Brenda and wishing I could see her more often.

CHAPTER

The Best Christmas

Since learning to drive my uncle's old van around the timber yard (I didn't ever get higher than second gear), I was fascinated by the Formula 1 Grand Prix on television, especially Graham Hill, my hero. When I watched him zooming around the streets at Monaco, I imagined I was him when I was whizzing around the yard in the old van. Unfortunately, I went a bit too fast when taking a corner at the top of the yard by the sawdust pile and ran over a long ladder, snapping all the rungs. I did own up to my uncle, and I feared he would not let me drive the van again. But all he said was "Don't worry, lad. It was an old ladder and wasn't safe. That's why it was there." Uncle Jim was so understanding, and he still let me drive the van. Imagine my surprise, on Christmas Day, I opened the biggest present ever:

a Scalextric model racing track and two cars, Graham Hill in a Lotus and Jim Clark in a Brabus I asked my father if he would help me set it up in the lounge.

"I can't," he said. "I hurt my hand at work. Ask your mother."

My mother whispered to me, "Hurt his hand bedamned, I bet he could still pick up a pint with it." I giggled but she did try to help and we soon had the cars whizzing around the track. Sheila and the others all wanted a go. So most of the afternoon, we played with that until the hand controllers started to smoke. Mum told us to let them cool down before we continued. So I set up Tommy's clockwork train set; he had enough track now to go around the lounge. Sheila had a brand-new pink girl's bike with tassels on the end of the handlebars and a little pink saddlebag. She loved it. Mary had a red 3 wheeled scooter. It had two wheels at the back to stop it falling over; that too had red tassels on the end of the handlebars. We all had other small presents as well, puzzles, books, etc. and Tommy had a toy Rifle that fired corks at a shelf of plastic bottles. He fired one cork off accidently and hit my father on the nose when he was asleep in the armchair, Mum and I laughed. He woke up, rubbed his nose, then went back to sleep again. That was a great Christmas. Mum must have been saving for months to afford all the presents, and we all thanked her before we went to bed.

We left all the train track and race track up all night so we could play the next day. We all came down the next morning excited, but I looked on in dismay. Somebody had stood on my Graham Hill Lotus and smashed it. Of course, my father denied it when Mum asked him if he had accidently stood on it. But we all knew my father was the last to come up the stairs and get into bed.

Mum let us stay up and see the New Year in on the television, but all the kids were well asleep by then, including my father, before Big Ben struck twelve midnight. The first part of the year I was more at the saw mills than I was at home, playing with Jonny and Jimmy and then working, emptying the sawdust pit and driving the old van. When I told my uncle what had happened to my model car, he was sympathetic. "I am sure it was an accident, son," he said. "If you work all week, I will give you extra money to buy a new car." He called me son, I thought. Oh, how I wished he was my father. He kept his word and gave me five shillings at the end of the week. With the extra two shillings from the block round on Saturday that Eddy slipped me, that was enough to buy the car.

I couldn't wait to get back to school, which Mum thought was unusual as I preferred to work at the saw mills. But I wanted to see Brenda. We had written a couple of soppy love letters to each other, which I opened before my dad could read them. (I knew what sort of remark he would make.) But I wanted to hold her in my arms and kiss her soft wet lips. So I was early that morning, waiting for the school bus to arrive so I could speak to her before lessons started. When she stepped off the bus, she looked gorgeous with her blond hair tied up with a red ribbon. And I noticed her breasts were bigger. It had only been six weeks since I last saw her, but they were definitely bigger, or else she was wearing a different sort of bra. I didn't want to embarrass her in front of the other children, so I said, "See you at lunchtime." She smiled and blew me a kiss, while the other girls started giggling.

We met at our usual place behind the coats in the cloakroom. I couldn't wait. I took her in my arms, closed my eyes, and kissed her, savoring the moment. I slipped my hand over her breasts and caressed them. When we parted, she pushed out her chest and said, "What do you think? Gran bought me a new Playtex bra for Christmas."

It certainly made her boobs stand out, so I said, "You've got a smashing figure, Brenda. I hope the other boys don't start hassling you."

She laughed. "I think you are jealous, but don't worry. You are my boyfriend, and I don't want anybody else."

Brenda and I continued to see one another. Over the next months, I continued weight training with Brian in the evenings, when he reopened his gym in the New Year. He still had the same lads as before, and we all got on with each other. I could now bench press my own body weight and enjoyed the other exercises Brian set us. Unfortunately, this was my undoing. I boasted to Eddy and Tom on the block round how much I could lift up, and they were impressed, so as we were delivering the sacks of blocks to one large house on our rounds, which normally had six sacks, Eddy picked up two sacks, one on each shoulder, showing off, and walked down the path. Not to be outdone, Tom did the same and walked off. I was left standing and decided to do the same and lift two sacks. I managed to get both sacks on to my shoulders and staggered down the path after Eddy and Tom. I knew it was too heavy when I felt a sharp pain in my back and had to drop them. Eddy came running back when I crumpled to the ground and helped me into the lorry. "You've just pulled a muscle," he said. "Take a rest until we get back to the yard."

I did feel a bit better when we returned to the yard and managed to bike home. I told Mum what had happened. She rubbed some hot cream on my back and told me to go to bed and rest it. I slept all Saturday night, but the next morning, I couldn't get out of bed. It hurt so much. I heard Mum discussing it with my father and him saying, "He'll be all right. He just wants a day in bed, with you mollycoddling him all day."

But after a few hours when it was still no better, Mum called Dr. Johnson. He came out within the hour and examined me. "What cream have you been putting on?" the doctor said to my mother. When she showed him, he said, "That's the wrong cream. His back is inflamed and swollen and needs cooling down. Hold a cold wet flannel on his back and get this gel from the chemist in the high street. It's open for emergencies." He wrote out a prescription and gave it to Mum. "Keep his back cool and the inflammation should go down," the doctor said. "He should be all right in a couple of days." Mum thanked the doctor, and he left.

"Sheila, cycle over to the chemist," Mum said, "and pick up this prescription." When she came back, Mum rubbed the cream on my back. God, it was cold, but it felt better.

My father had no sympathy. "Christ, I have bad backs every day riding on that bloody tractor." He sniggered. "And I don't get that treatment." The next day, my back was a lot better but Mum kept me at home and I started back to school on Tuesday. Brenda was a bit concerned when I told her, but put on a brave face and told her not to worry. I did cycle over to Brian's gym that evening, and after I told him what had happened, he advised me to rest it for another week before starting back. But that back injury was to plague me in later life.

Spring turned into summer, and my uncle asked if I would like to go out with them again in the summer holidays, felling trees. I jumped at the chance, and he said, "Let's see if we can make a real man of you." I couldn't wait, but first I had to say cheerio to all my friends, including Brenda on the last day at school. I asked if I could cycle over one Sunday and see her in the holidays. She said she would ask her gran, who was quite strict and always took Brenda to church on Sunday mornings. "I will write and let you know," she said as she boarded the bus. I did get a quick kiss before the bus drove away.

My fifteenth birthday was great. I had some extra track and two new cars to add to my Scalextric set. I also had two books. One was about Formula 1 and all the drivers and what teams they drove for. The other was a nature book. I thanked Mum and my father. He just grunted as usual, but I made sure all my electric cars were safely hidden away before I went to bed.

I had had no trouble with my back, but had only carried a single sack on my back since the injury. Now the block round had come to the end, I was looking forward to going to the forest with my uncle. We set off early on Monday morning, arriving about two hours later. I was immediately asked to light a fire while Tom cut down an enormous pine tree. Eddy cut all the branches off, then I put these on the fire. Jim then loaded the tree trunk onto the lorry. We stopped at midday for a break. Mum had packed me cheese sandwiches and some pickled onions and one of her rock cakes. I had a bottle of pop to drink. I felt like a real man sitting around the fire with the others. We continued until early afternoon before I removed all the branches and suddenly came across a nest. I looked inside, and there were four chicks still alive. I called my uncle over, and he said the nest must have been in the last tree we felled. I asked him what we should do with the chicks and he replied, "Nothing, lad, they are too young and will not survive without their mother, and now we have cut the tree down she will abandon them."

This made me feel bad. "Could I take them home and try to feed them, Uncle?" I said.

He could see I was upset. "Why don't you empty your lunch bag and put them in there?" my uncle suggested. "But I expect they will be dead by the time you get home."

But when I got home on my bike and showed Mum, they were still alive. "You can't keep them, Davy," Mum said. "The cat will probably kill them, and your father will go mad if he finds out."

"But he won't find out if I keep them in my bedroom under the bed," I replied. My mum relented. We found a big cardboard box and put some newspaper in the bottom then put the chicks in. They had some feathers but were a bit wobbly on their feet. Mum got some cat food, and I fed them with my hands. The chicks woofed the food down. Clearly they were very hungry. Mum then borrowed one of Sheila's dolls' drinking bottle and filled it with water. I opened the chicks beaks and squeezed the water down their throats. Then they all huddled together and went to sleep. I put the box in my bedroom under the bed. I had to show my brother Tommy the chicks before we went to sleep that night. But I made him swear not to tell anybody, including his sisters. Early the next morning, I was woken by the squawking chicks. I quickly pulled the box out and opened the lid. The chicks were all standing with their mouths open, clearly waiting for another meal. Sheila and Mary came into my bedroom before I could quieten the chicks, so I had to show them as well. Luckily, my father had gone to work, so I brought the box down into the kitchen. Mum put the cat outside and shut the door. (I expect Snowy wondered why he was being shoved outside so early in the morning.)

The chicks had made a terrible mess on the newspaper. So we each held a baby chick until I'd replaced the newspaper. I then set about feeding them as before. Sheila was not very happy that I was using her baby bottle to give the chicks a drink, but I said I'd buy her a new one so she was satisfied, and quite enjoyed squirting the bottle of water down their throats when I held the chicks' beaks open. A week later, when they had most of their feathers, I looked in my *Wild British Birds* book and found out they were sparrow hawks. My mum said, "As soon as they can fly, you will have to let them go, Davy." I knew this, but I was happy I had saved all four birds. A few days later, the birds were all trying to get out of the box. I took them out in the garden and gently put each one on the bird table. They all sat there for a few minutes looking at me. Then one flew off and landed in the nearest tree about one hundred feet away. The others soon followed. I watched them in the tree until they all flew off together.

I had a surprise the next morning. Two of the sparrow hawks were waiting on the bird table, so I put some cat meat out for them. They gobbled it up and then flew off. This happened for a couple of mornings before they eventually flew away. We did see them circling over the wood a few times, but whether these were the same birds I don't know. But it was nice to think they were. We had done all this without my father ever knowing.

I then started collecting bird eggs. Mum showed me how to prick a hole in each end and blow the contents out. But she told me, only take one egg out of the nest and try not to touch the other eggs or else the mother bird might abandon the nest. (Mum seemed to know about everything.) I did get quite a collection that summer and showed Billy a robin's nest in the wood that I had taken one egg from. He seemed interested but didn't say a lot. Next day, I checked on the nest to see if they had hatched and found all of the eggs gone. I knew it had to be Billy. He was the only person who knew where the nest was. We had a huge fallout when he next came over, and it was some weeks before we became friends again.

Brenda did write in August, and she arranged to meet at the entrance to the caravan park. I calculated it would take me about an hour to cycle over there, so I left in good time. I arrived at the caravan park about ten minutes early. But Brenda sat on the park bench, waiting for me. I put my bike behind the wall, and she came over and hugged me. "God, I so missed you," she said then kissed me. It was a beautiful afternoon, and I suggested we go for a walk along the river. So we set off along the tow path. She told me what she had been doing in the summer holiday, and it all sounded a bit boring.

"Your gran doesn't let you go out much, then?" I asked.

"No," Brenda said, "I am only allowed to play around the park. I had to plead with Gran to let me see you, and then she told me to be careful around boys." She smiled. "Especially you," she said. We walked a bit farther before we saw a gap in the fence and went into a cornfield. There were stacks of bales dotted around the field. We ventured over to one stack and slid down behind it. There was some loose straw on the ground. I rolled Brenda over and lay on top of her. She pulled me closer and kissed me, but this was no ordinary kiss. She pushed her tongue into my mouth, and I savored her juices. I was in heaven. Nobody had kissed me so passionately before. I became instantly aroused. I pulled away and pushed my tongue into her mouth. It felt exotic. My Willy was so hard it was bursting out of my trousers. I slipped my hand down and unzipped my fly and pulled my pants down. I then lifted her skirt and put my Willy on her bare legs and gently rubbed up and down. She was groaning and getting aroused as well, but then suddenly she pushed me away. "I do love you, Davy," she said, "but I'm scared. What happens if I get pregnant?"

"Don't worry," I whispered. "I will look after you." But the moment had gone. She sat up. I adjusted my trousers and did up my flies.

"I am sorry, Davy," she said and pulled me closer and kissed me again. I was still aroused, but respected her decision, so I did not try again. "Come on," she said, "let's finish our walk." We strolled back to the tow path arm in arm. I told her all about the tree felling with my uncle, and how I saved the sparrow hawks. She listened intently to my jabbering until we reached the end of the towpath. She then pulled me toward her and we kissed again. I slid my hand over her breast and squeezed gently, but she removed my hand. "You don't give up, do you?" she said, smiling.

"Not when I am on to a good thing," I replied. We turned around and headed back to her gran's. I thought she might invite me in to see her gran. But we parted by the caravan park entrance. We kissed once more, before I got on my bike and rode off.

"See you at school," she shouted after me. But I never saw Brenda again for a very long time.

That night, I dreamt about Brenda and me lying on top of her and rubbing my Willy against her legs. I seemed to explode with emotion. When I awoke the next morning, the sheets were all stiff, and I guessed I'd had a wet dream. Pete and I had talked about this sometime before, and he had told me he had started having them a year ago, so I must have been a late starter. But after that, I only had to dream about Brenda and the same thing happened. I don't know what my mum thought when she washed the sheets, but she never said anything.

School started again in September. I couldn't wait to see Brenda and kiss those soft lips. But she never turned up the first day. When I discussed it with Pete, he suggested she might be ill and her gran was keeping home for a few days. But those few days turned into weeks. I plucked up enough courage to knock on the headmaster's door. When he let me in. he looked at me sternly. "Jones, isn't it?" he said. "What trouble are you in this time?"

"No trouble, sir," I said, "I would just like to ask a few questions about a girl who's gone missing."

"Well, lad, you had better tell me all about her," said the headmaster. So I told him about Brenda. When I had finished, he was sympathetic and looked through the latest files and found her name. "It looks like she has finished school here and gone back to live with her parents in London. I am sorry. That's all the information I have. I don't even have a forwarding address."

I thanked the headmaster and left. I hoped she would write, but no letter arrived. Mum could see I was so depressed, and she found me crying one night. "I really loved her, Mum," I blurted out She gave me a cuddle.

"I know, son," she said.

CHAPTER

My Father's Accident

It took some time for me to forget about Brenda, but I started going to the youth club down at the village hall on Wednesday evenings and met a few girls. But none were very serious and only wanted to dance when the DJ came on and started playing the latest songs. So that didn't last very long. I did cycle over to Pete's dad's farm one Sunday, and Pete showed me the parlor where all the cows were milked. I tasted some fresh milk, straight out of the cow and screwed my face up. It tasted horrible. Pete laughed. "That's because it has not been treated," he said. "All the milk that the milkman delivers is pasteurized." He then showed me around the barns where all the straw bales and hay were stacked. We climbed right to the top of the bales, and Pete dared me to jump off into a huge pile of loose straw.

I looked down, and it seemed very high. "Go on," Pete said. "I do it all the time." And then he jumped, so I followed. We sank in the straw, then seemed to bounce back up. It was great, so we spent the rest of the afternoon jumping off the bales. I met Pete's mum before I left, and she made me a cup of tea and gave me a cake. It wasn't as good as my mum's, but then she made the best cakes in the world.

I still went to the gym twice a week and gradually got back into it. Brian advised not to do any squats with the bar on my back. "It might do more damage to your back," he said, so I mainly stuck to bench work. But I had not had any back pain for some time, and I think all the weight training might have strengthened it.

I was still busy doing the block round on Saturdays, but Billy stopped coming around. Every time he did come, I was always down at my uncle's, either playing with Jonny and Jimmy or at the timber yard, emptying the sawdust pit and driving the old van. I didn't go to the woods much as I had nobody to go with.

But we had a visit from a farmer from the other side of the village. He knew my mother and had often chatted down at the village shops. She must have told him about the sparrow hawks because when I opened the box he had bought with him, there was a tiny chick inside. "It fell out of the dovecote," he told my mother. "I don't think it will survive much longer. I wondered if Davy might try and save it."

"Of course I will," I said, and I thanked the farmer.

Mum was less enthusiastic. "You don't want to go through all that again, do you, Davy?" She asked, but I didn't mind. It was an ugly chick with hardly any feathers and an enormous beak. I did exactly as before, but kept an old jumper in the bottom of the box to keep it warm. It fed and drank well and soon started growing more feathers. I kept it under the bed at night, but when my father had gone to work, I bought it down and Mum soon started feeding it when I had to go on block round. It was a very pretty bird. The feathers were pure white and fanned out at the back, and its beak had turned a pinky-red color the following week, it flew but not very far, only onto the shed roof. We left it out that night, and it was still there the next morning. I threw some corn down on the grass, and Cookie, as we named him, flew down right near my feet. I bent down and picked him up and put him on my shoulder, and he stayed there as I walked around the garden, proudly showing him off to my mother and sisters. But it wasn't long before my father noticed the bird perched on the shed roof one morning. He immediately went and got his shotgun and was going to shoot the bird. "No," Mum cried out, "that's Davy's pet."

All my sisters started crying, and my father relented. "What's he want a bloody wild pigeon for?" he snarled. "Why can't he have a rabbit like everybody else?"

"It's not a wild pigeon, Dad," I said. "It's a fantail."

"Don't get smart with me, boy," he replied, and he cuffed me around the head.

But Mum said, "Leave the boy alone, Trevor. I said he could keep the bird. It's no trouble, and he can keep it outside." My father went off in a huff and put his gun away. Cookie stayed outside and became very friendly when he saw Mum or me and would fly down and land on our shoulders. He had a funny habit of pecking your earlobe when he wanted feeding, but it tickled more than hurt. Father grumbled at first whenever he saw the bird but soon got used to it and never carried out his threat to shoot it. Cookie even recognized my mum's black hair and would fly down and land on her shoulder when she got off the bus, much too everyone's amazement. It was a smart bird.

We still went over to Gran's occasionally, but it was a bit of a handful for Mum to organize with all four of us. But Gran always made us welcome. I did meet my uncle Bill, who lived next door. He was a paint sprayer and worked for the Morris Group at Oxford. He was a rare character, slim build with a big bushy black beard and a bald head. He was always joking around, and I didn't like him at first. But once I met him a couple of times, he seemed all right.

Christmas was cold, but it did not rain or snow. Cookie was still around, and I could feed him with corn out of my hand. He was so tame but only to me and my mother. He wouldn't go near anyone else. I think he thought we were his parents. He was crafty too. He had found a nice place to roost out of the wind and rain. A corner of the asbestos soffit over the porch had broken off, and he got in there and perched on the rafters. I kept an eye on it in case my father blocked up the hole and he couldn't get out. But the hole was never blocked up.

I wasn't expecting much for Christmas that year. We were all growing up fast, and money was a bit tight. I know Mum borrowed a lot on the Freemans catalog because I overheard the collector say it was ten shillings the week before Christmas, no wonder Mum didn't tell my father how much all this was costing. He would have hit the roof. I did manage to get Mum a headscarf and a pair of woolen gloves. I wrapped them up quickly before my sisters saw, or they would have blabbed to Mum. I also got Sheila a beauty set. She was nearly a teenager and had started using Mum's make-up. For Tommy, I bought a water pistol, which I got told off for because he kept squirting everybody. And for Mary, I bought a snakes-and-ladders game. I didn't get anything for my father. On Christmas Day, we all sat around the table and had turkey for the first time with roast potatoes, Brussel sprouts, carrots, and dumplings, with Christmas pudding and custard. We even had orange and raspberry Coroner pop. After we had cleared away the dishes and Father had fallen asleep in the armchair, we opened our presents. I was watching Mum's face when she opened hers. "Thanks, Davy," she said.

"They're from all of us," I replied, but Mum knew I had saved up and bought them. We all had little presents. Mine and Sheila's were clothes. Tommy and Mary had both a pair of shoes. We also had puzzles and a box of games. I set up the car racetrack upstairs in my bedroom, and Tommy set up his train set in the corner of the lounge so it didn't annoy Father. We all had a great time either playing games or watching the television.

The New Year didn't start off very well, at least not for my father. The day he started back to work, he had an accident. The cover over the PTO, or power takeoff on his tractor was loose and had not been fixed over Christmas. This was a shaft that came out the back of the tractor and was spinning all the time when connected to any farm implements. The cover was there to protect your leg or foot when you stepped off the back of the tractor, but as my father stepped on the cover, it broke away and his trousers caught in the spinning shaft and bruised all his leg. The farmer thought the leg might be broken, so my father was taken to hospital. Giles Bedford bought him home the same day. His leg was not broken but was heavily bandaged, and he limped through the front door and collapsed on the sofa. "Take a few days off, Trevor," Giles said. "I am sure when the bruising's gone down, you can come back to work."

I grinned when I saw him hobbling across the floor. "You can wipe that fucking smirk off your face," he yelled, "or I'll wipe it off for you." Mum told me to go outside while she took care of my father. I went back in later when he had calmed down, and kept out of his way. My father had Mum at his beck and call for the next two days, fetching and carrying for him all day. He even told her to go to the off-license and get a dozen bottles of beer. I told Mum I would go to get the beer if she gave me the money. But she only had a few shillings spare, so I took the rest of the money I needed out of my savings. We were both glad when he finally went back to work.

I started back to school and met all my friends. This was the last term at school. In the summer, I had to decide what I wanted to do. I really wanted to work down the saw mills with my uncle. But Mum flatly refused. "I want you to do an apprenticeship and get a proper job with qualifications," she argued, "not doing a casual job with poor pay." So I spent one evening with Mum going through the things I was good at. "Technical drawing," Mum suggested. I didn't to want to be stuck in an office. "A vet, then," she said. "There's a job advertised at the laboratory looking after animals."

"That's where they do the experiments on them," I said. "I wouldn't want that job"

"Well, you liked woodwork, what about a carpenter?" she suggested. So I agreed to try that. After all, I thought if it didn't work out, I could always work for my uncle. But Mum wrote to Belchers, the builders, and asked if they did an apprenticeship course for carpentry. She received a letter back, offering an interview in one month.

School was a bit boring that last term. At least Ian was made up to a prefect and was very proud of the fact that he was the first black boy to do this. It meant he had a turn at running the tuck shop and be in charge of the monies taken, quite a responsibility. But he was also in charge of one of the dining tables at lunchtime and made sure everyone had their equal share of the food. There were a few greedy prefects that had a big portion of their favorite pudding, and consequently, the younger kids had small portions. The prefects were supposed to stop this from happening.

We all still met in the playground but mainly talked about what job we would like to do. Mr. Tim's, the woodwork teacher, was impressed when I told him I had a job interview at Belchers, the local builders, and wished me good luck.

Those last few weeks were a little sad. I knew I wouldn't see many of my friends ever again. Ian had got a job as a graphic designer. I wasn't sure what that was. I knew it involved drawing and being in an office, which didn't appeal to me. Pete got a job on his farm, and Mick decided he wanted to help his uncle in a fruit-and-veg store. All our other friends got jobs in the local towns. I never knew what happened to Tugger Anderson, but then he lived ten miles away.

My sixteenth birthday was a week before the interview at Belchers, and I got a racing bike. It wasn't new, but it was a full-size frame with drop handlebars and three gears. I don't know how Mum kept that a secret, but I was shocked. I was never expecting that. "You will have to thank your father as well, Davy," Mum said. "He put in half."

I thought there must be a catch in this, as he'd never shown any interest in my birthday before. When I plucked up enough courage to thank him, he just replied, "Now you're earning a wage, you had better give it all to your mother. You eat more than you earn." He never had a nice thing to say.

CHAPTER

My New Job

The interview at Belchers went quite well. I was very nervous as the young secretary (she couldn't have been any older than eighteen) knocked on the door of the manager's office and let me in. The manager was in his mid-thirties, well dressed, and spoke with a posh accent. "Come in, young man," he said. "Would you like a tea or coffee?"

I replied, "Tea, sir, thank you."

"Tea for two, Miss Sims," he shouted to the secretary. He could see I was nervous. "Try to relax, lad. I'm not going to eat you," he said, with a smile. He held out his hand. "My name's Mr. Salisbury, and yours is?"

"David Jones, sir," I said as I shook his hand.

"David Jones," he said as he sat down and opened a folder on his desk. "Well, sit down, David. I see your mother wrote to us some time ago. You are lucky we have one apprentice course left starting in August. Your school report from Mr. Tim's is very good. Are you sure you want to sign up for a five-year apprenticeship?"

"Yes, sir," I replied. "I like woodwork and making things with my hands."

He passed me a document and asked me to sign at the bottom. He stood up and shook my hand again. "Welcome to Belchers," he said. "We'll see you in August, then." I was shown out by Miss Sims. The whole process could not have lasted more than ten minutes. I got on my bike and rode home. Mum was thrilled when I told her I had got the job.

At the beginning of August, my father bought home a Labrador puppy from around the farm. Giles Bedford had asked Dad if he would look after the pup as its mother had had a litter of six, and he was desperately trying to find a home for all of them. We all fell in love with the golden Labrador pup. "Can we keep him, can we keep him?" all the girls squealed. Mum looked at my father, who reluctantly nodded. So Ben, as we called him, became another member of the family along with Snowy the cat and Cookie the fantail pigeon.

The day finally arrived when I started work. Mum packed me a lunch box and a flask of coffee. It was a beautiful morning when I set off at seven, for the six-mile bike ride. I had to be at the building yard at 8:00 a.m., so I allowed myself plenty of time in case I had a puncture. When I arrived, the foreman introduced himself. "I'm Jack," he said. "I will show you around the buildings and then introduce you to the others. Follow me."

The downstairs was where the all the woodworking machines were placed: a saw bench, two spindle machines, a band saw, and a mortise drilling table. I shook hands with Dougie and Frank, the machinists. There was an inner staircase leading up the first floor. This was the workshop where all the items were made and assembled. The upstairs had five carpenter's benches in line, with two aisles either side of the benches, running the full length of the building. "This is my bench," said Jack the foreman, pointing to the first bench, then he introduced me to the other carpenters. "The first bench is yours so I can keep an eye on you," said Jack. The third bench was Richard's, the fourth was Steven's and the last bench was that of Piotr Kowalski, a Polish immigrant who had come over to England after the Second World War. I took an instant dislike to him. He had the same build as my father and had a short black stubbly beard that looked like he hadn't washed, and he resembled the bad man out of a gangster film. When I had met all the men, I went back down the stairs to the machine shop. "I will leave you with Dougie and Frank for the rest of the day," said Jack, "and we can start you upstairs tomorrow." He then went back upstairs. It wasn't long before Dougie had me cleaning out the sawdust from all the machines and sweeping it up into bins. We sat down at ten around an old tortoise stove. "We light this in the winter," said Frank. "It keeps it nice and cozy in here."

"And you can make toasted sandwiches," said Dougie. I was beginning to like these two men.

Frank looked at his watch and said, "Time to start work again, lad. We only have fifteen minutes in the morning. Thirty minutes for lunch and another fifteen-minute break at three." So I got up. "You can clean all the dust off the windows next," said Frank. I didn't like that job at all but cracked on with it till twelve thirty. Then we all sat down around the stove, and it wasn't long before they wanted to know if I had a girlfriend. When I told them I hadn't, Dougie said, "Well, what you think of our Jenny?" I looked at them blankly. "You know Jenny Sims the secretary?"

I nodded. "Yes, she's very pretty."

"Well, I'll let you in on a little secret," said Dougie. "Do you see that large window you've just cleaned?" I nodded. "Do you see the stairs running up outside? Well, the office staff use those stairs to deliver drawings to Jack the foreman upstairs, so they don't have to come through the machine shop." I nodded again. "Well," he said, "if you stand under those stairs and press your face against the glass, you can see right up Jenny's short skirt when she takes the drawings to Jack." They both laughed at this. All that time he took to tell me that. But I must admit she was very pretty with a petite figure, so I was intrigued. I could see why a middle-aged man would get quite excited about that. I spent the rest of the day clearing up until 5:00 p.m., then cycled home. I was tired out when I walked into the kitchen and flopped down on a chair.

The first thing Mum said was "Well, how did the job go son"

"Well," I said, "I didn't enjoy the first day. I was either cleaning out sawdust, sweeping up, or cleaning windows. And on top of that, I will be working alongside a pair of perverts and a gangster."

Mum didn't understand the last part, and I was too tired to explain. "Well," she said, "it's early days yet. Give it time and you will enjoy it."

But by the end of the week, the best job I had was sanding down some handrails to a staircase that Richard had made. I had my own bench, but had no tools. The lads lent me some basic tools until I could afford to buy them. The only real highlight was Jenny. I was sweeping up in the machine shop, when Dougie shouted to Frank, "Quick, here she comes." I looked through the window and saw Jenny walking toward the woodwork shop with a drawing in her hand. Quick as a flash, Frank shot up the inside stairs and out onto the roof and started coming down the stairs just as Jenny was starting to ascend the stairs. He met her halfway up, and she stopped. "I'll take those up to Jack if you like, Jenny," Frank said and kept her chattering on the stairs. Meanwhile, Dougie and I had our faces pressed against the window glass. And they were right. I could see right up Jenny's skirt, she had on stockings and white suspenders with a tiny pair of white knickers. I could see why this was Dougies highlight of the week.

ALAN WHICHELLO

By Friday, I had worked a full forty-hour week and Jenny brought the wage packets around. It was the first time I had seen her close up. She smiled as she handed me the packet "Your first wage packet, David," she said.

"Thanks, Miss Sims," I replied.

"There's no need to be so formal, David. You can call me Jenny, as you're part of the firm now." I blushed as I looked away. She was even prettier close up.

As she walked back to the office, Dougie said, "You're in there, lad. Did you see the way she looked at you?" I just laughed as I got on my bike and rode home. When I was alone, I opened the wage packet and looked at the pay slip: three pounds, eight shillings, and nine pence after stoppages. I showed Mum the pay slip. She could see I was disappointed.

"Just over three pounds for forty hours' work," I said. "I could earn more than that at the sawmills."

"Yes, but it's not a skilled job, son," she replied, "and you'll soon get a pay rise when you're seventeen." That wasn't much comfort, thinking I would have to wait for another eleven months.

All the men at the workshop had invited me for a drink on that second Friday night, at the local pub just down from the yard. "It's a traditional thing," they said, "for all of us to buy the new employees a drink to welcome them to the firm." I had told Mum I would be late back as I was being taken out for a drink by the lads at work.

She looked worried. "Don't get drunk, Davy," she said. "You know you're not used to spirits."

"Don't worry, Mum," I replied. "I can handle it." I cycled off to work. That day went quite quickly, and we all trooped off to the pub. The landlord had opened up early especially for me. I felt very proud. I was at last being treated like a man. "I'll get the first drink in," said Dougie. "What are you drinking, Davy?"

I looked around. There were about seven men that I knew from the workshop. So I said, "I'll have half pint of cider."

114

Dougie laughed. "You'll have a pint the same as us," he said. He bought the pint of cider. Most of the other men had beers. We got chatting about cars, holidays, and girls. Of course, by the time I'd had my fourth pint, my head felt dizzy. I couldn't understand it. Cider didn't really affect me that much.

"Come on, drink up. It's my round," I heard one of the lads say.

I gulped down the last dregs. "I think I've had enough," I said to Frank.

"What, aren't you going to have a last drink with me?" he said and put another pint on the table.

I picked it up and drank half of it down quick, so I wouldn't offend him. My head felt as if it was going to explode. The whole room started spinning, and I remember falling to the floor. I drifted in and out of consciousness and heard the landlord say, "Come on, guys. The lad's had enough. Somebody take him home." I could hear them all laughing, then somebody tried to take my trousers off but I kicked and struggled and he gave up. I remember somebody putting me into the back of a van and banging my head on my bike. Then I must have blacked out. I came to as somebody was helping me down the path to our front door. Then Mum came rushing out with the copper stick in her hand. "How dare you bring my son home in this state?" she screamed and started whacking the man. I dropped to the floor as the man ran off back to the van. Mum picked me up and helped me into the kitchen, where I was immediately sick all over the floor. I then remember Mum putting me on my bed and falling asleep. When I awoke that morning, I had been sick in the bed. I felt terrible. Mum kept giving me water, but I stopped in bed all that day. It wasn't until Sunday morning that I felt better and came downstairs. Mum was in the kitchen. "I can't understand, Mum, why I got so drunk," I said. "I like cider."

"I expect they were mixing it with whiskey or some other spirit," she said. "That's why you passed out. I hope this has taught you a lesson." It had. I vowed never to get drunk again.

Those first months at work were a bit boring. I had plenty of wet dreams thinking of Jenny with her stockings and white suspender belt. But I knew I was out of her league. Why would she want to go out with a boy two and a half years younger than her, and earning less than half her wage? But I could always dream. For some unknown reason, my father had become even more aggressive toward me since I'd started work. He had punched me several times when we were alone. It all became too much for my mother. She knew it was only a matter of time before I would retaliate and fight back. So she arranged for me to live with my gran. "It will be for the best, son. You and your father will never get on, and I'm scared you will get hurt," she said. I didn't want to leave, but I knew she was right. So that weekend, I packed my backpack with my clothes, then said my goodbyes to a tearful Sheila, Tommy, and Mary. "We can still come over to see you on the bus," said Mum. But we both knew it would never be the same. I gave her a hug and a kiss, got on my bike, and rode off to a new home.

CHAPTER

My Grans House

Gran welcomed me with open arms and made me very comfortable. I had my own bedroom with a big wardrobe and side table. Gran had her bathroom downstairs so I had to come down the stairs at night if I wanted a pee. She let me have my radio and a table lamp in my room, so I settled down the first night, listening to Radio Caroline. Gran didn't have a television. She didn't believe in them. I didn't sleep that well and was up early Sunday morning. Gran never got up very early. Well, she was in her seventies. But she made an effort and made me breakfast. It was a bit greasy but I was grateful she had tried. "I will be leaving early tomorrow, Gran," I told her, "and will make my own sandwiches and drink, so don't get up."

It didn't take me as long to get to work on my racing bike. I had devised a way of getting there quicker. I rode up fast behind a lorry and grabbed hold of the tailgate and got towed along. It was a bit dangerous if the lorry had to brake hard or swerve, but this rarely happened and I always managed to let go before anything happened.

The weeks went by quickly, and I did buy some secondhand tools at a garage sale. And Jack showed me how to make a carpenter's stool and I ended up making ten. These were all taken by other carpenters working on sites, so they must have been good. But I was never allowed to make things such as cabinets or stairs and banisters. All I did was sand the items down. For some reason, I did not get on with Piotr. He spoke in broken English but always seemed to smirk when I asked him something. I just don't think he liked me.

The weeks up to Christmas went slowly. Jenny always gave me a smile when she gave me the wage packet at the end of the week, and I always got encouragement from Dougie to ask her out. But I never did. As the weather got colder, it was my job to light the old tortoise stove so we could all sit around it at lunchtime and toast the sandwiches. I wondered if mum would invite me home for Christmas dinner. She and the kids had been over a couple of times but hadn't said anything about Christmas, so I was pretty depressed. Gran tried to cheer me up but, because of her age, didn't really know what to say or do. She never had a Christmas tree or put any decoration up. "I don't like all the mess the tree makes," she told me. It was my uncle Bill, who lived next door, who cheered me up. He hadn't been around very much since I had been living with Gran. But he suggested I strip my rusty racing bike down and respray it over the Christmas period. He said, "I can spray it any color you want as long as it's black." I knew he was joking when he laughed. So we chose a bright silver color.

Christmas Day, I bought Gran some gloves and a woolen bonnet to keep her ears warm when she went outside. On the following Monday, Mum and the kids came over on the bus and she cooked a nice roast chicken dinner. We all sat down with Gran and enjoyed the meal, and I realized what a good cook Mum was (I did miss her rock cakes). Mum and the kids did their best to cheer me up. Mum even gave me a Timex watch, but Christmas just wasn't the same as being home.

The next day, I started stripping down my bike in Uncle Bill's garage. He had it all kitted out as a spray shop. I think he did a lot of paint spraying on the side. I noticed a lot of Leyland paint pots on the side. "You will have to sand down all those rusty bits, Davy, before I can spray it," Bill said. When I had finished, he put the bike on a frame and gave me a mask to wear for the paint fumes. He then started spraying my bike. You could see he was a professional the way he layered on the paint. It didn't take him long. "It will take an hour or so to dry, before you can put it all back together," he said. He then took me into his house and I met his wife Berol.

She had bright ginger hair and was quite tall. She seemed a bit grumpy at first, but she smiled when she offered me a cup of tea. "I wish you would take off your stinky overalls, Bill, before you come into my kitchen," she moaned. "You smell of paint fumes."

"Oh, stop moaning, woman," Bill replied. I thought they might start arguing, but Berol didn't say any more. I did notice she walked funny and sort of threw her right leg rather than bending her knee. Bill noticed me looking, and when she left the kitchen, he whispered, "Berol lost her leg in a motorbike accident, and she has a prosthetic leg fitted." I was a bit embarrassed and was glad when we returned to the garage to see if the bike frame was dry. Two hours later, after Bill had helped me rebuild the bike, we stood back and admired our handiwork. It looked as if it came straight out of the showroom.

"How much do I owe you, Uncle?" I said.

"Nothing," said my uncle. "That's my Christmas present to you." I was very grateful at his generosity and thanked him. "There is something you can help me with though," he said. "When I have a car to respray, you can help sand it down." So it was agreed I would work for him on Sundays. Saturdays I helped with the block round at the saw mills, and the rest of the week, I worked for Belchers. As I was keeping all my wages from Belchers (I did give Gran a bit for food) and with the money I got from the block round and from my uncle Bill, I began saving for my dream car.

In the New Year I started back to work after the holiday and had to begin the apprenticeship course. I wasn't looking forward to this. I had to attend Reading Technical College for two hours in the evening, on two separate days, also all day on Fridays. It was an ordeal. I left work at 5:00 p.m., rode home to Gran's, gulped down some food, rode back to Wallingford, chained and locked my bike to some railings, and had to catch the six o'clock bus to Reading Station. I then had to hop on an electric trolley bus (they had all disappeared by the seventies) that drove past Reading Technical College. The lesson started at 7:00 p.m. (I was always a few minutes late) and finished at nine. Then I had to get to the bus station by ten to catch the last bus home. By the time I rode back to Gran's, it was gone 11:00 p.m., and Gran was fast asleep in bed. I had to do these evening classes on Mondays and Wednesdays. On Fridays, it was not so much of a rush as the lessons didn't start till 10:00 a.m. and finished at 4:00 p.m. Tuesdays and Thursday evenings, I still went weight training at Brian's gym. I was exhausted after a few months. But my money was building up fast. And by May, I had just over one hundred pounds. The trouble was I hated going to the workshop and loathed the tasks I was expected to do at work. In the nine months that I had been there, I'd cleared out the sawdust, swept up, cleaned the windows, lit the fire, and sanded various items that the other carpenters had made. Apart from the carpenter's stools, I had not made a single thing. Instead of me buying carpenter's tools, I would have been better off buying a new broom, dustpan, and brush. When I complained to Jack, he just said, "Be patient, lad. You were the first apprentice we took on, and you have to do the manual work first, until another younger apprentice joins the firm."

"But that could take months," I said. "I think that's unfair."

"You will have to take it up with management, if you're not satisfied," replied Jack. I stormed away, straight down to the manager's office. I was quite prepared to quit the job the way I felt.

I knocked on the office door, and Jenny let me in. I cooled down when she said, "I will see if the manager is free." A few minutes later, I sat in the manager's office and told him how I felt.

He was sympathetic. "I can see how frustrated you are, David," he said. "We don't want to lose you this far into your apprenticeship. How would you like to work on the site, under a skilled carpenter? You will still have to attend college, but I think you will find it more interesting." He looked at my folder, and he said, "I see you are due a pay rise in two months' time." This news cheered me up, and I accepted the offer straight away. "You will have to finish off the week at the workshop, but you can start work on site next Monday. Be at the yard at the same time, and the van will pick you up."

I left the office, and Jenny must have overheard part of the conversation. "I'll miss you," she said as I left the building. I felt flattered that she had acknowledged me. All the lads were sorry to hear that I was leaving, except Piotr. He just nodded. But I couldn't wait to start my new adventure.

CHAPTER

My Best Mate

Monday arrived, and I got to the yard early so I could pick up my tools. A Bedford van picked me up, and it all went quiet as I got in the back. There were about ten men sitting on benches along either side of the van. They squeezed up so I could sit on the end. The man next to me said, "I'm George."

"Oh," I said. "My name's Davy." None of the others spoke.

"Don't worry about them," George said. "They're a miserable lot of bastards." The men laughed, and that got them talking again. We arrived about half an hour later. The site was a private house. And Belchers had won the contract. Most of the brickwork was built up to the roof. "Come on, then, Davy, you're working with me," George said.

I couldn't have been happier. I took to him like a duck to water. George was about fifty but young enough to understand what I was thinking. He showed me how to hold a hand saw properly, how to hold a hammer and bang nails in without damaging the wood—simple things, but they made things easier for me. By the end of the day I had learnt more with George than I had in the last six months. It was just what I needed. I only had to ask, and he would show me how to do it, then let me have a go. I made a mess of it sometimes, but he never lost his temper. He let me do it again until I got it right. When I went home to Gran's that night, I looked forward to working with George the next day. But I still hated doing night classes, all that way just for two hours' work on science or English seemed pointless to me. What had that got to do with carpentry? I didn't mind the day class so much because you actually made scale models of roofs with real wood, and made joints, and saw how a house was constructed. All this was practical. That would be useful in the future. We also had technical drawing, which I was very good at, much to the annoyance of Cyril Gunner. He didn't like me from the start and hated me coming top of the class. I think in a fair fight, I would win, so I wasn't afraid of him. But apart from that one individual, I got on well with the other boys. There were no girls doing this course.

The weeks went by. I helped George cut and fix the roof of the house. Cut in dormer windows and clad the sides with timber. At the end of the fourth week, I could do things on my own. George was always there for advice if I got it wrong. The manager came out on site that week and asked George if I would make a good carpenter. I overheard George tell the manager that I was a hard worker and he was pleased with my progress.

My seventeenth birthday I had been working for a year. I had a pay rise as promised, an extra four pennies an hour, one pound sixty a week. I was very disappointed. But my money kept growing. I now had one hundred and sixty pounds saved up in the post office. I wrote off for a provisional driving license and then arranged for a driving lesson. That driving of the old van around the timber yard had paid off. I had four lessons before the examiner told me to get a driving test booked in about four weeks' time. All I had to do then was just wait.

Mum had knitted me a new mohair jumper. It had taken her ages, and I was very proud of it. So I wore it to the college on the following Friday. All the boys admired it except one. "You look like a hairy monkey," said Cyril Gunner.

I made a jokey reply. "At least I'm a warm hairy monkey." Some of the other boys laughed, and this infuriated Cyril. As we sat in class concentrating on drawing the sketch on the blackboard I smelt burning. Some boys were laughing. I didn't realize until it was too late. Cyril, who sat behind me, had set fire to my jumper with his lighter. I pulled the jumper over my head and threw it on the floor, all the mohair had burned off the back of the jumper. It was ruined. I flew into a rage when I saw Cyril was laughing. I launched at him and threw a punch that caught him right on the chin. We both fell between the benches, and I landed a couple more punches before the teacher pulled me off. He marched us straight over to the principal's office and told him what had happened. I grinned at Cyril when I saw one of my punches had caught him just above the eye and it had turned black.

"I will not allow fighting in our college under any circumstances. You will both be suspended for two weeks without pay," the principal said. "I shall also be informing your employers of my recommendation. I hope this has taught you a lesson." We both left with our heads bowed. But I had taught Cyril a painful lesson.

I didn't know how the manager at Belchers would react when I called in the next day. But I could see he was pretty annoyed when I went into his office. "You are an embarrassment to the firm, Jones," he said. "You are the first boy to be suspended in all the years I have been here. If it was up to me, I would seriously consider ending your employment with this firm. However, the principal has told me about your jumper and how you were provoked. So I agree with him, you will be suspended for two weeks without pay. Perhaps when you return, you will think twice about fighting."

I left the office feeling disappointed, but cheered up when Jenny showed me out. "Don't worry, Davy," she whispered. "His bark is worse than his bite."

I had a bright idea on the way home to Gran's and decided to go over to the saw mills instead. When I explained to Uncle Jim what had happened, he offered me a job for the next two weeks and said he would pay me the same wage as Belchers so I didn't really lose any money. I liked working with Eddy, Tom, and Bill felling trees and burning the brushwood, and the two weeks went by very quickly. I failed my driving test that week and had to book another test date, which was annoying as I thought I had passed easily. It was another month before I could retake the test. In the meantime, Uncle Bill had seen his mate's car for sale. "It's a sound car, Davy, and worth the one hundred and fifty pounds he's asking for it." When I saw it, I was a bit disappointed. The car was an old 1954 Hillman Minks. It was so old-fashioned but in excellent condition. It was a maroon color, which I was not keen on, and the engine was an old-fashioned side valve, which meant it didn't have much power. But it was within my price range and left me enough money for the insurance. The previous owner had just had an MOT and it was taxed for nine months, so I bought it.

The test was in Caversham, and I was not familiar with the area. Reg the driving instructor didn't think I would pass. "Just relax, son, and do your best" were the last words he said before the driving examiner got in the passenger-side door and told me to drive off.

I had to follow the examiner's directions and thought I was doing all right, until I overshot a right turn and reversed on the main road back to the junction. I saw the examiner write down something on his pad, and thought I'd surely failed. So I didn't worry anymore. When he slammed down his hand on the dashboard as an indicator for me to do an emergency stop, I nearly put him through the windscreen. (There were no seat belts fitted back then.) He wrote something else down on his notepad. I drove back to the office where Reg was waiting and pulled up outside, feeling disappointed. But the examiner leaned across and said, "Well, Mr. Jones, the emergency stop was a bit erratic, and the reversing on the main road would have meant you failed, but you kept calm and checked your mirrors to make sure there were no other cars about, so I am giving you a pass."

I couldn't believe it. When he stepped out of the car, I shook his hand. "Thank you, sir," I said. "You don't know how much this means to me." He smiled as he walked away. "I've passed, Reg," I blurted out. I was so excited.

Reg was pleased as well. "I'd better drive home until you have calmed down," he said, smiling as we drove away. I sat in my very own car when I got back to Grans. It may have been old-fashioned and a horrible color. But it was mine, and now I could go anywhere I chose.

The first place I went was Mum's. I walked into the kitchen, and she was alone, washing the dishes. "How did you get here?" she asked, surprised. "Shouldn't you be at work?"

"I passed my test, Mum, and drove over in my car."

She gave me a hug. "Let's go and have a look at it, then," she said. Mum liked the color and the car. "I think it's great, son," she said. "You've worked hard and deserve it, Davy."

"Do you want a ride, Mum?" I asked. She jumped in, and I drove around the village like we were royalty.

That car changed my life. I had worked solid for over a year and had not experienced any social life. I started driving over to Pete's farm at Wittenham on Saturday nights. I hadn't seen Pete or Mick since leaving school and had a lot of catching up to do. We then drove over to Mick's place and all went out for a drink. I had never been a drinker (after seeing how it affected my father), but I did enjoy a cider. Mick had done well for himself and had set up a fruit-and-veg round in an old Ford transit van. He drove up to Covent Garden in London twice a week to pick up fresh fruit and veg at trade price and sell at a good profit. Pete had joined his father on the farm and was in charge of the dairy herd. He had to do long unsociable hours, milking early in the morning and in the evening. He had not passed his driving test and was glad we had all got together. It became a regular pub meeting on Saturday nights, as I was the only one who had a car, Mick only had his van, and this was the only night Pete could get off.

I continued to help Uncle Bill with the paint spraying on Sundays and, one day, discovered what a wicked sense of humor he had. We were sheeting up an old car ready for spraying early one morning, when I discovered a false leg hidden under one of the sheets. I looked at my uncle, and he chuckled. "That's Berol's," he said. "She'll be looking for that, when she gets up." I didn't get what he meant. "You'll see in a minute," he said. "Watch out of that window."

I looked, and sure enough, a few minutes later, Berol came jumping down the path toward the garage, on one leg, dressed in her nightgown, shouting, "Bill, have you seen my false leg?"

And then Bill said, "There, I told you she would be hopping mad." He burst out laughing and I had to laugh too, but I knew it was a cruel thing to do. But that's what my uncle was like. He regularly hid the leg just so he could have a laugh, seeing Berol hopping around.

CHAPTER

I Suffer a Loss

When I returned to work, George said he would have done the same thing when I told him why I had been suspended. "I don't think that was very fair," said George. "At least the other boy should have been made to pay for your jumper." George always knew best.

While I had been away, George had nearly finished the carpentry on the house. And we were moved on to another project, a new primary school at Chalgrove. We had to build the single-story flat roof. It was an interesting job laying the big joists across the steel beams and then covering with plywood. We had to cut large holes in the ceiling for the roof lights. It took us over two weeks before the roof was ready for ashfelting (a waterproof membrane). Before that was done, the council building inspector paid a visit to check all the carpentry work was satisfactory. George didn't like building inspectors. "All they do is read books about building. They have no practical knowledge," George grumbled. "Ask him to saw a piece of wood or bang a nail in, and he wouldn't have a clue."

I think the inspector sensed that George didn't like him, and asked me to remove the bits of ply covering the holes in the roof. "I want to see if you have put all the correct joist hangers in," he said. He went around all the roof lights, checking.

"What a waste of time," George mumbled to me. Just as he said that, the building inspector vanished. One minute he was there, the next he'd gone. We looked around, and he had stepped back and fallen through a hole made for the roof lights. He was lying on the ground floor, motionless. We climbed down the ladder just as the site foreman came in. He took one look at the inspector and called an ambulance. He was still unconscious when they took him to hospital.

There was a big inquiry after that. The manager of Belchers came on site immediately. "What happened?" he asked George.

"Well, the inspector asked Davy to remove all the covers over the roof lights, and he did. He must have stepped back and fell through."

"Didn't you replace the covers when he had finished?" asked the manager.

"Not all of them," I said. "I didn't have time."

"Well then, you were responsible for the accident."

"Now just a minute." George butted in. "You can't blame Davy. He only did what he was told to do. If the inspector was concentrating on what he was doing, he wouldn't have fallen through the hole."

The manager looked at George and backed down. "You haven't heard the last of this," said the manager as he stormed off. I thanked George for speaking up for me.

"That's all right, son. You were not to blame. I bet we don't hear any more about this." And he was right. The inspector couldn't sue Belchers because their lawyers got away with a technicality. He didn't have the proper safety equipment on. But as George pointed out afterward, a high-visibility jacket, a pair of work boots, and a site helmet wouldn't have made any difference to the outcome.

Once the roof was waterproofed, George showed me how to swing a door and put the handle and lock in. I was a bit hesitant at doing this as it involved a drill and chisel and I was scared of scratching the doors. I did scratch one, but George managed to hide it with the handle cover. "Anybody can make mistakes, son," he said, "but it takes a good man to get over it." George was always saying little quotes like that. I told George all about my father and how he had mistreated me over the years. "Sounds like abuse to me, son," he said. "Didn't you tell the police?"

"I don't trust the police," I said, "not after they nicked me for apple scrumping." He laughed at that. What a nice man he was.

One Saturday night, Pete, Mick, and I decided to go into Oxford for a drink. I drove up and parked in a covered car park. We walked through Lombard Street and passed a pub that had a disco and decided to go in it was packed with lot of drinkers standing around with pints in their hands. We had to push our way through to the bar. There was a live band playing on a back stage, and people were trying to dance. Mick bought two beers and a cider, and we stood watching the band. There were plenty of girls around. When all of a sudden a large Irish man with a pint of Guinness in his hand knocked into me, he spilled his drink over the floor. He looked at me and growled, "You better buy me another pint, shit brain."

His other buddies laughed. "You can buy us all a drink." They cheered. I was petrified Pete and I backed away, not wanting to start a fight.

All of a sudden, a fist slammed into the Irishman's nose, and he fell to the floor. Blood poured from his nose, but he didn't move. All his mates carried him outside. We looked around. Mick stood there grinning. "Come on," he said. "We better get out of here before they come back." We piled out into the street.

The Irishman was still lying on the pavement out cold, with all his mates around him. They spotted us and gave chase. We ran back to the car, got in quickly, and drove off.

"Where did you learn to fight like that?" I asked Mick.

"I'm part Irish myself, and my older brother was a boxer. He taught me a few punches," he said. "And he always told me, always hit the leader of the group first, and his followers will back off." Well, Pete and I were glad Mick was there that night. Without Mick, we would have been beaten up for sure. But we never went back to that particular pub.

The summer was over. On Saturdays, I started back at the saw mills. I could cut the branches on the saw bench and was quite confident. I'd had no serious accidents. Sometimes the branch would jam and be wrenched out of my hand, but this didn't happen very often, only if the saw blade needed to be sharpened. It was easy now I had the car and relied on it to pop into Mum's on the way back from the saw mills. I had decided to make this Christmas one that Gran would never forget. I bought an artificial tree one that didn't make a mess, as Gran put it, and I bought some paper chains to decorate the ceiling in the lounge. I used to light the fire in the evenings. Now I could use my car to go to evening classes at college, I had a little more time. I was still saving some money, but with running a car, having a drink with Pete and Mick on Saturday nights, there was not a lot left to save. I used to make Gran a cup of tea on Sunday mornings and take it up to her in bed. She liked that. Then I went over to Uncle Bill's garage to see if he wanted a hand with sanding down or sheeting up for a respray.

This particular morning about a week before Christmas, it was cold. I crept downstairs early and put up the paper chains. I put the tree in the corner and decorated it. I then lit the small coal fire so it would be warm when Gran got up and then I could make her a nice hot bowl of porridge, just to say thank you for putting up with me for the past eighteen months. When I had finished, I stood back and admired what I had done. It was nearly as good as our own lounge at Christmas Apart from the artificial Christmas tree and even though it was decorated, it still was not as good as a real one. But Mum would be surprised when she visited. I bought Gran a warm coat, although Mum had bought it for me, I paid for it. I wrapped the coat in Christmas paper and stuck it under the tree. I made Gran a cup of tea and took it up to her. "Wake up, Gran," I said. "I've made you a nice cup of tea." It was cold in her bedroom, and she was snuggled under the blankets. I thought I would leave her a bit longer so she could have a few more minutes in bed. Then I came downstairs. "Do you want me to make you a bowl of porridge?" I shouted up the stairs. She didn't answer. So I started to make the porridge. Five minutes later, she had still not come down, so I took the porridge up to her. "Gran, I said I've made some porridge. Eat it before it gets cold." I put the bowl on the bedside cabinet and noticed she hadn't drunk her tea. I gave her a gentle nudge. She still did not move. I pulled the covers away from her face. She looked contented, so I nudged her again. "Gran," I said and felt her face. It was stone cold. I started to panic and shook her harder. "Gran," I shouted, "wake up." But deep down, I knew she was dead. Tears welled up in my eyes, and I cried like a little baby. I covered her back up and ran next door to Uncle Bill's and told him. He came around immediately and saw his mother. He didn't cry like I thought he would but went next door to phone for the doctor.

The doctor only confirmed what we already knew. "Your mother died peacefully in her sleep," the doctor said after examining her. Uncle Bill looked sad but did not break down. Gran was seventy-six. I offered to drive over and tell Mum and left, glad to get away from that cold bedroom. Mum was upset, and I drove back with her and the kids. Dad didn't really want to go and said he'd stay there and look after the dog. As it was Christmas, Gran was taken to a morgue for the burial after the New Year. Instead of being a joyful time of year, that Christmas was the saddest.

The council soon wanted me out when they were told of Gran's death, as they wanted to house another family.

I stopped in Gran's house on my own until Mum persuaded my father that I could come home. But I wasn't looking forward to moving back in with my father still there. I drove over a couple of days later and parked on the hard shoulder outside my mum's house. Cookie still remembered me and flew over when I held my hand out. He landed on my shoulder and started pecking my earlobe. He still hadn't forgotten.

It was hard to adjust to sharing a bedroom with Tommy after being on my own for so long but we soon got used to one another, and I think Sheila, Tommy, and Mary were all glad I was home. Even my father tolerated me being there, and we all looked forward to the New Year.

CHAPTER

My First Car Crash

After Gran's funeral, everything began to return to normal. I started back to work on the ninth of January and was reacquainted with George. I started college a week later. I still did the block round on Saturdays and helped Uncle Bill on Sundays. I started weight training with Brian, but only went once a week. I still met Pete and Mick on Saturday evenings. I did see my old adversary Gary Browning cycle past our house a couple of times. I nodded but he ignored me so I still think there was some bitterness toward me. I don't think he had a job and was on the dole, and it wasn't long after that I noticed scratches along my car. It could have been one of two people, my father or Gary, but as my car was parked in a lay-by outside our house, there was nothing I could do about it unless I caught them in the act. But as it turned out, it didn't matter. A few days later, we had a snowstorm that lasted all night. The snow settled then froze the following night, making the roads treacherous the next morning. I drove to work but slid on some black ice and crashed into the back of a lorry on the way there. My beloved car was a wreck. I was unhurt and scrabbled out. The front of the car was buried under the back of the lorry. The lorry driver jumped out of his cab and looked at the mess. "You were lucky you walked away from that, lad, and not be injured," he said. He then scratched his head. "We can't leave the car here. It's blocking the road." He pulled clear of what was left of my car and checked what damage I had done to his lorry. As far as I could see, only one of his rear tail lights was hanging off. He then connected a tow rope to the front axle and dragged the car into a lay-by. Then he took out a broom from the back of the lorry and swept the glass and broken bodywork into the ditch. When he had finished, he looked at me. I was shaking like a leaf. "Look, son," he said, "you will have to inform your insurance company, and I will have to take your name and address, because somebody will have to pay for my broken taillight." I told him I had to get to Belchers yard about a mile up the road and inform the manager. "Well, jump in, lad" he said. "I will give you a lift and then we can sort this out." He parked his lorry in Belchers yard, and we both went into the office.

The manager talked to the lorry driver and then they both went into the yard to look at his lorry. I saw Jenny running out with a checkbook and pen. The manager must have written out a check or something because the driver got in his lorry and drove off. "Follow me," the manager said sternly. I followed him into the office. He sat down and beckoned me to do the same. I was expecting a right bollocking. But he remained calm for a few minutes, as if thinking things through. "You don't seem to have much luck, do you, Jones?" he began. "However, Ben Fisher the lorry driver was very considerate and explained what happened. He accepted a check for fifty pounds for the damage to his lorry, which will of course be stopped out of your wages until it is paid. I don't think we have to inform the police, as I will get Barry our mechanic to tow your car into the yard. Then you will have to get your insurance company to sort it out, is that clear?"

"Yes sir" I said, relieved.

"But what do we do about your lack of transport?" he continued. "I don't want you to lose any more time off work. George needs a hand on the site. Would you be able to drive the van?"

"Well yes, sir," I answered in surprise. "I used to drive my uncle's van around his yard." (I didn't tell him the van was a wreck and wasn't fit for the road.) "So I'm perfectly capable to drive your van."

He seemed satisfied with that. He then added, "Of course, the van will only be used to pick up and drop off the men working on your site, which you will have to do. You cannot keep the van over the weekend and must be picked up Monday mornings and dropped off Thursday evening. You will have to make you own way to college on Fridays. Do you understand?" Again I agreed. "Well," he continued, "I suppose we will have to find you some work in the workshop for the rest of the day, until the van arrives back tonight and then you can take charge of it." I thanked him and shook his hand. I walked over to the workshop and went inside. I immediately felt an atmosphere as I spoke to Jack. (George had told me the joiners working there always thought they were better than the carpenters working on site, and hated the fact we were earning more money than them.)

"Well, the only job we have at the moment is in the machine shop," said Jack, so I went to see Dougie and Frank and was soon doing my old job, clearing out the sawdust and sweeping up. Oh, how I hated doing that.

I picked up the van when Simon, one of the bricklayers on site, drove into the yard. I explained what had happened and that I was taking over the driving. "Well then, Davy, you had better drive me home and then pick me up in the morning. Then I can show you the route I take to pick all the other men up." He seemed at bit put out that I was taking over his job driving the van, but he didn't say anything. So that night I drove over to Uncle Bill's in the van and picked up my bike. Luckily, it was stored in his shed and it still looked new. I gave Uncle Bill my insurance details and he said he would ring the company up the next day and get it sorted. I still had to ride my bike over to the yard to pick the van up on Monday morning and cycle home Thursday nights but I did have the van all week, so I used it to drive up to college Mondays and Fridays evenings. I don't think any of the staff at the college noticed a Bedford van with the words Belchers Builders advertised all over the side of the van, parked in their car park, and I was never found out.

Two weeks went by before I had a settlement figure come through the post from the insurance company. It was only half of what I was expecting: seventy-five pounds. "Is that all?" I said to my uncle Bill.

"Insurance companies are all rip-off merchants," he said, "They will only pay out the bare minimum, so think yourself lucky you got that much."

"But how am I going to pick up a car for that much?" I said, disappointed.

"Leave it to me, son," he said. Good old Uncle Bill—he may have had a wicked sense of humor, but he had a heart of gold.

His choice of car was an Austin A30 van, and it was in terrible condition. It had an MOT, and the engine ticked over. "It's not much yet," said my uncle, "but for fifty pounds, it's a bargain." I didn't share the same optimism. "If you sand all the paintwork down, I will spray it any color you want—"

"As long as it's black," I interrupted. "You said that gag before."

"Well then, you know what I mean." He chuckled. I knew what he meant: me doing all the hard work. But it would solve my problems and be useful for carrying my tools around. So I agreed to buy it. Two weekends later, it was complete. It meant I'd given up the block round for a couple of Saturdays, but it was worth it after Bill's mate tinkered with the engine and got it running well. I was pleased with the result. "If you sold that now," said my uncle, "you could double your money." I didn't want to sell it. It was such a cute little motor, and the insurance was reasonable considering I'd had an accident. So on the Monday, I drove to work, and Simon resumed the driving of the works van.

It was in June the block round had finished and Uncle Jim introduced me to his cousin's daughter Tracy. I liked her, and after a few weeks, we went out together. She was about five foot six tall with long black hair, a nice figure, and she wore the shortest miniskirt I had ever seen. When we went on our first date, I could see the tops of her stockings and suspender belt when she bent over. She was a real turn-on. She was not impressed with my little green van when I first picked her up. I had cleaned inside and it smelled all right. The first thing she said was "I thought you would have something better than this, Davy,"

So we only went for a drive that first night, and only kissed. We arranged to see each other the following week, and I took her to the cinema. We didn't see much of the film because we were smooching through most of it. She was a very good kisser. I did manage to fondle her breast, and she didn't object. So I slid my hand up her skirt and felt the tops of her stockings. But that got a reaction. "No, Davy," she said, "you are taking things too fast." I sat back in the seat and apologized. "It's not that I don't like you," she said, "but we have only been out twice."

We saw the end of the film, and I drove her home. But before she went in, she turned and said seductively, "Davy, I am learning to drive, and wondered if you could teach me."

I was flattered. "Yes, I can do that," I said.

"Can we start next week, then?" she said. I agreed, and as she got out of the car, her dress rode up and I had a full view of her white suspenders. I had another wet dream that night thinking of her.

I told George all about Tracy and her short skirts and white suspenders. "She's a great kisser," I said, "and has a gorgeous figure."

"Be careful," he said. "She sounds like a cock teaser." I thought he was just jealous, so I changed the subject. We carried on working together, and George and I made a great team. He was hard-working unlike many of the others, who were just along for the ride, only doing the bare minimum for their wages at the end of the week.

There was no work at the sawmills, and Uncle Bill had very little work for me. "How do you fancy doing some price work?" George asked me one day. I didn't know what he meant, so he explained, "I'll ask the manager if we can fit all the fire escape doors in the school on a price. We will both agree on a set price, and we can fit them in our own time, on Saturday and Sunday if you like. The more we do, the more we earn. We'll split the money fifty-fifty, so what do you say?" I thought this a great idea and agreed. So it was all arranged. The manager came on site and agreed to a price of four pounds per pair of doors, including all the safety catches. There were five pairs of doors so when we had completed all the doors, the price came to twenty pounds. George and the manager shook hands on the deal, and we agreed we would start that weekend. That Saturday, I picked up George in my van at 7:00 a.m we stopped once at twelve thirty for a quick lunch break, then continued to 5:30 p.m. We were both exhausted, but had completed three sets of doors before we went home. I slept well that night but was up at the same time on Sunday morning and picked George up. We had the last pair of doors on and finished by 3:00 p.m. By the time we cleared up, it was four thirty before we left to go home. In two days we had earned more money than a week's wage. We both arrived on site the next morning, shattered. It was a good job the day's work was easy. The manager came to the site at lunchtime and asked George how we got on over the weekend. "We finished all five pairs of doors, sir," he said.

"What, all the safety catches as well?" the manager replied.

"Yes, we did all the work you agreed with," said George.

"That's impossible," he muttered and went into the site office. About twenty minutes later, we saw him examining the door and trying the safety bars. He then came over to George and said, "I will have to deduct some of your wages, because you haven't fitted any deadlocks to the doors."

George was dumbfounded. I could see from his face that he was angry. "There was nothing in the agreement we had to fit deadlocks," George replied.

The manager smiled. "But they have to be fitted. It's the law."

To which George replied "Well, if we fitted a deadlock to each of the fire escape doors and somebody locked the doors, then how are people going to escape if all the doors are locked?"

The manager looked confused and didn't know what to say. "Well, er, I will have to check on that," he said and walked away.

I smiled at George. "That told him," I said.

"Did it?" he replied. "He's trying to knock some money off because we earnt too much." At the end of the week, we both checked our wage packets. We were both paid our normal wage plus ten pounds bonus, minus stoppages after tax and inadequate fitting of locks—seven pounds fifty pence. "The bastard," George raged. "The management has stopped five pounds for not fitting the deadlocks." He had cooled down by the end of the day. After all, we still made a good wage. (The deadlocks were never ever fitted to the fire escape doors.) So that scam put us off price work, and we never asked again.

CHAPTER

The Driving Instructor

Saturday night and I was all kitted out for the night of passion with Tracy. I had bought a pair of L plates and tied them to the front and back and thought how grateful she would be after the driving lesson and might be a bit more amorous. She was waiting in her front doorway when I arrived, and I saw her mum waving as she got into the car. She had a different dress on, but it was just as short and showed a lot of leg as she sat in the passenger seat. "I will take you on a quiet country lane," I said, "so I can see how you handle the clutch and brake pedal." I just remembered all the things Reg had taught me and went through them one by one. To be fair, she picked things up pretty quickly and soon we were whizzing along the country lane. "I think that will do for the first lesson," I said. "Pull in over in that lay-by, and we can swap places."

She did reluctantly, I thought, and we swapped places. As she got out, all her dress had wrinkled up again, and all the tops of her legs were on show. I don't know if she was doing this deliberately or the dress was way too short, but I immediately had a hard-on. I leaned across and gave her a kiss when she had made herself comfortable. Again she let me fondle her breasts and put my hand up her dress. This time, she let me feel all between her legs. I was getting very excited. Then she stopped me. "This van is way too small in the front. I can't get comfortable," she said.

"Well, we could get in the back," I suggested.

She giggled. "It's too dirty and there's nothing to lie on and I don't want to ladder my tights." I could see this was going nowhere. I sat back in my seat and sighed. She could see I was annoyed. "I think we should get going now," Tracy said. "Do you think I could drive back?"

"I don't think you are confident to drive on main roads yet," I said. "Maybe next time."

She looked disappointed as we drove home but still gave me a flash of her stocking tops as she got out of the van. "See you next Saturday," she said, then blew me a kiss as she went indoors.

On Sunday morning, Uncle Bill had to respray a side panel on a Mini. I was quite impressed when I sat in it. "One day, I am going to get a Mini," I said.

"You will have to save hard, then, Davy," Bill said, "Because they are quite expensive." I carried on sanding the panel down, then sheeted the car up, ready for spraying. We finished early that afternoon.

Bill said, "Do you want to watch a dirty movie, Davy?" I had never seen a dirty movie before, so I said yes. He pulled out a projector hidden under a sheet. "Cover that window with a bit of cardboard, Davy," he told me. When I had finished, he pointed the projector at a sheet hung over the back wall. The film was a bit grainy, but the title was *Debbie Does Dallas*. As the film rolled, I was shocked and a bit embarrassed watching it in front of Uncle Bill and sort of glad when it finished. "I show a different film every Friday night for the lads on the estate," he said. "You're welcome to come along, I only charge one shilling each, but you can watch for free." I was beginning to wonder if I really knew my Uncle Bill. What other secrets did he have hidden?

I was still doing the block rounds with Eddy and Tom. I really enjoyed going around all the houses. And my uncle had given me a good pay rise. "Well, lad, you do as much work as the others," he said, "so you deserve it." I worked even harder and finally came to Eddie and Tom's favorite house on the council estate. "I'm staying in the lorry," I said. "I don't want to sit in that kitchen and hear you bonking those girls and have to watch Phillis scratching her fanny." They both burst out laughing as they went down the path with a sack of blocks on their backs. I knew the lads would be gone for at least half an hour, so I started to doze off in the cab. I then noticed some young girls playing tennis in the road. They couldn't have been any older than fourteen or fifteen. But I watched them, fascinated. One of them looked vaguely familiar. But it wasn't until the tennis ball rolled over by the lorry and she came over to retrieve it, and then glanced up and saw me in the lorry. I couldn't believe it. She looked exactly like Brenda when I last saw her, same build and same long blond hair. "Brenda," I said, amazed.

"No, my name's Linda," she said, smiling, and ran off.

The lads came back then and got in the lorry. Both looked worn out. "We are both getting too old for this," said Tom, and he looked over to Eddy, "but it was worth it." They were both laughing when we drove back to the yard.

That evening, I cleared out the back of the van, borrowed a large piece of foam from Uncle Bill's garage and covered it with a clean dust sheet. (I made sure it didn't smell of paint fumes.) I cleaned the little ceiling light so I would be able to see what I was doing, then sprayed the inside of the van with a strong lavender scent, just as my uncle came around. "You've made that into a nice passion wagon," he said. "Are you on a promise?"

"I hope so," I said, grinning.

He went back into his garage then came out and handed me a small package. "Don't forget to put one of these on, then," he said, smiling.

I had never seen a packet of Durex before but said, "Thanks, Bill, I'll put them in the glove compartment."

"Make sure one of them is on the end of your cock before you start poking her," he said, grinning. God he was crude, but I still liked him.

That night when I picked Tracy up, she looked gorgeous. But the first thing she said before she got in the van was "Can I drive?"

"A bit later," I said, so she got in and sat down in a bit of a mood. She didn't speak for about five minutes as we drove out of the village. So I broke the ice.

"It smells nice in here, doesn't it, Tracy?"

She sniffed the air. "Yes, I suppose so." She then glanced in the back and saw the little bed I had made. She smiled. "Do you think I can drive now?" she said. So I pulled over to the side of the road and let her drive. She was quite good on the quite country lanes, but I didn't think she would be able to handle built-up areas quite yet.

We drove around for at least an hour. I kept looking at the fuel gauge and noticed it was under a quarter full. "We better pull into this lay-by," I said. "We are nearly out of fuel." She parked in the lay-by. It was perfect. We were on a single-track road that was rarely used, so we wouldn't be disturbed. I leaned across and kissed her. "Shall we get in the back?" I asked. "It will be more comfortable."

And she agreed. "But only if I can drive back home," she said seductively.

I would have agreed to anything. I was so aroused, so I said, "Yes, of course you can." So we both climbed in the back and I shut the door. I then turned on the little ceiling light. It felt very cozy, a bit cramped but we could at least lie down side by side and stretch our legs. I had remembered to put the pack of Durex in my pocket. I embraced her and she responded. I was all over her. I managed to push her short skirt up around her waist and undo her suspenders. I slid my trousers and pants around my ankles, all with one hand while still groping and kissing her. My hard cock slid between her legs, and I began rubbing myself up and down. I could hear her breathing heavily and moaning. She was clearly enjoying this. I then realized I was pushing against her knickers. I hadn't taken them off. I whispered, "I'll just put a Johnny on," and started fumbling around in my trouser pocket. My cock was so hard, thinking where I would be putting it in a few minutes. But then the moment was gone. She suddenly sat up and adjusted her skirt. "But," I said, "I thought this is what you wanted."

"I do, but you are pushing things too fast, Davy," she said. "I want to go home." I could see there was no point in pushing her, so I pulled my pants and trousers up and got out of the car, really frustrated and annoyed. I climbed into the driver's seat. "I thought you agreed I could drive back," she said.

I then lost my temper with her. "Look," I said, "every time we go out, you want to drive, and if I don't let you drive, you go into a huff. I'm not your boyfriend. I feel I'm being treated like a bloody driving instructor." We drove back to her house in silence. I looked across at her a couple of times, hoping she would say something. As I stopped outside her house, she got out, slammed the van door, and stomped up the path. She didn't even look around before she disappeared inside. That was the last I saw of Tracy.

I told my uncle Jim about finishing with Tracy, and he volunteered to try to patch things up with her. But I told him things should be left as they were. Anyway when I thought about it, I didn't really love Tracy. It was more lust than love.

I had driven over in my little van, and when I came out of Jim's office, Eddy was admiring the paintwork. "God, she does look smart," said Eddy. "Do you want to swap?"

"What have you got?" I inquired. He pointed over to a rusty Mini. When I examined the bodywork, it was worse than I thought. "It's a bit rusty, Eddy," I said. "What's the engine like?"

"The engine's fine. OK, the body's a bit rough, but with Bill's and your painting skills, you could make it better than yours," said Eddy. "And I've always wanted a van. You can get more stuff in it." I did like it and it was a car I'd always dreamed of. So with a bit of reluctance, we shook hands on the deal. I borrowed my uncle's phone, rang my insurance company, and got them to swap the insurances on the Mini. Then I drove off in my dream car. I took it over to Uncle Bill's garage. He had just finished spraying a front wing of a car. He looked at me then the car.

"What the hell have you bought now, Davy?" he said. "It's only the rust holding the bodywork together."

I got out. "OK, the bodywork does need a lot of work," I said, "but I'll do all the hard work if you spray it for me." And before he could make any witty remark, I said, "But not black."

I had to use the car for work the first week, and the lads at work took the mickey out of the car's rusty spots. But I didn't care. I knew what it would look like when it was finished. I didn't do the block round that Saturday and started on the car. Even Bill helped with the body filler and sanding down, and by Saturday evening, it was ready for masking up. We pushed the car into the garage overnight, and I cycled home. I arrived at Bill's the next morning early. I turned on the heaters to warm the garage up and began masking up the car. By the time my uncle showed his face about 10:00 a.m., the car was ready for spraying. He pulled off a sheet covering a bench, and there were about ten pots of paint hidden under the bench. "Choose a color you like, Davy," he said. I looked at the pots and chose a gold color. "It's a bit bright," said Bill. "It will stand out like a sore thumb."

"That's what I want," I said. "Everybody will know whose car it is."

We put on the face masks, and Bill began spraying the car. By lunchtime, the car was finished. "Let's go and have a bite for lunch and the car will be touch dry when we come back," he said. An hour later, we started peeling back all the masking tape and paper, then we refitted the chrome, and by 5:00 p.m., the car was finished. It looked brand new. It wanted a nice set of wheels, but apart from that, it looked gorgeous. When I drove to work Monday morning, all the lads thought the color a bit garish, but all agreed we had made a fantastic job of the paintwork.

CHAPTER

Money Problems with My Father

That Saturday, I drove over to the saw mills, and Eddy was surprised at the job we made of the Mini. "I like the color," he remarked. "It's unusual."

"I wanted it to stand out," I said.

"Well, it certainly does that." He laughed. We then loaded the sacks on the lorry and drove off on the block round We had delivered most of the blocks by 3:00 p.m. I looked out for Linda when we entered the council estate, but I couldn't see her. I wanted to find out more about her and how old she was. So when Eddy and Tom stopped at Phillis's house for their weekly nuptials, I got out of the lorry and started walking around to see where she lived.

She must have been looking out for me, because a few minutes later, she came out the front door of a semidetached house. "I didn't see you last week," she said.

"No," I replied. "I had to fix my car, but I'm here now," I said cheekily. She blushed. "Where do you work?" I asked.

"I haven't got a job yet," she replied. "I've only just left school."

"I'll see you next week, then," I said and blew her a kiss as I walked back to the lorry.

Eddy and Tom already sat in the lorry, waiting. "You bloody cradle snatcher," Tom said jokingly. "I bet she's only fourteen."

"She's nearly sixteen," I replied. "She's just left school and looking for a job." They kept quiet on the way back to the yard. But I noticed them winking at each other and grinning.

I had not been out for a drink with Pete or Mick since dating Tracy. I drove over that Saturday evening to see if they wanted to go for a drink. I went to Pete's house first and discovered him tinkering about with a minivan. "What do you think of the van?" He said. "I've just got it on the road."

"I didn't know you could drive," I replied.

"Well, it's been over six weeks since we last went out for a drink. I passed my test and bought a van since then." He looked over my car and liked the gold color. We set off to find Mick, then all went to the local pub for a pint. We chatted for most of the evening about the last six weeks, whom we had seen and what we had done. We agreed to meet the following week and go for a pub crawl.

I had been getting on quite well with my father since living back with Mum. He was speaking to me occasionally and not grunting. Now that all the family were growing up, Sheila was nearly fifteen, Tommy was thirteen, and Mary eleven. I think things had quieted down. He was still drinking, but was not coming home drunk. And one evening, he asked me if I would lend him ten pounds. "I will be able to pay you back at the end of the week when I get paid," he said.

I thought our relationship had improved, so I lent him the money. I forgot all about it by the end of the week, as we would be doing the final block round on Saturday and I was going out with Pete and Mick for a drink in the evening. I looked out for Linda when we approached Phillis's house on the council estate, but couldn't see her. When Eddy and Tom came back looking very pleased with themselves, there was no sign of her. I thought about knocking on her front door but decided against it. Anyway if she had wanted to see me again, she would have come out. So we left and drove back to the yard. It was a warm evening when I picked up Pete and Mick. We decided to go to Spread Eagle in Wallingford but didn't know anybody there, so we just had the one pint and moved on to the Coach and Horses and got chatting to a couple of locals. Mick looked at his watch and said, "Come on, lads, let's go to one more Pub and then call it for the night." We drank up and then drove over to the Fox, one of the pubs in my village. We went in and it was packed. We were about to leave when I heard a familiar voice boom out, "Hey, son, aren't you going to stay for a drink?" It was my father, so we pushed our way over. He insisted he wanted to buy us all a drink. Mick and Pete ordered a pint of draft beer, and I ordered my usual, a pint of cider. He immediately laughed out loud. "A pint of cider," he said. "That's a woman's drink." All his mates laughed and I felt about two inches tall. But I accepted a man's drink, as he called it, and had a draft beer even though I didn't like beer. I could see he'd had enough to drink. But he downed his pint and ordered another, just to impress my mates. But when the barman asked for the money, he felt in his pockets and discovered he'd spent it all. He pulled me closer and whispered, "Lend us a tenner, lad. I'll pay you back next week."

So I replied, "Just a minute, Dad, you still owe me ten pounds from last week."

All his mates in the vicinity went quiet; it was as if I had spoken through a loudspeaker. Then one of his mates said, "I'll get this, Trevor," and paid for his drink. That broke the atmosphere, and everybody started talking again.

We drank up and then thanked my father for the drink and left. Glad to get out of the pub, we sat back in my car, and Mick said, "You shouldn't have said that, Davy. You embarrassed your father in front of his mates." I realized I had made a mistake. I hadn't intentionally tried to embarrass my father and decided to apologize when I next saw him. That night when I arrived home, my father was already in bed, so I crept into my bedroom and went to bed. The next morning, my father had already gone out when I came down for breakfast. Mum looked at me. "What did you say to your father last night, Davy? Your father looked in a right mood when he left this morning." I didn't know how to explain, so I just made an excuse that we all had too much to drink. I didn't have a chance to apologize until that evening and then I don't think he forgave me. He hardly ever spoke to me again. (I never did get that tenner back.)

Summer was here, and just before my eighteenth birthday, Pete came over and suggested we all go on a road trip down to Devon. I was up for that and asked the works manager if I could have the next week off. "It's a bit short notice, lad," he said, then looked at the week's schedule. "Yes, I don't see why not. George can manage on his own next week." So it was all arranged. Mick would go in Pete's minivan. I would drive my Mini, and we would go camping in Devon.

CHAPTER

The Road Trip

It was raining when we set off early Saturday morning and decided to take the scenic route on the A303 to Amesbury and follow the road down to Exeter and then on to Dartmoor. The weather brightened up around 10:00 a.m., and it was great overtaking each other on the straight bits of road. We pulled into a roadside café just outside of Amesbury for an early lunch and sat down, pleased with our progress. We were all eating a fried breakfast, when a gang of Hell's Angels came in and they immediately helped themselves to the food displayed on the counter. They also started harassing the other customers and tipping over tables. Mick looked at me and Pete. "If they start any trouble," Mick said, "I'll take the biggest one on."

"There's too many of them, Mick," I whispered. "Let's get out of here before they spot us." Pete agreed, so we slipped out through the toilets block and out a side door and drove off without paying for our meal. Nobody followed us. I said afterward, "The counter staff probably called the police, so they were more interested in arresting the troublemakers than chasing after us."

Although we had eaten, we were all thirsty, so we stopped at a truckers' café at Wincanton. It was a bit of a dump but served a great mug of tea. When we came out, a couple of girls in short skirts and low tops showing all their cleavage came over and started chattering to us. Mick wasn't interested, and I must admit up close they did look like a couple of tarts. They had black eye shadow and bright-red lipstick. One leaned in my window. "Can you give us a lift to Exeter, governor?" she purred. "I'll make it worth your trouble." She leaned in further and dropped her bra, and both her tits flopped out. I was about to grab them, when Mickey and Pete drove off.

"Sorry, love," I said, "we are not going to Exeter," and I drove off after Pete.

I heard her shout after me, "Well, fuck off, then" and stick her two fingers up. We drove on to Honiton and pitched our tents up on a campsite. The site had a proper toilet block and showers and a little shop where you could buy milk, tea, coffee, and some food essentials. Pete had brought along a little camping stove, so we decided to have beans and sausages on toast. It was a disaster from the start. The sausages weren't done, and Pete managed to burn the toast. So we drank the last remaining cider and beer cans left and talked about the two scrubbers we had encountered and what we would like to do with them. Mickey was not that impressed. "If you can't do better than that," he said, "then you must be blind." He obviously had some sexual experience. But I was still a virgin at eighteen and determined to break that stigma. We did sleep reasonably that night, perhaps helped by the amount of beer we consumed. We awoke and went across to have a nice hot steaming shower; only we had a lukewarm drafty shower that only dribbled out over our heads. But at least the toilets worked. We didn't bother to cook breakfast and were on our way by 9:00 am and stopped just outside Exeter and had a bite to eat and a hot drink then we were on our way again. We drove down to Buckfastleigh and found a campsite. It was just a farmer's field really, but he did have some toilets and wash hand basins but no showers. After we had pitched the tents, we decided to explore Buckfast Abbey and sample some of their homemade wines and then drove around the River Dart beauty spots. We finally ended up in a local pub and had a meal. The locals made us real welcome, so we stayed there that evening, listening to some of their tales and having a good laugh.

We decided the next day to pick up some girls; after all, that was what we had come for. We decide to try our luck in Torquay and went down to the beach. It was a gorgeous day. We stripped off and went for a swim. We didn't stop in long. It was bloody cold. So we lay about on the beach, eyeing up the local girls. There were a few sunning themselves. Mick went over to them and started chatting them up. But after five minutes, he came back over and lay back down. "No luck, then," I said to Mick.

"All they wanted to talk about was what they had done and where they had been," said Mick. "I think they were lesbians. Anyway, they are going home tonight." We were not having much luck, so we decided to try a disco club that night. We had fish and chips washed down with a can of beer, then made our way to the local disco. We got there about 9:00 p.m., and apart from the bartender and DJ, who was playing an Elvis song, "Are You Lonesome Tonight?" which I thought was very appropriate, we were the only ones there.

"Will anybody else turn up tonight?" I asked the bartender.

He grinned. "They all turn up about ten," he said, "so you've got a bit of a wait. Can I get you a drink?" I had a local cider, or scrumpy, as the barman called it. Mick and Pete had the local beer. By the time the others started arriving, all three of us were pissed. I had never tasted cider so strong. We did chat to a few girls and had a dance with them, but even if we had been lucky and pulled one, I doubt any of us could have got a hard-on. We left about eleven and went back to the campsite. None of us slept well. I know my stomach was gurgling away all night, and it wasn't until I visited the toilets in the morning that I felt a bit better.

We decided to find the nearest café and have something to eat.

We slung our tents into the cars and set off. We headed out across Dartmoor, intending to see the famous Lydford Gorge on the west side of the moor and then on to Cornwall. We stopped at a mobile van that sold hot snacks and drinks. We sat and ate hot sausage rolls, packets of crisps, and a cup of coffee and felt a lot better. "Have you climbed Haytor Rocks yet, lads?" the owner said. "It's about a mile up ahead on the left. You can't miss them." We thanked him and drove off. He was right. A massive pile of rocks stood on a hill just in front of us.

We pulled up and got out. There were a number of backpackers climbing up the rocks, with all the gear on. We looked like we had just been to the beach with shorts, trainers, and T-shirts, but it was too hot to be dressed any other way. We climbed the hill then started clambering over the rocks. We got to the top, and all three of us stood there admiring the view. It was a bit windy up there, so we started climbing back down and were nearly there, when Mick suddenly cried out. He'd slipped between two large boulders and twisted his leg. We helped him up, and I could see all his leg was grazed. I thought then perhaps we should have dressed more sensibly. He seemed to have recovered when we got off the rocks and walked back down the grassy hill to the cars. "I shall be all right," he said. "It feels better already."

So we drove on to Lydford. We parked in the car park and walked around the two-mile scenic track through the woods and down along the river in the gorge. I noticed Mick grimace a few times, but he never complained. We finally ended up in the Devil's Cauldron. A small plank supported by chains hung over the massive hole where the river plunged into. You couldn't see the bottom because the spray rushed up and surrounded the natural cavern. It was worth the walk just to see this amazing spectacle. We climbed out of the gorge and went back to the cars. We decided to have something to eat at the café before moving on. It was nearly 5:00 p.m. before we got back on the A30 to Cornwall.

We drove on and on and took the wrong turning once and went about twenty miles the wrong way but eventually arrived in Bodmin. It was about 10:00 pm we were all tired and decided to find a campsite. We drove around for about an hour. It was dark and we were all fed up. "Let's just drive off the road somewhere and park up for the night," Pete said, "and we could just sleep in the van."

We all agreed and drove on for a few miles, before Pete turned off the main road and drove down a small track. I followed Pete through an open gap that said, "No entry" on a sign hung over the gate. Pete drove on for about half a mile before we came to a wide tarmac strip that was deserted. It was pitch black. He stopped and I pulled alongside him. "This will do," he said and climbed into the back of the van, and Mick followed. They looked quite cozy wrapped in their sleeping bags.

Mick complained his leg was hurting, so I gave him some aspirins to numb the pain. Then I pulled on my sleeping bag and curled up in the back of the Mini. It wasn't very comfortable, but eventually, I fell asleep. I was awoken by loud banging early the next morning. I looked out. A gray minivan with flashing blue light was parked next to Pete's van, and a security man was banging on Pete's roof with his fist. Pete opened the back doors and clambered out, dressed only in his pants. I heard the man shout, "What the bloody hell do you think you're playing at? Can't you see this is a private runway and a plane is waiting to land? Now get off immediately, or I will call the police and have you arrested for trespassing."

Pete got in the car and drove off, still in his underpants. I quickly followed. We pulled up just outside the gate with the "no entry" sign and got dressed. We glanced up and saw a small biplane coming in to land. We both laughed, but we didn't laugh when we saw the state Mick was in. He was still in his sleeping bag, and we helped him out. His knee was swollen to size of a football, and he was in agony. I managed to give him some more aspirins. "We'll have to get him to a hospital," I said, "something seriously wrong with his knee." Pete agreed. We looked on the map. The nearest big hospital we could see was in Truro about fifteen miles away. We laid Mick down in the back of the van and made him as comfortable as possible before we set off.

It took us half an hour before we found the hospital. We parked, and I went into the hospital to get some help. A nurse came out with a wheelchair and wheeled him inside. It was an hour before we were told he had a badly twisted knee and would be in hospital for the rest of the day and perhaps overnight as well. There was nothing we could do. It was still early, so we decided to head for the nearest coast and ring the hospital that evening to see how he was. We drove over to Perranporth on the north coast about twenty miles away. We stopped at a café on the way there and arrived about midday. We found a campsite right on top of the cliffs overlooking the beach. We pitched our tents and stripped off to our trunks and went for a swim. Pete and I lay on our towels, drying off, when we spotted a couple of girls eyeing us up. There was nobody else about. They came over and started chatting. I thought they were sixteen or seventeen maybe. The girl chatting to Pete was called Jacky. She was the prettiest. The other girl was called Zoe. She was all right, a bit short and plump, not the sort of girl I would normally go for. They were both dressed provocatively. Zoe had a very short checked skirt on and clearly didn't mind showing her white knickers. She had a loose-fitting top covering quite a large pair of breasts in a skimpy white bra that hardly kept them in. Zoe sat down beside me. "What's your name, then?" she asked.

"Davy," I replied.

"Are you on holiday?" she said. When I told her we were, she asked, "What car have you got?" I told her a Mini. "Would you take me for a ride?" she said. "I love Minis." I looked across at Pete. He seemed engrossed with the other girl. "I'm just going to take Zoe for a ride," I said. "See you back at the campsite." He just stuck his thumb in the air. When I got back to the tent, I took off my trunks and slipped on a pair of shorts and a T-shirt and got back in the car. I noticed straight away how she was seated provocatively with her dress pulled up to her knickers. "Where do you want to go?" I said.

"Anywhere," she answered. "I don't mind."

So I drove off toward St. Agnes. I kept looking at her legs and felt my cock getting hard. "I can show you a lot more than that," she said when she saw me looking. I didn't know how to reply to that, then she leaned across me, put her hand inside my shorts, and pulled out my cock. It was lucky there were no cars on the road because I swerved when she bent down and put my cock in her mouth. I had never felt so excited. I pulled over in a lay-by and let her carry on. It was not long before I ejaculated all over her. She didn't seem to mind and calmly wiped herself down with her hankie. "You enjoyed that," she said, "didn't you?"

"Yes, it was great," I said, shocked. I had never had a girl as experienced and forthcoming as this. She completely blew my mind.

"Can I see you tomorrow?" She asked. "Because Mum will be expecting me home for tea and I have to go out tonight to see my dad."

"Doesn't he live with you, then?" I asked.

"No, Mum and Dad split up when I was a baby, and I only see him once a month."

I looked at my watch and realized it had just gone 5:00 p.m. and we were supposed to phone the hospital at five. "Where do you want dropping off?" I said.

"Oh, just drop me off at the campsite. I only live down the hill." I drove back to my tent. And then she leaned across, put her arms around me, and kissed me. That was the first time I smelled her body odor. It was a bit off-putting. "I'll meet you up here at 9:00 a.m., then," she said. I nodded, and she ran off down the hill, still showing her knickers.

I raced over to the telephone kiosk and rang the hospital. It was a few minutes before I was put through to the doctor. When I asked him how Mick was, he replied, "Not good, I'm afraid. He's pulled some ligaments in his knee, and we have had to operate. He will need to stay in at least another day."

"Thanks, doctor," I said, then I put the phone down. Poor old Mick, he's not having much of a holiday, I thought as I walked back to the tent. I had just put my trousers on and a shirt when Pete came back on his own. He grinned at me. "Well, did you get your end away?" I asked.

"Not quite," he said, "but it's a sure thing tomorrow, when I take her out in the van." I then told him about Mick and how he might have to stay in hospital a couple of days. "I am sure he wouldn't mind us enjoying ourselves," Pete said. "After all, he is in the best place." (I don't think Mick would have thought that.) We went out that evening. There wasn't a lot to do in the village. They had a fantastic beach but no nightlife, so we ended up in the local pub and had a good roast dinner then drank the evening away talking to the locals. They were a very friendly lot down the pub.

The next day, Zoe was there outside my tent, dead on 9:00 a.m. I rather hoped she'd had a good shower and put some nice-smelling deodorant on. But when I opened the tent flap, she had exactly the same clothes on. Even her knickers looked the same. "Are you coming out," she said, "or am I coming in?" The tent was a one-man tent barely big enough for me, let alone her. But she pushed her way in and rolled over on top of me in my sleeping bag, trying to undo the zip. Again I smelled body odor when she tried to kiss me, so I pushed her off me, and half the side of the tent collapsed as the supporting ropes gave way. I unzipped my Sleeping bag and crawled out in my pants. It must have looked funny to see half the tent collapsed and someone's legs sticking out the side. I was a bit annoyed and went over to the car and put my shorts and T-shirt on by the time she had scrabbled out of the tent. "I'm so sorry, Davy," she said. "I will make it up to you, I promise." While I was repairing the tent, she sloped off and sat in the car.

I wasn't really annoyed with her. She hadn't damaged the tent, only pulled a few supporting ropes out, and she still looked incredibly sexy. I went over to Pete's tent. He was still asleep. I opened the flap. "Pete, I'm going out for the day with Zoe and won't be back until this evening." He grunted under the covers as if he heard me.

"Well, where would you like to go today?" I said when I got back into the car. "We could drive over to Tintagel and see King Arthur's castle."

"I'd like that," she said. So we set off. We stopped at a café halfway there, and I bought her a breakfast. I thought about stopping off at a chemist and buying her some deodorant, but thought that a bit embarrassing. After all, it only seemed to be under her arms. Perhaps she had a nervous reaction when she got excited.

We never got to see King Arthur's castle. As we were passing a hay field, she told me to pull over. When I had stopped, she suggested we go for a walk. It was a warm day, so we strolled down the side of the field, hand in hand. The newly cut hay still smelled gorgeous. We had only walked about half a mile before she sat down in the rows of hay and pulled me down beside her. She kissed me and pulled down my pants and began playing with my cock. I responded and pulled her knickers down and felt between her legs. She was incredibly wet as I worked my fingers up and down her fanny. She was moaning all the time until she suddenly stopped playing with me and pulled me on top of her. As soon as my cock touched her fanny, I ejaculated all over her. "I'm sorry," I said, and she replied, "Don't worry. I will soon make you hard again." But the moment had gone. I got off her and pulled my shorts up. It's a good job I did. As I glanced across the field, the farmer had just started baling the hay, and he was driving straight toward us.

We both rolled into the ditch at the side of the field and waited until he had passed. Then when he was at the other end of the field, we ran back to the car, got in, and drove off. It wasn't long before she was trying to get her hand inside my shorts again. What sort of girl was this? I'd only met her the day before. She wasn't interested in going places and seeing things but just wanted me to have sex with her. I couldn't have any respect for a girl like that. "You've gone quiet," she said after a while when I didn't respond to her groping.

I looked at my watch, and it was just gone 1:00 p.m. "Let's have some lunch," I said. "I'm starving." We stopped at a McDonald's, and I got out and went to the restroom and washed my hands and face. Zoe followed me in and went to the ladies'. I hoped she washed as well, then I came out and ordered two Big Macs and two Cokes. We sat outside on the tables. As we ate, I looked across at her. She was kind of pretty if she'd smartened herself up a bit and wore a little less colorful lipstick. But there was something about her innocent looks that made you lust after her. "What are you thinking?" she said, smiling.

"Let's go back to the tent," I suggested, "and finish what we started."

She couldn't drink her Coke down fast enough when I suggested that. So we drove off back to the campsite. Pete was still not there when we got back. And his van was gone, so I presumed he'd taken Jacky out for the day. I parked the car in front of the tent so it gave a bit more privacy I opened the sleeping bag and spread it over the floor so it made a thin mattress. Then when I came out, she went in. I waited a few minutes before I lifted the tent flap. She was laid on her back, completely naked with her legs apart. She did look tantalizing. I slid off my shorts and T-shirt and slid in on top of her. I fondled her breasts and sucked one nipple while rubbing myself up and down between her legs. She lifted her arms around my neck and pulled me closer, and I instantly smelled her unpleasant body odor. I pulled away, still trying to push myself into her. It was as if there was something stopping me going all the way. I rolled over on the side and put my fingers between her legs and worked them up and down until she moaned with pleasure. At least she was satisfied. What was wrong with me? I had a golden opportunity to have full sex twice and I had failed both times. I lay there thinking. "I will have to try again tomorrow," I said. "Maybe after a good night's sleep, I will be able to perform better."

"It will have to be after school then," she joked. "Jacky and I can't have any more time off."

I was shocked "I thought you were on holiday like us," I said.

"Oh no, we always bunk off Tuesdays and Wednesdays. It's the only two days we can get away with."

"Well, how old are you?" I said, becoming more alarmed.

"I'm fourteen but I'll be fifteen next month."

I opened my mouth in disbelief. I knew there was something wrong; it just didn't feel right. I had nearly had sex with a girl younger than my sister. I quickly told her to get dressed as I wriggled out of the tent and pulled on my shorts. I sat outside, wondering what to do.

She came out of the tent as if nothing had happened. "I will be able to see you after school, won't I?" She said. "I love you and want to see you again."

I said, "Yes, of course you can come over tomorrow. We'll still be here until the end of the week." She gave me a kiss on the lips and then walked off down the hill. She kept looking back and waving until she was out of sight. I immediately thought of Pete and then looked at my watch. It was nearly 5:00 p.m. I rang the hospital and spoke to the doctor.

"We will keep him in tonight, but I think we can discharge him about midday tomorrow," he said, "providing he doesn't put too much weight on his knee."

I thanked the doctor and said we would be there to pick him up. Pete didn't turn up until twenty minutes later with a big grin on his face. "You haven't had sex with her, Pete?" I said.

"Of course," he said, "twice, as a matter of fact."

"Do you know how old she is?" I said.

"Yes, sixteen, she told me"

"She's fourteen, Pete. I bet she's not seeing you tomorrow and has made some excuse."

"She's seeing her sister tomorrow," he replied.

"No, Pete, she has to go to school tomorrow. They have been bunking off for the last two days. They do it every week."

Pete still couldn't believe it. "I think we had better pick up Mick tomorrow and get out of here," I said, "in case she tells the police." I don't think Pete or me slept well that night, worrying about what might happen. We got up early, packed up the tent, and left before 8:00 a.m., desperate to pick up Mick and go home. There was no point staying. Mick would be limited to what he could do and would be better off at home, where his parents could look after him. We waited around the hospital until Mick came hobbling out on crutches, his whole leg heavily bandaged.

"I am sorry I messed up your holiday, chaps. I hope there no bad feelings."

We both shook his hand. "We don't care, Mick, as long as you're OK. Anyway, you might just have saved our necks," Pete said. "I'll explain on the way home. Let's get you in the van first." We managed to push the front seat right back so he could keep his leg straight then set off home. We only stopped once for something to eat and made it home by 9:00 p.m. I had to explain to Mum why we were back early, and finally climbed into bed about 11:00 p.m.

CHAPTER

28

Some Shocking News

That weekend, I went over to Uncle Bill's to see if he wanted a hand with any paint spraying, but he was only pottering about in his garage, tiding up. So I went over to Pete's farm, but he was busy milking the cows. "We can go for a drink when I have finished here," he said. I asked how Mick was doing, and Pete told me he didn't think he would be mobile for at least another week but we could go for a drink down his local. I went home and got changed and met them over at Mick's local, the Queen's Head, about 8:00 p.m. We talked about the holiday and noticed Pete had left out some of his personal experiences, so I did the same. "Sounds like it was very boring without me," Mick said.

I looked at Pete and grinned. "Yes, it was, Mick," I said.

I couldn't wait to start back to work on the Monday. George asked me how the holiday went. "I'll tell you all about it at lunchtime," I said, eager to get on with the work. We had the job of cutting and fixing thick asbestos sheets under the large entrance porch at the front of the school and around all the soffits under the fascia boards. It was raining, so we cut all the eight-foot sheets in one of the school classrooms. George had a small power saw with a tungsten-tipped blade that cut through the sheets like butter. But it made a lot of dust. George and I had to open all the windows, but we were still coughing when we sat down for lunch.

I told him all about Zoe and what we had done together. It was easy talking to George, He never criticized or made any sly comments and seemed to understand what I was saying. I never told him how old Zoe was however because I felt embarrassed. After I told him all the things we had done together he said, "I think you did the right thing Davy and walked away from that relationship. She sounds a right nymphomaniac and was probably trying to trap you into a marriage." I felt reassured after our conversation and finished off the day dusty but relieved. It took us all week to finish off the asbestos fascia, and we were glad to get the job finished.

It was a few weeks later when my mother and I were watching the six o'clock news when the newsreader said, "A girl was found murdered today near the beach at Perranporth. She has been identified as Miss Zoe Edwards. She had been spotted the day before, celebrating her fifteenth birthday. A twenty-year-old man has been arrested in connection with her death. Anybody with any information, contact West County Police."

Mum looked across at me. "Davy, what's wrong? You've gone as white as a sheet."

"It's nothing, Mum," I stammered. "I just have a bit of indigestion." But I felt sick inside. Whatever Zoe had done, she didn't deserve to be murdered. Pete was the only person to know Zoe's real name, so when we next went for a drink, I mentioned the news report. Pete hadn't seen it. "I wouldn't worry about it, Davy," he said. "They have arrested a man on suspicion of murder, so they must have some evidence that he did it." I wasn't convinced and didn't sleep well for several nights.

That dwelt on my mind for some time until I walked into the co-op at Wallingford for a snack bar, and there she was, working behind the cheese counter. "Linda," I said, "how long have you been working here?"

"About four weeks," she said. We were interrupted by the under-manager who gave a disgruntled look across at Linda. "I must get on," she whispered. "He's looking at me." I left and walked around the aisles, thinking of a way to ask her out. When I thought she was alone, I nipped back and blurted out, "Would you come out with me tonight?"

She blushed. "Yes, I would love to," she replied, then I spotted the under-manager coming over.

"I'll pick you up at eight," I said quickly as I walked out, not giving her a chance to reply.

That evening, I washed the car, hoovered the inside, and sprayed lavender perfume all around so it smelled romantic. I had a bath, put on a clean shirt and jeans, and wore a denim jacket. I looked in the mirror and thought, if this doesn't impress her, nothing will. She was waiting when I drove up outside her house. She didn't recognize my car as she'd never seen it, so I beeped the horn and she came over. She looked gorgeous. She wore a short pleated dress (but not too short), a white blouse, and a pink cardigan. Her long blond hair was tied up in a ponytail. She looked like a girl from a 1950s American movie with her little bobby socks and black slip-on shoes. I got out and opened the passenger door. Linda got in without showing any leg, and I shut the door. I drove off not knowing where to go. I could see she was very nervous, so I started the conversation. "You look very pretty, Linda," I said. "I like the way you've done your hair." That seemed to break the ice, and it wasn't long before she lightened up and started talking. I suggested we go to a little pub called the Swan, set in the woods just outside Woodcote. It was a very romantic place, which we discovered when on one of our pub crawls. The seventh-century pub had oak-beamed ceilings and a large brick inglenook fireplace in the center of the back wall. A log fire was blazing in the hearth. We sat in one of the coves at the side, watching the flames dance in the fireplace.

The pub was nearly empty with only a couple of old-timers supping at the bar. I bought her a glass of Coke and a packet of Smiths crisps, and I had a cider. It was a pleasure talking to Linda. She told me she had lived on the estate for as long as she could remember. She had two older brothers, Tony and Trevor, and both had girlfriends. Her father's and mother's names were Terry and Joan. Then I told her all about my family. We seemed to talk for hours and then Linda looked at her watch. "We better be getting back," she said. "Dad likes me to be in by eleven and gets very worried if I'm late."

We said goodbye to the landlord, and he replied, "Come again." I nodded (I bet he was glad of our custom even though we had only bought two pints of cider, two Cokes, a packet of crisps, and some salted peanuts.) We left just after 10:00 p.m.

I pulled up outside her house. "I really enjoyed this evening, Linda," I said. "Could I see you again?"

She leaned over, and I put my arm around her and pulled her closer and kissed her full on the lips. I don't know whether she was expecting this or I caught her by surprise because she didn't respond as expected. "Don't," she said. "Dad's looking."

I glanced across at her house and saw a man peering out of the front window. "I'm sorry, Linda," I said.

"Don't be," she replied. "Dad's a little old-fashioned and doesn't expect kissing on a first date."

"What about a second date, then?" I said. "Is it allowed then?"

She laughed. "Of course," she said.

"Well then, could I pick you up tomorrow about the same time?"

"Yes, I would like that," she said then got out of the car and hurried into her house. I drove home in a trance. I could tell she was very inexperienced in kissing and didn't think she had had many boyfriends. But when I was close to her, she smelled like a fresh young flower and her lips were wet and warm even though it was a fleeting touch.

Of course, I told George all about the first date when we were back at work. And he said, "She sounds a lovely young girl, Davy, and I would be concerned if she were my daughter. Show her some respect, don't push her into sex. That will all come in due course." I could always rely on George to give me some good advice. At last I had a girlfriend that I really liked, one that didn't tart herself up or tease me for a drive of my car, but one that was sweet and innocent.

We became a regular item, and as promised, the next kiss I had was mind-blowing. Her lips tasted of fresh sweet apples, and as the weeks went by, I knew I had fallen in love.

CHAPTER

My True Love

It was October. I had been dating Linda for four weeks, and we were very close. I had been around to meet her parents several times and had been invited to tea more than once. Terry, Linda's father, was a bus driver and worked for the Chilton Queens bus company. Her mother worked at a local florist's. They were far from rich but were smart, and proud of their council house, which they kept spotless. I met her two brothers later and found them both friendly. Tony was about the same age as me and Trevor about two years older—I think he and his girlfriend were about to get married. So I think her family liked me.

I still went out for a drink with Pete and Mick occasionally. Mick had at last bought himself a car instead of driving his old grocery van around. They had both had been out with different girls but none serious, and Pete always joked when I told him I was serious with Linda. "Ah, mate, you want to live by my motto. Find 'em, fuck 'em, and forget 'em."

But that Saturday evening when we all went out for a drink, Mick dropped a bombshell and said, "Pete and I have decided to go to Australia and wondered if you want to come."

I nearly choked on my cider. "Christ, mate, that's a bit sudden, isn't it?" I spluttered. "Anyway, I couldn't afford it."

"But it won't cost you anything. The Australian government has just brought out a scheme called assisted passage. They are short of skilled workers and giving British workers a free trip on a ship over to Australia."

"What's the catch?" I said. "Nobody gives anything for free."

"Well, there no catch," Mick continued. "As long as you've got a British passport and no criminal records, you're free to go, but you have to stay for a minimum of two years."

"Oh, what if you don't like it out there?" I said. "Can you come back home?"

"Of course," he replied, "you can come home anytime, but if it's under two years, you have to pay your way home."

"Come on," said Pete, "think about it: sun, sea, and all those suntanned Australian girls." I said I would think about it.

"Well, don't take too long," said Mick. "The ship sails in four weeks." I came away from the pub thinking of what to do. Mick and Pete were my best mates. We always stuck together, and I had known them nearly ten years. We'd had some great times together. But then there was Linda. I had never felt this way before. She only had to kiss me and I had an instant hard-on. I had managed to caress her breasts over her bra, but as George reminded me, "Don't push thing too fast, take your time," so I had, and I respected her for that. But it wasn't just the sex. I wanted to take care of her and to protect her. When I went to bed that night, I tried to think of the advantages of going to Australia and the disadvantages. What was I going to say to Linda? She would be devastated. I didn't think my mother would approve either. My father wouldn't give a monkey's and probably jump for joy. I fell into a deep sleep, wondering what decision to make.

Of course, I discussed the dilemma with George when I went to work, but he wasn't very helpful. "You will have to make your own mind up," he said. "On one hand, do you give up your girlfriend for two years and expect her to wait for you when you return? Or do you grab this once-in-a-lifetime opportunity and go and start a new life with your best mates? It's a tough decision, Davy, and it's one only you can make."

I dwelled on it all week until Linda asked one night when we were out sitting in the car, "There's something bothering you, Davy. Have I done something to upset you?"

I looked across at her concerned face and put my arms around her and kissed her gently on the lips. "No, darling, it's not you," I said softly.

"Then what is it? Please tell me," she pleaded. I had to tell her. When I had explained the situation and the choices I had to make, she sat for a while, thinking. "Davy, I have never loved anyone more than you, and one day would like to marry you and have your children," she said, "but I don't know if I can wait two years hoping you'll return and carry on where we left off." She looked at me with tears in her eyes.

I took her in my arms and kissed her wet eyes. "Don't worry, darling," I said softly. "I've made my mind up. I'm not going to Australia."

She pulled me in closer and gave me the most passionate kiss ever. "I love you," she said and gave me another hug.

Now all I had to do was tell Mick and Pete. I knew they would be disappointed but decided sooner would be better than later, before I could change my mind. So Friday night, I met up with them at their local pub. When I walked in, they were both drinking at the bar. They both turned, and Pete said, "You're not coming, are you?"

"How did you know?" I replied.

"You've got a face as long as this bar stool," he joked, "and I expect you're poking that Linda. You always let your cock make the decisions."

I laughed. "You are always so crude, Pete, but on this occasion, you are right. I couldn't leave her. She's so vulnerable and needs me to look after her."

"Christ, you have got it bad," said Mick, "but if you change your mind, you still have another week." I didn't change my mind and saw them off the following week at their local pub, which held a farewell party. I shook hands with them both, wished them well, and saw them drive off to Southampton docks. I wouldn't see them for another three years.

Linda and I grew closer and closer. Our smooching was getting more and more passionate, but there was little I could do in the back of a Mini. But my next car changed all that. We didn't have many arguments or fallouts, but on one occasion, we had an almighty row. Linda and a guest had been invited to the co-op Christmas party, so she invited me. I wasn't keen to start with, and a little jealousy crept in when I thought of all the young men working at the store. In a short skirt and tight top, Linda looked stunning, so I agreed to go. It started off all right. I had a few dances with Linda and a bite to eat at the buffet, with a couple of drinks at the bar. Linda had a few dances with her work colleagues, but toward the evening, people started having a bit too much of the free drink on offer, including Linda. She only ever had Coke when we went out and wasn't used to sprits. Whether somebody was spiking her Cokes I don't know. I had never suffered from jealousy before, but I was resenting her being mauled by her bosses trying to have a slow dance with her. I am sure she didn't know what she was doing and was laughing with them. The final straw came when the cheese manager who was her boss wanted a photo of Linda sitting on his lap. He was obviously drunk. As she sat on his lap, her skirt had risen up and you could see her stocking tops. The manager's hand was on her leg. As the photographer took the picture, the manager was being egged on by all his drunken mates. "Go up higher," they chanted, and he moved his hand up her leg.

That was the final straw. I stood up, marched over to the manager, grabbed Linda's arm with my left hand, and said, "This is my girlfriend. Take your filthy hand off her legs, you dirty bastard," and then I punched him right on his nose. I must have hit him hard because blood gushed from his nose as he fell backward. Before anybody came to his assistance, I pulled Linda outside and shoved her in the car and then drove off. She was so drunk she didn't know what was happening and fell asleep on the way home. I knocked on her door, and her father came out. I explained what had happened and told him somebody had been putting spirits in her Coke. "I've never seen her like this," I said.

"Don't worry, son. We'll take care of her and let her sleep it off." Linda's mum and dad helped her inside and took her upstairs to bed. Her dad came down a few minutes later and thanked me for bringing her home safely. I drove home that night wondering whether Linda would be disciplined for my behavior.

I did see Linda that next evening, and she was in a foul mood. We sat in my car outside her house. "What were you thinking?" she shouted. "I invited you to my work party, and you humiliated me in front of all my friends. I never want to see you again." She got out and slammed the door shut. She marched up the path, opened the front door, and slammed that shut as well. I was fuming, spinning the wheels as I drove off at a reckless speed all through Wallingford in the middle of the road. I didn't see the lorry parked on the wrong side of the road with no lights on. My car went under the back of the lorry, and I was thrown through the windscreen and landed in the road. I vaguely remember people running in the road before I passed out.

I woke up the next day in hospital, with my face heavily bandaged. My right arm and shoulder were in a sling, and both my knees were bandaged. I felt terrible. The doctor came around to see me and asked who my next of kin was and did I want the hospital to inform them? I know the farmer Giles Bedford had a telephone installed in our house when I was away on holiday, but couldn't remember the number and I think it was ex-directory. The only number I could get the hospital to ring was Uncle Jim's saw mills, which would be listed in the telephone book. So the hospital took care of that, then I thought of Linda. The last time I saw her, she made it clear she didn't want to see me again. That first day in hospital, I had to have another x-ray and found nothing was broken, only badly bruised. I'd dislocated my shoulder and had ten stiches in my face just above my chin where I had gone through the windscreen. "Can I go out, then?" I asked the doctor when he did his rounds.

"We will be keeping you in for the next couple of days," he said. "We would like to have your eyes checked first and make sure there is no damage from the glass. Also, your knees were severely bruised when they hit the dashboard, so we want to make sure you have full movement in them. You were very lucky, Mr. Jones, not to have done more damage to yourself." He then left to see the other patients.

Uncle Jim came to see me that evening. He had brought Mum and my sister Sheila along. They were all glad I was awake and talking. "I will ring Belchers tomorrow and tell them what's happened," Mum said. Sheila wanted to know what was the food was like, and did I get lots of ice cream?

My uncle piped up, "I suppose you won't be doing the block round this weekend, then." They all left about an hour later. I lay back in bed and thought about Linda. The third day, I was discharged, and my uncle picked me up and took me home. I had a plaster over my stitches and my arm was in a sling. All the bandages were off, but my knees still hurt a bit when I walked.

A couple of days later, I lay in bed, resting. When there was a knock on the door, Mum answered it. I could hear her talking to somebody, and a few minutes later, a policeman and a man knocked on the bedroom door and came in. "I'm Inspector Boise, and this is PC Stevens," said the inspector. I immediately thought of Zoe. Had they come to question me about her murder? "I'm from the fraud squad. Can I ask you a few questions about your Mini?"

I breathed a sigh of relief. "Yes, sir," I said.

He pulled out his notepad and began reading through it. "You were seen driving through Wallingford in the middle of the road at nine thirty on the thirtieth of September. Half your car went under the back of a parked lorry, hit the offside wheel, and you were thrown out. When the police removed your car, it broke in two, and they bought it to the police compound. I was called because the local police found none of the chassis numbers or engine numbers matched the log book." He then looked at me. "I am afraid, Mr. Jones, you have been driving around in a ringer, two different cars welded together and then sold on. We think your car originally came from Hammersmith. Could you tell us where you bought it from?"

I had to think a few minutes to take it all in. I stammered a little. "Well, sir, I didn't actually buy it. I swapped it for my Austin 30 van to Eddy. I don't know his surname, but he works at my uncle Jim's saw mills."

I noticed that PC Stevens was writing this all this down in his notebook. "Would that be Mr. James Beal?" he said.

"Yes," I replied, "but how does this affect me?"

"Well, I am afraid your insurance company may not honor your claim until we establish who the rightful owner is."

I was devastated. What was the point of having insurance if they didn't pay up? As the police prepared to leave, I asked, "How long before I hear from the insurance company?"

"It could take weeks," said Inspector Boise but let's keep our fingers crossed, we may be able to track this gang down pretty quickly.

After they left, Mum came upstairs, looking worried. "You're not in trouble, are you, Davy?" she asked.

I then had to explain to Mum what had happened. I lay in bed thinking I had not contacted Linda. I had no way of getting to work, and I had no way of getting to college. I dreaded getting my bike out, after having so much independence with my car and I felt completely depressed. That Saturday I could walk a lot better. My shoulder didn't ache so much, but I still had my stitches in. It was over a week since I last saw Linda. I needed to know if it was all over between us. I was thinking of cycling over to see her. But it was about ten miles, and I didn't think my knees would cope. Then my uncle Bill came up with a solution. "I could lend you my car in the week, because my mate picks me up and drops me off at my place. But I will need it back at the weekends."

"Thanks, Uncle," I said, "you saved my life."

I caught a bus over to Bill's Sunday evening and picked up his car, ready for work Monday morning. I told George and the others what had happened. I was a little stiff but managed to do a day's work. I decided to skip college that evening and make up some excuse. I got home, had a quick wash, and was out again about six. "Don't you want anything to eat, Davy?" Mum said as I raced outside.

"I'll have some when I get back," I shouted as I got in the car and drove off. I sat outside Linda's house about six thirty, wondering whether I should go and knock on the door. I got out and was about halfway down the path when the front door burst open and Linda came running up to me, crying her eyes out. She gave me a huge hug, and I winced with pain.

"Oh, Davy, I thought you had left me for good," she said between sobs. "I didn't mean to say those awful things. Will you forgive me?"

"Of course I do," I said. "Let's go inside, and I can explain where I have been all this time." We sat down in the lounge. Her mum and dad must have been in the kitchen because I could hear them making a cup of tea. I began explaining all the things that had happened since the row. She snuggled up to me all the time and didn't interrupt until I had finished.

She felt the scar on my face. "Is it sore, Davy?" she whispered.

I replied, "Not anymore."

She leaned closer and gave me a passionate kiss on the lips. "I don't think I could bear to be apart from you again," she whispered. "I love you."

I looked into her damp eyes and knew she meant every word. "I love you too, Linda," I said and kissed her again.

She then said, "Have you got a different car?" I explained that I was only borrowing it until the insurance was sorted out. "Can we go for a ride?" I was hoping she would ask that. I said we could. Then she dashed upstairs and, five minutes later, came down. "I've put on my new suspender belt," she whispered then winked at me. I couldn't get out the door fast enough.

"Don't be late," I heard her father call after her.

"I won't, Dad," she replied as she sat in the car. She looked around the car as we drove off. "There's a lot more room in this car," she said with a smile.

I drove up to our favorite spot in the woods and parked the car so I had clear sight of anybody approaching the car. "I don't suppose I could see your new suspender belt," I joked. She leaned across and kissed me. Then she put my hand on her leg. I slid my hand up her dress and felt the soft smooth skin between the stocking top and her knickers. She opened her legs so I could feel her vagina. She pushed her lips against mine. My penis was so hard I thought it might poke out of my trousers. I then slipped my fingers inside the leg of her knickers and felt the warm sticky slit right up to her clitoris. She moaned as I rubbed it up and down faster and faster until she let out a groan and climaxed. I slowly pulled my hand out.

"That was fantastic," she moaned and kissed me again. I was a bit frustrated and wanted to go further. I fumbled with my zip and took out my hard penis and placed her hand on it. She didn't seem to know what to do, so I slipped my hand over hers and moved it up and down. She soon got the hang of it and rubbed harder. Her small soft hands soon made me climax all over her hand. I don't think she had ever done anything like this before and seemed a bit embarrassed. I gave her my hankie so she could wipe her hands. "I think we should be getting back now," she said. "We could stop off at the pub for a drink before we go home."

"You know I would never force you to do things you didn't feel comfortable with," I said, trying to reassure her.

"I know, Davy," she said. "I do trust you." We stopped at the pub on the way home, and we had the usual a pint of cider and a Coke. At least she was cheap to take out and didn't expect a four-course meal and a bottle of champagne.

I saw her twice more that week before I had to return the car. She never let me go the full way. I respected her for that and was prepared to wait. When I did return the car, the first thing Uncle Bill said when he sat in the car was "Blimey, it smells of fanny in here. What have you been doing, Davy?" He laughed then said, "Let me smell your fingers." I laughed. He had such a crude way of saying things, but I liked him. He drove me home that night.

CHAPTER

In Trouble with the Police Again

I remembered one evening we all sat in the lounge, watching the television when a news flash interrupted the program. President Kennedy had been assassinated. Nobody could believe such a powerful man could be killed so easily. He was the most famous person after the queen. Everybody was talking about it for weeks after.

That same week I had a check for two hundred and forty pounds with an accompanying letter from my insurance company explaining that the previous owners had already been paid for both cars. The front was a 1960 model Mini and the back had been registered as a 1959 model; therefore, they were paying the above payment for the later car.

I was over the moon. That was twice what my car was worth. My uncle helped me pick another car, a Morris 1000 Traveler. It was a bit old-fashioned but was in good condition, so I paid the asking price of two hundred and twenty pounds. It didn't leave me much savings, but I had just enough for the insurance. So on the last day of November, I had my very own car again. Linda loved it and thought it quirky. I didn't tell her the other reason I had bought it: when the back seats were folded down and my old sleeping bag spread across the back, it made a perfect bed. But it was some time before I persuaded Linda to try it out. I had taken her out a few times twice to a disco and once ten-pin bowling. She didn't like that much and could only just pick up the bowling ball. We had gone to the cinema a few times but never saw all of the film because we were snogging in the back row must of the time. Our favorite place was the woods. We would stop off at the pub, pick up a couple packets of crisps, two Cokes, and some chocolate bars then drive up the track in the woods and park for the evening.

I had persuaded Linda to get in the back with me, just to see how comfortable it was. She was laid out and I started to fondle her small breasts. I managed to unbutton her blouse and slid my hand around her back and unhooked her bra while kissing her. I looked at her naked pert breasts. They were perfectly formed. I slid down and sucked her erect nipples. She didn't push me away and seemed to enjoy this new experience. The windows were all steamed with all the heavy breathing.

Then suddenly there was a beam of light penetrating the back windows, and I immediately thought some pervert had been watching us. Linda quickly adjusted her blouse, then somebody knocked on the car roof. "Come on out. This is the police," somebody said. I opened the back door and climbed out. "I'm PC Dicks, and we have recently had a report of a rape in these woods," he said. He took out his notepad and continued, "Could I have your name and address, young man?" I gave him the details he wanted. Then he shone the torch into the back of the car. Linda was hiding under the sleeping bag. "You better come out as well, young lady," PC Dicks said. He waited until Linda came out. Luckily, she had fastened her bra and looked respectable. "And your name and address, miss?" he asked. Linda looked embarrassed but gave her details as well.

He wrote all this down then shone the torch into Linda's face. "Are you by any chance Terry Boswell the bus driver's daughter?"

"Yes," Linda said, "that's my father."

"I know him well," said PC Dicks. "I thought you were still at school. Does your father know where you are?"

"Yes, he does," she said, rather disgusted at being asked these questions, "and I'm sixteen and a half and have a job. This is my boyfriend Davy."

"Well, I will be asking your father about you when I next see him," PC Dicks said. "You look far too young to be gallivanting about in these woods with this man. Now both of you get off home." We got back in the car started the engine and drove off.

Linda was furious. "Who the bloody hell does he think he is, talking to me like that and treating me like a little girl?"

I looked across at Linda and her smudged mascara and lipstick and chuckled. "But you do look like a young girl, Linda," I said, "a very pretty and sexy young girl who I hope to marry one day."

This cheered her up and she beamed. "You say the nicest things, Davy." She leaned across a kissed my cheek. PC Dicks did speak to Terry Linda's father, a week later and joked that he was going to have me arrested for going out with his daughter.

That Christmas, I bought Linda a nice fake-mink coat. She looked like a film star when dressed up. She bought me a suede leather coat and black roll-neck sweater. I took her home for Christmas dinner. Mum liked her, and my father, whom I thought might try and embarrass me in front of her, was the perfect gentleman. I once caught him leering at her petite figure and wondered what dirty thoughts he was thinking. But I don't think anybody else noticed. Linda got on great with my sister

Sheila as she was only about six months younger. They went up to Sheila's bedroom after dinner and stayed there most of the evening, talking girly talk and playing records. Mum had a chat with me as I was helping with the washing-up. "She's very young, Davy. Do her parents agree with you going out with her?"

"I've met both of them, Mum," I said, "and I like them. You would too if you met them. I told them I would take care of her, so stop worrying."

She looked at me seriously and said, "You will be extra careful, won't you, son?" I think this was my mum's way of telling me about the birds and the bees, but I knew what she meant. That Christmas was great, and New Year's Eve I spent with Linda's parents Terry and Joan. Her brothers Tony and Trevor were out all night partying. I had asked Linda if she wanted to go out and see the New Year in, but she said she would rather spend it with me and her family.

CHAPTER

Dr. Wilkinson

We decided to cool off a bit with our lovemaking. I had still not had full sex with Linda, but our smooching was getting very touchy-touchy, and it was only a matter of time before we would have full sexual intercourse. We both decided to see Linda's doctor and discuss whether Linda could go on the pill. We waited in the small reception room until a green light flashed over Dr. Wilkinson's door and could go in. His office was a bit old-fashioned, as was Dr. Wilkinson. He was about sixty-eight and should have been retired. He sat behind his desk, looking over the top of his reading glasses as if studying us. "And what can I do for you, young lady?" he said pompously.

Linda stammered a bit, and I could see she was embarrassed to ask the doctor. So I spoke for her. "Doctor, Linda and I have been dating for some time now and love each other. We have started to have a sexual relationship and wondered if she could go on the pill."

He looked at me with horror across his face. "I don't believe I am hearing this," he said. "Linda's only just left school, and you want to have sex with her. Do your parents know what you plan to do, Linda?"

Linda plucked up enough courage to reply, "Well, no, doctor, we haven't told them yet. We thought we would ask you first."

"Well, I am disgusted with you both," he said, "especially you, Linda. I shall be talking to your parents and will certainly not recommend you go on the pill at such a young age. That will be all." The doctor got up and opened the door then showed us out.

I couldn't believe what I had just heard. We had asked for his help in our relationship, and he had condemned it. "What a pompous old-fashioned twit," I said to Linda when we were back in the car.

"I know," said Linda. "He's been the family doctor for as long as I can remember." What were we supposed to do? We came away disappointed.

Would I ever lose my virginity? We did find another place in the woods away from the track so we were less likely to be disturbed. The only thing was it rained one night and we hadn't noticed until I tried to get back on the track and the wheels just spun on the wet leaves. It was dark, and I said to Linda, "Would you get out and push? And I will keep trying to get some grip on the tires." She put her new pink anorak on and got out in the rain and began pushing behind the driver's side wheel. The car started to move. "That's it, Linda," I yelled out of the window. "Keep pushing." I floored the accelerator until I was back on the track, waiting for Linda to catch up. As I caught sight of her in the headlights, she looked like a drowned rat that had rolled in the mud. Her nice pink anorak was filthy from the mud spraying up from the spinning tires. She took her anorak off and got in the car.

"I'll have to wash this before Mum sees it," she said. She looked over to me. "What are you grinning at?" She asked.

"Have you seen your face?" I said.

She looked in the driver's mirror. Her face was covered in mud. "Have you got anything to wipe my face?" she cried.

I joked, "I wouldn't worry, Linda. People pay good money for a mud pack." She didn't laugh, so I got out and found an old towel in the back and gently wiped the mud from her face, then I pulled her close and kissed her lips. "I don't care what you look like," I whispered. "You're still beautiful to me." We drove home and stopped at our favorite pub and sneaked into the outside toilets, and Linda cleaned herself up as best she could, then we drove home.

Everything continued as normal: the work at the school with George, the trips up to the college, and me working on the block round on Saturdays, although that would be ending soon as July was approaching and the weather was getting warmer. I still went over to see my uncle Bill occasionally and had to endure his crude comments about Linda, but I knew he was joking. Just before my birthday, I asked Linda if she would like to go on a camping trip to Devon for a week. I knew some of the best places to go after having the last trip there shortened. Her mother and father agreed to let her go. Terry, her father, pulled me to one side just before we left. "I trust you, Davy. Look after my little girl. She's all I have."

I was touched by this and shook his hand. "I will, Mr. Boswell." We drove off Saturday morning and began the long trek down to Devon.

I had borrowed my uncle Bill's tent. It was much larger and could sleep four adults. We drove all day and reached the outskirts of Dartmoor by dusk. We found a lovely campsite overlooking the river Dart and pitched our tent. We decided not to cook and buy our meals out. We made our tent comfortable, then went to the nearest pub and had an evening meal. By the time we'd had a few drinks, it was 11:00 p.m. before we got back to the tent. I switched on the small battery ceiling light that illuminated the tent in a soft glow. I was shattered after driving all that way, but became quickly aroused as Linda started to undress. I had never seen Linda completely nude, and when she had stripped to just her skimpy white knickers, my penis was bone hard. I slipped off my pants and she asked, "Did you bring any johnnies?" I slid a packet of Durex out of my trouser pocket and attempted to put one on over my erect penis, she slipped off her knickers and lay there completely nude. She had the most perfect body imaginable. Her small pert breasts stood out and she had just a small patch of fair hair covering her vagina. She looked up at me with innocent eyes. "Be gentle with me, Davy," she whispered as I lowered myself onto her. I slipped my fingers into her vagina as she opened her legs. I kissed her lips, working my fingers up and down until she was wet with excitement. She opened her legs wider and I guided my hard penis into her. I didn't push all the way but gently, with each thrust went deeper and deeper until my whole penis was in up to my pubic hairs. I then quickened my pace as she writhed under me, moaning. I heard her gasp and relax just as I ejected into the rubber Durex. I rolled off her, to one side. She pulled me close and kissed me hard on the lips. "That was wonderful, darling," she said. "You didn't hurt me at all."

That was it. I was no longer a virgin. I lay there thinking for a moment. Snuggled up to a gorgeous young girl, what else could be better than this? We both slept well in our own sleeping bags. The next day after a wash, we left the tent and drove to a teapot factory and pottery center then spent the rest of the day exploring the moors. That night was great as we repeated the sexual adventure from the night before. For the next few days, I took Linda to the places we had visited on our road trip the previous year, mostly around Dartmoor. But the more we had sex, the longer it took for me to climax. I think the main problem was putting on the Durex. I think the early ones felt like they were made out of car inner tubes and I was gradually losing the feeling. Sometimes my penis started to go limp before I had fully pulled the Durex on. Linda didn't seem to mind as I was still satisfying her, but it was worrying me. I thought it might have something to do with me being circumcised and I was losing the feeling with the rubber Durex on. The rest of the holiday went by quickly, but it was taking me longer and longer to climax and I think sometimes Linda became a bit sore, but she never complained. The last day it rained, so we packed up the tent and drove home. It had been a great holiday, apart from that one problem.

I celebrated my nineteenth birthday down at the pub. I didn't want Mum to make a fuss. After all, I was a man now in more ways than one. I never told George my worries. But I did tell him that Linda and I were having sex. "I told you if you took your time, the rewards would follow," he said. "But be careful, Davy. You don't want to get her pregnant. You're both very young, and you don't want that burden on your mind." I always took George's advice. After all, he had been around a lot longer than me. Linda had bought me a watch and Mum bought me a sweater for my birthday, and I had a lot of cards wishing me well on my nineteenth.

When I came home from work in the evenings, Cookie would always fly down from the chimney top and land on my shoulder. He amazed me how brazen he was. If the kitchen door was open, he would calmly walk across the kitchen floor, keeping a close eye on Snowy the cat, and Ben the dog, but the cat never seemed to bother Cookie even though he was always catching birds and mice and eating them. Then he would fly up on Mum's shoulder and peck her earlobe, a favorite trick of his. And even when all the wild pigeons came in the fields after the corn had been cut, to feast on the dropped corn, he would never join them. But one evening, Cookie didn't fly down to me. I asked Mum if she'd seen him.

"No," she said, "I haven't seen him all day, but I expect he's found a mate." I had my doubts. In the four years we had him, he'd never left the house. My immediate thought was of my father. He had never liked Cookie. "Pigeons are all vermin" was his motto and should be eaten or shot, so did he have anything to do with his disappearance? He had mellowed over the years, and I doubted he would have killed Cookie after all this time. After a week, Cookie was still missing. Mum was convinced he had found a mate and flown off, but I wasn't convinced. It was not until it started getting colder and Mum called in the chimney sweep to clean the chimney before we lit the fire and the grisly mystery was solved when the chimney sweep removed a very skinny black pigeon. Cookie had fallen down the chimney, couldn't get out, and starved to death. I could see a tear in Mum's eye as she took Cookie outside and we buried him in the garden.

I took Ben for a walk that evening, thinking about what George had said about getting Linda pregnant. I Knew Mum would go mad, my father would probably laugh and poke fun at me, and Linda's parents would probably kill me—if not, her brothers would. Ben looked up at me as we walked down the lane. He could sense something was troubling me. He was a good dog, but not quite so good as my first dog Bruce. I didn't see Linda that night.

CHAPTER

Pregnancy

The following Friday evening after college, I gulped down my dinner as I wanted to get to Linda's early. "You eat your dinner far too fast," my mother shouted as I ran outside and got in the car. I wanted to take Linda to the cinema for a surprise treat. She wasn't quite ready when I arrived, but we raced over to Wallingford and just got in just before the main film started. I knew she liked lovey-dovey films, so I thought *Gone with the Wind*, starring Clark Gable and Vivien Leigh would put her in a very romantic mood. And my wicked thoughts worked. As we left the cinema, she said, "Shall we drive over to our favorite place, Davy?" giving me a wink. So we ended up having a quickie in the back of the car, only it wasn't a quickie. It took me ages to climax, and I was sure Linda was a bit sore, because all of a sudden, I felt a new feeling, a warm sticky pulsating pressure and I exploded into her. She looked at me, surprised. "That felt different, Davy. I didn't think you were going to climax. It took so long."

I didn't say anything but guessed what had happened. I pulled my limp penis out and looked in dismay. I had poked a hole right through the end of the Johnny.

Linda saw it and burst out crying. "I'm pregnant," she said and became hysterical.

I gave her a hug and tried to reassure her. "It doesn't mean you're pregnant," I said. "The chances are very slim on becoming pregnant the first time, and sometimes it takes ages."

That seemed to calm her. "Do you really think that, Davy?" She said, still sobbing.

"Yes, I do," I replied. "Now let's go home before your dad sends out a search party." Linda cleaned her smudged mascara off her face, but you could see in her eyes that she had been crying. I just hoped her mother and father didn't notice. A week later, she had her period, much to our relief. But things didn't turn out quite as planned. Our next sex session, I managed to persuade Linda to have sex without a Johnny fitted after that last feeling. "I will be very careful," I said. "I will take it very gently and pull it out before I climax." She wasn't sure but let me make love to her. Everything worked out fine. The difference was like chalk and cheese. The sensation I felt was mind-blowing, and I think Linda enjoyed it more too. I pulled out just in time and ejected all over her belly. It was a bit of a mess, but she was relieved I had kept my promise. Over the next few weeks, we had sex quite a few times and we both felt the feelings were much more intensely, but I was leaving it later and later before pulling my penis out. Then one evening, the sensation was so great I climaxed inside her. She felt it too. "Do you think it will be all right, Davy?" Linda asked worriedly.

"Of course," I said confidently. "It was only the once." But a few weeks later, she missed her period. "Don't panic," I reassured her. "You may be just late."

"But I'm always on time," she said. "I have never missed a period and I have started being sick in the mornings, and I'm sure Mum's noticed."

Linda's mum had noticed. "You're pregnant, aren't you, Linda?" She said one morning after Linda had been sick again.

"I don't know, Mum," Linda replied tearfully. Her mother took her to see her doctor that morning, and he confirmed Linda was pregnant.

Of course, the next time I went over to pick up Linda, her father called me into the lounge, where we were alone. "I am disappointed in you, Davy. I guessed you were both having sex, but couldn't you have taken some precautions?"

"I did, sir, but one split on me" was the only thing I could think of saying and still save face.

"Well, she's now pregnant," said Terry, "and you have only one choice. Joan and I are completely against abortion, so you will have to marry her as soon as possible. Have you discussed this with your parents yet?"

"No, sir, I haven't told them yet," I stammered.

"Well, I suggest you go home and discuss this with your parents," said Terry, "and I hope you do the honorable thing and marry my daughter." I had never seen Linda's father so angry. I left without even seeing Linda.

I was not looking forward to informing Mum that Linda was pregnant. But when I got home, my father had gone to the pub. Sheila had gone over to her friends, and Tommy and Mary were outside, playing. I found Mum in the kitchen alone. I sat down at the kitchen table, and Mum looked across at me. "What are you doing home so early?" She asked. "Have Linda and you had an argument?"

"Sort of, Mum," I said.

"Well, spit it out, then," she replied rather harshly.

There was no easy way of telling her, so I came straight to the point. "Linda's pregnant, Mum, and her parents want me to marry her."

Mum was quiet for a few seconds before she asked, "Do you love her, Davy?"

"Mum, I have never felt this way about a girl before," I replied. "I do love her, and I want to do the right thing"

"Then you will have to marry her. Do you know how far she's gone?"

"Her doctor reckons about six weeks," I replied.

"Well, we need to meet Linda's parents and discuss the arrangements." That went better than I thought. Linda's parents Terry and Joan came over to our place, with Linda in their car the next evening. My father didn't want to discuss my problems. His only comment was "He's made his own bed. Now he's got to lie in it," and he went off to the pub. Mum got on very well with Terry and Joan as they were of similar age and had the same moral values. Neither of our families were wealthy, so we all agreed that Linda and I get married at the Henley registry office as soon as possible. Terry would ring the registrar the next day and arrange a date. It was all very hasty. The earliest date was the last week in September, about two weeks away, on Saturday at 11:00 a.m.

On Monday, I had told George everything. I trusted him to keep it a secret. He asked where I was going to live after we were married. I'd never given that a thought as I was so engrossed on the wedding. George suggested I speak to Belchers' manager and ask if we could rent a flat as they owned quite a few properties in the area. So that evening, I arranged a meeting on Tuesday evening after work. The manager seemed pleasant when he showed me into the office. All the other staff had gone home. "Thank you for seeing me so promptly, sir," I said.

"That's all right. Jones, isn't it?" he said. "What can I do to help?"

I explained the situation I had got myself into and was desperate for somewhere to live. "Can't one of your parents take you in?" he asked.

I exaggerated a bit and said both parents were living in a three-bedroom council house and all rooms were occupied with their families, which wasn't far from the truth.

The manager took down a folder from a shelf and glanced through it. After a few minutes, he said, "You are lucky, Jones, we have a one-bedroom ground-floor flat in Wallingford that has just come on the market. It's twenty pounds a month, but because you work for Belchers, we give our employees a 50 percent discount. Do you think you can afford it?"

I did the sums in my head, and it only left me just over fourteen pounds a month. With my Saturday work down at the sawmills, I could just about afford it. "Yes, sir," I said, "I would be able to afford it."

"You do realize that if you leave the firm," the manager said, "You will have to vacate the property immediately." I agreed with the terms and signed on the dotted line. "You can pick up the keys next week," the manager said, "and the monthly payment will start on the first of October." I shook hands with the manager and left, very excited.

I couldn't wait to tell Linda and her family my news. Of course, the whole site knew I had put a girl in the pudding club by the end of the week. We celebrated Linda's birthday window-shopping, looking at all the furniture for the flat we couldn't really afford. I knew money was going to be tight, especially when Linda had to finish work and we would have to live on just my wage. I had a little money saved up, but worried I had taken on more than I could manage.

The day we were to marry finally arrived. Things started to go wrong right from the start. My car wouldn't start, and I flattened the battery trying to start it. We did manage to bump-start the car, but I was already an hour behind schedule. Linda was going in her father's car with her mother. I was taking my mother, two sisters, and brother in mine. Dad didn't want to go and made an excuse that he had to meet somebody. I was relieved as it would have meant one of my parents would have to be picked up by Linda's parents.

When we arrived at the registry office, Linda and her party were already there waiting. Linda looked beautiful in her blue-and-white top dress. Her hair had been backcombed and done up in a bun. We then realized nobody had brought a camera to capture our special moment. We had to hurry on with the ceremony as we were ten minutes behind schedule. It was then halfway through, when I discovered I had forgotten to bring the wedding ring. Linda's mum quickly took off her engagement ring and lent me that to put on Linda's finger to complete the service. The whole ceremony was a shambles, but at least we were married.

We were then supposed to go over to our place for an afternoon's tea. But my car wouldn't start again. So the whole family had to push the car as I sat in and let the clutch out and it finally started. Mum had put on a nice spread, but the cat had got up on the table and under the covering over the food and started to eat the salmon sandwiches, so they had to be thrown out. My father had still not returned, which we were all glad of. But apart from that, the rest of the day went quite well.

Linda and her parents left about 5:00 p.m. My mum did take a photo of us the next day dressed in our wedding clothes, and that is the only photo of our wedding we ever had. I had asked Belchers if I could have a week off to furnish the house. The manager was a bit reluctant but agreed. The first thing Monday morning, we drove over to Pettit's, the furniture store in the high street, and bought a brand-new bed on the condition that they could deliver it the same day, which they agreed to. This was the only thing we bought new; everything else was secondhand from used-furniture stores or bric-a-brac shops. That Monday evening, Pettit's kept their promise and delivered the double bed and assembled it for us. The van driver said to me, "Good luck tonight," on the way out and gave me a wink. I knew what he meant, but I don't think Linda did. That night was the best sex ever, and we well and truly christened the bed.

The flat was not far from the town center, so it was easy for Linda to walk to work the following week. We had got most of the furniture. It was a very small flat, so with a three-piece suite, a small dining table and a sideboard in the lounge, a wardrobe and double bed in the bedroom, that was it. The kitchen already had an electric cooker fitted with a small fridge under the worktop. We never had a washing machine but took our clothes to the launderette in town. There was a glazed door from the lounge into the small garden, which was overgrown with weeds. I had just two pounds left out of my savings to last us till the end of the week, before we both got paid. The petrol gauge on the car was reading nearly empty, so I had to preserve the fuel for work only. The good thing was evening classes at college had finished and I had passed the English and science exam but only just. (I still didn't know what those two exams had to do with carpentry.) I had to attend all day at Reading College on Fridays, but I was in my final year.

By Christmas, Linda hadn't put on much weight although she was five months gone. You would never have known she was pregnant. The baby was due in early April, but the doctor couldn't be sure as Linda was so small. We had a great Christmas, having spent half the time around her place and half around mine. I got on well with her two brothers. Now they were my brothers-in-law and I was looking after their little sister, they had accepted me as part of the family. Most of our presents were for the house, which we appreciated. My mother gave Linda a large illustrated cookery book. (I told her she was a lousy cook.) We gave each other silly little things as neither of us could afford much. The flat looked great to us, but when I took my mother over to see it after Christmas, she commented, "It's very nice and cozy, but where are you going to put the cot for the baby?"

I must admit I hadn't thought much about the baby, so I said, "We can sort that out, Mum, when the time comes." I think she was impressed with what we had achieved.

CHAPTER

Fatherhood

By February, Linda was only showing a small bump in her stomach, and her doctor was becoming a bit concerned. "It's either a very small baby," he said "or she's not carrying very much water. I think we had better have you in hospital for a few days so we can monitor you and do a few tests, just to be on the safe side."

I drove Linda over to the Wallingford Cottage Hospital on Saturday morning. Her bed was one of six beds in a ward. The doctor asked her to get undressed and put the white hospital dressing gown on as he drew the curtain around for some privacy. I was allowed to stay for a few minutes. She looked like a child lying in bed. "I'm scared," Linda said. "What if there's something wrong with the baby?"

I could see she was on the point of crying. So I lay on the bed beside her and gave her a passionate kiss. "Don't worry, darling. It's just a precaution," I said. "I bet you'll be out in a day or two, and I'll be up to see you tomorrow." The nurse came back and asked me to leave. I blew Linda a kiss as I left the ward.

It was very lonely in our double bed that night, and I missed the warmth of Linda's body. I went to pick up Linda the following evening. She was glad to get out of the hospital. She told me on the way home that after all the tests and poking about, as she put it, they found nothing seriously wrong, apart from the baby having a slight heart murmur, nothing to worry about, the doctor had said. So that evening, we made love. I was very gentle with her, and we both enjoyed the experience. Linda had to go to the hospital every week just for a quick checkup and to monitor the Babies heart. She usually walked there and back as it was a good exercise. You could see the bump in her stomach by the end of March, but she was still very small. And on the second week in April when the baby was due, there was still no sign of it. So she was admitted to hospital Linda's waters broke that afternoon and the nurse gave Linda castor oil to help with the birth. The hospital wouldn't let me see Linda or the birth, and I had to stay in the waiting room until they called me. It was in late evening. Linda had been in labor for three hours and finally had a little girl. The doctor told me they would be keeping the baby in hospital for a couple of weeks as it was so small. She only weighed three pounds ten ounces and had to be placed in an incubator to help her breathe, but he assured me it was common practice for a baby this small. When I was finally allowed to see Linda, she looked in a terrible state. The nurse told me they had to give her gas and air as she got very tired toward the end of the labor, but she should recover very quickly, she assured me. When the nurse left and drew the curtain around, I walked across to the bed, picked up her hand, and kissed it. She turned, her eyes full of tears. "They took my baby away," she sobbed. "I think there's something wrong with her." I tried to reassure her and told her what the doctor had said, but she didn't seem convinced.

I stayed all evening, trying to cheer her up and asking what name we should call her, but she was still upset when I left. I went home to Mum's and phoned all our relations and told them the good news. Linda's mum was over the moon that her daughter had had a little girl and couldn't wait to see her. "I wouldn't go and see her yet. She's a bit upset that we can't bring the baby home with us, because it's so small, but the doctor said I should be able to bring Linda home tomorrow evening if she's recovered enough, so you can see her then." I then put the phone down.

Mum seemed pleased that Linda and the baby were OK. "Davy," she said, "now you have a family, you will find things much more difficult. You will only have your wage to rely on, and Linda will need you more than ever to help with the baby, so if there is any way I can help, please ask me."

"I will, Mum," I replied, "and thanks." Little did I know that I would need a lot of Mum's help in the next few months?

It was six weeks before the doctor finally let us take the baby home. After a lot of discussion, we had decided to call our little girl Catherine "Katie" Jones and had her christened at the local church a week later with just the immediate family attending. The baby was still very small at just under five pounds and needed feeding every three hours. Linda had tried breastfeeding but her breasts carried very little milk and she didn't know how much the baby had drunk, as she was always crying. So the midwife suggested she should try bottle feeding, then she could monitor the Baby's intake. This seemed to work, but we were still being woken up through the night. We had managed to squeeze a small cot into our bedroom, but it was only about two feet away from me trying to sleep. We both took our share in feeding the baby, but it was taking its toll. I felt like a zombie when I started back to work a week later. Linda pleaded with me not to go and leave her on her own. She was crying as I left. I felt really guilty as I drove off, but I couldn't afford to stay home any longer. I confessed all my troubles with George at lunchtime and told him about Linda panicking when I left her alone. George told me Linda was probably suffering from post-natal depression. He said, "You've got to remember, Davy, Linda's still only a child herself, and to be left alone with a baby is a great responsibility and she's frightened of hurting the baby." I understood what George was saying. He seemed to know what Linda and I were going through.

On the way home, I stopped off at my mother's and explained how Linda had become upset when I left for work that morning. "Would you like me to come over on the bus tomorrow and stay with her for the day?" my mother said. I thought that was a good idea and agreed. I stopped off at the local store and bought Linda a bunch of flowers and a box of chocolates. I couldn't really afford them but thought the gesture was worth it. Linda threw her arms around me as soon as I entered the front door. "I missed you so much, darling," she said and kissed me passionately when she saw the flowers and chocolates. I checked on little Cathy, and she seemed contented. She did look beautiful laid in her cot, a miniature Linda with wispy blonde hair. That evening, Linda seemed confident around the baby, feeding it and then putting the baby over her shoulder and winding it. I had a go at changing the nappy, which I thought I made a pretty god job of.

Linda had tried to make a cauliflower cheese, mashed potato, and sausages for dinner out of Mum's cookbook, but it was a disaster. The cauliflower wasn't cooked, the mashed potato was lumpy, and the sausages were burnt, but I still ate it. "That was horrible, wasn't it?" Linda said when I'd finished.

I replied jokingly, "Well, I don't think Fanny Cradock would have approved, but keep practicing and you'll get better."

At least she laughed. When we went to bed that night, we made love for the first time after the birth. Afterward, I hoped Linda had remembered to take the pill the doctor had prescribed. I didn't want another child, well, not yet anyway.

Again I had the upset and tears when I left for work the next morning still half asleep, I had told Linda that my mum would be coming over on the ten o'clock bus and she was going to stay until I got home. But she was still upset that I was leaving her as I drove off. I had to go to college that Friday, so I knew I would be back just after 5:00 p.m. When I did get back home, I could see things had changed. Linda seemed much more confident. The flat was tidy, and Linda had cooked a big shepherd's pie, with Mum's guidance. I thanked Mum and took her back in the car before my father got home, or he would be complaining the dinner wasn't ready. That evening, I sat down to a perfect meal. Linda beamed with delight when I praised her up. "It was quite easy when your mum showed me," she said, "and I am more organized now."

After dinner, Linda then showed me what Mum had brought with her, my sister Mary's old pram. I don't know how she got it on the bus, but in those days, the bus conductors were more helpful. "We could take Cathy out for a walk tomorrow," Linda said excitedly. I had planned on working at the saw mills that Saturday for some extra money, but after looking into Linda's pleading eyes, I didn't have the heart to say no.

The next day was warm and sunny, and we went for a walk along the river. I felt very proud pushing my daughter along with my wife by my side, a perfect family. It was amazing how many people wanted to see the baby and congratulate Linda, who was beaming with pride. Cathy had put on a bit of weight, and the midwife was pleased with her progress. "I shan't have to come anymore," she told Linda. "You seem to be coping quite well now."

And she was right. Linda was coping. We still had sleepless nights having to feed every three hours, and one night when it was my turn to do the feed, Cathy started to cry. I was so tired I ignored her. The trouble is, lack of sleep makes you skip important things, and I just couldn't be bothered. Anyway, she stopped crying after a while, and I drifted off into a deep sleep. The next morning, I was awake first and Linda was still fast asleep, so I got up and checked on Cathy. No wonder she had been crying—the poor mite had been sick in the night and she was covered in it. It had congealed around her face and neck, and it smelled revolting. The smell made me heave. I could change the smelliest of nappies and even wash them out, but sick I couldn't deal with. I had to wake Linda, who wasn't too pleased, but she cleaned Cathy up and gave her a bath and Cathy was soon smelling like little babies should.

CHAPTER

Money Problems

Now that Linda had settled down to a routine, I tried to earn as much money as possible to try and save some for Christmas. The beginning of July, the block round had finished some time ago. Jim had given me some work on Saturdays but not every week. Uncle Bill usually had some work on Sundays, spraying cars or repairing them. But understandably, Linda wanted me home a least one day a week so we could spend more time together as a family. "I only see you in the evenings," she complained. "You're becoming a workaholic." It was true. At least Cathy was sleeping better and only woke once in the night. So I had a lot more energy, but I was seeing them both less and less.

I decided to go and see the manager at Belchers and ask for a pay rise, after I had discussed the problem with George. "It's worth trying, Davy," George said. "But it will be like getting blood from a stone." He was right. The manager was all chatty and pleased about how well I was working with George, but as soon as I mentioned a pay rise, he coughed then took down a folder and opened it.

"Ah, Jones," he said, "I see you are earning slightly more than the other apprentice." (I didn't know they had another apprentice.) "So I can only raise your money two pence an hour extra, but that's only if you promise to keep this to yourself and not tell anybody, or they will all want a pay rise." I had to agree. It was disappointing as it worked out less than a pound a week. But it was better than nothing.

George laughed his head off when I told him what the manager had said. "He uses that ploy every time," he said, "saying you're already getting paid more than the others. That's why he told you not to tell anyone. Nobody knows want the next man is earning. But you did do well to get that measly amount." That night, I thought about all the things I could finish or cut down on. I had already stopped going to the gym just before the baby was born. I hadn't been for a pint for over two months. I had tried smoking as most of the other lads did, but quickly kicked the habit as I worked out how much it was costing a week. I was worried the tax and MOT were due on the car and I didn't have the money to pay that. I thought I would get away with it as I only used the car locally. There was nothing I could do except work longer hours, but where?

My twentieth birthday was in a week's time, and I would no longer be a teenager. But I wasn't looking forward to it. All my mates had left the country and the only other mates I had were at work and they were all a lot older than me. Linda tried to make me happy and dressed up that night in her white knickers and suspender belt and bent over so I could just see the tops of her stockings pretending to do housework. It worked. I soon had a hard on and made love to her on the settee. She still had the most perfect figure even after the baby was born. But I soon dropped back to my depressing thoughts. "Don't worry, darling," she said as we curled up in bed. "Something will turn up."

It did just after my birthday, but it only made things worse. I was on my way home from work and took a corner too fast. It had been raining all day. I hit a large puddle of water and skidded off the road, over a small bank, and into a field. I got out and had a look around the car. There was no damage to the car apart from the mud splashes, but the car was well and truly stuck in the field.

I looked around to see how I could get out of this mess. I was only about two miles from Uncle Bill's place, when I saw a police car pull up and park on the side of the road, with his little blue light flashing. He came across to me and asked if I was all right. I thought he was going to help me tow the car back on the road. But he took out his notepad and wrote my cars registration down. Then he asked for my name and address (I thought about giving him a false name and address but he had my number and make of car so decided against it.) After he had written this all down, he walked slowly around the car and noticed the expired tax disc. "Is this vehicle yours, sir?" he said. When I replied it was, he continued, "I shall need you to produce your driving license, insurance, MOT, and tax to your nearest police station within the next seven days, sir." He gave me a ticket, said, "Good day, sir," and walked back to his car. It was five thirty. I should have been home by now. Linda would be worried.

The only solution was to see if I could cadge a lift off a passing car. I started to walk back to the road then noticed a farmer on a tractor in the next field. He stopped the tractor when I approached him, and I explained what had happened. He couldn't have been nicer, especially when he found out my name. "Are you related to Trevor Jones, who lives over in the Baldwin's?" he asked. When I told him that was my father, he replied, "I know your father well. We've had many a pint together over at the Lion Pub. Well, lad, let's get you out of this field and back on the road." He tied a chain around the front-bumper fixing brackets and pulled the car over onto the road. I thanked him and wished I had some money on me to give him a tip. "Don't worry, lad," he said. "You can buy me a pint down at the pub if I see you in there sometime." I drove home thankful for the farmer's kindness, and I didn't even know his name.

I got home about an hour late and explained to a worried Linda that I had skidded off the road. "You're not hurt, are you, Davy?" She asked.

"No, only my pride," I replied, "for making such a silly mistake." I didn't mention the ticket I got for the traffic offense. I thought Linda had enough worries looking after the baby, without anything else to worry about.

Seven days seemed to go quickly, and on the last day, I arrived at the police station and produced the ticket with all the documents. The desk sergeant looked through them slowly, then said, "Your MOT ran out last year. I see your insurance is still in date, but I am afraid as the MOT has run out, your insurance is invalid. So you will be contacted through the post as to the amount of fine you will receive."

"Do you know how much it will be?" I asked.

"That depends on the courts, lad, and who's sitting on the bench." He looked at me over the top of his spectacles. "Let this be a warning to you, lad. You shouldn't have a car on the road if you can't afford to maintain it." At least he hadn't mentioned about the tax expiring, so I thought I'd got away with it. It was two weeks before I received a summons through the post. I tore the letter open that morning before Linda got up. I had been fined ten pounds and three penalty points on my license for each offense, to be paid within fourteen days of the date stamped. And I got a further fine a week later from the tax office of another ten pounds for nonpayment of vehicle tax and three more penalty points. Thirty pounds and I had no means of paying this amount. I didn't want to sell the car but could see no alternative. I was so depressed that week and Linda knew something was wrong, but I didn't tell her. I had to sort this out myself.

It was Uncle Bill that came up with a solution. He had plenty of work on over the next few months and offered me fifty pounds in advance to pay off my fines and get the car back on the road, if I worked for five pounds a day over the next ten Sundays. It was a lifesaver. I knew Linda wouldn't like me working all those Sundays at Bill's and Saturdays at the saw mills, but I really didn't have a choice. At least I would still be able to drive the car.

CHAPTER

Losing My Driving License

I did get a bit of luck the following week. George and I had finished all the work we could do at the school, and we were assigned a new job at a hospital. It was only a mile from the flat, so I didn't need to use the car but could cycle or even walk to work. But it wasn't an ordinary hospital. It was a huge old Victorian building that housed insane or disturbed patients. Belchers had held the contract for the maintenance of the building for the last three years, and it was an interesting job. We had not only the maintenance but also some alterations to some rooms inside the hospital and a new modern office block being built out the back. So there was quite a big task force on site. We had our lunch in a large wooden shed on site, but you could go down to the canteen in the hospital and buy a meal with the staff. But most preferred to eat in the shed as some of the rooms smelled of pee.

We did meet a lot of characters in the passageways, walking from one job to another, and got to know some of them. A lot of the inmates were on drugs to subdue them and were allowed to wander around the hospital unattended. I had not been there long before we bumped into Rosy. She was a wrinkly old lady about sixty years old and had a rather rude party trick the other lads had told us about. Even though we hadn't spoken to her, we had seen her walking around. As George and I approached her one morning in the passageway, George said, "Hello, Rosy, give us a flash."

She looked at us both, lifted up her dress as high as she could, and flashed her gray hairy crotch at us. "What do you think of that, boys?" she said, then dropped her dress and walked off.

George and I both laughed. Apparently, she never wore any underwear at all and flashed her fanny at anyone who asked. That was just one of the tricks the other lads played on me that first week.

We had all been warned not to go near dormitory D as this was where they kept the violent patients, who were all heavily sedated but still moved around the ward. They were more like walking zombies. (This all might seem a bit barbaric, but in the sixties, this was the norm, with drugs and electric shock treatment commonplace.) Some of them were a bit frightening when you saw them, usually being accompanied by a male nurse.

On this one occasion, the site foreman had sent me over to the other side of the hospital with some plans for the bricklayer. I was told the directions through the hospital, along a passageway through the dining room along another passageway and the bricklayer would be in the end room, simple really. I set off and soon found myself in the dining room. Unfortunately, most of the inmates were sat down eating their lunch in this huge hall. I couldn't see any staff, so I walked briskly through the tables to the other end. But when I turned the door handle it was locked.

I rattled it a few times, but that didn't work. This had drawn attention to me, and some of the patients started staring at me. I panicked and ran back to the door I had come in, and that was locked too. I didn't know what to do as I was now the center of attention. I stood rooted to the spot. They all had knives and forks in their hands, and I started to imagine what damage they could inflict on me. Then a cook emerged from the kitchen, carrying a large bowl of rice. He looked at me and saw the panic in my face. "Do you want letting out?" he said casually. I nodded and he came over. "Where are you going?" he asked and I pointed to the other door at the far end of the room.

"Through there," I said, "but all the doors are locked."

He laughed. "You're not the first to be caught out. I bet the foreman sent you this way." We walked across the dining room, and he pulled a key from his belt and opened the door. "All the doors leading in and out of some rooms have these locks fitted to stop the patients wandering off during mealtime," he said. "You needn't have worried. All the knives and forks are made of plastic for their own protection. So next time, ask one of the staff to open the doors for you before you enter the room, OK?" I felt such a fool to be caught out like that and delivered the plans to the bricklayer, but avoided going back through the dining room. I was the butt of the jokes when we next sat down for lunch.

I enjoyed the work at the hospital with George and cycled in to work to save on fuel. I still had to use the car at the weekends, but I was keeping up with the work at the saw mills and Uncle Bill's. But I was knackered when I got home.

Cathy was growing up fast, and after six months, she had her front two milk teeth and she was crawling around on the floor. Linda quite often took her out in the pram and had made several friends in town. Occasionally, she had been invited back to their place for a cup of tea. Linda seemed quite happy and contented with her lifestyle but would rather have had me accompanying her.

I had just finished paying off Uncle Bill and was looking forward to Christmas and decorating the tree. I had been rushing over to Jim's saw mills as I was late for the last block round before Christmas. We usually got some good tips from our customers, and I was relying on this to buy some presents. I hadn't taken much notice of my speed. But I was stopped by a policeman just outside Wallingford, waving his arms for me to pull in. "I just clocked you doing fifty in a thirty-mile-an-hour speed zone," he said.

"I don't think I was driving that fast, officer," I replied.

He held up a gun-shaped object. "This is a speed gun," the policeman said. "It's just been released to the Thames Valley Police and is accurate within five miles an hour, and you can't argue with that." He gave me a ticket. "You will be notified by the courts within fourteen days," he said, smiling. "Perhaps, Sterling Moss, that will teach you to slow down."

Very funny, I thought as he let me continue my journey. Eddy and Tom had nearly finished loading the sacks of blocks, when I got to the yard. I helped them finish loading then jumped in the lorry, and we set off. I didn't tell them why I was late, or else they would have taken the mickey about my driving. We did well with the tips, and Eddy and Tom split the money three ways as I was doing as much as them. My share was nearly ten pounds, which combined with the four pounds my uncle was paying me to help with the block round, came to more than a week's wage from Belchers.

Linda was pleased when I got home that evening. "We've been invited over Mum's for Christmas dinner." She beamed. "And I can show off Cathy's new pink coat and matching leggings."

"Where did you get the money for them?" I asked.

"Oh, it's all right, Davy," she replied. "I just opened an account with Freemans catalog. It's really cheap. It only costs one shilling a week, and the man comes around on Fridays to pick up the money." I didn't want to spoil her dreams but remembered how my mother had got into debt over the same thing.

Christmas was good because Linda didn't have to cook many meals, being invited to her parents for Christmas dinner then Boxing Day at my mother's. Cathy had been spoilt rotten and had enough clothes and toys to last the whole year, which was good for us. We bought each other a watch to save money as I knew the court case would be in the New Year. I had about twenty pounds in the bank and was hoping the fine wouldn't be much more than that.

But I had a shock when I opened the letter on the sixth of January. Under the toting-up scheme, I had acquired twelve points including the latest speeding fine and would have to attend Didcot Crown Court on the twentieth of January at twelve noon. When I started back to work, I asked George for some advice.

"Well, Davy, twelve penalty points is an automatic ban from six to twelve months, depending on the magistrate," said George. "You need to hire a good solicitor to plead your defense or else you could end up with a hefty fine and a driving ban for twelve months."

That lunchtime I went to see the site manager and asked him if he knew a good solicitor that was cheap. He laughed. "No solicitor is cheap, lad, but I do know Jonathan Hodge. He's been our solicitor for years, and I could ask him if he would be willing to defend you in court."

A few days later, I had a letter from Mr. Hodge saying he would be able to act as my solicitor on the day. The standard cost would be fifty pounds for his services. If that was agreeable, then I should sign the document along the dotted line and return it to him within seven days. I was shocked at the price more than four times my weekly wage. But I had no choice, so I signed the document and posted it off. I met Jonathan Hodge on the morning of the trial at the magistrate's court. He was a lot younger than I had imagined. He was tall and slim with a neat little moustache under his quite large nose. We shook hands, and he proceeded to tell me what to say and to let him plead my case. "With any luck, Mr. Jones, you should be able to keep your driving license, but you might have to pay a larger fine," Jonathan said. "Trust me. I know the magistrate, and he's a fair man." (Fair? I didn't think it was fair.)

I kept my license after Jonathan pleaded that I would lose my job and, with a young family to support, find it very difficult to find other work without a car. The magistrate fined me two hundred pounds and told me the twelve points would stay on my license for three years. If in that time I committed another driving offense, then I would automatically lose my driving license for two years. Jonathan did ask for time to pay, and I was granted one year to pay the fine.

Where the hell was I going to find that sort of money? I had found just enough money to pay off Mr. Hodge the solicitor, but that had left me overdrawn in the bank. There didn't seem any point in keeping the car if I couldn't afford to run it. I would just have to get on my bike or catch a bus, like millions of other people did. It was as if somebody with a big boot was treading on me, trying to keep me down. I had never felt so miserable. I confided in George about my problem when I got to work the next morning.

After thinking it through, he said, "You have two options, either to go to Belchers and ask the manager for a loan and get them stop so much a week out of your wages." He continued, "But the problem with that is, you will be committed to Belchers until the loan is paid off, which could take years. Your apprenticeship finishes soon, so you would have a chance of leaving and find another job that pays more money." I'd never thought of leaving Belchers. Most of the employees had been on for years and had never left, including George.

"What is the other option?" I asked?

"Well," George said, "you could make an appointment with your bank manager and see what options he can offer. At least you won't be tied to Belchers." I decided on the second option and made an appointment to see Mr. Sullivan, the branch manager at Barclays. The latest appointment he could see me was

5:30 p.m. on Friday. I skipped the last class at Reading Technical College so I could be at the bank on time.

I was shown into Mr. Sullivan's office. He held out his hand, and I shook it. He was quite a short tubby man with a rounded face, and he seemed warm and friendly. "Sit down, Mr. Jones," he said. "What can I help you with?" When I explained the situation I had got myself into and asked if he could help, he smiled. "Of course we can help," he said. "I have been looking through your bank details and notice the payments into your account are not very consistent. At the moment, you are ten pounds fifty pence overdrawn, which is slightly above your agreed overdraft limit. I suggest you ask Belchers, your employers, of paying your check straight into your account, then we can monitor your outlay and open a budget account. We could offer you a loan of three hundred pounds paid over five years, which will allow you to pay off any outstanding debts. What do you think, Mr. Jones?" I thought that a great idea and signed the paperwork. "The money will be transferred into your account tomorrow, Mr. Jones," the manager said as he stood up, and we shook hands. "It was nice doing business with you, Mr. Jones. I hope everything works out for you."

I came away very happy and planned to pay the magistrate s fine off and Linda's catalog and still have nearly one hundred pounds left in the bank. At last my luck had changed, or so I thought.

CHAPTER

Self Employed

A month before my twenty-first birthday, I sat my final exams at college. I had my doubts as to whether I would pass, having missed so many lessons over the years. But I did pass just, with a minimum grade of C on my City of Guilds certificate, qualifying me as a skilled carpenter and joiner. I proudly showed George the gold-colored certificate when I got back to work on Monday.

He shook my hand and congratulated me. "Belchers no longer have a hold on you, Davy," he said. "You're free to look for better-paid jobs." I'd never thought of that seriously, and I was quite prepared to stay with Belchers. After all, their work was interesting and varied. But I noticed on my monthly bank statement, my savings were dwindling quite rapidly. I was simply spending more than I was earning. I was beginning to worry.

But on my twenty-first birthday, my in-laws took me for a drink to celebrate my coming of age, as Terry put it. We were all having a quiet chat, Linda, Joan her mother, and Tony, one of Linda's brothers. (We had left Cathy with my mother.) When somebody tapped me on the shoulder, I turned and was startled. Mick was standing there grinning like a Cheshire cat. He hadn't changed one bit. "Good day buddy," he said in an Australian accent, "how you keeping?"

I hadn't seen Mick for nearly four years since leaving for Australia with Pete. I quickly introduced him to all my family. Mick said he couldn't stay and suggested we meet at his local the following week to tell us about their adventures in Australia. I agreed and shook hands with him before he left. I told Linda's parents all about Mick and Pete, how we'd met at school and such until the barman called last orders. (I think they became a bit bored with my chattering and were glad the barman had called time, but I thanked them for the evening and they dropped us off at our flat after picking up Cathy from my mother's.)

Mick and Pete's homecoming had cheered me up a bit. I had missed them and looked forward to our get-together the following week. However, I had an unexpected problem that week. I knew it would not be very long before I would have to replace the tires on my car as the garage had pointed out to me at the last MOT, and that was over eight months ago. I looked at all four tires; the front two were just still legal, but on the back tires, the canvas was clearly visible, having worn away the tread. It was a bit dangerous to drive in this condition, and I knew if the police stopped me, then that was the end of my driving career. But I took a gamble and drove over to see my two best friends the following week. They greeted me with a hug and warm handshake.

Pete bought the first round then sat down and chatted. Pete had gone back on the farm and was helping his father. Mick, on the other hand, was doing something completely different. While over in Australia, they had both got jobs on a building site, even though Mick or Pete had no previous experience. They had persevered, and the local tradesmen on site taught them the trade. Pete had done plastering, and Mick had gone tacking (nailing up sheets of plasterboard to ceiling and walls). They had both saved up the money and decided to come home and start a business back in England. Mick had gone self-employed and had gone tacking on large building sites, getting paid by how many sheets of plasterboard he could fit. Pete hadn't fancied the building trade and had gone back on the farm with his dad.

They then asked me what married life was like and I told them the sex was good, but the responsibility was overpowering. "I never seem to have any money left at the end of the week," I said, "and it's always a struggle."

"Well, I hope you have enough money to pay for the next round," Pete said jokingly. I was a bit embarrassed when I told them I hadn't any money at all.

Mick bought the next round. "Why don't you come on the building site with me?" He suggested. "There's plenty of work for carpenters, and you could earn twice as much as you do now." I said I would think about. "Well, don't leave it too long," said Mick. "There's plenty of blokes after jobs like that." We parted on the best of terms and arranged to meet the following week. "Bring some money next week," Mick joked. "It's your round."

I thought about what Mick had said all week and discussed it with George. "Take it," George said excitedly. "You may not get another chance. You don't want to be stuck on this firm for the rest of your lives like all the other lads." So I gave a week's notice to the manager when I called into the office that evening.

When I told Mum what I had done, she was furious. "All that apprenticeship and training Belchers have given you over the past five years," she said, "and you're throwing it away on some mad-brained idea of your friend, who hasn't even got a family to support. I think you are crazy to even think of it." When she had calmed down, I tried to explain the reasons I was leaving. But Mum wouldn't listen, and we parted company not speaking to each other. I felt sick. This was the first time Mum had fallen out with me, and I was beginning to think whether I had made the right choice. A few days later there was a knock on the front door of the flat at around 6:00 p.m. We had just finished one of Linda's special dinners, a chicken curry, which wasn't cooked enough but I ate most of it. I opened the door, and an old man with a great bushy beard stood on the doorstep. I didn't recognize him at first until he said, "Hello, I'm Mr. Belcher. Could I come in, please?"

I had never met the man in person but had seen him going in and out of the office a few times. "Yes, sir," I said, "come in." Linda had cleared the table and Cathy was laid on the settee, so we all sat down at the dining table.

"What a lovely baby" were the first words Mr. Belcher said. "What's her name?"

"Cathy," Linda said.

"What a lovely name," he replied but then his altitude changed. "What I've really come about is your resignation. We have given a lot of time and expense to train you, and you repay us by leaving."

"It's the money, sir," I said. "I am going on a site that pays you by the amount of work you do."

"Self-employed, you mean," he replied. "You don't know what you're letting yourself into, my lad. You will not get any sick pay, you will not get any paid holidays, and you will have to pay your own liability insurance. Do you realize that?"

Mick had told me all the drawbacks about being self-employed, but the benefits outweighed these by far. "Yes, sir," I replied, "I have thought of that but still think I have made the right decision."

"Very well," he said, "I will expect you to vacate this property by next week."

"But, sir," I pleaded, "couldn't I pay you the full rent as some of the other private tenants do until we can find alternative accommodation?"

"Certainly not," Mr. Belcher replied rather angrily. "We need this for another employee somebody who's a bit more appreciative." He got up and went to the door and opened it. He turned just before he left. "Don't forget one week and I want you and your family out of this flat" He shut the door and left.

Linda burst into tears. "What have you done, Davy?" she sobbed.

I put my arms around her and kissed her wet eyes. "Don't worry, darling," I said. "He was just trying to frighten us so I wouldn't leave the firm."

By the following week, I had worked my weeks' notice and said my final farewell to George. I was a bit emotional. George had been there when I needed a man's advice; he was more like a second father to me and had taught me more than any college did. I gave him a hug, and he said, "Don't forget, Davy, nobody ever gives you anything for free. If you want something, then you have got to work for it." I remembered that for the rest of my life.

I had still not found anywhere to live. I figured on paying a month's rent, so I went along to Belchers office and spoke to Jenny. "I'm sorry," she said, "but Mr. Belcher gave me strict instructions not to take any money off you." I said goodbye to Jenny, knowing that would be the last time I saw her. "Good luck," she whispered as I left and then blew me a kiss. I often wondered if she felt some attraction toward me.

The following week, I started the new job at Grove, a huge housing estate. I was told to see the site foreman who had the carpentry contract on the site. He looked at me apologetically. "I am sorry, son. I have just given that job to another carpenter that came last week. But we might have something in about a month." That wasn't what I wanted to hear. I went to the site to find Mick and explain what had happened. He was tacking a ceiling upstairs in one of the houses. "I told you, you had to be

quick because the job could go," he said. "But being as you're
here, I can give you a job helping me until another carpenters
job comes along." That cheered me up. At least I had a job
for the time being. When I got home, there a letter from the
magistrate's court addressed to Mr. Jones, instructing me to
attend a hearing at Didcot Magistrate's Court on the twenty-
sixth of September, which was less than two weeks away.

That week was the hardest I had worked in years, humping
eight by four sheets of plasterboard in houses so that Mick could
tack them on the ceilings. I don't know how he had managed
it on his own, holding a full sheet of plasterboard with one
hand and nailing it to the ceiling with the other. I was glad a
carpentry job came up the following week and I could earn
some real money. But it wasn't as easy as I imagined. I was given
the job of second fixing a whole house; that included hanging
all the doors, including the locks and handles, the architraves
around the doors, the skirting, and fitting all the wardrobes in
all four bedrooms—in total, twenty-two interior doors, all for
the sum of sixty pounds.

It did look daunting, but I began hanging the doors as I had
been taught by the college and Belchers. At the end of the first
week, I had completed nearly half the house, but I didn't get paid
until the house was finished.

So I went home with nothing that week. The court hearing
was on the Monday, so I took the day off and went along. I
saw Mr. Belcher leave the magistrate's office before the hearing,
and he looked across at me and grinned. It was all a formality
really. The magistrate said since I had not been paying any rent,
I was squatting illegally and must vacate the property within
seven days; failure to do so would be seen as a criminal act, and
I would be arrested for trespass. Then I realized why Belcher
would not except any rent money, the crafty old sod.

I had to break the news to Linda when I got back home,
"What are we going to do, Davy?" Linda cried. I tried to calm
her down. Mick said we could borrow his old van and store the

furniture at his dad's old barn. "But where are we going to live in the meantime?" Linda moaned.

"First thing tomorrow," I replied, "we'll all go to the council offices in Wallingford and show them the eviction notice. They will have to rehouse us, especially with a child." Linda calmed down then, and we had a peaceful night, now that Cathy was at last sleeping through the night.

The next day, we all sat in the council offices, waiting to be interviewed by the housing officer. I disliked the woman the moment I saw her. Linda explained what situation we were in and we had nowhere to live. She looked down on us as if we were scum. "I can accommodate your wife and child in a hostel, Mr. Jones," she said arrogantly, "but as you are self-employed, you can afford to find your own accommodations."

"But we don't want to be split up," cried Linda. "We are a family."

"Your husband should have thought of that, Mrs. Jones, before he quit a perfectly good job," she said. "Now do you want to take up the offer or not?"

I was furious with the woman for being so unsympathetic and rude. "You can stick your offer right up your fat arse," I said as I grabbed Linda's arm and walked out with the baby. I didn't know who to turn to, so I went home to Mum.

"There is one solution," my mother said after hearing what predicament I was in. "You could stay here, and Linda and the baby could go back home if that's all right with her parents."

I didn't really want us to be separated, but we both could see no alternative. "I can come over every night to see you and Cathy," I said," so it won't be too bad." But after two weeks being separated, we were both fed up. This wasn't a marriage; it was more a partnership. We hardly ever made love in case somebody heard us. Linda's mother Joan questioned the way Linda was bringing up the baby and wanted it done her way, which was upsetting Linda. So I knew something had to change and fast.

I was earning a bit more money but not as much as I had hoped when Alan, another carpentyer showed me a quick way of hanging doors. "You'll never earn good money doing it that way," he said. "You're taking too long." I took his advice, and instead of hanging six doors as I would have done at Belchers, I had hung fourteen by the end of the day. I was getting quicker and quicker each day.

Then I had an idea when I saw an old caravan for sale as I was leaving the building site. The next day, I spoke to the site foreman and asked if I could set a caravan up on site. "I don't see why not," he said, "as long as you put it well away from any houses being built." I bought the caravan from an elderly man just down the road. He was glad to get rid of it, so he let me have it quite cheap. That evening, I persuaded Brian the dumper driver to pull it on site to a patch of ground that was allocated for a playing field for the estate when all the houses were finished. It needed a bit of work doing to it. But after a week, it was ready to move in. I had bought all our old furniture from Mick's barn over in his van and arranged it in the caravan.

Linda was over the moon to be at last leaving her mother's interfering ways, after putting up with her for more than ten weeks. She was a bit disappointed at how old-fashioned it looked, but once inside, she was amazed at the conversion I had done. We now had two bedrooms, a bathroom, a kitchen, and a lounge diner with a parkway coke-burning stove, which heated the whole caravan. It was nowhere as big as a house, but it was cozy. That night when we had put Cathy to bed in her very own bedroom, we snuggled up in our double bed. That night, we made love. It was so nice to take our time and not be worried by how much noise we made and it seemed to last for ages before we finally fell asleep in each other's arms.

CHAPTER

Money, Money, Money

At last I was earning serious money. I could now complete a house in six days. But I was working ten hours a day and earning sixty pounds a week, more than four times what I was earning at Belchers and the saw mills combined. I had my heart set on buying one of the new terraced houses we were building on site. I had worked it out: if I could earn at least sixty pounds a week every week for two years, then I could afford to buy the £2,500 house. I would probably need a small mortgage to top up the deficit, but we could manage. I remembered what George had said on the last day. (If you want something bad enough, then you got to earn it.)

I worked hard for six months, often from dawn to dusk. Linda often came over the site to see when I was coming home for tea. "You're doing too much," she would say. "Let's take a few days off." But all I could see was the money growing in my bank account, and this spurred me on even more.

Christmas came and went, and we did the same thing as we did before, dinner at Linda's mums then at my mum's. Cathy was growing up fast, and in April, she was two years old. She was walking well and could speak a few words. It was then I had a brainwave. Linda was right. I only ever spent a few hours on Sundays with her and Cathy. I was so tired in the evening I usually dropped off to sleep as soon as I had my dinner. So as a surprise, I booked a week's holiday for two adults to Lorete de Mar in Spain. I figured it would be too hot for Cathy and she wouldn't remember it anyway at her age. I had asked Linda's mum Joan if she would look after Cathy for a week. She was of course delighted to look after her granddaughter all by herself, without her daughter interfering. I told her it was a secret and not to tell anybody, and she promised not to say anything. After we had dropped Cathy off at Linda's mums, we made our way up to the airport in a taxi, as my old car was not very reliable.

Linda and I had never flown before, and we were both excited when we entered the airport terminal at Gatwick, carrying our suitcases. Linda knew we were flying abroad but didn't know where, until the announcement over the tannoy system informed us to proceed to gate number 6 for the Lorete de Mar flight. We both enjoyed the two-hour flight to Spain, looking out over the clouds below us. It was magical.

When we were picked up by the bus, it was sweltering, and I was glad it was only a ten-minute journey to the hotel. The hotel was a bit disappointing and not that clean, but it was cheap with full board included. After we had found our room and put our clothes away in the wardrobe, we came down to our evening meal, which was another disappointment. Fish paella with unshelled mussels—it tasted disgusting.

I wish I had listened to my mother. She was always saying, "You get what you paid for. You don't get champagne for a lemonade price."

That evening, we walked through the town and found a restaurant that served English food, and we ate traditional fish and chips. There was not a lot of nightlife but we did come across a little bar that was playing disco music, so we stayed for an hour before we headed back to the hotel for the night. The next morning, we had a French breakfast, which we both enjoyed, then walked down to the small beach. We stayed there all day, laying on the beach and soaking up the sun. I noticed Linda was getting a lot of the local boys gaping at her petite body in her orange bikini. But I didn't take much notice.

We did a coach trip out to Barcelona the next day to see the tourist attractions and met a couple of people staying at our hotel, Paula and Ken. Paula was about our age, but Ken was in his early thirties and a bit weedy. He should have done some weight training and put on a bit of weight. I couldn't see what attracted Paula to him. She was very attractive, and he was the opposite. But they were both friendly, so we stuck around with them all day. The next couple of days we spent around the hotel swimming pool, sunbathing. But Ken didn't like the midday sun, so he mostly stayed in the bar area under the canopy.

That night, Linda and I had a furious row in our apartment. She accused me of looking at Paula breasts, which I must admit were bigger and firmer than Linda's. "She hasn't had a baby!" she screamed, and became hysterical, imagining I fancied Paula. I slapped her across the face to shut her up and immediately regretted it. Was I becoming like my father slapping my mother around? I gave her a cuddle and said I was sorry. It would never happen again. She did forgive me, and we had a great night of lovemaking.

On our last day, we all decided go to the disco bar that evening, just down the road from the hotel. It was packed as I think everybody had the same idea as us. Paula and Linda were drinking vodkas all evening, and Ken drank the local beer but it upset his stomach and he went back to the hotel early. Paula and Linda sat together laughing. I looked around the dance floor and realized there were only about a dozen people still drinking at the bar and most of them were Spanish. I looked at my watch. It was gone 11:30 p.m.

"That's it, girls. Let's go back to the hotel. It's getting late," I said.

"Oh, just one more drink," Linda replied, "as it's our last night." I could see both girls had enough drink, but relented and went up to the bar for a couple more vodkas. When I came back, two of four Spanish lads were sitting next to Linda and Paula with their arms around the girls' necks, chatting them up. I think both girls were oblivious to what was happing and seemed to like the attention they were getting. I admit I was frightened more for the girls than me. I put the drinks down on the table. "Leave the girls alone," I shouted. "They're with me." And I pulled one of the lads out of the seat onto the floor. The barman came across and ordered the Spanish lads out of the bar. He didn't speak much English, but I understood "no fighting." I left the drinks and pulled Linda up. "Come on, Linda," I said, "let's get you both back to the hotel." Paula followed us out of the bar.

All four of the Spanish lads were waiting outside on the road. I knew I wouldn't stand a chance against all of them, so with the girls behind me, I eyed up the lads. One of them was the loudest and was gesturing with his arms what he wanted to do with the girls. I didn't understand anything they were saying except the word *fuck*. I remembered what Mick had told me: go for the biggest and loudest. So I punched the one giving all the lip right on the nose, and he went down like a sack of shit. Before the others had helped him to his feet, I said, "Run, girls." They didn't need telling twice and were off down the street, with me right behind them. The lads gave chase, but we were in the hotel foyer before they got to the hotel gates. The next morning, we caught the bus to the airport then a train from Gatwick back to Didcot and then a taxi home. It was an experience, but we were glad to be home. That night, we slept in the caravan alone and picked up Cathy the next day.

The money was building up nicely in the bank, and after a year, I had saved up just over six hundred pounds. Then another man and his girlfriend had the idea of putting another caravan about ten feet away from mine. The site foreman had given him permission, so I couldn't argue. His name was Michel Polanski, and he seemed quite pleasant at first. He was a first fix carpenter, fitting all the joists, stairs, and roof trusses before the next trade came in. After a week, I noticed he was very religious and never swore, so he did not fit in with the other men, whose every other word was the word *fuck*. His girlfriend was English and got on well with Linda, and they would often go for a walk together. We lived in perfect harmony until the New Year. I had been living in the caravan for just over eighteen months, and Michel and Katrina, his girlfriend, had been in their caravan for about six months.

Cathy was quite grown up and would be three in April. Then Linda broke the news one night that she was pregnant. Whether it was accidental or she planned to get pregnant I never knew. But that spurred me on to get the house and move in before the birth, which I hoped would be a boy. Michel got stranger and stranger as the months went by, often confiding in me that the Lord God would punish all who blasphemed against his name (which I thought would include half the men on site). I played along with him, but I was getting nervous with Linda and Cathy being so close. He had bought Katrina his girlfriend a black Labrador puppy to keep her company while Michel was working on the site. I think she was getting a bit broody after knowing Linda was pregnant again because she treated the pup like a baby. I had never known Michel to lose his temper or curse, but he would often come home talking to himself.

The next day, Linda asked Katrina if Michel was all right. Katrina admitted that he was acting strangely and they had not made love in over a month. "I think he's just tired," said Katrina, "but he has started talking in his sleep about God." Then on Friday morning, we heard Katrina screaming, and she came running over to our caravan.

"Quick, Davy, do something. Michel's gone mad," she screamed. I told Linda to pick up Cathy and go over to one of the occupied houses on site and phone the police. Katrina followed me over to Michel's caravan.

Suddenly, the door burst open, and Michel came out carrying the frightened pup. "See what you have done," he shouted at Katrina, spitting and foaming at the mouth. "You have turned this beast into Satan. I will not stand by and let this happen." He then grabbed the pup by its front legs and ripped its legs off. Katrina was sick, and I had to look away as he began to tear the pup into pieces. Michel then threw the dead pup to the ground and stormed off up the road. I put my arm around Katrina and went back inside my caravan. She was still sobbing when the police arrived. I told them what had happened and showed them the remains of the black pup. "Stay in your caravan," the police advised us, "Until we have caught him."

But I left soon after they had gone to find Linda and Cathy. They were staying at the house Linda had called the police from. I thanked the owners for their help, then helped Linda and Cathy back to our caravan. Katrina was still there, when one of the policemen knocked on the door. "It's all right, Mrs. Polanski, we have caught your husband, but I'm afraid he's been admitted to Broadmoor mental hospital for his own safety."

"Oh, he's not my husband, constable," said Katrina. "I only met him a year ago."

"Well, miss, here is my contact number if you require any more information," said the constable. "Sorry for all the stress you have suffered." He then left.

"I am sorry I can't go back in that caravan tonight," said Katrina. "Could I stay with you for the night and then I will make arrangements tomorrow for somewhere to stay?" I couldn't refuse, after all that she had been through. Linda made up a bed on the settee, and Katrina stayed the night. The next day, I went into Katrina's caravan and packed her clothes into her suitcase. She thanked us for all the help and left. That was the last time we saw either of them.

CHAPTER

Our Own House

At the end of the summer, I thought I had enough money saved to put a good deposit on the house and only have a small mortgage. Linda was due to have her baby in December, so we had plenty of time to sort out a mortgage. But we had a shock when we discovered the price of the house we hoped to purchase had shot up to over four thousand pounds, double what we had budgeted for. There was no time to waste. The rate house prices were shooting up outstripped what I was earning. I contacted a mortgage broker, and the most money he could raise was two thousand pounds based on the money I was earning over a twenty-five-year period. With what I had saved, I was still nearly a thousand pounds short. The only solution was to take a second mortgage out with a different company. We found one but they wanted double the interest rate, but we had little choice. So the mortgage broker arranged all the documents, and I signed all the paperwork. He shook my hand and said, "Well done, Mr. Jones, you are now the proud owner of your first house."

I had done it: 25 Albermarl Drive was our new end-terrace house. It had two bedrooms, bathroom and toilet upstairs and kitchen and large lounge / dining room downstairs with the open stairs going up from the lounge. There was a small porch over the front door, and the back door led from the kitchen to a small garden at the rear. It was costing us one hundred and thirty pounds a month with the combined mortgage, but I thought we could manage if we lived within our budget.

I got two hundred pounds for our old camper van, which wasn't a lot, but the new owner could take it away, which saved me a lot of hassle.

We had new neighbors move next door about a week after us. Bev and Ross—they were both about twenty-five. He was a milkman, but I never did find out what Bev did. They must have won some money on the football pools or something, because they could never afford a mortgage on a milkman's wage. But she was a bit of a flirt, often doing the ironing in the back garden on a sunny day with just her bra and knickers on. Linda didn't like her from the start and tried to avoid her as much as possible.

Toward the end of November, Linda had got quite a big stomach, and it was obvious she was going to have a bigger baby than before. We had arranged for Linda's mother to have Cathy if Linda had to go into hospital for any length of time, so I never lost any time at work. On the seventh of December, Linda started having pains in her stomach, and she was admitted to Wallingford Hospital as a precaution. I worked all the next day and drove over to see Linda in the evening. The doctor decided to keep her in until she'd had the baby.

When I returned home, Bev invited me into her house for some tea. I asked where Ross was, and she replied, "Oh, he's had an accident at work and been taken to hospital. He won't be home for a couple of days." She didn't seem all that bothered. She poured me a vodka and said, "I bet you could do with a drink to help you relax." I could see where this was leading as she'd had a few drinks herself. She sat across from me on the settee and was dressed in a short loose skirt and white blouse that was unbuttoned most of the way down, showing her skimpy bra. She parted her legs provocatively, and I could clearly see she wasn't wearing any knickers. "Can you see anything you fancy?" she said. Bev was quite attractive, and I was tempted. I hadn't had sex for over a month and felt quite aroused. But I imagined what Linda would think if I started an affair with the next-door neighbor. So I made an excuse and left without drinking the vodka.

Linda had a five-pound two-ounce baby girl on the twelfth of December. I didn't get to the hospital on time, so I missed the birth. Linda and the baby, whom we both agreed to call Gemma, were discharged the next day, and I brought them home. I'd had a telephone fitted by BT while Linda was in hospital, as a surprise. She could then phone her mother if she suffered the same problems as last time. But she was fine and coped very well, which allowed me to carry on working. Seven days after the birth, I started pestering Linda for sex, but she said it was too early to think about that. So I phoned the doctor and asked his advice. He was sympathetic and said, "It is up to Linda when she feels ready to carry on lovemaking." He continued, "But Linda has been taking the pill on and off for the last four years. She told me she had been suffering headaches and nausea during pregnancy. We don't recommend that women take the pill for more than four years, so I suggest she be fitted with a coil to stop any more pregnancies. It's a simple procedure, and I can fit one if she pops in, in the next few days." Linda had a coil fitted the next day to stop me pestering her. I was gentle the first time but it didn't feel quite the same, and I wondered if it was still too early and her vagina hadn't gone back to its normal size.

We celebrated Christmas with Linda cooking her first turkey with roast potatoes and all the trimmings. But she forgot to remove the plastic bag containing the neck and all the giblets from inside the turkey, and it didn't taste very nice. But she had tried, and the Christmas pudding was excellent. We had a nice Christmas tree with all the presents underneath. I had built Cathy a Wendy house under the stairs, with a real opening door and window, and she spent most of her time in there. Gemma was the complete opposite of Cathy and slept through the night, without having to be feed her every three hours. We all went over to Linda's family for a party to celebrate and see the New Year in.

The New Year didn't start that well for me. Our old Morris Traveler finally blew a head gasket; it seized up the car's engine and wasn't worth repairing. So I bought the nearest and cheapest car, just down the road from our house, a Vauxhall Viva, but it was still three hundred pounds. I used the money I had saved for the mortgage, so knew when the bank received the standing order, the bank would probably decline it. But it was a risk I had to take. I needed a car. At the end of each month, I was always overdrawn on my account. Since having the mortgage, I hadn't taken into account how much it cost running a house with the council tax, gas and electricity bills, and of course, my public liability insurance. I just never seemed to have enough money even if I worked eighty hours a week, which I did sometimes.

The months dragged by, and one evening I was having sex with Linda and it was great. We both climaxed at the same time when I gave an extra thrust at the end. I pulled out my penis, and the coil fitted inside Linda's vagina came out as well. We were both worried, so Linda went and saw the doctor the next day.

"It shouldn't have come out," the doctor said after examining Linda. "Maybe we fitted the coil too soon after your birth and your vaginal canal had not fully deflated. That's the only explanation I can think of. This has never happened before." The doctor was very apologetic and refitted a new coil. We thought that was the end of the mystery, but the next month, Linda missed her period and, just for peace of mind, went back to the same doctor. After examining her, he confirmed that she was pregnant again.

"But that's impossible," Linda moaned. "Davy only had sex with me that night."

"It is possible, Mrs. Jones," replied the doctor, "If your husband dislodged the coil before he ejaculated." Linda was devastated and left the surgery in tears. I found it hard to believe when Linda told me. We both worked out the months, and the baby should be born in December, the same month as Gemma. At least it didn't matter whether the coil fell out or not, now Linda was pregnant.

I pressed on through the year, had my twenty-fourth birthday, celebrating it with Mick and Pete at the local pub. I confessed to Mick that I was struggling with the mortgage repayments, but he wasn't a lot of help. He was still single, earning a lot of money, and still living at home with his parents. He had bought himself a nice Jaguar car and had foreign holidays. I was quite envious of him. If only I hadn't got Linda pregnant, I could have been like him. Pete, on the other hand, was still at home but he was seeing a girl. I don't think it was serious because he was always out with Mick drinking, but he had got himself a nice car and was earning a good wage. I wondered when my luck would change and I would be rich enough to take my family abroad for a holiday. At the moment, it seemed a long way off.

In October, two months before Linda's baby was due, I decided to have a vasectomy. We had talked it over with the doctor, and he advised Linda not to have any more children. Either Linda had to have a hysterectomy, where the womb is removed, or I had a vasectomy. I decided to go for the latter, as Linda had suffered enough through childbirth. The doctor had warned me if I had the operation, it would be permanent and I would not be able to have any more children. I was booked in at the Churchill Hospital at Oxford and had the operation two weeks later. Boy, did my balls hurt afterward, and it was another two weeks before I felt better.

I had a letter a few days later from Mr. Sullivan the bank manager, asking me to make an appointment to see him. I knew I was overdrawn again and dreaded having to confront him. But I made the appointment and went to see him a week later.

He invited me into his office, and I sat on a seat opposite him. He was looking through a folder, and I had time to study him for a while. He had a habit of stroking his gray beard while thinking, and he kept mumbling "hm" every so often. He suddenly looked up at me. "Mr. Jones, it has come to my attention that you are three months behind with your payments to your building society," the bank manager said. "You have also exceeded your overdraft limit by thirty pounds. Have you any means of repaying this amount off?"

"Well, no, sir," I replied, "I am working over sixty hours a week but still don't seem to earn enough."

"Yes, I can see that," replied the bank manager. "I have been looking through our files and have a solution that will help with your finance. The interest rates on both your mortgages are very high, and it's obvious that you are struggling with the repayments. We can offer to pay off your existing mortgages if you take out a single interest only mortgage with Barclays over twenty-five years. This will reduce your monthly payments by half." He hesitated then said, "There is a drawback though. If we lend you two and a half thousand pounds, you will still owe the bank this amount after the twenty-five years, or until you sell the house and can repay the bank back." I couldn't thank Mr. Sullivan enough and signed the papers for the new mortgage. At last I would be able to manage and not work so many hours. When I got back home, Mick's Jaguar was parked outside our house. I went into the kitchen, and Mick and Linda sat drinking a cup of tea. "Mick's had a wonderful idea," said Linda excitedly. "Why don't we sell up and buy an older place that needs doing up?"

"I know a place in Didcot," said Mick, "that's got three large bedrooms and a big garden. That's what I've come over to tell you."

"Please can we go over to see it?" pleaded Linda. I agreed, and we all got in Mick's Jaguar and drove over to Didcot. I was a bit jealous as I sat in the front seat. It was a beautiful car with all cream leather seats and mahogany dashboard, and I wished someday I could have a car like this. I snapped out of my dream when Mick pulled up outside the semidetached house. At first glance, it didn't look too bad. It was advertised by a local estate agent. I jotted the number down and said I would ring the agent when I got back home. When Mick took us back home, I pointed out to Linda we hadn't even got our house on the market yet and the house could be sold before we sold ours. But she was adamant, so we contacted the same estate agent and our house was put up for sale.

In December, Linda was admitted to hospital for the birth of our third child. This time, there were no complications, and on the twelfth of December, I held Linda's hand as she gave birth to a healthy baby boy. I was over the moon—a son whom I could teach how to ride a bike, could take fishing and show him how to build soapbox carts, all the things that I did when I was a kid. I loved Cathy and Gemma, but they were girls and liked doing girly things with their mum. We had decided to call him Ivan, my choice not Linda's, but as she'd named the other two, she relented. So Ivan Jones or Ivan the terrible as Linda sometimes called him when he played up.

CHAPTER

Renovating

That Christmas we had an offer on our house which we accepted. It wasn't quite the asking price, but it was double what we'd paid for it, and as the other house hadn't sold, we got that a bit cheaper too. In January, we moved into our new house. Mick let us borrow his truck to move all our furniture, which was now becoming a bit tatty.

The house had been lived in by an old couple. The old man had died and the woman had moved into a care home, so the whole place needed decorating. I put my skills to good use and divided the large front bedroom into two smaller bedrooms so each of the kids would have their own bedroom and we had the large bedroom on the end. But the big job that I hadn't foreseen was the roof. It leaked. I had a local roofer, Carl Andrews, to have a look at the condition of the roof for me. "It's not good news, Davy," he said. "Quite a few old tiles need replacing, but your biggest problem is there is no felt under the tiles, so if it rains, there is nothing to stop the rain from seeping through the damaged tiles."

"So what will it cost me to put right?" I asked.

Carl scratched his head then went over to his van and took out a notepad. After writing a few numbers down, he said, "In total, it will cost you £1,200."

"That sounds a bit expensive," I replied, but after he told me that included all the scaffolding around the house and replacement of any damaged tiles, I realized it was a realistic price, so I agreed and shook hands on the deal.

But I wondered where I was going to get that amount of money.

Two weeks later, the scaffolders came and erected the scaffolding around the house. One of the lads was quite young and good-looking. He fancied himself as a ladies' man and kept looking and chatting to Linda. I could tell she was flattered by his advances. After all, she'd had three kids, and this lad who must have been ten years younger was taking an interest in her. I did feel a bit jealous, but when I confronted her, she just laughed and told me not to be so silly. But that was the first sign that Linda had taken any interest in other men.

The following day, Carl started the roof. I was a bit worried as we were still in March and the weather didn't look good. "Don't worry, Davy. We'll strip the tiles off, then cover the roof with a large tarpaulin sheet for the night, then we'll felt and batten the next day." Carl seemed to know what he was talking about, so that night we slept under what seemed like a large tent stretched over the roof. Unfortunately, that night we had one of the worst storms of the year. I was awoken by a constant drip, drip of water splashing down on my face. I looked up and could see stars. Part of the ceiling had come down in our bedroom. I quickly got out of bed and turned on the light. There was a loud puff as the lights went out, and I realized the water had seeped into electricity board and blown all the fuses. I pulled on a pair of trousers and shoes and ran outside and climbed the ladder on the scaffolding to the roof. One side of the tarpaulin had come away in the wind and was flapping about. It was still raining, but I managed to tie the sheet down with the ropes. I was soaked, and it wasn't until the morning that I could see the full damage. Luckily, it was only our bedroom that the rain had got in. But our bed and all the Linen was covered in wet plasterboard and debris from the loft. At least it had stopped raining when Carl and his boys arrived. I had cleared up the bedroom, and Carl said he would get an electrician in to fix the fuse board and he would refit the sheet of plasterboard in our bedroom. It could have been a lot worse, and the kids slept through it all and never woke up. After that catastrophe, the work was completed within a week. I kept a close eye on the young lad when they came to take the scaffolding down, which only took a day. Carl knocked £100 off the bill for all the damage the rain had caused, which I appreciated, and I thanked him for doing a good job.

The kids were growing up fast. Cathy would be five in April and start primary school that summer. Gemma was eighteen months old, and Ivan was six months old. It had worked out that Gemma and Ivan were born on the same day, December 12, exactly a year apart. The odds on that were very rare.

I decided that year to buy a long-wheelbase transit bus. I took most of the seats out and just left the front row, so there was plenty of room for Linda and all the kids and I had the idea with all the windows in the sides, I could convert it into a camper van at a later date. It would be useful for fetching and carrying materials for renovating the house, and I could get some materials off site. The perks of the trade, as my mates called it, and everybody seemed to be doing it. I could then claim the van against my tax when my accountant filled in my tax return at the end of the year, another expense that I had overlooked since being self-employed. I had found a good private accountant that had been recommended by the other carpenters on site and was reasonably cheap.

The job at the house-building site was coming to an end. There had been over two thousand houses built since I started there. And it was time to move on. My boss James Gardener, who employed most of the carpenters on site, had won a contract in Whitchurch, which was about thirty-five miles away and was quite a journey for me in the old van but he promised us more money, so I accepted the job.

I was the best second fixer my boss James had, so he favored me to do all the interior woodwork, and I was earning good money. The only downside was the traveling and having to pick up the site foreman Jimmy Edwards. He was a character, a very large Scotsman with a red bushy beard and a very red face to match. With the amount of whiskey or cheap wine he could drink, I don't know how he got the job. From when I picked him up at Newbury on the way to work, to when I took him home he was drunk. I don't think he was married, he had been caught drink driving so he couldn't drive himself. But he was a nice chap and I got on with him well, especially when he let me take home some materials in the van.

But all good things come to an end. After only six months, he got fired, not for being drunk, although that was part of it. He tried to grope one of the women who had recently moved into one of the houses. When she told her husband he informed the police and Jimmy Edwards was arrested and escorted from the site. I never knew what happened to him, but he must have cost the company thousands of pounds with the amount of materials that was disappearing off site. The new site foreman started the next day and turned up in a smart new Jaguar. I didn't like him from the start.

He was the company chairman's son. He was a stuck-up, arrogant little bastard. He may have had management qualifications, but he didn't know how to speak to the building workers and treated us all like shit. He didn't ask you if you would do something politely; he ordered you to do it. How he didn't get a punch on the nose from the bricklayers, who were as hard as nails, I don't know because he was always criticizing their work. I kept out of his way, and he didn't bother me too much and never criticized my work. But I had other worries driving all that way in the old bumpy van. My back ached constantly when I got home in the evening, and I had to go to bed to rest it. Whether it was from the injury I suffered from the block round, when I tried to carry two bags of blocks all those years ago, I don't know, but I couldn't manage to make love to Linda that night. It was too painful. I did manage to dose myself up with painkillers and rub some deep heat on my back before I went to work, but the pain was always there.

That day, I had to fix the skirting around all the rooms in the house, a job I could easily do in a day normally. By lunchtime, however, I had done less than half and had to leave the site and go home. The drive home was agonizing. Every little bump sent a stabbing pain through my back. I tensed my back in the seat, trying to minimize the pain. Sweat was pouring off me as I parked the van in my drive. I sat there unable to move until Linda came out to see why I hadn't come in. Somehow she got me in the lounge and laid me on the floor with just a pillow under my head. Linda called the doctor, who came out within the hour.

I had never seen her before, but after seeing how much pain I was in, she rang up a private orthopedic surgeon and took me over to see him in her car. She and the surgeon half carried me into the surgery and laid me on a table. He gave me a quarter-zone injection straight into my back, and within a few minutes, the pain was nearly gone. He gave me some strong painkillers and told me to rest it for a week. I had been half carried into the surgery, but I walked out unaided, what a relief. I took his advice and rested up for the rest of the week. At least my back had improved by Sunday, and I drove to work the next day. I felt fine and finished the skirting I had started the previous week. Then the site foreman came barging into the house and started mouthing off about the amount of time I had taken off. I tried to explain I had hurt my back, but he didn't let up and said I should have got his permission to take the time off. I did point out that I was self-employed and only answerable to my boss James Gardener. He went ballistic telling to pack my tools and get off site.

I lost my temper and said, "I'll go when my boss tells me to go, not by some jumped-up arrogant creep who only got his job because he's the boss's son." Perhaps I was a bit rude, but that was the last day on that site. My boss James moved me to a site a bit closer to home, and I never came into contact with the boss's son again.

CHAPTER

The Camper Van

Cathy had now started school and looked quite grown up. Gemma was two and Ivan one. That Christmas was the best ever on our own. I had spent a fair bit of money on the house, and most of my savings were gone. But I didn't care. Linda's mum looked after the kids on New Year's Eve so Linda and I, Mick and Josie (his new girlfriend), and Pete and his sister Patsy came out for a meal. I had never seen Patsy before, but she soon started having fun after the meal and the drinking started. It was getting toward the magical hour, and we had been dancing and drinking a lot. Linda was drunk and seemed to want to dance all the smouchy slow dances with Mick, so I danced with Josie. But I got a bit jealous when Mick kissed Linda under the mistletoe and she seemed to enjoy the prolonged embrace. They both laughed it off when I butted in, saying, "I wanted the last dance before midnight." But apart from that, it was a great evening, and he was my best mate.

I started converting the transit bus into a camper van. I had to make it so I could still use it as a works van as well. Linda was against the idea from the start. "Why can't you get a decent car like Mick's?" She said one day. "Or teach me to drive and then I can get my own car instead being driven around in this old van."

"Mick's not got a family to support or a mortgage," I replied angrily.

"But he has got a house," Linda said, "he told me." I wondered why he had never mentioned that to me. But I thought Linda being able to drive was a great idea. She had never shown any interest before, but it would save me ferrying all the kids back and forth to school when the time came.

So I arranged to have a few driving lessons for Linda with the instructor from Wallingford. I knew it wouldn't be long before she would want her own car.

I started working longer hours so I could get Linda a car and put the renovation of the camper van on hold. About two weeks later, Uncle Bill phoned about a Mini his mate had for sale. It wasn't in bad condition, so I bought it. It took some time for Linda to pass her test, having failed it twice, and it wasn't until August that she passed.

She was as happy as Larry driving around on her own and going where she pleased. Meanwhile I carried on finishing the camper van at weekends, and by the end of August, it was ready for the first test run.

We drove down to the New-Forest-Hampshire for the weekend and camped at a caravan park as I had not installed any toilet facilities in the van. But the four hammocks I had rigged up were excellent and very comfortable. We did have our own gas cooker and fridge, a small sink and draining board. Linda and the kids seemed to enjoy the break, and we came back Sunday night tired but contented.

The only thing that upset me a bit was one Monday evening, I'd be playing with the kids and Linda made an excuse that she had to go over to her mate's to pick up some clothes that she had ordered on her mate's catalog. When I challenged her about this, she replied, "Well you made me cancel my Freemans catalog, and it's easier to buy clothes off her." I didn't want to start an argument, so I let the matter ride. She did dress nicely and always looked smart, and the kids did too. But I didn't know how much this was all costing until Mr. Sullivan the bank manager sent me a letter asking me to arrange an appointment with him. And when I did see him, he asked why my account was overdrawn again.

I had no idea. "You do know your wife opened up an account with Barclaycard and at the moment,"—he looked down at the account—"she has five thousand five hundred pounds on credit and is only paying off the interest monthly." The bank manager looked at me for my reaction.

I didn't know what to say. Linda was a bit coy when I asked her about clothes and things. She always said she took it out of the housekeeping money I gave her each week, but she was obviously buying it on credit. "I will put some money back into the account at the end of the week and clear the debt" I said.

"Make sure you do, Mr. Jones," the bank manager replied, "or else we'll be charging you interest on the amount overdrawn."

When I got home, I asked Linda why she had opened an account without asking me. She immediately lost her temper. "You're a skinflint with money," she moaned. "Mick never treats his girlfriend like that. He's always buying presents for her, and what do you buy me?"

"Maybe you should have married Mick, then," I said angrily.

"Maybe I should have," she replied and stormed off upstairs.

We had never argued like this before since having the children. I knew money was tight, and we never seemed to have enough even when I worked a sixty-hour week occasionally. Something had to be done, so I decided to put the house up for sale and buy something smaller to renovate. Linda had calmed down by the evening, and we were on speaking terms again. I talked through the idea I had with her, and she agreed. And the house was up for sale the following week. We had been looking around Didcot for something and found a three-bedroom end-terrace house in need of modernization. We had only had our house for eighteen months, and we had three people wanting to buy it within a week of it going on the market. We eventually agreed to a price over double what we had put into it. This renovating business was very rewarding. I was able to pay off my mortgage and Linda's Barclaycard loan and have a small mortgage on the house in Didcot, and ironically, I bought Mick's old Jag when he part exchanged it for a new one. We now had three vehicles to run, but we did have a smaller mortgage. I worked all week on site and did the renovating at the weekends. We planned to live in the property for only a year and then resell it at a profit. We did live in a pigsty for a few weeks until we had installed a new downstairs bathroom and shower. I decided to sell the camper van. We'd had quite a few weekend holidays in it, but it was expensive to keep and only did sixteen miles to the gallon. I advertised it in the local paper and had three different people offering to buy it for cash. So I took the highest offer.

Uncle Bill worked up at the Morris Factory at Oxford in the car-spraying section, and he could get me a brand-new Morris van at 20 percent discount. I put the money from the camper van toward a brand-new Morris van, which was much more practical.

We did complete the house, but it took eighteen months, and in all that time, we had one mishap on Christmas Eve. We had all sat around an open log fire, watching television. The Christmas tree was in the corner with all the presents placed underneath. The whole living room looked very pretty with the decorations up, and suddenly, the log fire began to roar as though it was being sucked up the chimney. I ran outside and looked up. The chimney pot was spitting out flames and sparks, and I realized the chimney was on fire. I ran back inside and rang the fire brigade.

I didn't think on Christmas Eve they would be very quick, but within ten minutes, they were inside my house, dousing out the fire. They made a bit of a mess, but all the living room was undamaged. I gave them a couple bottles of wine as a thank-you present, as I realized they had sacrificed their own family Christmas Eve celebrations to put out my fire. But it could have been a lot worse. We soon had the place back to normal, and the kids all remembered the big red fire engine, especially Ivan, who now wanted to be a fireman when he grew up.

That summer, we sold the little end-terrace house for £28,000. Linda had spotted a detached four-bedroom house just down the road. It had been on the market for some time. It was on a big plot of land, and I couldn't see why it hadn't sold, until the estate agent showed us around. The house only needed redecorating, but it overlooked a graveyard and people were superstitious about its past history. It was a modern house built around the early fifties for the pastor of the local church. He'd been involved in a sexual affair with a choirboy, and the boy had been found murdered in the graveyard. I remembered reading about it in the paper. Apparently, they caught the man, but the pastor was involved somehow and he had to leave the area for his own safety. Then the church had put the house up for sale, not wanting to get involved in the bad publicity. But after some negotiations, we agreed on a price, and we bought it. We had to have a bigger mortgage with Barclays, but at last we had the house we always wanted.

For the first time, I had money in the bank and decided to treat the family to a holiday in Spain. Pontian's, the holiday specialists, had advertised a family package all-inclusive holiday to Majorca, which I booked. It was cheap because it was a cancelation, but we had to go in two weeks. It was a rush but the kids loved going to the airport and seeing all the planes, and when we took off, they were thrilled as we soared up into the clouds and emerged into bright sunshine. We arrived at Palma Airport two hours later, and a bus took us to the apartment. The kids wanted to go in the swimming pool straight away. Cathy and Gemma could both swim but Ivan needed arm bands, so I took them all down to the pool while Linda unpacked. We were having a smashing time when Linda joined us and spent the rest of the day relaxing by the pool.

There were a lot of Germans staying at the camp, and they regularly occupied all the best spots around the pool by putting their towels on the sunbeds early in the mornings and then going off to get their breakfasts. I got fed up with this and, one morning, waited until they had left for breakfast and moved all their towels from the sunbeds and put them in a large heap on the grass, then I put our towels on the sunbeds. They complained to the management, but there was little they could do as none of the sunbeds were reserved. It wasn't the first time I had arguments with the Germans. They were always pushing to the front on the queue for the self-service food and taking all the best treats. This annoyed me and some of the other English holidaymakers, and there was always a tension between us.

Two days before we returned home, Cathy slipped on the side of the pool and cut her chin. I could see the cut was bad and she had bitten her tongue and was bleeding badly. Somebody fetched the camp nurse, and she managed to stop the bleeding. She told us in broken English Cathy would have to go to the hospital and have some stitches in her chin. She arranged a taxi and I took Cathy to the hospital while Linda looked after the other two kids. We came back two hours later. I had to pay 2,500 pesetas for the stitches and 500 for the taxi there and back. That took a big chunk out of our holiday money. The doctor told me I could claim the money back on my insurance company, but that wouldn't be until I arrived back home, which didn't help me with our immediate money problems. So we spent the last day around the camp and just had enough money to last until we arrived home later that evening. I sent off the receipts and claim form to my insurance company, but they would only pay out on the hospital fee as they did not cover travel to and from the hospital. I never trusted travel insurance companies after that.

CHAPTER

The Dream House

It wasn't long after the holiday that Linda started complaining about her old car. She wanted a newer model, "something I can be proud of," she said. I did point out we had the Jaguar and she could drive that. "I don't like driving that. It's too big and it's an automatic," she said. "I want something small and fast like a Mini Cooper."

I was a bit annoyed. We hadn't even finished the decorating, and she was already moaning. I just couldn't seem to keep up with her demands. I cheered up when I was playing with Ivan. He was nearly four, and I took him fishing one Sunday morning. Cathy and Gemma didn't want to come, preferring to stop with their mother and try some new clothes on. Cathy was the splitting image of her mother and, at eight and half, was growing up and putting make-up on, which I didn't approve of. "Don't be such a prude," Linda would say when I objected. "She's a young lady now."

Ivan didn't mind. "I like going with you, Daddy," he said. "I don't like playing with my sisters." I gave him a hug and told him he was a good boy. So we went fishing on our own. We found a spot on the river near Wallingford Bridge and put out a line in the water. I had bought my son one of the tiniest rods you could get, but he struggled to cast in. His concentration was good, and he kept his eye on the bright-red float as it bobbed up and down. "I've got one," he suddenly cried out excitedly as the float disappeared beneath the water. I pulled the rod out and a tiny gudgeon was dangling on the hook. I took the hook out of its mouth and was about to throw it back, when Ivan said, "Aren't we taking it home so Mum can cook it?"

I laughed. "No, son, it's far too small, and you're not supposed to take fish out of the river. If everybody did that, there would be no fish left." We stayed by the river most of the morning, lying on the bank and throwing stones into the water (no wonder we didn't catch any more fish). We packed up our gear and went home because we were both hungry.

When I arrived home, Micks car was parked outside. The two girls came running out, and Cathy cried out excitedly, "Daddy, Daddy, we've been out in Uncle Mick's new car."

Mick came out a moment later. "I just took Linda and the girls out for a quick drive in the new Jag," he said. "I hope you don't mind."

"No, of course not," I said, trying to control my temper.

"You've made a good job of the house so far," Mick said. "Linda's given me a guided tour. The bedrooms are huge. You and the family will have to come around to our house for tea one day. I am sure Josie will be delighted." I thanked him, and as he got in his car, he said, "Keep in touch" then waved to the kids as he drove off. Cathy and Gemma waved after him. I was fuming, and when I caught Linda alone and the kids were in the garden, I asked "Why are the kids calling him Uncle Mick? He's not their uncle," I said, "although he's around here often enough."

"Don't tell me who or what friends I should see," she raged. "Mick just popped around to see how we were getting on that's all."

I went out into the garden to cool off and played with Ivan on the swing. Things were a bit frosty between us for a few days, but gradually, we carried on with the decorating and the argument was forgotten.

I still went out for a drink with Pete and Mick at the local pub, and I asked him if he was going to marry Josie in one of our conversations. "Not likely," he said, "I like a woman a bit more independent. Josie's all right in bed and keeping the house tidy, but she's useless at cooking, she'll be all right for the time being." Pete, on the other hand, had been going out with Susan, whom I hadn't met, and he was hoping to marry her in the following summer.

The subject got around to houses and I said, "When are you going to invite us around to your house, then, Mick?"

"As a matter of fact, in two weeks' time, I am having a bring-what-you-drink party, and you are both invited." I thought I wouldn't give that a miss after all the boasting to Linda about how fabulous his house was. So when the date arrived, Linda got her parents to look after the children, and we went along to the grand house.

I must admit it was far superior to our house. It was overlooking the golf course at Frilford. Mick was on the bar as we walked in the front reception area. I handed my usual six-pack of cider and a bottle of vodka for Linda. He poured me a cider and Linda a vodka and tonic. Most of his guests I knew from the building sites, and one chap, a fellow tacker whom I'd met in the pub with Mick before, handed over a cheap bottle of wine for him and his wife. "What do you and your wife want to drink, then, Steve?" Mick said.

"I'll have a large whiskey, and my wife will have a gin and orange," replied Steve. Mick then opened the cheap bottle of wine, filled two glasses, and handed the drinks to Steve, who looked dumbfounded. "But I asked for a whiskey and gin and orange," protested Steve.

"And I served you with what you bought with you," replied Mick. "If you wanted something different, then you should have bought that, instead of a cheap bottle of wine." I laughed, but Steve and his wife left without even having a drink.

Josie, Mick's girlfriend, showed Linda and me around the house. Mick wasn't kidding about it being grand. It had an indoor swimming pool, games room, and enormous lounge with the biggest television I had ever seen. Mick certainly didn't do things by half. There must have been a dozen people there already, milling around the house, holding drinks in their hands. After Linda and I had left the party, Linda asked, "Well, what do you think of their house, then, Davy?"

"I was very impressed," I said, "but it must cost a bomb to maintain."

"There you go again," Linda replied. "You always look on the negative side of things, one day we could have a house like that."

"Not with bringing up three children and a wife to support," I replied. Linda sat and moped all the way home and didn't speak to me all evening.

CHAPTER

The Tragedy

The following week was Ivan's fourth birthday and Gemma's fifth. I had bought Gemma a doll's pram and baby doll so she could push it around when we went for walk. For Ivan, I bought a Scalextric car-racing set just like mine when I was a kid. But this set was far more advanced, with bridges, pit stops, and banked corners so the cars stayed on the track longer. I was more excited than my son, thinking of us setting up the track in his bedroom and racing each other with the cars, now the house was finished.

December the twelfth and the council decided to repair the road right opposite my house and had installed a set of traffic lights, which was a bit inconvenient as it was Gemma's and Ivan's birthday party. "Could you nip out and get some more fizzy drinks, Davy?" asked Linda. "We have nearly run out."

I didn't know whether the kids were tipping it down the sink or drinking it. But I ran outside, got in the car, and drove off to the shops. Ivan was up at the lounge window, waving me off. I waved back and blew him a kiss. I was not gone more than ten minutes and returned home. Ivan was still at the window when I returned. I had to wait at the traffic lights as they were red before I could turn into my drive. I looked across at Ivan, expecting him to be at the window, but he wasn't there. I was distracted when a car pulled up behind me and honked his horn. The next minute, Ivan was running across the road toward my car. I looked on in horror as a car came racing through the traffic lights and hit him. He was flung across the bonnet, hit the windscreen, and landed in the road. I screamed, got out of the car, and ran over to Ivan. He wasn't moving. Blood was trickling out of the corner of his mouth. The other drivers had stopped and held up the traffic. I ran inside my house and called the police and ambulance, then went back outside. Linda followed me, wondering why I was so distraught and saw Ivan lying in the road. She burst out crying and rushed over to him, trying to shake him awake. "I wouldn't do that, lady," a man said. "He may have some broken bones."

I took off my coat and covered his little body, praying the ambulance would get here quickly.

We heard a siren, and the police arrived. They quickly dispersed the crowd that had gathered trying to see what had happened. The ambulance arrived a few minutes later and examined my son. They put an oxygen mask over his face and put him in what looked like straitjacket then lifted him onto a stretcher. "Will he be all right?" I cried.

The paramedic replied, "Well, he's still breathing, so he stands a good chance of recovery as long as he has no internal bleeding." I went with the ambulance to the hospital at Wallingford. I had to stay in the waiting room while they took Ivan into the operating theater. I seemed to be there for hours before a doctor came to see me. "Is he all right?" I asked desperately.

"Come with me," the doctor said and led me into a private room. "Sit down, Mr. Jones," he said. "I am afraid your son never regained consciousness, and he died."

I broke down and between sobs, said, "But he can't be. The ambulance man said he was breathing and would be all right."

"We did everything we could, Mr. Jones, but your son had massive bleeding to the brain when he hit the road, and we could not stop the bleeding." My head was in a whirl. It couldn't be. My son was gone. I would never be able to play with him again. I curled up in the chair and wept.

It was some time after when a nurse came in with a cup of tea and sat with me. "At least he didn't suffer, Mr. Jones," she said soothingly. It didn't help much, but I thanked her. I drank the tea, then left in a daze, thinking, how I was going to tell Linda and the girls their little brother was dead? When I walked in the front door, all the children had gone home and the party things were cleared away. Linda burst into tears when she saw my tear-streaked face and hugged me.

"He's dead, Linda," I sobbed. The girls came over, crying, and I hugged then both.

"Won't Ivan be coming back home, then, Daddy?" Gemma sobbed, not understanding what had happened.

"No, darling," said Linda, "he's gone to stay in heaven."

It took some time for the family to get over Ivan's death, me especially.

Linda and the girls grew closer, taking comfort from their mother. I became bitter. The one thing I had cherished had been torn away from me.

It wasn't long before Mick came around, offering his condolences. He seemed to show great sympathy toward Linda and the kids, then shook my hand. "I am so sorry, mate," he said. "Why don't you come out for a drink with Pete and me tonight just to cheer you up a bit?"

I didn't really feel like I needed his company to cheer me up, but I accepted his invitation anyway and met him and Pete at the Vine public house in Wittenham. The conversation quickly got onto Pete's wedding plans for the summer. "Of course you and your families are all invited," said Pete.

"Oh, it will only be me coming," replied Mick. "Josie and I have split up." I looked at Pete, and he was as shocked as I was.

"What's gone wrong, then?" I said. "I thought you too suited one another."

"No," Mick replied, "she was all right in bed, but I figured I could do better." As he had got older, Mick was becoming more arrogant, not like the best mate I had known since our schooldays. I left sometime later, feeling I had lost a friend as well as my son.

It was some months later I decided to treat Linda to a surprise holiday. I had asked my mother if she would look after our two girls for a week so I could take Linda away. She agreed, so I booked a holiday to Barbados in February, flying with British Airways. It was costing me a packet, but I figured it was worth it with all the tragedy we had suffered over the last year. I didn't tell her until a few days before we flew. "Pack your bags. We are going off on holiday for a week," I said excitedly. She immediately thought we were heading off to Spain again. I had arranged a stretch limo to take us to the airport, with a bottle of champagne in the back. If Mick could do it, so could I. Linda still didn't know where we were flying to when we arrived at the airport until it was broadcast over the loudspeakers. I said, "That's us, Linda. We're off to Barbados."

She didn't believe me at first until we were boarding the 747 jumbo plane and sat down. She beamed with delight. "However could you afford this, Davy?" she whispered in my ear.

"A lot of hard work," I replied, "but I've got another surprise for you." She snuggled up to me, trying to find out what it was.

We were halfway through our flight when the captain announced over the speakers, "It's Mr. and Mrs. Jones' tenth wedding anniversary today, and I would like to invite them up to the flight deck." Linda couldn't believe it when the stewardess invited us to follow her, and we stood up amid a rapturous applause. Then we went up the stairs through the first-class section into the cockpit. It was very small, and it was a bit cramped with us in there. The captain and second pilot shook our hands and explained some of the controls. He told us we were in autopilot, and the plane was virtually flying itself. I was amazed how small the windows were for such a large aircraft. We thanked the captain, and the stewardess showed us back to our seats.

Our first stop was Maine in America, where we had to take on more fuel. All the passengers had to leave the aircraft for an hour but were not allowed outside the airport terminal. We then flew on to Barbados and landed at Grantley Adams Airport. In all, it had taken us eleven hours. When we finally climbed out of the aircraft, the heat was unbearable, and we were glad of the air conditioning in the terminal. We got a taxi to Inn on the Beach in Holetown, a quaint small hotel set right on the beach. It was a spectacular setting, the beach fine white sand and the sea a pale blue. Linda and I had a great week soaking up the sun and swimming in the warm Caribbean Sea. We went out on several excursions, to Welshman Hall Gully, Harrison Caves, and the Flower Forest. By the end of the week, we didn't want to leave. We were picked up Friday night and taken back to the airport for our return journey. All the passengers sat in the airport for three hours before it was announced that the flight would be delayed for twelve hours and British Airways would pay for an extra night for all 375 passengers. We heard the next day that one of the engines had to be replaced and flown in from America. The engineers were still replacing it when we started to board at 11:00 am everybody had their fingers crossed that the job had not been rushed and the engine had been fitted properly. But it was nerve-racking when we took off. The plane touched down in chilly Gatwick ten hours later. It had been a holiday to remember, and I vowed one day to take the whole family, a vow I would never keep.

CHAPTER

My World Collapses

My life returned to the same routine, work and more work. I had to get my finances back in order, before the bank manager gave me a call. Linda had only been back a week when she started dropping hints about her car. "Can't we get a new Mini Cooper on finance?" she asked one day. I couldn't believe what she was saying. "I've just taken you on an all-expenses paid holiday that cost me nearly £3,000, and now you want a new car," I said angrily. "Perhaps you should ask Mick if he could buy you one."

She stormed off in a huff, and Cathy and Gemma looked at me as though it was my fault. "You are always arguing with Mum," Cathy said. "Can't you make her happy?"

"I am trying, love," I replied, "but your mummy wants things I can't afford." I don't think Cathy or Gemma understood what money was or its value.

Things did improve over the next few weeks, and I met up with Pete for a drink one night. Mick was there and greeted me with a handshake. "Can I buy you a drink, mate," he said, "and cheer you up a bit? I hear you are going through a bad patch with Linda."

I thought, how did he know that? I hadn't mentioned it to Pete or anybody else, but as the evening wore on and the drinks flowed, the subject changed and we talked about our road trip and the adventures we had with the two girls all those years ago. I went home glad that Mick and I had eased the tension between us.

About a week later, my old boss James Gardener rang me up and offered me a job at the Ideal Home Exhibition at Earls Court in London. He was building a team up of bricklayers, carpenter, tilers, and electricians. We had four weeks to build a fully functional house for the public to view, an exact replica of the houses we were building on site, in the hope that this would encourage sales. There were about seven other companies we were competing against. I snapped up the offer when he offered me double the day rate. The only problem was we were working double the hours.

Linda was not pleased that I would be away so long. "The kids and I will hardly see you," she complained, but when I told her the extra money could go toward a new Mini Cooper, her face brightened up and she agreed that I should go.

James picked us all up at six in the morning in a minibus and dropped us off at seven in the evening. It was long hours but the work was interesting, and we had three canteen breaks during the day. The hot food was excellent and at cost price, was great value. But there were a few drawbacks: we all had to join the workers' union and one person from each company had to attend a meeting every day. When it was my turn to attend, I went along, not knowing what to expect. There were about fifty people sitting in rows, and the speakers sat at a table on a raised platform. The union elders were asking people to vote for a shorter eight-hour day. But I thought, how are we going to complete a house in four weeks by working fewer hours? It didn't make sense to me. So I didn't raise my hand when they took a vote. The next item on the agenda was the amount of tea they were serving in the canteen. Apparently, the canteen company was serving tea in polystyrene cups smaller than the recommended size. I couldn't believe what I was hearing, having to sit here and listen to all this twaddle, when I could have been working. I was glad when the meeting was finished.

I heard over the next four weeks that it was costing each company £50,000 to build a house. The only perks the company got was all the smaller businesses would have to pay our company to advertise in our house, such as curtains, carpets, light fittings, and furniture. There was even a fully fitted gym in one of the bedrooms and a brand-new car in the garage, all advertising their company. I could see why this was such a profitable business. We finished early on the last day, and I asked James if he could stop off at a flower shop so I could buy a bunch of flowers for Linda. All the lads cheered when I got back on the bus with a big bunch of red roses. "Are you going to get your end away tonight, then, Davy?" one of them joked.

I laughed. "Yes, I hope so," I replied. I got James to drop me off at the end of the street. I knew the kids would be still at school, so I let myself in quietly, planning to sneak up behind Linda and thrust the roses in front of her. But the house was quite apart from some muffled noises coming from upstairs. I sneaked up the stairs and pushed open our bedroom door.

Somebody was on top of Linda in our bed with their arse going up and down having sex. I stood there dumfounded and dropped the roses. Linda opened her eyes and screamed when she saw me. Mick looked around and grinned. "Hello, mate, I didn't expect you back so early." I just ran out of the house and drove off in my van, tears streaming down my face. I parked up in a quiet spot in the woods and broke down. How could my best mate betray me like this? How long had he been shagging

Linda behind my back, while acting like my friend? I was devastated. All we had built up together, the surprise holiday to Barbados, and all along, she'd been seeing that bastard behind my back. I sat there until the pubs were open and I could drown my sorrows. I didn't feel like talking to anybody and left at closing time. I sneaked into the house, hoping everybody was asleep and not have to confront Linda. I got as far as the lounge, hoping to sleep on the sofa. But Linda had been waiting up for me and came marching into the lounge.

"I want a divorce," she demanded. I had never seen her so angry, and I was in no state to argue with her.

"Can't we talk about this tomorrow?" I replied. "I'm exhausted."

"No, we can't," she snapped. "You were never here when I needed you, and Mick was," she said. "And I hate you for that."

"So it's my fault," I replied. "If you didn't demand so much, I wouldn't have to work so hard to pay for it."

Linda hated losing an argument. "Well, you can sleep down here from now on," she shouted, "because you're not sleeping in my bed." She then slammed the lounge door and stormed up the stairs. I was too drunk to care and soon nodded off on the sofa.

I went over to Mum's the next day and poured my heart out to her. She gave me a cuddle. "Maybe it is for the better," she said, "but I doubt the kids will understand." I hadn't thought about Cathy and Gemma and what effect it would have on them if we divorced. "If you want my advice, Davy," Mum said, "get yourself a lawyer and ask his advice." I did that the next day, and he advised me to wait until Linda filed for a divorce and on what grounds.

"But you could lose the house, Mr. Jones, because your wife has two youngsters to support," the lawyer said. "But let's wait and see. It may not come to that."

I moved out of the house and back in with Mum. It wasn't too bad really as Sheila had moved out and was living with her boyfriend and Mary and Tommy were both in their early twenties, so I slept in Tommy's bedroom in the spare bed.

It wasn't long before my lawyer received the divorce papers from Linda's lawyer citing that I had neglected her and the children and that I treated her unfairly. She was claiming half of the house and her car and I could keep the Jaguar and my van. "So will the house have to be sold?" I asked the lawyer.

"Yes," he replied, "unless you agree on a settlement figure and she can raise the money and pay you off." I doubted that would happen, so I asked an independent estate agent to value the house. He came back with a figure of between £45,000 and £50,000, quite a bit more than what we paid for it. But what surprised me and the lawyer was a week later, Linda offered to buy me out for £25,000.

"I would take that offer," replied my lawyer. "She's offered the top end of the estate agents' price." I wondered how she could have got that sort of money and then realized Mick must have lent it to her. "She's also claiming £100 a month for each child, until they are sixteen," my lawyer continued, "and the cost of her lawyer's fee."

"That sounds a bit steep," I said. "Can she do that?"

"When it involves children," he said, "the courts always favor the mother, so yes, she can."

"What about access to my children?" I asked. "I want to see them regularly."

"Linda cannot deny you the rights to see your own children," the lawyer replied, "unless she can prove you are a danger to them. But let's get the ball rolling. We can argue about that at a later date. Do you accept her offer?"

"I don't think I have much choice, do I?" I replied.

"I'm afraid not, Mr. Jones, unless you want to fight the case but that could take months and could cost you a small fortune." So after some thought and on the advice of my lawyer, I agreed to the terms and signed the paperwork. On leaving the lawyer's office, I thought, why would Mick want to lend Linda the money when she had no means of paying him back? I was about to find out six weeks later when my visiting rights were approved. I could see Cathy and Gemma the first day of every month for four hours in the morning unsupervised. I had to pick them up and drop them off at her house. Four hours a month I couldn't even take them out on day trips to the zoo or to the seaside. I was devastated. But I did look forward to seeing them when the first day of the month arrived I cleaned the Jaguar inside and out so it would smell nice for the girls. I planned to take them to the park for a picnic.

I pulled up outside our old house, expecting to see the girls run out excitedly to see their daddy. I sat there for ten minutes, and eventually got out of the car and knocked on the front door. An elderly woman answered the door. Thinking that she was a cleaning lady, I said, "I've come to pick up my children."

"What children?" the elderly woman replied. "There are no children here. My husband and I rented this property last week from Mr. Michael Bolton." I looked at her and my mouth opened but no sound came out. She then shut the door.

Mick the bastard had not only stolen my wife and my children; now he had stolen my house. My best friend had taken everything from me. I felt like killing the bastard. I drove over to Mick's house, intending to confront him. As I pulled up outside his house, the electric gates swung open so I could drive in. A brand-new red Mini Cooper stood in the driveway. As I got out of the car, Linda and Mick came out of the front door. "How are you doing, mate?" Mick said, with a smile.

"You're no mate of mine," I shouted and lunged forward. I caught him with a punch to the side of his face, and he fell backward. I expected him to retaliate, but he didn't.

Linda went to his side and helped him up. "You better get out," she screamed, "before I call the police."

I got in the car and drove off, completely forgetting the kids. I'd hardly got back home before the police arrived and arrested me for assault. I had to go to the police station and make a statement. "But it's only his word against mine," I protested.

"I'm afraid it's not as simple as that, Mr. Jones. You see, your ex-wife swears it was an unprovoked attack, and it's all been recorded on Mr. Bolton's CCTV." He'd done it again. That was why he hadn't retaliated and punched me back. He'd set me up and recorded it all. He must have planned this all along.

The following week, I was back up at Earls Court, dismantling the house we had built in four weeks, but we only had one week to clear the house from site before the International Boat Show started. I had a letter from the courts a few days later, stating that all charges would be dropped against me if I did not come into contact with my ex-wife or family. I had lost everything; even my kids had turned against me. I felt utterly defeated. That was the first time I thought about taking my own life.

I started drinking heavily, often sleeping on park benches and buying cheap bottles of wine until the pubs were open. My £25,000 share of the house had dwindled to less than £18,000 by the time I had paid all the lawyers' fees, court costs etc. The £200 was being taken out of my bank account every month for the upkeep of the girls. That was a laugh. Mick and Linda didn't need that money; they were just humiliating me, and they had succeeded. One evening, I was slouched in a corner of the pub in a stupor, when a chap shook my shoulder. "Hello, Davy," he said. "Boy, you look as though you've hit a hard time. Haven't you got any work?" I looked at him through my bleary eyes, but I didn't recognize him. "It's Brian," he said. "We worked together on the building site where you and Linda had the caravan." He slowly came into focus.

"Oh hello, Brian," I replied, "do you want a drink?"

"I think you've had enough already, mate," he said. "I'm glad I bumped into you. I'm going back out to Saudi Arabia next week and wondered if you would like to come."

"What, on holiday?" I replied.

"No, to work," Brian said. "I joined a firm last year that flies skilled building workers out to Jedda. You do a six-month stint then they fly you home for a couple of weeks to see your family. The pay is fantastic, and every expense is paid for. Well, what do you say, mate?" I didn't have to think for very long. There was nothing left for me here, so I shook his hand and agreed to go.

CHAPTER

My New Life

A week later we landed in Saudi Arabia and were bused over to the compound just outside Jedda. It was huge. There were all sorts of tradesmen there, from building workers to truck drivers, crane operators, welders. I should think every trade imaginable lived in this complex. There was a huge dining hall where you could help yourself to any meal three times a day. They even had a small cinema and games room. The whole idea was to keep you in the compound. The company didn't like their men mixing with the locals and getting into trouble. And it wasn't really safe at night as some locals resented the fact foreigners were corrupting their way of life. But Brian and I settled in. I was glad he was with me as he'd done all this before and knew the layout. We had the contract of building a new school in Jedda itself.

We were bused in every morning and taken back every evening and took a packed lunch until the evening meal. I was allocated a local young man to work with me and teach him some skills in carpentry. He didn't speak much English, so we had to get by on sign language. But it was quite difficult to learn the Muslim ways, as every so often, he would down tools, take out a little prayer mat, and pray to Allah. I found out his name was Rashid but not much else. It was slow work teaching him, and sometimes he was more of a hindrance than a help. Some of the lads did leave the compound at night and go in search of other entertainment, but as there was no drinking outside the compound, I didn't see the point. I knuckled down and worked all the hours I could and after the six months were up and we flew back home, I had saved £6,000. After the two weeks at home, I decided to fly out with Brian and do a final six months in Saudi Arabia then look to buy a house on my return and start a new life.

Those six months went very quick, and I was soon looking for a house to buy. Unfortunately, my total amount of savings came to £27,000, but it was enough to put down a good deposit and only have a small mortgage and I ended up buying 27 Albermarl Drive right next to our very first house. But it was an end-terrace, and there was enough land at the side to build an extension. I rented the property for a year while still living at Mum's, because this was another income to build up my bank balance. It had been nearly three years since splitting up with Linda, and I hadn't seen her or the girls in all that time and I did miss them.

James Gardener called in at my mother's house about a week later, offering me the job at the Ideal Home Exhibition in London again. It was a different house from before, but the terms were as before, double the day rate. I agreed immediately. "I'm trying to get the old team back together," James said, "and I would like you to be in charge of the carpenters."

"As long as I don't have to go to any union meetings," I replied.

He laughed. "I think I can arrange that. I'll pick you up on Monday about 6:00 a.m., OK?" So I started being picked up at 6:00 a.m. and dropped off at 7:00 p.m. every day for the next month.

It was shattering work having no break from the grueling schedule. On the last day, as we had completed the house early, we decided to celebrate and have a drink in the nearest pub. I bought the first round and noticed a girl staring at me from a cubicle in the corner. I didn't take much notice, but somehow she looked familiar. There were six carpenters plus the boss, James, who was driving, so he only stuck to soft drinks. I got up to go to the toilet, and when I came back, the girl who had been sitting in the cubicle stood up and said, "You're Davy, aren't you?"

"Yes," I said, "do I know you?"

"It's Brenda," she said, "from school, remember?" I looked at her more closely. It had been over fifteen years since I last saw her, and she had changed a lot. Gone was her sleek blond hair; it was now dyed black. Her skin was dry and she wore no make-up. She still had a petite figure, but looked aged.

"God," I said. "What happened to you?"

"It's a long story," she said, "and not a very nice one." She was about to tell me then James called all the men together and it was time to go.

"Give me your telephone number and I'll give you mine," I said, hurriedly jotting the numbers down. "I'll be back here in two weeks at the exhibition," I shouted as we all got in the bus and drove off. All the chaps wanted to know who the girl was, but I just said it was my cousin. That evening, I tried to phone the number Brenda gave me and got a "number not available" answer. Either I had taken down the wrong numbers or Brenda had given me a false one. But why would she do that? She seemed excited to see me. So I'd just have to wait until she called me. I waited all week, but she did not call. I had told her to phone in the evening, but perhaps that was not possible. I thought of all the possible excuses imaginable, but she never phoned.

Two weeks later, we went back up to London to start demolishing the show house in the exhibition and that evening I sneaked along to the pub about an hour before we went home. I sat in the same cubicle and was on my second pint before she came in. She was in a worse state than before. Her hair hadn't been combed, and when I looked into her sad face, she had a swollen eye. "Who did this?" I said angrily.

"My boyfriend"—she sighed—"when he found the telephone number you gave me and ripped it up."

"Can't you leave him?" I said.

"I would," she replied, "but I have nowhere to go."

"You could come and live with me," I said. "I would look after you."

"Would you really, Davey?" She sobbed. "It's a bit more complicated than that. I have a son and he's only eight years old. I couldn't leave him with his father—he's violent."

I looked at my watch. "I've got to go in a minute, but could you meet me here at the same time tomorrow?"

"I'll try to," she said, "but wait for me if I'm a bit late." We parted, and I kissed her on the cheek.

That night, I was thinking of how I could look after them both. My house had another two months before I could not renew the tenant's contract and legally move in the house myself. The only alternative was to rent somewhere until we could all move in together. I had a plan all worked out by the time Brenda and I next met. Brenda was a few minutes late again and hugged me when she saw me. "I didn't think you would turn up," she said, "after seeing me like that."

"Listen," I said, "if you really want to live with me, then you will have to sneak away one evening with your son. I could pick you up here on Friday about 9:00 p.m., in my car."

"Could you make it 10:00 p.m.?" said Brenda. "I could get him drunk by then and slip a few sleeping pills into his drink."

I left her that evening and went home and asked Mum if she would put Brenda and her son up for one night so I could arrange some board and lodgings on Saturday. "Do you know what you're taking on, son?" she said. "You hardly know the girl, and she's got a little boy. Does the boy's father agree with what you're doing?"

"He doesn't know, Mum," I said. "He's abusing Brenda and the boy, and I want to rescue them before he can do any more harm."

"Can't she go to police and report him?" Mum said.

"She's scared stiff, Mum. He's got a lot of mates. This is the only way she'll feel safe." Mum eventually agreed.

Friday night, I set off in my Jaguar and stopped just down the road from the pub. I waited until ten before going inside, expecting Brenda to be inside but there was no sign of her. I sat in the cubicle and bought a pint. Time slipped by, and when the bartender called for last orders, she was still not there. I was beginning to wonder if her boyfriend had discovered her plans and locked her in. I was leaving the pub disappointed, when she came running down the road, pulling a little boy behind her. In her other hand, she held a suitcase. "I'm sorry I'm late," she said. "It was a long time before my boyfriend went to sleep. This is my little boy Steven." And she pushed the little boy forward. He put out his hand to shake mine.

"Nice to meet you, Steven," I said, and noticed he was a half-caste little boy, but I didn't make any comment. "Let's get in the car before anybody sees us," I said. "We've got a long journey back, and I expect Steven's tired." He was very tired. As soon as Brenda laid him on the back seat, he fell asleep. She put the suitcase in the foot well to stop him rolling off the seat then climbed in beside me. I set off through London onto the M4 motorway.

Then Brenda told me most of her story on the way back home. "When I went back to live with Mum, she was living with a new boyfriend. He was all right to me, and I liked him. He wasn't the best-looking chap Mum had been out with, but Mum treated him like dirt. I got a job working at the co-op as a checkout girl. He offered to teach me to drive in his car when I was seventeen, and I passed my test the first time. But I would never be able to afford a car on a till girl's wage, as Mum spent most of my wages on booze. Not long after that, he left Mum because of her drinking.

"I tried to persuade Mum to change her ways and cut down on the drinking, but she took no notice. 'I can get a boyfriend any time I want,' she said in a drunken rage, 'and I don't need a girl barely out of school telling me what to do.'

"But her next boyfriend was a big black African man called Coffey. He was scary, and I couldn't understand what attracted Mum to him. I didn't like him from the start, and he often beat Mum up when he was high on drugs. I managed to keep out of his way most of the time, but he kept pestering me for sex. I rejected him every time, and when I told Mum, she wouldn't believe me. Mum went out one evening to pick up some more booze. As soon as Mum was gone, I heard Coffey coming up the stairs. I had locked the door of my bedroom, but that didn't stop him. He burst into my bedroom and threw me on the bed and started ripping off my clothes. He was like a madman. I tried to fight him off, but he was far too strong and he raped me. I finally fell pregnant after he'd raped me several times after that. Mum helped me when I had his baby then as soon as I could, I ran away.

"I met Matt one evening. He seemed kind and, after listening to my story, offered to take me home. He was a lot older than me and lived on his own. But I had to sleep with him in exchange for him looking after us. I later learned he was also a drinker and became violent when he was drunk. I was so scared."

"So this latest man isn't the boy's father?" I asked.

"No," she replied. She then burst out crying. "Do you know what it feels like, sleeping with an older man I didn't love? I had to look after Steven somehow and he was kind to us to start with, until he started drinking." It seemed like Brenda had experienced a horrible start in adulthood. I just wished she hadn't left her grandmother's and I could have looked after her. I did feel sorry for Brenda and her little boy and wanted to change their tragic lives for the better.

We arrived at Mum's just before midnight. I let myself in and crept up to the spare room. Mum had spruced up the room and had laid out the fold-up bed for Steven in the corner. Brenda and I would have to share the double bed. We quickly laid Steven in his bed. He was still half asleep and snuggled under the bedclothes. Brenda quickly got undressed to her bra and knickers and climbed into bed. I soon followed and cuddled up to her back. She seemed to tense up and said, "Davy, I do love you and appreciate what you have done for Steven and me, but could we just cuddle tonight?"

I did so want to make love to Brenda after not having sex for so long. But with all the trauma she had been through, I thought it best to let her make the first move when she felt the time was right. So I just cuddled her until we both fell asleep.

The next morning, we both slept in and didn't wake until 9:00 a.m. I got out of bed and drew back the curtains, and the morning sun flooded the bedroom. "Come on, sleepy," I whispered to Brenda, "time to get up." She seemed reluctant to move, so I jokingly pulled all the covers off her. She then sat up, and I noticed all the cigarette burns on her body. I had to fight back the tears as she stood up. "Oh my god, Brenda, what has that bastard done to you?" I cried.

She came over and hugged me. "It's all right now, Davy," she said. "They will heal. At least he didn't touch Steven." I couldn't control my emotions any longer. Tears filled my eyes, and I wept on her shoulder.

It was some time before I controlled myself and got dressed. We woke up Steven and gave him a quick wash then dressed him as well. It was obvious Brenda had only packed the bare essentials as there were not many clothes in her suitcase. But we looked presentable as we went downstairs and into the kitchen. I was glad my father had gone to work, because he would have made some comment about Steven's color. My mother did look at him and you could see she was a bit surprised, but she recovered and smiled. "Hello, young man, and what is your name?"

Steven held out his hand and said, "My name's Steven, ma'am."

My mum shook his hand. "No need to call me ma'am, Steven," she said. "You can call me Auntie Eddie." She then looked at Brenda and shook her hand. "You have a very polite young son, Brenda. I can see you have taught him some manners and looked after him well." Brenda thanked Mum for putting them up for the night at such short notice. We all sat down for breakfast and then went out in my car to search for some accommodation for the next two months, until we could all move into my own house.

We found a room at the local hotel. It was expensive, but we managed to negotiate the price after I told the manager we would be stopping for at least two months. It was a nice big room with our own toilet and shower room. But obviously there was not much privacy with Steven sleeping in the same room.

I had to go back to work on the building site, so I left my Jaguar at my mum's and used my van. Brenda amused herself and Steven by walking around Wallingford and looking in all the shops and then down along the river. I would come back about 5:00 p.m., swap the van for the Jaguar at Mum's, and take them for a ride out somewhere. It all worked out pretty well and the two months soon went by, before we finally moved into our new house together as a family.

CHAPTER

My New Family

We soon settled into a routine. Luckily for me, Brenda had passed her driving test. She had never owned her own car and was a bit nervous at having to drive the Jaguar around, especially as it was an automatic, but after a few weeks, she became quite confident and dropped Steven off at his new school. We had a few problems in the first week with bullying and racist taunts, but after I went in to see the headmaster and explained what a tragic upbringing Steven had had, he promised he would keep an eye on him and stamp out any bulling.

To be fair, he kept his word, and Steven seldom complained he was being teased. I grew quite attached to Steven. He was always polite, a bit shy sometimes, but once he got to know me, I think he liked me too.

My only regret was I would never be able to have a child with Brenda. I did go and see the doctor about reversing the vasectomy operation and he said they could try but there was only a 5 percent chance of it working. So I didn't bother and Brenda didn't seem to mind. I think she had been through enough turmoil in her life, without having to worry about another child.

After about six months of living in our house. I had my mother over our house one evening and she was playing with Steven. Brenda was upstairs making the beds, when there was a knock on the back door and I went to open it. A big black man burst in. "Where's my boy?" he shouted. "I know you've got him, so don't deny it." He took me by surprise, and I stumbled with an answer.

Brenda had come down the stairs when she heard the commotion. "He's here," said Brenda, "and he's staying here where he's safe and out of the reach of your bullying ways, Coffey."

"You fucking bitch," he snarled and pushed past me into the lounge. Steven was cowering behind my mother. "Hand him over, granny," Coffey said, "or else you get a slice of this." He pulled out a knife about nine inches long. My mother screamed, and I grabbed his arm holding the knife from behind. He struggled and swung around and slashed my arm with the knife. I had to do something quick, so I picked up a chair and smashed it over his head. The chair broke, but he didn't go down and had taken most of the force on his arm holding the knife. I grabbed the hand holding the knife, and he pushed me back. I fell over the broken chair, and he fell on top of me. The knife must have gone into his stomach as he made a gurgling sound and stopped struggling. His eyes bulged, and I could see the hatred in them. He slackened his grip then let out a final breath and lay still. I pushed him off me, and he rolled over on his back, the knife still in his stomach.

Nobody moved, then Brenda came over and tried to stop the bleeding on my arm with a towel. Mum reached for the telephone and called the police and ambulance. Poor Steven stood traumatized, shaking with fear, until Mum went over to him and gave him a cuddle. The lounge was a mess, the carpet covered in blood. We left the body on the floor and waited for the police. It wasn't long before an armed response team came to the house, and Mum let them in. The ambulance wasn't far behind. They examined the body of Coffey and told us he was still breathing. They put an oxygen mask on over his nose and mouth then took him away on a stretcher. I had to wait for another ambulance after the paramedics said my injuries were not life-threatening. Mum made us all cups of tea while the police took statements from us all. Then Steven asked the police officer, "Is he dead?"

"No, they might be able to save him," the officer replied.

"Well, I hope he dies," said Steven. "Then he can't hurt Mummy anymore." The officer looked surprised but made a note in his diary.

When the police had gone, the other ambulance arrived and took me to hospital. I was released after the doctor put ten stitches into my arm and gave me a tetanus jab. "You were lucky it was not that deep and didn't sever any arteries," the doctor said, "but don't do anything with that arm until we can take the stitches out."

I got a taxi back and arrived back home about an hour later. Mum and Brenda had rolled the bloodstained carpet up and just left the underlay. "You will have to buy a new carpet," Mum said. "You'll never get those bloodstains out." I thanked Mum for all the help and drove her back home. When I finally got back home, it was gone 11:00 p.m., so we all went to bed. Steven wanted to come in our bed because he was afraid Coffey would come back for him when they made him better. So just for one night, we all slept in our bed.

Steven needn't have worried as we later learned that Coffey had died on the way to the hospital. The next day, I was arrested on a manslaughter charge and held in custody. My mother got me a lawyer, and I was released on bail until the trial date. My lawyer told me not to worry as he would claim self-defense as we had a lot of witnesses' statements, including the next-door neighbors who had seen Coffey burst into the house. But the wait for the trial was worrying. What if I was found guilty? In truth, I didn't want to kill him. It was an accident. I suppose we could have tried to stop the bleeding, but I didn't want to pull the knife out in case it bled more.

It was two long weeks before the trial date, and I entered the courts shaking. I had to stand and swear on the Bible that I would tell the truth, the whole truth, and nothing but the truth and hesitated when I was asked if I deliberately tried to kill Coffey Johnson. "No, sir," I said, "he was still fighting me as the knife went in." That was the hardest thing to say, but after that, the questions were easier to answer and the prosecutor seemed satisfied. It was later proved that Coffey was an illegal immigrant and had been in trouble with the police before, for violence and drug trafficking. So that went in my favor, and after just a day, the jury found me not guilty and I was bound over to keep the peace. I thanked the lawyer and walked out a free man.

At least we could get on with our lives. Steven seemed more relaxed and wanted to come fishing with me at the weekend. He reminded me of Ivan a little with his mannerisms and politeness, all down to Brenda's upbringing, and I couldn't imagine what horrors she had endured, trying to protect her son from such a horrible, violent man. I bought Brenda a bunch of red roses and a box of chocolates on the way home. "What are these for?" she said, smiling as we came in the door.

"They're for you, darling, and Steven," I replied, "for agreeing to live with me and making my life complete." She looked at me, and her eyes watered. She had grown out her black locks and now her long blond hair glistened in the light. Her skin looked radiant. She looked like the girl that stayed with her granny all those years ago. That night, she forgot about all her past worries and we made love as never before. My life was complete.

CHAPTER

A Death in The Family

It was several years later that I went over to Mum's and she told me that my father had prostate cancer and they couldn't operate because he had pneumonia. Mum moved his bed downstairs as he refused to go into hospital. "If you go into those places," he told me, "you only come out in a box." My father was old-fashioned in his ways and very superstitious of hospitals, but as I saw him lying in bed, looking like a beaten man, I didn't feel the hatred I had carried all those years when he had beaten me with his belt and I had vowed to get my revenge. I actually felt sympathy for him and wished him well as I left.

He didn't get well. Mum had the doctor out a few times, and he told Mum, "Your husband seems to have given up, Mrs.

Jones. If he refuses to be admitted to hospital, then I'm afraid there's not a lot we can do."

"But he's not eating anything, doctor," Mum protested, "and what he does eat he vomits back up."

"Keep feeding him sugared water," the doctor replied. "He should keep that down. But be prepared, Mrs. Jones. Your husband will not last long on just that alone."

I visited my father nearly every night and watched him slowly shrink from a seventeen-stone giant to an eight-stone skeleton. He had just given up, and no matter what Mum or the doctor tried, he died two weeks later in his sleep.

We had the funeral at the local church. He was laid to rest in an open coffin for one day before the burial so people could pay their respects. I went along to see him with my brother and sisters. I didn't like what I saw. His face was plastered with make-up and his body plumped up to make him look normal. But he looked unreal like a manikin from a dress shop. We all came away saddened by his appearance, he was not like anything we remembered.

We buried him the next day, and we were surprised by how many people turned up for the service. He must have had a lot of drinking buddies that we didn't know about. But the service went well, and we all left satisfied with the outcome. Mum got over my father's death very quickly as she had realized it was only a matter of time before he died. She asked me to go up in the loft and fetch an old suitcase down, as there were some important documents inside concerning my father's will. When I was up in the loft, I came across my very first Scalextric racing car set that had been packed away all this time. I wondered if it was worth any money as it was over twenty years old, so I brought it down with the suitcase. I put the suitcase on the kitchen table, and Mum opened it. There were a lot of papers in there, and we both went through them, looking for my dad's will. I found an old birth certificate that had my name on it. I read through it and was shocked to find it stated "father unknown." I asked Mum what it meant, and she made an excuse that there had been a printing error and the registration authorities had sent a replacement birth certificate. I then asked her, "If I was born in 1945, why my birth was first registered in 1948? It doesn't make sense. I thought you had to register a birth within forty-two days, not three years later."

She looked baffled for a few minutes and didn't say anything. "Well, Davy," she said, "I do owe you an explanation, and now your father has died, I can tell you the truth about your birth."

CHAPTER

My Mother's Confession

"During the war when you reached sixteen years old, you had to do something for the war effort. I chose to work on the farm and became a land army girl helping to feed the nation who were relying on us for food as most things had to be grown on British soil. I worked on a massive farm over at Witney along with about twenty other girls. We were all young and we had to do the jobs of men as they were all overseas fighting the war. The farmer and owner was Mr. Alfred Reacher. He was about thirty-eight years old and quite a ladies' man. He was married to Gloria, and they had two boys about fourteen or fifteen years old. Gloria was older than him and was suffering from dementia, although the doctors were not sure if there were other problems as well as she was very sick. Alfred seemed to like me and confided in me about all his problems. It wasn't long before he seduced me, and we started an affair. He confessed he hadn't had sex for over five years as his wife's mind was muddled and she didn't know what she was saying. Eventually, she was admitted to a care home. We carried on the affair, and eventually, I fell pregnant even though he took precautions. He panicked. It would not look good to the farming authorities if a land owner seduced one of his working girls, especially as I was only seventeen. He said his career would be ruined.

"Alfred was a very wealthy man, and I trusted him. It was arranged for me to go to a private clinic in London before I started showing my bump. He rented a one-bedroom flat in Hammersmith for a year which shared a first-floor bathroom with the other tenants. His idea was for me to have the baby and then return to the farm later on and then he would look after me. But things started to go wrong before you were born, Davy. I suffered some complications and had to have a caesarean operation. The umbilical cord was wrapped around your neck, and you were not breathing when you were born. So it wasn't a very good start, and we spent a week in hospital before I was discharged. I then bought you home to the flat. Alfred did come up and see me and his baby when you were born and gave me £100 to buy some baby clothes, nappies, etc., but it didn't last long. Alfred was killed in a car crash on the way up to see me the following week. I was devastated, stuck in a dingy flat with a newborn baby and nobody to help. I survived the first year on social security, but when the money ran out and Mr. Bridger the landlord wanted the rent, I was desperate.

"He propositioned me into doing his washing and housework and sharing his bed. I know that sounds disgusting to you, but I would have done anything for you, even that. It wasn't too bad the first year. He was a lot older than me, but he treated me well. I used to take you for a walk in the park, and sometimes for a treat, I took you on a London double-decker bus and we sat upstairs at the front. But there wasn't much to see. Most of the houses had been bombed and turned to rubble. Ragamuffin kids would search in the rubble for anything of value so they could sell it to the pawnbrokers. Times were desperate then Davy, and I thought myself lucky that I had a roof over my head and food in my stomach. But then it all changed. Mr. Bridger took on two new tenants, and I didn't like them from the start.

"They were Irish laborers bought in by the government to help clear the streets after the war. The first week, they were all right. Then they found out I was sleeping with the landlord to pay my way, and they wanted me to sleep with them as well. I refused their advances, but they threatened to harm you Davy, unless I agreed. I stalled them and said I would think about it. I wrote to my sister your Auntie Stella, and asked her to help me. I told her my address and what a desperate situation I was in. Luckily, two days later, your uncle Jim drove up here and saved us. He drove back to their house, and I stayed there until I met Trevor. He was working on the local farm, and as we had so much in common, I started seeing him. I didn't really love him, but back then, he was kind and very affectionate and eventually he proposed to me. I said I would marry him if he would adopt you. At first, he refused, suggesting putting you in a children's home. But I stuck to my proposition, and we eventually married. We had to have another birth certificate drawn up to include Trevor's surname so we could become a legitimate family. Then we moved into our first farmhouse at Lower Balding. The rest you know about."

When Mum had finished, I sat silently for a few minutes, thinking things through. It all made sense: the dreams I had when I was a toddler about the red bus and the children playing in the rubble and why my father hated me so much, having to adopt me when all he wanted was Mum.

My mother waited and finally said, "Well, aren't you going to say something, Davy?"

"Have I got any brothers or sisters that are still alive?" I asked hopefully.

"As far as I know, your two half-brothers are still running the farm over at Witney," my mother replied. "But they must be quite old by now."

"But I could find out where they live and go over to see them," I said.

"Do you think that's a good idea, Davy?" Mum replied. "After all these years, they might resent you bringing back all those painful memories of their parents."

I looked at her and felt sympathy for all the sacrifices she had made for me. But then I felt bitterness that she had not told me about my father or my half- brothers. "But why didn't you tell me sooner, Mum?" I said.

She took my hand and said, "I was going to, son, but would it have made any difference?"

"Well, it would to me," I replied. "Then I could understand why my father hated me so much." My mother began to cry, and I realized what a trauma it had been to finally reveal her early years and my birth. I stood up and hugged her then kissed her cheek. Tears welled in my eyes. How could I have been so horrible to my mother with all the heartache she had endured?

We said our goodbyes and I went home determined to find out about my long-lost brothers. I wasn't difficult to find the location of the Reacher farm at Witney, and I drove over there on my own at the weekend. Mum was right. It was a huge farmhouse. I parked in the farm yard, among the outbuildings, got out of the car, walked down the garden path, and knocked on the back door. After a few minutes, an elderly man opened the door. "Can I help you?" he said.

"Yes," I replied, "but it might be better if I could come inside and talk to you, as I have some important information that needs to be discussed." He invited me into his kitchen, and we sat down at the table. "Could you tell me your name, sir?" I asked.

"My name's Brian Reacher," he said.

"Well, Brian," I said, "my name's David Jones. Can you remember back in 1945 when all the land army girls came to work on your farm, and one of them was called Edith?" He looked at me, wondering where this was all leading, and finally said, "Yes, I do recall a girl by that name," he replied.

"Well, your father Alfred had an affair with her. She became pregnant and was sent away to London to have her baby," I said. "I was her baby, Brian, so that makes you my half- brother."

He didn't say anything for some time. He just looked at me, thinking of something to say, and then he became angry. Instead of me hoping for a joyful family reunion, it turned into a loud shouting match. "If you think you can come in here," he shouted, "with some cock-and-bull story about my father having an affair with your mother, I just don't believe it and would like you to leave." He got up, went to the door, and opened it. I protested and tried to explain but he ushered me out of the house and slammed the door behind me. There was no point in me staying. Brian wasn't interested and probably thought I was trying to claim part of the farm. I should have listened to Mum's advice and not stirred up the past. I drove away disappointed that Brian and I had not become friends.

I was determined to make my mother proud of me after all she had been through and somehow treat her to a surprise she would never forget. I told Brenda all about my childhood when we were in bed. And she listened intently as I told her about Mum and all the sacrifices she had made. "Why don't we take your mum on holiday?" Brenda suddenly said. "I bet she would enjoy that, and she gets on well with Steven." I thought about Brenda's idea and decided to call on the travel agent on the way home from work and look at what was on offer. There was a special package holiday to Majorca for a week. It meant that Steven would miss five days of school. But I decided to book it anyway and risk getting into trouble with the school governor. It would be the first time that any of them had been abroad.

Two months later, we caught a plane from Gatwick and flew to Palma in Majorca and checked into a three-bedroom villa with its own swimming pool. It was great. Steven loved the sun and was in the pool every day. Mum enjoyed herself and loved going to the local market for fresh vegetables and cooking new recipes. Brenda liked walking down to the sandy beach and sunbathing. One day, we all went to the beach and sat in a café having our lunch. Although it was hot, there was a red flag flying on the beach, which meant nobody was supposed to go swimming because there was a strong wind that was whipping up the waves. Steven climbed over the barrier and sat on a rock overlooking the choppy waters. I looked out to sea and noticed a huge wave coming in fast. I jumped over the barrier as the wave hit the rock. I just reached him and grabbed his arm, and we were both covered by the wave. We were both safe, but I think Steven would have been swept off the rock and cut himself on the jagged rocks if I hadn't grabbed him. We all decided to go back to the villa and enjoy the rest of the day by the pool. It was a smashing week, and I think we all enjoyed the break, especially Mum.

CHAPTER

My Hopes Dashed

I was earning good money and Brenda had found a job as a self-employed accountant doing work from home. She listed all the receipts then filled in the forms and sent off the books to the Taxation Office once a year for other self-employed building workers, including me, which was helpful. During that winter, we had very bad weather. I was all right as most of my work was inside. But my poor workmates would get soaked trying to fit floor joists in the rain and to fix roof trusses (premade large wooden triangles ready for assembly on the roof).

Of course, if they did not work, they did not get paid, and a lot had families to support and a mortgage, the same as me. So sometimes I slipped on my boots and raincoat and went and helped push up the roof trusses onto the scaffolding above. The trusses were about one hundredweight each, but it wasn't the weight; it was the awkwardness of their shape. It needed two people on the top scaffolding pulling them up and one pushing from the bottom. I was always on the bottom, pushing them up. There were normally about a dozen trusses, depending on the size of the house, and it normally took about half an hour, so I didn't mind helping out occasionally. This particular day, it had been raining all morning, then stopped suddenly. It was very muddy at the bottom of the scaffolding, and as the two lads grabbed one of the trusses and I let go, it slipped out of their hands and came crashing down. I saw it falling and went to run, but my boots were stuck in the mud and I fell over. The roof truss fell across my legs, and I was trapped in the mud. By the time the lads came down the ladder and lifted the roof truss off me, I knew from the pain that I had broken my leg. The lads called an ambulance from the site office, and I was whisked off to hospital. I was laid up for six weeks, unable to work on site. It was a good job Brenda could drive and had her little business running, or else I would have been overdrawn again, but we managed.

I did the football pools most weeks and had never won a sausage, but the last week I was off work, we had a letter through the door from the football pools company stating I had won £3,000. I couldn't believe it, the one time when I needed a bit of luck and it had been granted. Brenda and I planned what to do with the money: put it toward a new extension on the house, then we could sell it and make a big profit. We had it all worked out and then our hopes were dashed. A man from the pools called in the next day and told us there had been a huge mistake and it wasn't Mr. David William Jones that had won the pools but a David William Johns living in Benson. He said it was a typing error. We were both devastated. He did give us a bottle of champagne as compensation and again apologized for their mistake. I remembered what my old friend George had told me. We don't ever get anything for free. You have to work for it—how right he was.

Even with Brenda working, my savings were nearly all gone by the time I went back to work on the building site. I had to get some money up together and fast. I could sell the Jaguar and get something smaller for Brenda, but the Jaguar was getting old and wouldn't fetch much money. So we ditched that idea. There was a job on site, cleaning the newly built houses ready for occupation. Brenda applied for the job and got it. I liked to think I had some influence on the site foreman as he knew I had broken my leg and had to have six weeks off work, so perhaps he had a bit of sympathy for me.

Brenda relished the new job and employed another girl to help. She had to pay Trish the new girl in cash, but between them, they were cleaning about a dozen houses or flats a week. After taking out Trish's money, Brenda still made nearly £200 a week profit, and with her private account business, some weeks she earned more than me. Perhaps our luck had changed.

We built a garage extension with a bedroom and shower room above. I used some of the subcontractors working on site to do the bricklaying, plumbing, wiring, and plasterwork, and Brenda and I did the rest. As soon as the place was finished, we put it on the market and it sold within in a month. Trish wanted to take over the contract cleaning the houses. So Brenda and I decided to start buying rundown properties, repairing them to their original condition, and selling them on at a profit. This worked well for us but not for Steven. He was now nearly sixteen and had drifted away from us a bit. He didn't like living in a half-finished house and then moving on every six months. We did manage to keep him in the same school with all his friends, but he was mixing with the wrong crowd. There had been an influx of colored immigrants coming and settling in Reading, and some of them went to Steven's school. They tended to stick together, and he joined a gang when he got himself a small motorbike, which we gave him for his sixteenth birthday.

Steven wasn't interested in the building trade. He said he wanted to do something more intellectual. But he had no idea what he was going to do when he finally left school, preferring to claim benefits off the government and dossing over at his friend's house in Reading. Brenda tried to talk some sense into him to make something of himself. He hated being told what to do and often told his mum, "I'm a man now. I can do what I like." I didn't like to interfere. After all, he wasn't my child, but it did hurt when he rebuffed me after all the contact I had with him when he was younger. Brenda and I kept buying and repairing houses and had made a tidy profit by the time Steven turned eighteen and Brenda was no longer his legal guardian. He left home, still with no job, and Brenda feared he might be taking drugs with his mates in Reading. There was nothing we could do, only be there if things turned out bad for him. Brenda got a Christmas card that year, telling her he was living in a commune and had a girlfriend, but he didn't leave a contact number or address.

Brenda and I celebrated our ten years together. We were both forty-six years old and at last had a four-bedroom detached house with no mortgage and a nice car. I did get into trouble because we had such a big turnover that year we should have registered for VAT. Brenda and I had the VAT men visit us one evening. They wanted to look through the bookkeeping and weren't impressed when they found a lot of discrepancies. Brenda was not very good with VAT records and made lots of mistakes. We agreed to pay an extra £8,000 in lost VAT over the last three years just to keep the tax man happy. But apart from that, the rest of the year went well for us.

My mother was only in her early sixties when she got pneumonia. She was not that strong and had to be admitted to hospital. Sheila, Mary, and Tommy all rallied around and kept a constant vigil at the hospital. Mum had been moved up to a private room on the top floor when I visited. "They have bought me up here to die, Davy," she whispered, with tears in her eyes.

"Don't be silly, Mum," I said, trying to cheer her up. "Remember when you had that heart attack on the way to work and fell off your bike. You soon recovered and cycled over to the hospital and asked for a checkup. You survived that and you'll survive this."

Mum smiled as she recalled that day. "I was a lot younger then, son, and in much better health," she whispered.

I tried to say something that would cheer her up but I could see she was getting tired. "Get some sleep now, Mum," I said. "Sheila will be up in about an hour, and she's got you some books to read." She looked at me, squeezed my hand, and closed her eyes. "I'll see you tomorrow, Mum," I said and kissed her cheek and left. When Sheila arrived an hour later, Mum had died in her sleep. She was just sixty-three years old.

Mum's funeral was held on Saturday, and half the village tuned up for the service. I didn't know Mum had so many friends. I gave the last speech about how Mum had looked after us through all the difficult times, and as I was speaking, I could feel myself becoming more emotional. I had to stop before I broke down and embarrassed myself. Sheila then took over and finished the speech. Mum was buried in the local churchyard next to her husband, my stepfather. It was a sad day. We all went back to a reception at the village hall and talked about old times, some of which I did not want reminding of. Everybody paid their respects and left, leaving us to clear up.

There was only my stepsisters and stepbrother left. Sheila had set up home with her boyfriend. Mary was living with a boy and was about to get married, and Tommy and his friend shared a flat in Wallingford and worked at a local garage. Brenda and I went back home and, that night while lying in bed, discussed our future together. I decided we should go on a week's holiday to Spain just to unwind from the past year's work.

One month later, we arrived at Benidorm and booked into our hotel. It was not a quiet break as I imagined. We hired a small car for the week and drove around all the local beauty spots, then went to a different show every night, which were all free as long as you bought some drinks. Most of the bars were owned or managed by Brits who had immigrated to Spain. We got chatting to some of them and were impressed by how easy it was to start up a business out there. The next day, we visited a small town just outside Benidorm called Albir. It was a lot quieter and not so busy. The beach was good, with plenty of watersports nearby, so we stayed there during the day and then ventured back into Benidorm for the nightlife. We had a great week and finally arrived home tired but happy.

CHAPTER

The New Start

Brenda and I kept working for another two years but were becoming bored with our way of life. We both wanted something different. The lure of Spain was overpowering. The warm Mediterranean Sea, the carefree lifestyle, and the nonstop entertainment were too much of a temptation, and in 1996, we sold up everything and moved to Spain. We had opened an account with the local bank in Albir and had all our money transferred over to Spain. We then rented a flat to start with and got friendly with a Spanish estate agent who could speak good English. He showed around several villas that were in our price range and eventually choose one overlooking Albir. Carlos the estate agent recommended a Spanish lawyer who could speak a little English. So we hired him to do all the paperwork and were surprised how quick the process was. We signed all the paperwork, and within a week, the place was ours.

The paperwork was all in Spanish and there were a lot of things the lawyer did not explain to us or didn't think we needed to know. On the first day when we were moving into our villa, an English-speaking Dutch lady visited us as we were unpacking. "Welcome to your new home," she said, holding out her hand, which we both shook. "My name's Monica, and I am the community's president. I will need your full names so we can register you on the committee and you can attend this month's meeting."

"What community?" I said, rather surprised.

"Since you bought this villa, you automatically become part of our little community of six residents," Monica replied, "whom you will meet shortly then we can discuss your monthly payment to the community." This was all news to me. Our lawyer had never mentioned a community when we signed the paperwork. When we attended the first meeting at the town hall a week later, we were in for some other shocks as well. Monica informed me that as our villa was the biggest, I had to pay the largest amount, 37 percent of the total budget for the year, which worked out at 1,000 pesetas a month. When I enquired what this payment was for, I was told it was for the maintenance of the other villa and flats in the next building and all the gardens. I was also told that although I owned the villa, I did not own the surrounding land or gardens, and they were all owned by the community. We left after meeting the other residents who were all Spanish apart from Monica. At least we could relax in our nice swimming pool and spend the rest of the day sunning ourselves on the veranda, drinking ice-cold beers.

The first couple of weeks, we rented a car but looked around the local garages, intending to buy one and finally bought a little left-hand-drive Ford Escort. At the next community meeting we had, one of the residents approached me. Her name was Conchie, and she could speak a little broken English. I didn't really like when we were first introduced. She seemed to hate the English and detested us buying up all the surrounding properties. "You no own villa," she snarled, "built on my land." I was a bit concerned and asked Monica what she meant.

"Oh, don't take any notice of her," replied Monica. "She doesn't get on with anybody and is always stirring up trouble with the other residents." But it got me thinking. Was there anything else the lawyer hadn't told us?

I looked around the town for another English-speaking lawyer and found one, advertising renting or buying properties. I met Anna Brooks, who was English and had lived in Spain for the last ten years. Her rates seemed reasonable, and I asked her to find out about our lawyer whom the estate agent had recommended and see if he was genuine. I met her a week later, and she told me that Fernando, the lawyer I had hired, was in fact a fake. He had studied law and attended a college but had no qualifications. "You had better bring me in all your documentation of the sale," Anna said "then I can check what you have actually bought." I left thinking, I might have made the biggest mistake of my life investing all my money in the Spanish way of life.

A few days later, Anna rang me and arranged a meeting the following day. "It seems most of the documents are all legal," she said. "However, there are a few gray areas that need looking into. For one, did you know that on the plans you gave me, your villa had two bedrooms, with bathroom, kitchen, and lounge on the first floor, with double garages on the ground floor? Somebody has changed the first-floor garages and built two more bedrooms and bathroom and put an internal flight of stairs leading up to the first floor, all of which are not on the plans."

"It was like that when I bought it," I protested.

"It doesn't matter, Mr. Jones. If the town hall finds out that all this was done illegally, they could make you knock it down." I was shocked that an estate agent could sell an illegal property. "It happens all the time, I'm afraid, Mr. Jones," Anna said. "There are thousands of illegal extensions and buildings throughout Spain. It's a very corrupt business. I think your best bet is to keep quiet and hope nobody reports it to the town hall." That wasn't what I wanted to hear, but I took Anna's advice. I did tell Brenda my fears when I got back to the villa.

"We'll worry about that when the time comes," she said, "but let's think about renting a bar in Benidorm first and make a bit of money." Brenda was right, of course. Our savings wouldn't last forever, and we both needed to work to be able to stay in Spain.

As we were going to be living and working in Spain indefinitely, we both had to become Spanish citizens and pay our taxes in Spain. We signed all the relevant paperwork, handed our British passports in, and were issued with new Spanish passports a few weeks later. Brenda and I had discussed buying a bar and cafeteria, but it would mean we would have to have a Spanish mortgage. So we decided to rent a place and discovered a tiny café and bar just off the main street in the old part of town. Although we had no experience of running a bar or cafeteria, we hired Manuel, a Spanish chef who could speak quite good English.

The business was very slow to start with. After paying Manuel, we were left with just about enough to pay the rent and make a reasonable wage but nowhere near as much as we had earnt back in England. It was a lot cheaper to live here though and you had the glorious weather, so we thought it was worth the compromise.

The first year, we made a modest profit but not the amount we had hoped for. Sheila and her husband came over and stayed with us for a week, but thought it a bit hot and clammy as we had no air conditioning, so I didn't think they would be returning. Mary, my other stepsister, didn't like Spain at all and couldn't understand why I ever wanted to live there in the first place. Tommy came over with his friend Sebastian toward the end of the year, and I found out he was more than just a friend and they had been living together for some time. They loved the old town in Benidorm where all the gay and colorful people congregated. Brenda was a bit surprised at first, but welcomed them both into our home. Tommy and Sebastian left after a week and asked if they could come over the following year as they had both enjoyed their stay with us. I agreed and wished them a safe return home.

At our monthly community meetings, I had made friends with Conchie, and when we all voted on something, I usually voted with her just to keep the peace. After the meeting, Monica spoke to me in private. "I wouldn't get too pally with Conchie," Monica said. "She's up to something and can't be trusted." I knew there was no love lost between Conchie and Monica and there was often shouting between them at the meetings. I was always the piggy in the middle, but it was obvious that Conchie thought she should be president and not some foreigner.

Things didn't improve when one of the Spanish couples sold their two-bedroom flat a year later to an English gay couple, Peter and Gordon. Brenda and I got on with them both as we had a lot of gay and lesbian couples in our café and bar, which was normal in the old town. But Conchie detested them both as they often sided with Monica, so things got very heated at some meetings. But it wasn't until six months later that we got into some very serious trouble.

CHAPTER

My Hopes Destroyed

At our first meeting after the New Year, Conchie submitted some plans for a new extension to her villa. Her villa was directly behind mine, so my villa spoilt her views over Albir town. She wanted to build up above her single-story lounge, creating another bedroom with uninterrupted views. But that created a problem for me: not only would she be able to see straight into my property, but also she would severely restrict the sun to my swimming pool. I voted with the others to reject the plans even though she had the town hall's approval. Conchie was furious. "I will get revenge," she spat when she left the meeting, and I wondered what revenge she could take, but I soon found out at the next meeting.

Conchie couldn't find anything that would affect the other residents but showed us all plans of the original drawing from the town hall. She pointed to my property. "See, no villa, only garage," she said. "Town hall say you knock down."

I looked across at Monica for some support. But all she could say after looking at the plans was "I think you had better find a good solicitor."

I made an appointment with Anna the next day while Brenda and Manuel looked after the café. "I hoped this would not happen," said Anna, "and would be overlooked. But this Conchie must have friends in the town hall to be able to go through all the original plans and bring this to light. She must hate you, David, to do something like this."

"But can you do something, Anna?" I asked desperately.

"Well, from what I can see," Anna replied, "you have two options. You can ether apply to the town hall with revised drawings of your property, which my architect can do, hoping they will pass the plans and not charge you too much. Or you could sue the estate agents for the original price of the villa. But that could take years, knowing how long our legal system works and they could say they sold it in good faith with the information they received from the sellers." I took Anna's advice and had new plans drawn up and submitted them to the town hall. This was all costing me a fortune, and our last bit of savings dwindled out. Now we were just relying on the income from the café and bar.

We seemed to live in limbo for the next eight months waiting for news from the town hall. Conchie wound everybody up at the next few meetings and even had Gordon in tears by saying, "he should have his balls cut off for being gay." She was such a vindictive person.

Brenda and I finally got a letter from the town hall telling us the plans had been rejected and we must demolish the property within a month, or the town hall would send in contractors to do the job and charge us for the bill.

Brenda burst out crying, and I felt like crying myself—all we had gambled on and worked for, dashed. It felt like somebody was against me. Whatever I tried to do seemed to fail. That evening, we lay in bed wondering what to do. We couldn't live in the café. There was no accommodation. Anyway, the Spanish owner we were renting off wouldn't have helped us; he was only interested in the rent money. Our only other option was to rent a small flat if that was what it came to. We hung on for another month, enjoying our last days in our villa, hoping for a reprieve from the town hall. The final day arrived, and nothing happened. We thought they might have overlooked us. The next day, the subcontractors delivered us a letter telling us we had twenty-four hours to remove all our belongings in the house or else they would be destroyed. I contacted a clearance firm that specialized in buying secondhand furniture and utensils for cash, which we thought would tide us over for a couple of months as we had found a small furnished flat not far from the café. We kept our bed and a few personal items but the rest we sold. We couldn't bear to see our lovely villa demolished, so we left when the subcontractors arrived with their heavy machinery. Conchie waved at us and grinned as we drove off. We did claim on our insurance company, hoping to get a substantial pay out, but they rejected the claim, insisting the property was built illegally; therefore, the insurance was void.

Brenda and I moved into our little one-bedroom flat that day and spent the next day trying to make the best of things. At least the business was doing well, and we seemed to be managing. We did go back and see what was left of our old villa and found nothing left except the swimming pool, which Conchie had claimed belonged to her. She now had what she had always dreamed of, an unrestricted view over the town.

Our new inspiration for the business lasted for two weeks. Then a letter was posted through our letterbox claiming 120,000 pesetas for the demolition and landscaping work done by the subcontractors. Payment should be paid within a month or else interest would be added and we would be taken to court. It was the final nail in the coffin for both of us. We both became very emotional. That night, we both sat in the bar and had a few beers to drown our sorrows after knowing it was impossible for us pay that amount of money.

I then did the most stupid thing I had ever done in my life I drove Brenda over to see Peter and Gordon, the gay couple who had bought the two-bedroom apartment next to our villa. We thought they might let us stay with them temporarily, as they had two bedrooms. As we drove out of Benidorm, we came to a sharp curve in the road. I had driven on this road thousands of times, but this time with a few drinks inside me, I was driving too fast and ended up on the wrong side of the road straight into the path of a lorry. I swerved, but it was too late. The car hit the lorry head on.

I remember waking up in hospital, not understanding what had happened. My arm and shoulder were in a sling, my ribs hurt when I coughed, and I had a splitting headache. I called a nurse over and asked her what had happened. She did not speak English and went off to find a doctor. A few minutes later, she returned with a male doctor. "I'm Dr. Vincent," he said in an Oxfordshire accent. "I understand you're a bit confused about what happened. Don't you remember anything, Mr. Jones?"

"I remember hitting a lorry," I said, "but nothing else."

"Well, Mr. Jones," replied Dr. Vincent looking at the spreadsheet. "You were admitted unconscious eighteen days ago with a severe head wound, a dislocated shoulder, and three broken ribs. You are lucky to be alive, Mr. Jones. When we x-rayed your ribs, we also found a dark ring around your lungs. We think you have asbestosis, Mr. Jones. Have you worked with asbestos or been in close contact with it recently?"

"No, I don't think so," I said. Then I suddenly remembered Brenda was with me in the car. "Is Brenda all right?" I said.

The nurse took the doctor to one side and spoke to him out of earshot. Then he said, "There was a woman admitted to the hospital that night, Mr. Jones, but I'm afraid she died on the way to the hospital."

"No, that can't be," I cried. "She was right beside me, and I survived."

"I'm afraid that side of the car took all the impact," the doctor said. "She wouldn't have stood a chance." I was in shock. I didn't know if I should scream or cry when I realized I had just killed the only person I had truly loved.

The nurse gave me a strong sedative, and I fell asleep almost instantly. I came to in the middle of the night, still with the nightmare vision of Brenda lying by my side, dead. I realized I had to get out of that hospital fast, or else I would go mad. I looked around the darkened hospital ward and found my clothes, shoes, and wallet in a bedside locker. I quickly got dressed even though it hurt when I put my shirt and cardigan on. I sneaked through the hospital and out through a fire escape door at the side. I didn't know what I was doing or where I was going. I remember walking through Benidorm. There were still a few bars and people about. So I bought two double whiskeys (which I drank quickly), a sandwich, and pork pie. I rummaged through my wallet and gave the bartender all the money I had. I don't remember how I got to the motorway on the outskirts of the town, but I do remember walking to the middle of the footbridge and standing looking down at the night traffic tearing along under the footbridge.

I had nothing to live for. I had one foot on the safety rail, about to jump off when I felt something tugging at my trouser leg preventing me lifting my other leg I looked down and saw a mangy-looking dog gripping my trouser leg. I kicked out, but the dog wouldn't let go. I climbed back down, and the dog let go. He looked half-starved. I reached into my pocket and pulled out my pork pie and gave it to the dog. He woofed it down as though he hadn't eaten for days. The dog walked off then looked around for me to follow. He seemed to know where he was going, so I followed him. We must have walked about half a mile, and I found myself in an old disused quarry. The dog disappeared into an old mineshaft and lay on the floor on some old canvas sheeting. It was clearly his home, so I curled up beside my new friend and fell asleep.

CHAPTER

I Become a Vagrant

I awoke later in the day, my head still throbbing and looked around the darkened space. The dog was gone. I staggered out of the dismal tunnel into the bright morning sunshine and sat down on a large stone boulder. The quarry had not been used for years; already there were trees and shrubs covering the area. It was a good hiding place and wasn't visible from the road. I stood on the boulder and could see Benidorm in the distance, the tall skyscrapers glistening in the sun. My mouth was dry and I was hungry. I sat down again and wondered what to do. It was all coming back to me: the crash, Brenda by my side, still looking beautiful, her long blonde hair tied in a ponytail. I started to sob. I couldn't help it. Tears rolled down my cheeks, and I knew I would never see her again. Suddenly, the dog appeared from nowhere and sat by my side. I think he sensed I was distraught. I looked at his sorrowful eyes. He was quite an old dog and clearly had been living wild for some time. His brown shaggy coat was dirty. I put out my hand, and he licked it.

"What shall I call you?" I said. The first name that came into my head was Bruce, my very first dog. So that's what I called him. He didn't respond to the name at first but quickly cottoned on when I kept repeating it. I needed some food, change of clothes, and a shave. I hadn't shaved since I'd been in hospital. I looked in my wallet and realized I'd given all my money to the bartender the previous evening. I still had my credit card and wondered if I should risk drawing some money out of the bank although I doubted there was much money left in my account. But it was worth the risk. I walked back to the town and Bruce followed. He was a smart dog and was clearly streetwise, siting at the side of the busy roads until it was safe to cross. I entered my bank and went to the cashier. I noticed her looking at my worn dirty clothes, but she recognized me even with my face stubble. "Could I draw out two hundred pesetas, please?" I asked.

The cashier checked out my account and replied, "I'm afraid you only have 130 pesetas left in your account, sir. Do you want to withdraw that amount?"

"Yes, please," I said, "I will be putting some more money into my account by the end of the week when I get paid the money that is owed to me."

She handed over the money, then said, "Would you take a seat over there, Mr. Jones? The bank manager would like to have a word with you." I sat down on the seat nearest the door. Bruce sat outside, waiting. I looked around the bank at all the customers queuing at the cashier's desk and left the bank without being noticed. Bruce and I ran down the next street to the market. I went straight to the hot meat counter and bought a full rack of ribs and a bottle of cola for only fifty pesetas. Bruce and I found a quiet spot at the side of the market, and I scoffed the lot, giving Bruce the leftover bones. After drinking the bottle of cola, I felt much better. I realized I needed to tidy myself up a bit. Should I risk going back to my rented flat? I was a least a month behind with the rent and could not afford to bump into the landlord. I crept back when it got dark and tried opening the door with my key. The bastard had already changed the lock, and I couldn't open the door. I looked around and found a couple of bin liners dumped next to the garbage bin. All my clothes and personal things were stuffed inside. I grabbed the bags and walked to the nearest bar then went in the toilets and washed. I walked out feeling much better. I left the beard on so not many people would recognize me. I bought some sandwiches and a drink, then followed Bruce back to our den in the quarry.

The tunnel was dry and warm. I had picked up a mattress from a skip and made the space quite comfortable. Nobody would find me here. I felt safe and it was free. Bruce was good company and snuggled up to me in the evenings.

I eventually got a job as a cleaner sweeping up and washing down floors after the café was closed for the night. The owner knew I was a vagrant and paid me in cash, enough to feed me and Bruce. I knew the police would be looking for me as I owed money everywhere: the subcontractors who demolished my villa, the hospital for the insurance bill, the owner of the rented property, and the bank wanting to know when I was going to put more money in my account. The job suited me. It was late at night, and the owner didn't ask any questions. I managed to stay hidden from the police for a year, staying with Bruce in the den and working the late shift at the café. We became very close. Bruce even let me wash him late at night, under the showers on Benidorm's beach.

I knew I could not keep up this lifestyle, living from day to day, not venturing out during the day in case anybody recognized me, and living in such squalid conditions. If only I could get back to England. I was sure one of my sisters would take me in until I found a job. But I only had my Spanish passport, so would I become an illegal immigrant. I needed help and money. And then I thought of Peter and Gordon, the gay couple living in Albir. Surely they would lend me the money for the fare home. After all, they were British. I said goodbye to Bruce. If he had not been on the bridge that night, then I would have jumped. He saved my life. So I bought him a whole cooked chicken and shared it with him as a final parting gift. I left him in the den. He seemed to know I was leaving him for good and whimpered as I left. I just had one bag for a change of clothes and walked to the main road out of Benidorm. I thumbed a lift to Albir about six miles away and was dropped off on the outskirts of town. It was still dark when I reached Peter's flat and decided to wait until the morning before I knocked on their door.

He didn't recognize me at first with my big bushy beard and darkened complexion. I had aged considerably from the last time I had met him, but once I explained who I was, he welcomed me inside. I told Peter and Gordon the whole story since I last saw them. They were saddened to learn that Brenda had died in the crash and agreed to help. They rang the airport at Alicante and paid for a flight back home. Peter even offered to drive me to the airport the next day. I went through passport control, handing over my Spanish passport. The woman asked how long I intended to stay in England and, I replied, "Oh, just fourteen days, it's a holiday." She hesitated when looking at my photo and kept looking from my face to the photo. I had a dreadful thought the police were still looking for me and my description had been circulated through all the airports. But she smiled and said, "You really have to shave your beard off, Mr. Jones, or get another photo on your passport." She stamped the passport, and I went through to the departure lounge and waited for my flight. I arrived back in England two hours later and stepped off the plane, glad to be back home.

CHAPTER

Home at Last

I had a bit of trouble at passport control Gatwick and was asked what my intentions were in England as I had no return flight booked. I said I would like to stay as all my family were here.

"Then you will have to reapply for a new British passport, Mr. Jones. And it may take longer than two weeks, in which case you will have to return to Spain and wait there until the passport has been approved." I agreed to that, and she let me through. I had a little spending money that Peter had given me, and I used this to buy an English breakfast and a coffee then thumbed a lift from the airport back to Oxford. I slept in a bus shelter that night and, the next day, went to the Social Services for some help. As soon as they discovered I was a Spanish citizen, their attitude changed. "I'm afraid we can't help you, sir. You will have to go to the Spanish embassy in London."

I walked out in disgust and decided to find Sheila, my stepsister. I knew she still lived in Abingdon Road, Oxford, but didn't know the number. I walked the street, knocking on people's doors, asking if they knew a Sheila Jones. I didn't know her married name as she had married a different guy that had come over to stay with me in Spain. I gave up as the evening approached, and I crept back to the bus shelter and slept on the seat. I felt very cold as the temperature was a lot colder at night than it was in Spain. I kept waking up as I was so cold and hungry. I roamed around the Oxford streets and copied what and the other homeless people were doing, sitting in a doorway to a large department store with a plastic container, begging for a few coins so I could buy some food. I did this for two years, often getting abuse from young teenagers or being told to move along by the police. Nobody seemed to care until you came along and asked me to tell you my story.

EPILOGUE

A Sad Ending

I didn't publish Davy's story until 2022, having tried writing other books but having limited success. In 2005, Davy was admitted to the John Radcliff Hospital in Headington, Oxford. I was contacted by them after they found my card in Davy's pockets and had phoned my number. The doctor said Davy was very sick and had asked for me. I went up to the hospital that evening but was told he'd died just before I arrived. I asked how he had died The doctor replied they had found asbestosis around his lungs and it had lain dormant for some time, but it had turned cancerous and spread throughout his body very quickly, shutting his internal organs down. "We might have saved him if we had caught it earlier," the doctor said, "but it didn't help him sleeping rough in all weathers during the last few years. Davy told us he could have caught it when he was an apprentice working with a chap called George. He didn't make a lot of sense just before he died, but he asked me to give you this. He said you would understand." The doctor handed me a folded piece of paper. I unfolded it, and there was a childish drawing of a red London double-decker bus with the word THANKS scribbled underneath. I knew what it meant. He was reliving that childhood dream.

David Jones was buried in a pauper's funeral two days later at St. Johns Church, Oxford. He was just sixty years old. I was the only person that attended the funeral. There was a simple black plastic name plate stuck in the mound where he was buried. I visited his grave some years later to lay some flowers on the grave, but I couldn't find it. There was only a hump in the ground. It looked like it had been mowed over, and David Jones had been erased from memory.

The End